THE
STRATEGIST

D1550873

THE
STRATEGIST

A GRISHAM & SULLIVAN THRILLER

JOHN HARDY BELL

SECOND
SIGHT
PUBLISHING

This is a work of fiction. All of the organizations, characters, and events portrayed in this novel are either products of the author's imagination or are used fictitiously.

For more, visit www.johnhardybell.com

Acknowledgements

Despite the solitary existence inherent in a writer's day to day life, none of us can say we've achieved anything of value by ourselves. If we're fortunate, we have lots of help, lots of voices speaking to us (aside from the ones in our heads), and lots of cheerleading pushing us along every step of the way.

I'm definitely one of the fortunate ones.

Thank you to my early readers Amanda Lopez-Askin, Dawn Kirby, Cheryl Remedi, Jennifer Sutter-Wixson, Bettye Williams, Anna Theisen, and John Ulmer.

Thank you to Michael Turner for providing the visual inspiration.

Big thanks to Mercedes Blea-Davis for keeping the day job fun and always being there with optimism and support. Go SFAM!

To the Bells and the Ulmers (including the extended Chicago clan), thanks for always being there, always supporting, and always inspiring. I'm proud to call you my family. To Yvette, for the unconditional friendship and support.

And last, but certainly not least, to my amazing Jackie, thank you for being the great love of my life. Your constant encouragement has gotten me through some tough writing times, and I'm proud to say I've made it this far in large part because of you. You are the best wife, partner, and friend that I could ever ask for, and I am so honored to share this with you and our wonderful Logan.

To everyone else who had a hand in the final creation that is *The Strategist*, I thank you. Some of your contributions were big, some were small, but all were invaluable. I will forever be grateful.

For Mom

I'm here because of you, a dreamer because of you, and a writer because of you. I hope your smile is as big as I imagine it to be.

THE
STRATEGIST

In times of universal deceit, telling the truth becomes a revolutionary act

~**George Orwell**

CHAPTER 1

SAFEKEEPING

Her hand trembled as she tore the flash disk from its plastic casing and inserted it into her computer. She had spent most of the night compiling the nearly nine hundred files she would need to transfer, so she anticipated the actual upload process would be relatively painless. Still, she worried that something could go wrong. A file could be missed, the disk could be corrupted, men in black suits and sunglasses could show up at her front door in search of answers she wasn't the least bit prepared to give.

But she knew that was merely the paranoia working over her already fragile mind. Every file had been accounted for. The disk was brand new, so the chances of corruption were minimal. And as far as she knew, men in black suits were little more than figments of Hollywood's imagination. She smiled at the thought of Will Smith and Tommy Lee Jones chasing aliens, but the sense of dread that inspired her actions remained.

Once the document transfer began, her nerves slowly settled. Watching each file make the split second journey from her computer's hard drive to the disk, she couldn't help but marvel at the sheer amount of information that could be stored on such a tiny, portable device. Data that was once only accessible on a mainframe computer the size of a broom closet could now fit comfortably inside her pocket, but unlike a mainframe, the files on that pocket-sized device could potentially be accessed by anyone in the world, provided it was not adequately safeguarded.

Her disk would need safeguarding that went far beyond adequate. Some would undoubtedly consider her methods extreme. Given what could happen should its contents ever become public domain, she still wondered if it would be enough.

For now, it would have to be.

In a perfect world, there would come a time when the information was no longer relevant and could be discarded before it was ever seen. The world she inhabited was far from perfect, however, which meant that an outcome other than the one she routinely saw in her nightmares was not very likely.

The transfer took half an hour to complete. She spent much of that time thinking about what was to come. The last twenty-four hours had been tense. The next twenty-four would offer no let up. She had already arranged to take tomorrow off – no easy feat when your employer is one of the most powerful law firms in the western United States and you're smack dab in the middle of defending the region's largest grocery chain against a multi-million dollar lawsuit. But she needed the time if she was going to accomplish everything she needed to.

She would begin the day by making two very important trips. The first would ensure the safekeeping of the disk. The second would bring the arrival of the one person in the world she could completely trust with it. In her circle of influence, trust was not an easy thing to come by. Actually, it was non-existent. The exception to that rule was coming back into her life tomorrow morning after nearly eight years away.

The thought of having Camille home made her heart dance with anticipation, but the prospect of ever having to reveal the contents of that disk to anyone, let alone her best friend in the world, made her empty stomach feel queasy.

When the transfer was finally complete, the flash disk held 397 Excel spreadsheets, 473 Word documents, 22 PowerPoint slideshows, and one very important movie file. After performing one last sweep to ensure that she had gathered all the necessary data, she proceeded to wipe the entire contents of her computer's hard drive – every picture, every password, every temporary file – until the tropical sunset on her desktop was replaced by a blue screen and the error message: *0xc000000f boot section failed.*

A $2500 laptop killed with just three mouse clicks.

Once she shut down the now useless computer, she sealed the disk in an envelope. A note that she had spent a significant portion of the night writing went inside a second envelope. She buried both deep inside her handbag.

After some quality time with her kids – two Dalmatians named George and Gracie – she armed her security system, turned off the lights, and prayed that tonight would finally bring restful sleep. As she had done every night for the past week, she looked through the foyer window before going upstairs. She had no good reason to suspect that she would see anything out there that she wasn't supposed to, and so far she hadn't.

But she knew better than to think it could stay that way forever, given her knowledge and her willingness to share it with the entire world if she had to.

Yet Julia Leeds continued to hope, despite what everything in her heart told her to the contrary, that it would never come to that.

CHAPTER 2

JULES

The flight from Washington D.C. to Denver was approximately three hours and eight minutes, a full twenty minutes ahead of schedule. Under normal circumstances, Camille Grisham would have welcomed the efficiency. But as she walked off the plane and into a world that she wasn't the least bit ready to navigate, she knew the term 'normal circumstances' no longer applied to her.

Aside from a TSA pat down at the Reagan National Airport security checkpoint – a personal intrusion that her FBI credentials allowed her to bypass before now – the trip was uneventful. She had expected to spend the time mentally preparing herself for the inevitable onslaught that would accompany her arrival home. Once the plane descended and the familiar Denver cityscape came into view, Camille realized she was no more prepared to be here than when she quit the Bureau two months ago; and nothing short of a connecting flight to another region of the solar system was going to change that.

Her chest felt heavy the moment she stepped onto the jet bridge. By the time she entered the concourse, she was completely out of breath. Camille may have spent the first twenty-two years of her life here, but she lived the last twelve at sea level, which meant that the thin Colorado air had the same debilitating effect on her that it had on anyone else who wasn't used to it. She was light-headed, her legs felt unsteady, her stomach was queasy. Classic signs of altitude sickness. She sat down in a chair near the gate in hopes that the feeling would subside. It didn't. The more she tried to focus her eyes, the cloudier her vision became. Each swallow of air brought on a wave of nausea that nearly overwhelmed her. Ten minutes into her brand-spanking new life, and she was already going to be sick.

It was a feeling she had grown accustomed to since that otherwise beautiful July morning in Lancaster, Pennsylvania when her life took the sharpest left turn imaginable. Once mundane tasks that required minimal physical exertion now left her drained.

During her last counseling session before leaving the Bureau, the head-shrinker assigned to her suggested this to be a symptom of acute emotional trauma. He even threw around the words 'post-traumatic stress' and 'mild depression'. Camille laughed at the suggestion and promptly walked out of his office. In retrospect, she realized there was nothing funny about the diagnosis. Ending the session so abruptly had been nothing more than a defense mechanism against a truth about herself that she was not equipped to face.

What Camille felt right now may have truly been nothing more than altitude sickness; an ailment easily cured with a couple of Dramamine and a ginger ale. But part of her wondered if this wasn't something more elemental to who she now was; the new normal. Perhaps if she hadn't stormed out of the shrink's office, she would have had a chance of finding out. Perhaps the answer would still reveal itself in time. Most likely, she was simply over-thinking the whole damn thing.

Whatever the case, she didn't have time to worry about it. Her ride was due to meet her at exactly nine-thirty A.M., which meant that she only had a few minutes to get her luggage. After taking in the deepest breath she could muster, Camille stood up. She immediately felt the urge to sit down again, but instead pushed her way through the concourse. Desperate for something to sooth her stomach, she made a quick trip to Starbucks for a green tea.

She skimmed through a *Denver Post* while waiting in line. The front page read like the front page of every other major news daily. Crime stories that once occupied prime space were now relegated to the second and third sections in favor of the more pressing issues of high unemployment and depressed housing markets, but the grim economic forecasts didn't bother Camille in the least. She certainly preferred that to the story about the latest missing toddler or shooting rampage that would inevitably pop up had she kept reading.

The last such story to capture the nation's attention involved her and it had been only a couple of weeks since her name last appeared in the *Washington Times-Herald*. Camille's fifteen minutes were particularly infamous, and at its height, the D.C. field office was handling some fifty-interview requests per day. Very few were granted, but that didn't stop her picture from ending up in virtually every printed news outlet in the country. By the time she finally decided to leave Washington, she would have been hard-pressed to walk the streets of the city without someone recognizing her.

So far, no one here had given her a second glance, and she intended to keep it that way. Her pace quickened as she walked out of the Starbucks, up the escalator and into baggage claim. Even though she took great pains to blend in, she still felt anxious. In one of the many worst-case scenarios that played out in her mind before she got here, she imagined that some enterprising investigative reporter who had gotten wind of her arrival would be waiting with her luggage – notepad, microphone, and a thousand difficult questions in tow.

What Camille saw instead as she rounded the corner to baggage carousel number six brought a smile to her face so broad that it physically hurt.

The words were written on bright red poster board, in a meticulous script that she instantly recognized.

BREAD LINE FOR DOWN AND OUT FBI AGENTS BEGINS HERE

There was only one person Camille knew who would have the audacity to write such a thing under the circumstances, and because that person was her best friend, she was the only one who could actually get away with it.

"For once in your life you're on time," Julia bellowed as she lowered the sign. "Unfortunately the bread won't be out of the oven for another twenty minutes, so I'll need you to wait behind the white line."

Camille's eyes welled up as she choked back laughter. "Giving up law for comedy I see?"

"It wouldn't be much of a stretch. Some people think they're one in the same anyway."

"I have yet to meet a lawyer with anything approaching a sense of humor. I'll give you credit for trying though."

"It's better than being the ruthless witch that everyone always expects me to be."

"Who on earth would call you ruthless? That's just flat-out rude."

Julia laughed. "Apparently I'm not the only comedienne here."

"It's better than being the loser former FBI agent that everyone expects me to be."

Julia's smile faded as she pointed to her sign. "Down and out FBI agent. Get it right. Loser doesn't apply to you. Never has, never will."

"If you say so."

"I do say so. Now shush and give Auntie Jules a big ol' hug!"

Camille chuckled at the ridiculously bad West Virginia accent that Julia was fond of speaking in when she felt the random need to channel her Appalachian ancestry. "You are such a geek."

"I love you too, Cam."

As Julia approached, Camille could see that her eyes were beginning to water. "Hey, I don't need you getting all hysterical on me."

Julia dabbed at her eyes with one hand and reached out to Camille with the other, discarding the sign as she did. "Shut up. You're crying too."

Camille's tea fell to the floor as she pulled Julia close. For a long moment they were silent, the only sound between them being Julia's muted sniffles. Camille had wondered what her first encounter back home would feel like. Would her fear of change outweigh the absolute joy that would come with seeing her closest friend for the first time since she'd last visited D.C. over two years ago?

Much to her relief, the answer was a resounding no.

"I guess neither of us is as hilarious as we pretend to be," Camille declared.

"Guess not," Julia concurred as she bent down to pick up her sign. It was then that she noticed Camille's Starbucks cup. "You might want to pick that up, honey. You never know when a cop will be around."

"Aren't you clever? But as far as I know, you're the only person in the history of the world who has gotten a ticket for littering."

"Admittedly, my rap sheet in college was lengthy, but getting a ticket for throwing a Burger King wrapper out of a car window is complete nonsense. Even you have to acknowledge that."

"The only thing I'm acknowledging is my desire to get the hell out of this airport. You can regale me with tales from your wayward past later."

"Who says my waywardness is in the past?" Julia asked in a tone that briefly made Camille wonder if she was really joking.

When they simultaneously burst into laughter, Camille no longer had to wonder.

"My bags just came up," she said, pointing to two red suitcases lying side by side on the baggage carousel. "You can take the heavy one."

"Thanks, Cam. You always were the generous one in our relationship."

Camille walked a few paces behind Julia as they made the short trip from the terminal to the parking garage. Physically, Julia hadn't changed one bit in the two years since Camille last saw her. If anything, she looked more radiant and healthy. From their telephone conversations, Camille knew that Julia's career had come to dominate her life. She was a corporate attorney on the fast track of some major law firm, which undoubtedly meant long hours, little sleep, and zero social life. But she wore the stress well. Her strawberry blond hair fell lazily below her broad shoulders. Her chocolate brown eyes looked rested and alert. Her ready smile took up a comfortable residence on her sun-soaked face. And as Camille could tell from her yoga pants and fitted warm-up jacket, her shapely body benefitted from a lot of time spent in the gym. If there was one constant with Julia in the sixteen years that Camille had known her, it was the attention paid to her appearance. Whatever else was going on in her life – and with Julia there was usually a lot – she never failed to look the part of the smart, successful, disgustingly beautiful go-getter.

Camille hoped that the confident beauty she saw walking in front of her now wasn't merely a matter of looking the part.

"Did I mention you look amazing?" Julia said over her shoulder, as if she were reading Camille's mind.

"You're too sweet," Camille answered with a sarcasm that masked her mild embarrassment.

"I'm serious, Cam. You have a Rosario Dawson with curly hair vibe going on. It's a great look."

Camille's cheeks burned. "Please. I don't look *anything* like Rosario Dawson."

9

Julia stopped mid-stride and turned to Camille with a genuine look of shock. "Oh my God, you totally do. No one has ever told you that?"

"Only my well-intentioned, yet completely delusional friend here."

Camille was no stranger to compliments, but when she looked in the mirror, the last thing she saw was a movie star. A pro beach volleyball player or track and field sprinter perhaps. Her toned, five-foot-nine frame certainly made each a possibility. But Rosario Dawson? Even with their similar skin tones and hairstyles, Camille considered the comparison to be a monumental stretch at best.

"I know more than a few guys who would seriously beg to differ," Julia insisted.

Camille sighed. "Had those guys seen me half an hour ago, I don't think they would have been begging for anything."

"What do you mean?"

"Let's just say my stomach was having a hard time adapting to its new environment."

"Did you get sick on the flight?"

"As soon as we landed. The thin air almost knocked me out."

"Are you talking about altitude sickness? You spent most of your life here. How could that possibly be an issue? Besides, that whole thing is a stupid myth anyway. It's not like we're living in the Alps or something."

"Okay Doctor Leeds. What does your vast medical experience tell you the problem is?"

Julia pondered. "Honestly? I think you've been scared to death."

"Of what?"

"Coming back. Seeing me. Seeing your father. It's been a really stressful time, and I think it finally caught up with you this morning."

Camille stopped walking.

"Don't get upset, Cam. I'm not saying that as a negative thing."

"But it is a negative thing."

"Given the circumstances, I'd say it's perfectly understandable."

Camille's grip tightened around the handle of her suitcase. In her heart of hearts, she knew that Julia was right, but admitting so would unleash a flood of emotions that she had fought for months to contain. "I've been scared of a lot of things lately, but seeing you definitely isn't one of them."

"Okay," Julia said with a nod. "Just know that I understand how you're feeling. Probably more than you realize."

Camille relaxed her grip on the suitcase as they started walking again. "I know you do. That's the only thing that makes this situation tolerable. It scares me more to think of how things would be if you weren't here."

Julia's face stiffened.

"What's the matter?" Camille asked, noticing her sudden change in demeanor.

"Nothing," she answered, her expression unchanged.

"Are you sure?"

Julia drew in a shallow breath as she stopped in front of a burgundy Range Rover. "Your chariot awaits."

Camille's concern was suddenly replaced with awe. "I guess someone is doing quite well for themselves."

"The eighty-hour work week does have its privileges." Julia opened the hatch and put both of the suitcases inside. "Memento?" she asked when she saw the FBI Academy duffle bag Camille was carrying.

"No," Camille sighed as she took the bag off her shoulder and threw it in the car. "Just another piece of luggage."

CHAPTER 3

LANDMARKS

The pair spent the first few moments of the car ride in silence. The dull gray sky had recently turned black, bringing with it thick sheets of rain. Camille stared absently out the window as they passed green fields of empty earth. So far, nothing about this place felt familiar, and had it not been for Julia sitting in the driver's seat next to her, Camille would have wondered if she hadn't landed on a different planet altogether.

"I'm afraid it hasn't changed much since you were last here," Julia said as she kept her eyes trained on the wet road. "But at least you know what you're in for: great skiing, a marginal nightlife, and a ton of people who will be over the moon to see you."

"Not to mention zero prospects for a job, an undersized bed in my father's house, and a soul I seemed to have left somewhere on the east coast."

Julia shook her head. "Talk about dramatic."

"I'm simply seeing the situation for what it is."

"Look, I know what happened was horrible, but I'm not going to pretend that I'm unhappy you decided to come home. This is the best place for you right now. You need to be in a familiar environment with people who know and love you. And personally speaking, my life is going to be a lot more bearable because you're in it."

"That's a big statement."

"It's true, and I'm not the only one who feels that way. I don't know if you want to hear this, but no one is crying over you right now. You want to know why?"

Camille's stomach tightened. "I'm not sure I do."

"Because you're stronger than any of us even realize. No one is crying because if there is anyone on the planet who can go through all of this heinous crap and eventually become a better person, it's you. You're down right now, we all know that. But you're not staying down."

Camille rolled her eyes. "I feel like I just walked into a Tony Robbins seminar."

"Screw you, I'm being serious. You dealt with stuff every day that the average person only sees in movies, and you kept your head together through most of it. Everyone has a threshold, and you finally reached yours. That doesn't make you a failure. It makes you just like everybody else. Honestly, I would be more concerned if the things you saw didn't bother you."

"I wasn't supposed to be like everybody else, Julia."

"No one expected you to be super-human just because you carried a gun and an FBI badge. I know there was all this pressure because of who your dad is, but he of all people should understand what you were going through. You don't think in all the years he was out there that he never thought about quitting?"

"So what if he thought about it. He never did it."

"You did the only thing you could do. There's no way he's going to think any less of you because of it."

Camille shook her head and bit down on her lip. "I love you, and I love that you're trying to make me feel better, but can we please change the subject?"

Julia looked like she had more to say, but responded with a simple nod instead. "Of course." Then after a long silence: "What do you want to talk about?"

Camille looked in wonder at the smooth, leather upholstered interior of Julia's car. "How about we start with this Range Rover? The last time I was here, you were in a Toyota Camry that was, let's just say, well-driven. When did you graduate to this?"

Julia smiled as she stroked the steering wheel. "She's a beauty, huh? And it only took seven hundred billable hours to pay for her."

"I'm sure you loved every second of it."

"Love is a very strong word."

"Please. You're the biggest workaholic I know."

"Maybe my priorities have been out of whack."

"So does that mean you're ready to quit your job too? Maybe we can start a knitting circle with all the other washed-up hags."

The smile faded from Julia's face and she tightened her grip on the wheel. "I just made junior partner, Cam. I think it's a little late for that."

"Easy. I was just joking. It's called lightening the mood."

Julia eased her grip on the wheel. "Sorry. I guess I get a little bent when it comes to work these days."

"Clearly." Camille looked around the car. "The perks seem good."

"It's not about that."

"Since when?"

Julia laughed as if she was on the verge of becoming annoyed. "Since I began to see what can happen when people value the perks too much."

"By people you mean all those snobby Yale-educated lawyer types you work with?"

"Watch it. I'm one of those Yale-educated lawyer types."

"True, but notice you left out the word snobby. Besides, there is nothing wrong with having nice things. Try spending eight years driving around in a government-owned Grand Marquis that needs an oil change every five hundred miles."

"I'm not saying there's anything wrong with having nice things. I work hard for my money and I enjoy spending it. But I also know how to keep things in perspective. I'm not one of these idiots who lives and breathes for money. Look around my firm and you'll realize within five minutes that I'm in the clear minority. It's almost criminal how shallow they are."

"If it's that bad why don't you do something else? Wasn't the plan to go to law school to be a prosecutor? There's always a market for that."

"That was the plan if I stayed at CU. Unfortunately I got accepted into Yale, which made my track very narrow."

"Just because you have a big student loan bill to pay doesn't mean you have to be miserable doing it. You have options."

"Not as many as you think."

"Okay, now you're getting all cryptic on me. I'm not a fan of cryptic."

Julia's posture became rigid and tension hardened her soft features. "What can I say? I hate my job."

Camille was quiet as she studied Julia's face. Eyes that were bright and curious minutes earlier were now strained with worry.

"Are you sure that's all it is?"

Julia shifted in her seat. "It's not like I'd be the first person in the world to despise what they do for a living. What else would it have to be?"

"Did you suddenly forget who you're talking to?"

"The woman who knows me better than I know myself? How could I possibly forget?"

"Be sarcastic if you want to, but you know it's true. Remember, I once made a living out of reading people. Most of the time they didn't have to say two words to me before I knew exactly what they were thinking, and that was after knowing most of them for no more than five minutes. Imagine what I can do with you."

"Okay, so what are your finely-tuned instincts telling you right now?"

"That you're holding out on me. About what, I don't know. But something tells me it doesn't have anything to do with the shallow idiots you work with."

Julia looked at Camille with damp eyes. "The FBI's loss truly is my gain."

"What does that mean?"

"It means that they'll be hard-pressed to find someone as talented at reading people as you."

"In other words my instincts are right."

Julia sighed. "We'll talk about it."

"When?"

"Soon. For now just let me enjoy having you home."

Camille sat back in her seat, willing to let the subject go for the time being. "Don't think you're going to get away without it coming up again."

"I know you entirely too well to think otherwise."

They spent the next few moments in silence. Julia directed her focus back to the water-soaked road while Camille stared out her window. Now instead of empty green space, she saw empty industrial space, but at least she sensed the makings of civilization.

In less than a mile, they would be off the highway and into the northeast section of the city that Camille had called home her entire life. Surreal didn't come close to capturing what it felt like to be this close after being away for so long.

Before she reached her father's house, she would pass one landmark of her former life after another: her elementary school, the Catholic Church she was baptized in, the park she and her mother used to run through on days when the chemo treatments weren't so bad.

But she wondered if those landmarks would still have any of the meaning that they once did. She wondered if too much time had passed and too many connections had faded. She wondered if she really could go home again, and if she could, would it ever truly feel like home?

"Is it finally starting to sink in?" Julia asked as they passed the precinct house that Camille's father worked in for most of his career.

Not even a little bit, she thought.

When they made the turn onto her father's street and Camille saw that every inch of curb space was occupied by a car, the queasiness that she felt at the airport suddenly came back. This time she knew it wasn't altitude sickness.

"Julia, I need to ask you something, and you have to be completely honest."

"*Completely* honest? I guess I can give it a try."

"Does my dad have something planned here?"

Julia bit down on her lip in an attempt to stifle the smile that had already formed on her face. "I don't know what you're talking about."

"Like hell you don't. It's written all over that spray-tanned face of yours."

"Okay, but you have to promise not to tell him that I spoiled it."

Camille shook her head. "I knew it. How bad is it going to be?"

"I don't know. Twenty-five, maybe thirty people. He didn't want to make too big a deal of it, but there's a lot of excitement surrounding your return and he thought it would make you feel good to see that."

Camille grunted as she looked at the house. "You were in on it too?"

"He needed me to pick you up so he could finish the prep work, but he didn't bother to fill me in on the details."

"Because he knew you couldn't keep your mouth shut."

"Yep, and he was obviously one hundred percent correct. So when you go in there you need to act surprised. He's finally at the point of trusting me with you. I don't want to screw that up now."

"What are you talking about? My father loves you."

"He always thought I was a bad influence on you."

"You are a bad influence on me."

"Just remember to act surprised, smart-ass."

Camille's pulse quickened as they pulled into the driveway. She thought she saw a head peek at her from behind the living room curtains then quickly disappear. Suddenly the chaos of D.C. didn't seem so bad after all.

"Act surprised," Camille said as she unbuckled her seatbelt and pushed the car door open with an unsteady hand. "That shouldn't be a problem."

She figured she had been acting for the past eight years anyway. Why not thrill them all with one last command performance?

CHAPTER 4

CRYPTIC

Camille had expected to be bombarded with a *'For she's a jolly good fellow'* chant the moment she opened the door, but she and Julia were instead met with the silence of an empty house.

"I thought this was supposed to be a party," Camille whispered as she looked into the foyer.

"I thought so too," Julia replied, seemingly as confused as Camille was. "I'm sure he told me ten o'clock when we talked yesterday."

"You mean you didn't confirm with him this morning?"

Julia rolled her eyes. "I got caught up in stuff."

Camille couldn't help but laugh. "Jules, you're the smartest person I know, but sometimes…"

"All I know is he told me ten o'clock. I got you here at exactly ten o'clock. I did my part. Who knows, maybe no one bothered to show up."

That option would have been just fine with Camille. "People should have better things to do on a Thursday morning anyway."

"No they shouldn't. Not on this particular Thursday anyway. What the hell happened?"

"It really is okay if no one's here. The last thing I wanted was some hero's welcome anyway. I just want to settle in, grab a late breakfast somewhere, and decompress."

"Maybe I should just check the kitchen," Julia suggested, apparently not hearing one word Camille had said. "They have to be around somewhere."

"Could you please just help me get my bags upstairs?"

"Don't you at least want to look around a little bit?"

The confusion of the moment hadn't allowed Camille to focus on the fact that she was standing in the foyer of the house she was born in; a house she hadn't seen for the better part of eight years. She knew the couch in the living room was the same one her mother had bought twenty-five years ago. She knew most of the pictures hanging on the wall were of her. She knew her father's office was just five feet to the right. And she knew the kitchen that was once home to the best chocolate chip muffins in the world was right around the corner. But she didn't feel the slightest bit of connection to any of it.

"No need to look around," Camille answered as she picked up the suitcase and started up the wooden staircase – a staircase inscribed with the words of a precocious nine-year-old. 'Cam was here'.

Hard to believe that was once true.

The door to her bedroom was closed. She half expected to walk in to the sight of fifty people crammed inside her closet, ready with shouts of surprise and songs of good cheer. But just like in the living room, she only saw emptiness. And just like in the living room, she was not disappointed.

She put her suitcase on top of the double bed she bought when she was in high school. The comforter was purple with white tulips. She had never seen it before.

"You can put that suitcase in the corner," she said to Julia. "I'll get to it later."

Julia complied, dropping it on the floor with a heavy sigh. "My concierge duties are officially done. I'm going downstairs to grab some water. Do you want anything?"

"No thank you," Camille answered without looking up from her suitcase.

"Okay then. I'll be back."

Julia walked out of the room and down the staircase. Camille took a deep breath, then cast her eyes around the bedroom. Except for the comforter, the space was exactly as she left it when she went away to college in the mid-1990s, right down to the Metallica poster hanging beside her bed. As far as she knew, she was the only person in her neighborhood with a Metallica poster on her wall. Then again, she was the only person in her neighborhood to do a lot of things.

If Camille had her way, she would never have even seen this room. The plan was to book a hotel suite and retreat to it the moment she got off the plane. Her father insisted that she come home instead. Camille vehemently protested. But as the criminals who encountered him over the twenty-five years that he served as a Denver police officer could all attest to, it never did any good to protest anything Paul Grisham said.

Now here she was, squatting in a room that hadn't been hers for nearly two decades. And the worst part was that for all of her father's insistence that she be here, he couldn't be bothered to greet her when she actually showed up.

"Oh, this is gonna be a swell time," Camille muttered as she unzipped her suitcase.

From behind, she heard the sound of footsteps entering the room.

"Any sign of that crazy father of mine?" Camille said without turning around.

Her question was met with silence.

"Julia? I said have you seen my dad anywh—" Camille's voice caught in her throat as she turned around to see her father standing in the doorway. The broad smile on his bearded face instantly obliterated the force field she had planned to hide behind once she saw him.

"Are you just going to stand there? Or can this crazy father of yours actually get a hug?" Paul asked as he extended arms so long they looked as if they could wrap around Camille twice with room to spare.

She wanted to run straight into those arms, to lose herself in the warmth and safety of an embrace that had comforted her more times than she could remember. But she was frozen where she stood. The scenarios of this moment played out constantly in her head since she decided to come home. None of those scenarios, however, involved her suddenly losing the power of speech.

"Judging by your lack of forward movement I'm assuming a hug may not be in the cards," Paul continued, his smile slowly fading.

"I'm sorry," Camille finally answered. "I didn't think you were here. Julia and I came in and the house was empty."

"Actually the house is quite crowded."

"What are you talking about?"

"I suppose Julia told you about our little get-together?"

"As a matter of fact she didn't," Camille said with a straight face.

"I'm not so sure I believe that. In any case, there are about twenty people downstairs very eager to see you."

"Were you all hiding in the basement or something?"

"We were waiting on the patio. Good thing it's enclosed with the way this rain is coming down, otherwise my plan would have gone completely to hell."

"And what was your plan?"

"I wasn't going to have twenty people bombard you the second you walked in the door. I wanted you to have whatever moment you needed in here before you saw anyone. Once you made your way into the kitchen, you would see everyone and make your own decision about when to join us. And if you didn't want to join us that would be okay too, but I certainly wanted to try. You're very much in demand down there."

Camille felt the corner of her mouth curl up in an involuntary smile. "And what about the demand level up here?"

Something quivered in her father's face and a tear pooled under his eyelid.

"It's off the charts."

This time when he extended his arms, Camille didn't hesitate. She sunk her head into his barrel of a chest and kept it there for a long time. There were no words spoken between them. And in the best case scenario that Camille envisioned for this moment, there didn't have to be.

After what felt like an hour, Camille lifted her head and looked in her father's face. His smile made her feel more accepted than the world's largest welcome home party ever could.

"So what do you feel like doing?"

Camille was hesitant to answer. For as nice as it was that people took time out of their day to see her, she wasn't sure she was up for the role of party hostess.

Paul continued. "If you're not comfortable I'll understand and so will everyone else. Well, everyone except your Aunt Helen."

"You invited Aunt Helen?" Camille bellowed with a feigned look of dread. "I'm surprised she hasn't already marched up here wondering where the hell I am."

"Exactly. And the longer you keep her waiting, the more likely that trip will be."

Camille took a deep breath to steel herself. Paul put a hand on her shoulder and offered a nod of reassurance. Her first steps into the unknown. She was as ready as she was ever going to be.

"I guess we'd better not keep her waiting."

Aunt Helen wasn't the least bit put off by Camille's delayed appearance, and neither was anyone else. Though her father said the guest list numbered at twenty, Camille counted at least fifteen more. Unlike the vision that played out in her mind, there was no spontaneous cheer when she arrived; no cake and ice cream; no party hats or streamers. Just smiles, hugs, and plenty of encouraging words.

Despite her initial misgivings, she couldn't help but feel touched by the outpouring. Most of the people here were family and close friends who knew Camille long before she had even considered joining the FBI. Many of them had barely even known Camille the FBI agent, aside from what they heard from her father or read in the newspapers. Much to her relief, not one of them appeared interested in learning anything more.

As the day went on and news of her arrival had apparently spread, more people came. Before Camille realized it, the once modest gathering of well-wishers had morphed into a full-blown party. Dixie cups were replaced with beer bottles. Quiet remembrances became raucous storytelling sessions. And for the first time in years, Camille was beginning to remember what home felt like.

At some point during the festivities, she had lost track of Julia. When Camille last saw her, she was talking to her cousin Jonathan, a bear of a man who was the sweetest soul Camille had ever known. He was also a shameless flirt. Even though Julia never had an issue holding her own in social situations, and Cousin Jonathan was as harmless as they came, Camille still felt the need to come to her friend's assistance. But before she could reach them, she was inadvertently pulled into a debate regarding the qualifications of the two local candidates running for U.S. Senate. Beyond the fact that she knew nothing about the candidates, Camille would rather gouge her eyes out than discuss politics on any level. By the time she managed to remove herself from the conversation, Julia was gone.

Camille searched the kitchen, then the living room, then her father's office, but saw no sign of her. Afraid that she may have left, she stepped onto the front porch. Julia's car was still parked in the driveway. Unsure of where else to look, she used the most dependable locating method she knew of.

Julia answered her cell phone after one ring. "Hey."

"Hey stranger. I haven't seen you for a while. I was worried my cousin sweet-talked you into the closet or something."

Julia chuckled. "He's a cute man, but not that cute."

"So where did you go?"

"I'm actually up in your bedroom."

"Oh my God, he's not up there with you is he?"

"You are so gross. I just needed some quiet."

"Don't get your yoga pants in a knot. I was kidding." Camille expected another chuckle to let her know that everything was okay, but Julia was silent. "Are you alright?"

"Yes and no."

"Do you want me to come up?"

Julia made a noise that sounded like a sniffle. "Yes and no."

"I'm ignoring the no."

Camille quickly made her way up the stairs. Even though the bedroom door was ajar, she still knocked.

"You can come in, Cam. I'm decent."

Camille opened the door and saw Julia sitting on the side of the bed. She was scrolling through her cell phone with the intent of someone desperate to find a long lost message.

"I figured I would be the one hiding out up here," Camille said as she walked in.

Julia looked up from her phone with heavy eyes. "Sorry. I had to make a few calls."

"Everything okay?"

Julia nodded.

Camille closed the door and sat on the bed. "I'm getting that cryptic vibe from you again."

"I don't mean to do that."

"For someone who doesn't mean to, you're doing an awfully good job of it."

"It's just a weird time, that's all."

"Preaching to the choir, sister."

Julia sighed. "I know, and I'm sorry."

"For what?"

"Everything you've gone through and you have to come home to a basket-case of a best friend. Not exactly the welcome home that you deserve."

"Right now I'm not worried about what kind of welcome home I deserve. I'm worried about what's happening in my best friend's life that's got her feeling like a basket-case."

Julia abruptly stood up and walked to the window. "There sure are a lot of cars out there," she said as she peered through the blinds. "I told you there were a ton of people eager to see you."

"Don't you dare change the subject," Camille barked. "Get back over here."

Julia rolled her eyes. "Okay mom. You don't have to be so mean about it." She sat down on the bed with a huff.

"Talk."

"I guess the interrogation has officially begun."

"If that's what it takes. I've only lost the desire. I haven't lost the skill. Remember that."

"I don't doubt your skill for a second."

"Then why do you insist on testing it?"

"I'm honestly not trying to be difficult about this. I just don't feel the need to burden you with my screw-ups the day you get home."

"I've been burdened with your screw-ups from day one," Camille said with a half-cocked smile she hoped would ease the tension that was beginning to fill the room.

26

Julia's quivering lip let her know the tactic hadn't worked.

"Bad joke. I'm sorry."

"Hey, it's not like you're lying."

They had first met as roommates during their second year at the University of Colorado. As a way of ushering in their newly minted friendship, Julia invited Camille to a house party for the sorority she wanted to pledge. On her first night as Julia's roommate, Camille not only bore witness to drunken outbursts that would make a sailor blush, she also had to endure the indignity of being thrown out of the house after Julia decided she would rather steal a Delta Gamma pin than pledge for it. If the sorority president hadn't been wearing the pin at the time, Julia may have actually gotten away with it.

When they finally stumbled back to their dorm room, she spent the entire night apologizing. But Camille was far from upset. In Julia she saw the rebellious free spirit that she could never be; the yin to her yang. And though on the surface they appeared to have little in common – Camille played basketball on the cracked asphalt of the Skyline recreation center while Julia played golf on the pristine greens of the Cherry Hills Country Club – they quickly realized that theirs was the recipe for a perfect friendship. Camille needed someone to show her what it was like to walk on the edge, and Julia needed someone to pull her back when she went too far. Sixteen years later, the recipe may have changed, but their friendship was still perfect.

"Jules, you may be a lot of things, but you're far from being a screw-up."

"Don't be so sure about that."

"Fine. I'll reserve judgment until I actually hear the story. Is that fair?"

Julia nodded, her eyes cast down at her feet. "Fair."

Several beats of silence passed between them.

"That was your cue to tell me the story."

"Not now."

Camille clenched her jaw in an attempt to fight back her mounting frustration. "What is the big deal? You've never held out on me like this. Did you kill someone or something?"

"Of course not."

"Then it couldn't possibly be that bad."

Camille was met with silence.

"Could it?"

Julia's cell phone chimed with the sound of tubular bells. She anxiously read the text message then turned the phone off and pushed it in her jacket pocket. "I hate to do this to you, but I have to go."

"You're kidding, right?"

Julia rose to her feet and started for the door. "Unfortunately I'm not. Something's come up at work and I have to go put out the fire."

For reasons she couldn't explain, Camille didn't believe her. "So we're just leaving this up in the air?"

Julia stopped short of the door. "Why don't we do dinner at my house tomorrow? I'll grill some steaks, we'll open a couple of bottles of wine, and I'll totally spill my guts."

"No more holding out on me?"

"No more holding out," she answered with a smile that Camille could only hope was sincere.

"It's a date then."

"Good. I'll write down the address. Do you think you can get a ride?"

"Now that I'm finally old enough to drive maybe my dad will let me borrow his. By the way, do you still have those dogs?"

"Of course. Those are my two babies."

"They're Dalmatians. I doubt there's anything baby-like about them."

Julia shook her head. "You dealt with the world's most hard-core killers on a daily basis, yet you're still petrified of dogs. I'll never understand it. But if it will help, I'll make sure they're in the backyard when you come."

"Thank you," Camille said. "And by the way, I'm not petrified of dogs."

"No? Then what would you call it?"

"Hopelessly petrified."

She and Julia shared a much-needed laugh. After she wrote down her address, Julia extended her arms. "Hug please? A big one?"

Camille promptly obliged.

"To say it's good to have you home would be the understatement of the century," Julia said.

"You make being home a lot easier to deal with."

"I really can't help but wonder how different things would be if you had been around more."

Camille pulled away from Julia's embrace. "What do you mean?"

Julia paused to measure her words. "You're the only person in my life who has ever been able to reel me in when I step too far out on the ledge. Most people I know could watch me fall off head first and not lose a moment of sleep over it."

"Jesus, what kind of crowd are you running with these days?"

"The kind you probably wouldn't approve of."

"If you're talking about those money-hungry idiots you complained about earlier, then you're absolutely right I don't approve."

Julia's face twisted in disgust. "It's not about money for these people. Money is simply a byproduct."

"A byproduct of what?"

"The game."

"The game?"

"Every move they make every second of the day is spent finding new ways to manipulate a system they've already thoroughly corrupted. Most of us have boundaries we won't cross.

Most of us live a life of limits. These people don't understand limits. They aren't bound by morality or conscience or empathy, because they've never had to be. They're in the business of accumulation and control. Be it money, institutions, or people's lives, it makes no difference. To them, it's nothing more than sport." Julia paused for a long beat. "Unfortunately, that's the kind of crowd I've been running with."

Camille was nearly rendered speechless, needing to take a deep breath before responding. "Well, thanks for freaking me the hell out."

"I haven't freaked you out yet," Julia declared as she moved toward the bedroom door. "Just wait until you get some wine in me. I'll tell you some stuff that will positively blow your mind."

"I know I haven't been the most available friend lately, but whatever this is, you could have talked to me about it before now."

"Trust me, I couldn't have."

Camille needed another breath. "Wow, you certainly know how to build suspense, and I can't say that I particularly like it."

"I'm sorry. I shouldn't have even gone there. Just forget I said any of that."

"Not likely."

"Okay. At least forget about it until dinner tomorrow."

"Why do you think things would be so different had I been around?" Camille asked, not yet ready to forget.

Julia appeared to lose herself in thought. "It doesn't matter. You're here now."

"And that ledge you were talking about? Do I still need to pull you back in?"

"Believe it or not you've already started to," Julia said with a deep smile. "But more about that tomorrow. I really do have to go."

"Not before I tell you something," Camille said, stopping Julia in the doorway.

"I'm all ears."

"Thank you for being there for me this morning. Thank you for always being there for me, but especially this morning. I don't think I could have managed any of this without you." Camille felt a lump in her throat and knew that if she said any more the dam of emotions that had held up for the past few hours would burst wide open.

Julia dabbed at the corner of her eye with her shirtsleeve. "The feeling is more than mutual, my friend."

After another extended hug, Julia walked down the staircase.

Camille lingered in the bedroom long after she was gone. Though their conversation ended on a positive note, it still left her feeling uneasy. She couldn't remember a time when Julia spoke in such vague terms, especially when it came to personal matters. And though most of the conversation centered on Julia's work colleagues, Camille knew there was something much more personal behind it all.

She couldn't pretend to know what that something was. She hoped it was nothing more than some pre-midlife crisis that made Julia want to quit her job and join the Cirque De Soleil. It was a preposterous notion, but one that Camille knew she could handle.

In reality, she knew that the situation was not the least bit preposterous, nor was it any kind of pre-midlife crisis. And considering Julia's hesitation in revealing that situation, Camille wondered, with mounting fear, if it would ultimately be more than she could handle.

CHAPTER 5

PLAN B

The last guest didn't leave until six that evening. Even though Camille was thankful for everyone who came out, and tried to give each person a word of gratitude, she could barely contain her joy when the house was finally empty. It was as long and emotionally draining a day as she could remember having, and she wanted nothing more than for it to end.

After she closed the door for the last time, she settled into the recliner that had been her father's favorite for nearly thirty years. It was surprisingly comfortable, and Camille thought that if she actually reclined in it she would be asleep within five minutes.

Before she could close her eyes, her father came into the living room and took a seat on the couch next to her. He looked tired, and Camille imagined it had been a long day for him too. But behind his heavy red eyes, she saw a familiar gleam. She saw that same gleam after every dance recital she ever had. She saw it when she graduated from college. She saw it when she showed him her FBI shield for the first time. Tonight, the gleam said, *I couldn't be happier to have you home.*

The two sat in comfortable silence for several minutes before Paul finally spoke. "So is everything how you remember it?"

From the built in bookcase on the east wall, to the green couches that were supposedly imported from Italy, to the hideously outdated popcorn ceilings, most everything in the room had remained unchanged from when Camille was a child.

"Feels like 1992 all over again."

Paul smiled. "I'm not big into updating."

"You realize that you can actually hire people to do that for you, right?"

"I'm more of a do-it-yourself kind of guy. My idea of remodeling is patching up the cracks, changing the light bulbs and stopping the leaks. I don't need anyone else's sense of style wrecking this place."

Camille thought about her mother and wondered what she would have to say about that. The image of her face put a knot in Camille's throat so large she could barely fight it back.

"I'll see if I can change your mind," Camille replied, her voice cracking.

Paul noticed. "Are you okay?"

Camille took a moment to steady herself. "I'm fine. It's just strange, that's all."

"Being back here?"

She nodded.

"I know it's going to be an adjustment, but right now it's the best thing. You need time to get yourself–"

"I should probably start cleaning up this mess," Camille said as she abruptly stood up and began picking up paper plates and beer bottles.

"Camille, stop."

She continued as if she hadn't heard him.

"Sit down please? We've hardly had a chance to talk since you got here. This other stuff can wait."

Camille promptly stopped and sat back down in the recliner.

"I just want you to talk to me," Paul continued.

"About what?"

"About whatever is on your mind."

Camille stood up and started collecting beer bottles again. "There isn't anything on my mind right now except cleaning up this place."

"Cam, sit down."

This time it wasn't a request. Camille let out an exasperated sigh as she complied.

"Listen, I know this has been a difficult time, and you've had to make some decisions that you never thought you would have to make. Believe me, I understand—"

"How could you possibly understand?" Camille interrupted. "You've never quit on anyone or anything in your entire life. You were a cop for twenty-seven years, and you were out there every single day, no matter how shitty it got."

"There were plenty of times I wanted to quit."

"But you didn't."

"I never had to deal with anything close to what you had to deal with, even on the worst days. I saw some things in my time on the street, but never anything like..." He paused as if to clear his mind of something very much unwanted. "I don't know how I would have handled it."

"It was my job to handle it."

"Just because you had an FBI badge didn't mean you weren't human. They didn't train you to be some unthinking, unfeeling robot whose sole mission was to hunt down terrorists and serial killers. Everyone has a limit, Camille. You reached yours and you rightly walked away. And it was the best thing you could have done for yourself. I've worked with plenty of men who exceeded their limits and thought they could fight their way through it. If you want to know how that worked out for them, ask their wives and children, because quite a few of those men are no longer here to answer for themselves."

Camille felt her knees buckle and was glad she was sitting. "You certainly know how to drive a point home."

"It's more like trying to drive some sense into you. It's been killing me to see what you're doing to yourself over this. Before all of this Circle Killer stuff, I never used to worry about you. I knew from firsthand experience how dangerous it was out there, but you were part of the finest law enforcement agency in the world, which meant you knew how to handle yourself. But there's no amount of training in the world that could have prepared you for what you encountered with Daniel Sykes. I've never worried more about you than I have for the past two months. From the night you called to tell me you were thinking about quitting, I hadn't been able to sleep, not because you wanted to quit, but because things had gotten so bad that you felt like you had to."

When Camille's mouth began to quiver Paul put a hand on her knee. "When you finally told me that you had decided to leave, I couldn't have been more relieved. Yes, I was over the moon that you were an FBI agent. Yes, I bragged about you every chance I got. But before you were a federal agent, you were my daughter. Contrary to what you may have thought, I never saw you as someone who decided to take the easy way out because you couldn't do your job. I only saw my little girl in a tremendous amount of pain. When I told you I supported your decision to leave, I meant it. What I didn't tell you was how overjoyed I was at the news. I slept like a baby that night."

Camille smiled as she wiped the tears running down her cheeks. "I always assumed you were disappointed."

"Hopefully this sets the record straight," Paul said as he gave Camille a box of Kleenex. "You did what you had to do. Whether I agree with it or not is ultimately irrelevant. All that matters is that it was the right decision for you."

"It was. I had so many people in my ear telling me that I just needed time; that counseling would help; that I was too good to leave. Obviously that wasn't true."

The expression on her father's face hardened. "Stop right there. You're not getting away with that one. You were more cut out for the job than anyone I've ever known, myself included. I know how much respect you had in the Bureau. There was a reason the agent in charge of your unit was falling all over himself to get you to stay. And it wasn't just because you're pretty."

"That doesn't exactly help me feel better."

The creases in Paul's furrowed brow softened. "I'm only telling the truth. I was a cop for almost thirty years, so I know what it takes to be a good one. You were a damn good one, Camille. Don't ever forget that."

"Keep up with this pep talk and I might have to consider going back."

"I'm afraid it's too late my dear. I finally have you home and I'm not giving you back."

Camille leaned into her father with outstretched arms, burying her head in his broad shoulder. "Dad, what the hell am I going to do with myself? It's not like I had a plan B."

"Most cops don't. But it isn't something you should worry about right now. You're home with people who love you to death. You're safe here. Take as much time as you need to figure it out."

Camille finally managed a smile. "So does that mean I can crash here?"

"You can crash here as long as you like, but on one condition."

"What's that?"

"After tonight, the pity parade ends."

Pity parade. The words stung, but Camille couldn't be mad at him for saying them. She had become quite adept at wallowing in self-pity. And as much as she wanted to tell him that she would snap out of it, that from here on out she would be the headstrong, confident, fearless Camille that he had raised, she didn't want to make promises she couldn't keep.

"I'll give it a shot, dad."

"That's good enough for me."

"Now, I have some conditions of my own," Camille said as she leaned back in the recliner.

"I'm almost afraid to know."

"The first is that you help me figure out that plan B. The second is that you give me a lenient curfew."

Paul smiled wide. "The first one I can deal with. The second one will require some major negotiation. What do you say we start the bidding at eleven P.M.?"

"I'm almost thirty-five-years-old, dad. At least give me twelve forty-five."

"How about I just ground you altogether?"

"You wish old man."

"Fine. We'll save the house-rules conversation for another day," Paul relented as he stood up and scanned a living room littered with plates and beer bottles. "Let's just get this mess cleaned up."

"I thought you'd never ask." Camille grabbed the closest stack of plates and took them into the kitchen. As she walked in, she heard her cell phone ringing. Tossing the plates in the garbage, she ran over to the kitchen table where her phone was sitting, but she was too late to answer it. The call had come from Julia. Camille held the phone for a moment, waiting for a voicemail notification. When one didn't come she set the phone back on the table and went into the living room. If she remembered, she would return Julia's call when she was finished. But if she didn't, she could always talk to her tomorrow.

As it turned out, Camille didn't remember. She went to bed shortly after cleaning the house, not giving a second thought to the missed call. Settling into the double bed that felt entirely too small for her, she could only think about how thankful she was that the day had finally come to an end, and how she hoped that tomorrow would finally be the start of something good. There may not have been a plan B in sight, but for the first time in months, she felt reasonably optimistic that she would find it.

Unfortunately, the feeling wouldn't last.

Tomorrow would definitely be the start of something. But it wouldn't be good.

CHAPTER 6

SILENCE

Julia was startled awake by the sound of heavy bass. Underneath the rhythmic thumping, the whiny, indecipherable lyrics of some cotton-mouthed rapper scratched at the edges of her brain like sandpaper. Her bedroom windows shook, and as the volume of the music increased, Julia feared its sheer force would be enough to shatter them entirely. Then just as she rose out of bed to go to the window, the bass began to fade. A few seconds later, it was gone. Living in the city, she was accustomed to hearing rap music blasting from car speakers at volumes too earsplitting to be legal. But it was rare to hear it in this neighborhood. It was even rarer to hear it at 12:30 in the morning.

Downstairs, George and Gracie were barking up a storm, and Julia guessed the music had gotten their attention too. It normally took very little to whip the two of them into an absolute frenzy, especially when they were startled. As guard dogs went, Julia could not have asked for a better pair. Gracie was normally curled up on the floor in front of Julia's bed while George held down the kitchen. It made for a good night's sleep knowing those two were always around, always reliable, and always ready to bite the nuts clean off of anyone who didn't belong there.

In fact, George and Gracie were the only reason Julia was able to sleep at all. She'd had a security system installed the day she moved into the house, and it was armed every night. But she never fully trusted it to keep her safe. It couldn't sense the danger before it arrived, nor did it have the instinct to protect her to the death. It was a machine, which meant it could be tricked, manipulated, and ultimately defeated. As far as Julia was concerned, none of those things could happen to her Dalmatians.

Tonight, more than any other night that she could remember, she was grateful for their presence.

Julia feared there were people in the world who meant to do her harm because of what she knew about them. Before yesterday, there had been no direct evidence to substantiate this fear. There weren't any menacing phone calls or emails, no warning shots through her bedroom window, no failed car bomb detonations. There was only the disk and the safeguards she took to ensure that no one else was aware of its existence. And as far as she knew, no one else was.

But when she saw the black Audi trailing her as she left Camille's house yesterday afternoon, Julia knew that it was time to rethink that notion.

She first noticed the car three days ago on her morning drive to work. She had always had a thing for Audis and the arrogant dickheads who drove them, so she paid close attention to the car the instant it pulled up behind her at a stoplight. Though the darkly tinted windows prevented her from getting a good look at the driver, he wasn't difficult to imagine. She had dated men like him by the dozen; most of them tax attorneys who preferred money clips to wallets, ate sushi instead of red meat, and prized their trophy mistresses over their blindly committed wives. The man she pictured sitting behind the wheel fit the profile to a tee. He undoubtedly sat ramrod straight in his seat, his left hand – absent a wedding ring – tightly gripping the top of the steering wheel. And though she had no way of knowing for sure, she couldn't escape the feeling that his eyes were fixed on her.

Her mouth curled up in a tight smile at the thought.

Whenever she glanced in her mirror, he was there. When she switched lanes, so did he. When she ran a yellow light, he ran the red one. And so it went for the entire eight mile drive to her office. She didn't want to read too much into it. He was most likely just another three-piece suit-wearing idiot running late for work. The morning commute was full of them. But a small part of her still hoped that his attention was something more than fellow motorist.

She let the thought pass quickly, however. It was that line of thinking that always seemed to get her in trouble. And the last thing Julia could afford more of was trouble.

By the time she reached the parking garage of her office building, the Audi was gone. *Nothing like a playful game of cat and mouse to start the day*, she had mused to herself. *Maybe I can do the following next time.* Julia knew that she had probably seen the last of the Audi and laughed at herself for even indulging in such a thought.

The next time she saw the car, that same morning during a cross-town trip to a client's office, she was not laughing.

Much like it had done earlier, the Audi followed at some distance behind her – too far to be an obvious threat, yet close enough to be noticed. This time she was positive the driver's eyes were trained on her. But of course they couldn't really have been. Like the Audi, the windows of her Range Rover were darkly tinted, making it nearly impossible for a person driving behind her to see inside. Still, she couldn't help but dwell on the possibility.

Not possible, she thought. *No one is watching you. It's purely coincidence.* She repeated the word until she finally lost sight of the Audi two blocks from her destination. *Coincidence.*

But what were the odds that the same car would end up behind her twice in the same day by strict coincidence? Far greater than that car ending up behind her intentionally, she concluded.

She decided right then that she would not succumb to the fear that was beginning to settle in over her; fear that had caused her to believe that the dickhead in the Audi had either the time or the inclination to follow her; fear that she was slowly losing her grip on reality.

The roots of that fear had begun to take hold long before the Audi, but seeing it that day only served to bring her situation into clearer focus. It reminded her of what could happen if she wasn't careful; what could happen if she didn't begin to make better decisions; what could happen if the trouble she currently found herself in reached the levels that she knew it had the potential to.

The thought was too much to consider and she decided to push it as far out of her mind as she could. For the most part, she had succeeded in keeping it out.

Until yesterday.

When she saw the Audi for the third time, she finally understood that it wasn't coincidental. She also knew that his attention was far more than that of fellow motorist. It didn't matter how good-looking she imagined him to be, or how many guys like him she had dated in the past. Dangerous men in black suits may have been figments of Hollywood's imagination, but dangerous men in black Audis were very real.

Eying the car in her rearview mirror, she knew there were only two options: call the police or put her foot on the gas and try to outrun him. She wasn't crazy about either one. Calling the police was the most logical thing to do, but it would also open her up to scrutiny that she was desperate to avoid. Outrunning the Audi was simply not realistic, especially if he was the least bit motivated to keep up with her.

Instead, she continued to drive as if nothing were wrong until she came upon a fast food restaurant. She pulled into the crowded parking lot, hoping like mad that he didn't follow. Much to her relief he kept going.

THE STRATEGIST

After fifteen minutes, the trembling in Julia's hands calmed down enough for her to put them back on the wheel and pull out of the lot. Her eyes were locked on her rearview mirror for the entire fifteen-minute trip home. The Audi had not come back into view, but Julia knew he was out there somewhere; and she knew she would probably see him again.

After arriving home, she strongly considered checking into a hotel until she could meet with Camille and figure out her next move. But she didn't know any of her neighbors well enough to take the dogs, and their overly-rambunctious nature made the doggy-daycare folks a little too nervous. That meant leaving them alone for the night. And no matter how uneasy being in the house made her feel, she couldn't leave them alone.

So she closed the blinds, armed the security system, and told George and Gracie to stay extra-vigilant. Judging from their reaction to the music, they were doing just that.

Aside from the sound of clawed feet scurrying against the wood floor downstairs, the night had fallen back into silence. Julia put her head on the pillow and closed her eyes. She saw the Audi in her mind, and wondered if it had been outside of Camille's house while she was there. *It couldn't have been*, she concluded. If it were, she would have noticed it sooner.

But what if it had been there? And if it had been, how many other times could she have missed it? For all she knew, he could have been following her for weeks. Something was making her nervous enough to look outside before she left the house every morning. Yet she was always quick to dismiss her fear when she saw nothing to support it. Now she knew that the fear was legitimate, and its source had apparently been in her rearview mirror all along.

When she called Camille earlier in the evening, she had done so reluctantly. She wanted to tell her about the Audi and all the reasons she believed it may have been following her, but she was afraid to hear what the words would sound like as they came out of her mouth. It is one thing to think someone may be stalking you. It is another thing to give an audible voice to it. She was almost relieved when Camille didn't answer and she gave no thought to leaving a voicemail. She couldn't even fathom how such a message would begin.

Julia had wanted to tell her so much more about what was happening: work, the affair, the flash disk, and how the three were so intricately intertwined. But like the child who promises to bring her failing report card home to show her parents, she chickened out.

It was true that Camille was dealing with a lot, and Julia adding her own problems to the mix would probably be more than her already full plate could handle. But Camille was also the kind of person who could easily cast her own problems aside to come to the aide of someone else, especially when that someone else was her best friend. The fear of being a burden wasn't the reason why Julia couldn't bring herself to tell the story. It was the fear of being judged by the one person in the world who still thought the absolute best of her; the one person who would never believe her to be capable of doing the things that she had done; the one person who still saw enough good in her to be disappointed by the bad.

But Julia now realized that it no longer mattered if Camille judged her or looked differently upon her. Despite the image she may have displayed to the world, the truth of who she actually was lay in the files of that disk. Camille had to know that truth, not merely for the sake of having a more accurate picture of Julia's life, but also in the interests of saving it.

When she glanced at her alarm clock, it read one twenty-eight. It had been nearly an hour since she last heard the music. Now nothing moved around her. Even George and Gracie had settled down. Julia looked toward the foot of her bed to see if Gracie had come back up undetected and taken her usual resting spot, but she hadn't. George, ever the charmer, must have convinced her to stay downstairs.

44

Julia felt a deep sense of calm as she rested her head on the pillow, and within moments, she was fast asleep.

She heard echoes of the dogs barking in her dreams. The barks were weak, pleading, and distant. In her dream, she and Gracie were running through Congress Park, the same as they did every morning, when a man wearing a black hooded sweatshirt suddenly came up behind them and kicked Gracie in the ribs, sending her hurling to the ground. As she fell, she made the most horrendous sound that Julia had ever heard come out of a living being.

The man stood over Julia as she cradled Gracie's limp body in her arms.

"Look at me," he said in a voice that didn't sound human.

When Julia refused to divert her eyes away from her injured dog, the man kicked Gracie again. "I said look at me!"

Julia screamed as she leapt to her feet and turned to face him. But he wasn't there. She was instead looking directly into a narrow beam of light so bright that it instantly blinded her. Julia shut her eyes in an effort to fight off the glare, but she couldn't escape it.

There was a hard yank on her shoulder and for an instant, she thought it was Gracie trying to pull her to safety, but Gracie was lying motionless at her feet.

The sight of her dead dog instantly pulled her out of the dream.

The light that she woke up to wasn't nearly as bright as the one from her dream, but it blinded her just the same. She felt a throbbing in her shoulder and realized that something had indeed yanked at it. She instinctively called out to Gracie, then to George.

When the circular beam of light that had been shining in her face suddenly shut off to reveal a massive silhouette standing directly above her, she realized that neither one of them were coming.

CHAPTER 7

THE OPEN DOOR

If Dale Rooney had his way, he would live in a two-room cabin cloistered deep in the Sangre de Cristo Mountains of southern Colorado; so far removed from anything resembling civilization that even the world's most sophisticated GPS wouldn't be able to find him. He imagined a simple life of living off the land, surrounded by trout-filled lakes, lush evergreen trees, and limitless space for his German Shepard Ike.

But in sixty-seven years of life, Dale rarely got his way. He knew there would be no frontier living with Ike the German Shepard. Dale didn't even have a German Shepard. What he did have was a house in the city that he wished he had sold fifteen years ago, a wife who somehow convinced him not to sell it, and a little runt of a Pomeranian that she seemed to love a hell of a lot more than she loved him.

Fifteen years ago, when he had first considered selling, the neighborhood was much different than it is now. There were no uppity hipsters who were young enough to be his children yet treated him with the reverence of a garden tool; no inflated property taxes because misguided parents insisted that their children's schools have state-of-the-art everything; and no cars driving up and down his street all times of the night blaring that jungle thump that passed for music.

What Dale wouldn't have done for the opportunity to go back; to act when he still had the chance. He would certainly have had that cabin by now – with his wife and Pomeranian or without them.

But now he was stuck here, and as much as he may have fantasized about it, there would be no escaping the uppity hipsters, the high taxes, or the jungle music.

Of everything that was wrong with his neighborhood, the music bothered him the most. It was especially bad last night. He had dealt with the obnoxiously loud bass before, but what he heard outside his window a few hours ago bordered on criminal.

He had just fallen asleep on the couch, which he seemed to do a lot more of these days, when he was awakened by what he thought was a sonic boom. When he looked outside he immediately saw the source of the noise. A light colored Chevy Impala that he instantly knew should not have been there idled in the middle of the street, its engine running and its stereo on full volume. Dale pressed close to the window. The car's windows were tinted, but he had no trouble imagining the kind of person who sat behind the wheel.

After thirty seconds or so, the car pulled up to the curb a couple of houses down. The engine continued to run, but the music abruptly stopped. A thousand alarm bells instantly went off in Dale's head and he had the immediate thought of calling the police. But before he did, he decided to get a closer look. If he needed to give the police a description, he wanted to give the most accurate one possible.

From his front porch, he could see the car clearly. It was light gray or silver with four doors. Looking closer, he could see that the passenger's side window was rolled down, though his vantage point did not allow him to see inside. He couldn't see the license plate either, which he knew he would need to write down. He had to get closer but didn't want to leave the cover of his front porch, so he decided to go back inside to retrieve a pair of binoculars that he kept in the foyer closet. He liked to have them on standby specifically for occasions like this.

But as soon as he turned to walk inside the house, he heard the music start up again. By the time he turned back around, the Impala had pulled away from the curb.

Dale stepped off the porch and on to his front lawn, scouring the street like a surveillance camera. He kept watch until he was completely satisfied that neither the Impala nor its God-awful music was returning.

When he finally made it up to his bedroom, it was 12:56. He shook his head when he looked in the bed to see his wife Maggie spread eagle in the middle of it while Trinket the prized Pomeranian slept soundly on Dale's pillow.

"Dale Rooney bites the dust again," he said in a voice that he hoped was loud enough to wake up Maggie or the dog. Neither of them flinched.

Back on the couch, Dale fantasized about the cabin he never had, and the solitude he would probably never experience. He wasn't sure if he had fallen asleep or if the fantasy was so real that it felt like he was asleep, but the next time he looked at the clock it was four seventeen a.m.

Dale never needed more than a few hours of sleep a night to function properly, so he got up, brewed himself a pot of coffee, and basked in the silence of the early morning. There was very little in Dale's life that he would describe as ideal, but these early mornings came close. When the world was this quiet, it was almost like it didn't exist. He was free to be alone with his thoughts; to dream of the life that could still one day be his.

This morning, he reflected on the strange car and the loud music and wondered if he should have called the police. He supposed it was possible that the car had a legitimate reason for being on his street – a late night pizza delivery, a boyfriend of one of the rebellious teenage girls across the street — but the car was just as likely filled with a bunch of gang-bangers casing the neighborhood.

As was usually the case with Dale, he waited too long to act. Calling the police would be pointless now. The car was long gone. If it was filled with gang-bangers casing the block, all he could do was pray that his wasn't the house they targeted.

Dale finished his second cup of coffee, then as was customary, especially on mild mornings when the rain or snow was kind enough not to interfere, he slipped on a pair of sweatpants, grabbed his wooden walking stick, and set out for a quiet stroll around the neighborhood. It was the absolute perfect time to go. Most of his neighbors were still asleep, so he didn't have to put on the tired act of being interested in them.

He whistled Bob Seger's *Turn the Page* as he walked to the front door. But before he could make it outside, he heard an unfortunate noise from upstairs that stopped him cold in his tracks.

Trinket started barking.

Dale rolled his eyes. Once that dog started, she didn't stop. He knew what was coming next. Unfortunately, he didn't have to wait long to hear it.

"Dale? Sweetie, are you awake?"

Maggie knew damn well he was awake, but he refused to answer her. The dog started barking even louder and now he could hear her paws scratching against the hardwood floor.

"Dale honey? Are you here?"

Dale grunted and walked to the base of the staircase. "Yes I'm here! What do you want?"

"Would you do me a favor and take Trinket out? She's really agitated and I think she needs to relieve herself!"

"Come on, Maggie! You know that dog always gives me grief when I take it out!" Dale used the same argument every morning. It had yet to work.

"Please? It'll only take a minute!"

Dale grunted again. It would have been easy for him to just walk out the door without saying anything, but he didn't. *A willing accomplice to my own misery*, he thought as he braced himself for what he was about to say next. "Bring her down!"

Dale stood on the front porch holding a flashlight while the dog did her business in the bushes. He had learned to bring a flashlight along because Trinket had the most annoying habit of running away whenever she grew tired of sniffing the rose bushes or digging up Dale's grass; and finding a black Pomeranian in the pitch dark of early morning is next to impossible without the assistance of a heavy duty Mag-lite.

Less than thirty seconds into her bathroom break, Trinket held true to form. Before Dale could take a step to try to stop her, she had bolted off the lawn and down the sidewalk.

Dale gave chase as fast as his artificial knees would take him.

"Trinket what are you doing? Get back here!"

The dog briefly stopped to look at Dale, then ran up the grassy hill of the house two doors down.

"If you think I'm climbing these stairs to get you, you're out of your mind," Dale snapped in between labored breaths.

When he reached the house, he saw Trinket standing on the front porch. She was making that incessant 'yip' sound that was her version of barking, and it was about three octaves louder than usual.

"Trinket! Shut up and get back down here!"

The dog briefly stopped to look in his direction then redirected her attention to the house. The yipping continued.

Dale mumbled a string of curses as he slowly made his way up the stairs leading to the porch. "I don't know what you're barking at, but if you don't stop right this minute…"

When he reached the top of the stairs, he saw exactly what Trinket was barking at.

The entire house was cast in a deep shadow of black. There was no porch light, no lights on in the house, even the street lamp in front of the house was out.

Yet the front door was wide open.

Dale's blood ran cold. He called out to the dog. "Trinket, get away from there." This time his voice lacked anything resembling authority.

He vaguely knew the woman who lived here. From what he had gathered, she wasn't particularly social, not with him at least. She was just another one of the young, upwardly mobile types who were taking over the neighborhood; a neighborhood that they saw as nothing more than a place to lay their heads when they weren't working.

When Dale made it to the porch, he could see inside the house. It felt cool and empty, like no one had lived there for a long time. The alarm bells went off in his head again, twice as loud as before. And this time he was determined to act.

As Trinket stood next to him, still yipping, her eyes seemed to be focused on something inside. Dale stepped into the doorway, hesitated briefly, then stuck his head inside the foyer. For a moment, he could see nothing in the darkness. Then the natural light from outside began to filter its way in and he could make out objects: pictures on the foyer wall, an armchair, an end table with a lamp on top of it. Then he saw something else about ten feet away from the door. His eyes did a double take, then a triple-take, yet he still couldn't quite believe what he was seeing. As he took another step inside, he finally turned on the flashlight. Suddenly, the horror was very real.

The Dalmatian was lying on its side directly in front of the staircase, motionless. Were it not for the pool of blood, Dale would have assumed it was asleep.

He stumbled backward as he put his hand over his mouth to stifle a scream. All he wanted to do was run, but he knew he couldn't.

With the flashlight turned on, Dale could now see a lot more of what had apparently happened inside the house. There was broken glass on the floor. A potted plant had been smashed near the dog. The couch was turned over as was the dining room table and china cabinet. It was as if a tornado tore through the living room and left nothing standing in its wake, not even the Dalmatian that he had seen so many times before.

He knew there were two dogs, but he couldn't see the other one. "Where is it?" he silently mouthed to himself. The same place as its owner, he suspected.

Dale ran back onto the porch to dry heave, then scooped up Trinket and hobbled home to call the police. As he ran, he thought about the strange car, and his failure to act when he should have, and how his wife always talked him into walking her stupid dog – just like she always talked him into so many things. Mostly, he thought about that two-room cabin in southern Colorado.

Right now, it never felt so far away.

CHAPTER 8

SCANNER

Despite a major bout of jet lag and a night of sleep that could best be described as inconsistent, Camille was out of bed, showered, and dressed by six-fifteen A.M. The two-hour time deficit and drastic change in scenery had done little to alter a morning routine that had been a constant since her days in the academy. Old habits apparently die very hard.

She smiled as she walked past her father's closed bedroom door and down the stairs. When Camille was a child, he was usually gone long before she woke up. Even on days when he didn't have to work, she was often awakened by his heavy footsteps padding down the staircase one to two hours before the sun made its first appearance. Now, six years removed from the daily grind of making his doughnut run in time for morning roll call, Paul Grisham had apparently found another way to enjoy the hard-earned fruits of his labor aside from regular trips to the driving range. He slept in.

You've certainly earned it, big guy.

Before she went to bed, Camille set the coffee maker to start brewing at six, the same as she had done in D.C. every morning for the past eight years. By the time she came downstairs, the smell of fresh coffee had wafted into practically every corner of the house.

As she sat at the kitchen table, skimming the business section of the previous day's newspaper and sipping on a cup of *Seattle's Best*, she realized that this could have been the start of any other morning. But it wasn't like any other morning. There would be no briefing from the Bureau chief, no psych profile to review, no bagel and cream cheese breakfast with her partner and friend Agent Sheridan. There was only a cup of coffee, an outdated newspaper, and the first full day she would face in a long time with absolutely nothing to do.

Despite her own lack of an agenda, she was positive her father would have something in store for her. As he had declared last night, her pity parade was officially over. He may have respected what she had gone through and supported her decisions along the way, but he also fully expected her to crawl out of the murk that she had been slogging through, and to do it quickly. That meant no sitting on the couch watching *The Young and the Restless* while she half-heartedly plotted her re-entry into the world of the productive. How far he was willing to go to ensure that such a scenario was never allowed to play itself out remained to be seen, but as long as she lived under his roof, Camille knew that she would have no choice but to play along.

For now, she simply wanted to enjoy the stillness of a house that she had yet to fully reacquaint herself with. As she walked around each room, she tried to focus on something that would help re-establish her history with it.

In the kitchen, there was the red and green vase that she made for her mother in eighth-grade ceramics class. Despite its cracked rim and overall hideous appearance, someone always made sure there were fresh flowers in it; a tradition her father currently maintained with pink and red carnations. On the living room floor was the gold afghan that her mother shampooed at least once a month. On the mantle over the fireplace was the outstanding service award that her mother received from the Colorado Bar Association for her five years as a district court judge. Next to that was a picture from the 2001 Race for the Cure. Camille and her mother stood arm in arm at the finish line, both of them dressed in pink from head to toe.

In spite of an always-radiant smile, the chemo had taken a major toll on her mother's appearance at that point. Most of her hair had fallen out, and her once bright face was gray and gaunt. She had been diagnosed with breast cancer eight months earlier and signing up for the race had been her way of declaring war on a disease she was determined to beat. For that day, with Camille running beside her for the entire three miles, Olivia Grisham did beat it. Early detection, a double mastectomy, and aggressive chemotherapy had given her hope that there would be many more races to run.

But there wouldn't be. The cancer spread much faster than the doctor's anticipated and had quickly become inoperable. Olivia died three weeks before her daughter was accepted into the academy.

When Camille decided to apply, her mother was the first person she told. Though she expressed initial misgivings the same as any parent would when their only child tells them she wants to be the next Clarice Starling, Olivia eventually embraced the idea. Whenever she found a story related to the FBI, she would clip it from the newspaper. When Camille shared her dream of living and working in Washington D.C., Olivia convinced Paul to start looking at houses in the area. Near the end, when the hospice nurses would visit the house, she always told them they had to work extra hard to keep her alive because her daughter was on her way to becoming an FBI agent, and she planned to be there to see her first big arrest. She told them that it would be one of the proudest moments of her life.

Unfortunately, that first big arrest came long after Olivia passed away; and nothing about it, Camille concluded, would have given her reason to be proud.

As she continued looking around, Camille realized that most everything here was a reminder of her mother. She had been dead for nearly nine years, but the house was still decidedly hers. Camille knew that her father's disinterest in changing the décor had very little to do with his lack of style. It had everything to do with preserving the memory of his wife. Keeping the house unchanged meant keeping her alive; just like keeping Camille's room unchanged was his way of keeping her home.

But no matter how much her father tried, home could never be what it once was. Camille's connection to it died along with her mother. And every year that she found an excuse not to come back, every Thanksgiving and Christmas that she flew her father out to D.C., the cold reality that her mother would never be there to hug her stung a little bit less.

As she walked out of the living room, Camille finally understood why this house felt so foreign: she needed it to be that way. For as much as she wanted to feel the safety and security of being home, she knew that she had the ability to be little more than a temporary guest here. To try to be anything else threatened to open up wounds that she had neither the strength nor the will to endure. All it took was one glance at a decade old picture of her mother to remind her of that.

"So much for enjoying the stillness," she muttered to herself as she walked into her father's office and sat down at the desk.

The room was filled with the standard memorabilia that came from twenty-seven years of being a first-rate cop: service awards, pictures with four different mayors, a gold plated replica of his badge, and a framed retirement banner covered with the signatures of practically every member of the Denver Police Department. Her father was as respected as any officer in the department had ever been, and the testaments to that were on proud display all around her.

Of all the rooms in the house, Camille felt the most out of place in this one. In the past, it had been a source of inspiration.

She spent countless hours staring at pictures of him in his uniform, reading the true crime books that lined his bookshelf, listening to dispatch chatter on his police scanner, and dreaming of the day when she would get to wear a badge just like his.

Now the room felt like a shrine that she was desecrating by her mere presence.

I really should have checked into a hotel.

As she stood up from the desk, her eyes drifted to the bookshelf where she noticed that most of the true crime and procedure books she grew up reading had been replaced with historical novels and golf magazines. But one thing hadn't changed.

The handheld police scanner sat in the same corner of the top shelf as it always had. Judging by the thick blanket of dust covering its face, it probably hadn't been touched in the decade since she last used it. By this point, it was more ornamental than functional anyway; another sentimental keepsake from a bygone era.

Camille picked it up off the shelf and sat back down at the desk. She blew away a mound of dust and hit the power button. To her surprise, the green LED display lit up and the sound of crackling static emitted from the speaker. The 200-channel scanner could hone in on frequencies as far south as Houston and as far west as Los Angeles, but it was automatically set to pick up Denver police dispatch.

After about thirty seconds, the static gave way to the sound of a female voice.

"Corner of twelfth and Logan. We have a Hispanic male, late forties, early fifties, possibly homeless, lying on the sidewalk unresponsive. Need EMT support, over."

"Copy that, twenty-four," a male voice answered. "Stand by for paramedics."

After a few seconds of silence, a different voice. "Traffic lights on Colfax between York and Colorado Boulevard are malfunctioning. We have major tie-ups in all directions. Requesting units to help monitor traffic flow."

"Two one copy, we'll send units that way now."

It was the kind of garden-variety chatter common to police scanners. There were domestic violence reports, requests for back up on suspicious traffic stops, reports of elderly people in need of assistance because of chest pains. Before the Bureau, Camille could have listened for hours on end. But now that she understood the true nature of police work, and the fact that most of these calls would end uneventfully no matter how exciting they may have started out, there wasn't much to hold her interest.

She left the scanner on the desk while she walked back to the bookshelf, hopeful that she could find something in her father's book collection mindless enough to distract her for a few hours. She had begun skimming through a Tom Clancy nonfiction book about nuclear submarines when something came over the scanner that redirected her attention.

"This is six two eight, we've located the vehicle possibly belonging to the deceased in an alley on the 3800 block of Gilpin Street. Burgundy Range Rover, license 289 Alpha Charlie X-Ray. All four wheels have been lifted and it looks like most of the engine has been stripped."

"Roger that six two eight," a female voice responded. "Do we have confirmation that the SUV is registered to the victim?"

"Affirmative. The plates came back as a match. There's a possibility the suspect or suspects may still be on scene. Requesting additional units to secure the Range Rover and sweep the area."

"Copy six two eight. Additional units are en route to your location."

Camille dropped the book and walked over to the scanner. Burgundy Range Rover. The same as Julia's. But there had to be hundreds of them in the city. Besides, why would her car be anywhere near 38th and Gilpin? She lived clear on the other side of the city.

Another voice on the scanner.

"Detectives have been dispatched to the original crime scene. Any word on the status of animal control?"

"Animal control is on scene but forensics has requested that they not remove the dogs until their cause of death can be confirmed."

"Roger that eight two. And there were two of them?"

"Correct. Dalmatians, I believe."

Then a second feed cut in. "Be advised of increasing media and spectator activity outside the victim's residence. We need units to cut off outside traffic over a three-block radius starting at the 400 block of Monroe Street."

Camille remembered the address that Julia left for her. 335 Monroe Street. An immediate shockwave of numbness surged through her body and she could no longer feel the scanner in her hand.

"Copy that. Additional units are en route to the original crime scene and forensics is standing by at the secondary site to survey the victim's vehicle."

After that, the scanner lost the frequency and went silent.

Camille stood frozen, desperately trying to process what she had just heard. She knew what her instincts were telling her, but no other part of her could come to terms with it. Though there was no confirmation of the victim's identity, the fact that he or she drove the same car as Julia, lived in the same neighborhood, and had the same breed of dog meant that coincidence should have been officially off the table as a possibility. But Camille held tight to the possibility anyway.

Fighting back the panic that was beginning to surge through her, she calmly walked into the living room and turned on the television. This time of morning, the local newscasts were primarily concerned with the traffic and weather and she had to switch between three different stations before she finally found one actually reporting the news. After more bleak reports about the job market and an overblown account of the latest political strife in the

Middle East, the scene switched to a high helicopter shot above a large, two-story house that was roped off with yellow tape.

"We want to update you on a developing story we've been following involving a possible homicide in this home on the 300 block of Monroe Street," the anchor said as the helicopter shot continued. "Police are now saying that an SUV possibly belonging to the victim has been found in an alley in northeast Denver, though that information has not been officially confirmed. Authorities have apparently identified the victim but are not releasing her name. What we do know is that a woman was found dead in the home sometime early this morning. Details surrounding that death are still not known, but sources have told 7 News that homicide detectives are on scene and are currently pursuing tips related to the SUV. We will have continuing coverage of this developing story all morning and will pass along more information as it becomes available."

Camille had no memory of running through the house frantically searching for her father's car keys, nor did she remember getting into his Chevy Suburban and peeling out of the driveway. It was as if she made the drive to Julia's house in a complete state of unconsciousness, unaware of the traffic around her, how fast she was going, or how she even got there.

But she became fully aware when she came upon the patrol cars blocking entry onto Julia's street. The two officers standing guard eyed her with suspicion as she came to a stop in front of them. She had considered telling them that she lived in the neighborhood and needed to get through, but quickly thought better of it. Instead, she turned the car around, parked half a block away, and made her way to Julia's on foot.

The further she walked the more activity she saw. Neighbors were standing in the middle of the street talking to each other, their subdued conversations punctuated with shock and disbelief; satellite news trucks were lined up in caravans along the curb while television reporters scrambled to prepare for their live feeds.

She had already put in back to back calls to Julia's cell phone, but there was no answer either time. As she made a third call, she still somehow believed that she would come upon Julia's house and see her standing outside with the rest of her neighbors.

Listening to Julia's voicemail greeting for the third time, Camille finally saw the house. There were no satellite trucks, anxious reporters, or gawking neighbors standing in front of it; only police cars and uniformed officers as far as she could see.

The outside of the house was illuminated with standing floodlights. Behind the closed blinds, she saw shadows and the occasional pop of a camera flash. The police set up two perimeters of yellow tape in front of the house – one on the sidewalk near the curb and one across the front porch. Camille crossed the first police line without a second thought. A uniformed officer quickly made his way over to her before she could get any closer. But she didn't need to get any closer. She already saw what she needed to see.

The custom-made address plate above the front door was green with gold letters, written in a fine cursive script eerily similar to Julia's. When everything else around her went black, Camille could still see the plate as if it were burned into her brain.

335 Monroe St. Leeds.

.

CHAPTER 9

CRIME SCENE/ DO NOT CROSS

"Ma'am, you need to step behind the line right now. Do you hear me? This is a crime scene. If you don't step back I will arrest you."

The words sounded as if they were coming from somewhere distant, even though the officer who spoke them stood only a few feet away. Camille looked away from the address plate and into the patrol officer's strong, beet-red face.

"I'm only telling you one more time," he said with lips that were coiled tight with rage. "Get behind the line."

Camille continued to stare at him with a blank expression that only seemed to fuel his anger. There was a tug on her shoulder as the officer attempted to move her backward, but she didn't budge. Instead, she brushed his hand away and sidestepped out of his reach. When the officer put a hand on his holster and took a defensive posture, she immediately realized her mistake.

"I'm a federal ag—" Camille nearly bit through her tongue as she stopped herself from saying the word 'agent'. That had almost been as big a mistake as raising a hand to him, but the words were instinctive.

"What did you say?"

Camille tried to swallow but couldn't. "I know her."

As the officer approached with his hand still on his holster, Camille extended her arms to ward him off.

"Please. My friend lives here. I'm just trying to figure out if she's okay."

The officer stopped, though nothing in his icy blue eyes communicated sympathy. "You still need to let us do our job. I don't want to physically put you across that line, but I will if you don't—"

"You don't understand. I can't leave. Not until I know that she's..." her voice trailed off as something heavy moved from her chest into the back of her throat. She grabbed his thick forearm with both hands. "Can someone please help me? I don't care who it is. I just need someone to tell me that Julia's okay. She's not answering her cell phone and I just need to hear..." The heaviness in Camille's chest and throat suddenly expanded into her mouth, and before she realized what was happening, she let out a guttural scream that sounded almost inhuman in its agony.

The officer struggled to pry her clawed grip from his forearm. Once he did, he walked her to the base of the grassy hill leading up to Julia's front porch. "Sit here," he said flatly as he helped her down. Then without saying another word, he ran up the stairs and into the house, brushing past two large men in suits standing in the doorway.

Completely unaware of the scene she had made, Camille was shocked to see that the eyes of most everyone out there – police, neighbors, news crews – were trained on her. She tried to meet their unfeeling stares with a hard glare of her own, but her eyes burned from tears that wouldn't stop flowing and the only way to manage the pain was to keep them closed.

From behind, she heard the jingle of handcuffs and knew the officer was returning.

"That's her," she heard him say.

"And she says she knew the victim?" a female voice asked in response.

"That's correct, ma'am."

"Okay. I'll take it from here," the female voice said from a position directly behind Camille. "Thank you, Officer Davies."

Camille opened her eyes in time to see the officer crossing the sidewalk in front of her. He kept his hard glare fixed on her until he reached a small group of officers huddled in the driveway of the house next door. Soon, they were all staring.

"Miss, you really shouldn't have crossed the police line."

Camille jumped as she looked away from the officers to the woman now kneeling beside her.

"I'm sorry if I startled you," she said with a thin smile. "Officer Davies told me that you were a friend of the victim. I wanted to come out and talk to you. My name is Chloe Sullivan. I'm a detective with DPD homicide." She extended her hand.

Camille looked at it without extending her own. "Her name is Julia."

"Pardon me?"

"Julia Leeds. That's the name of the victim you're referring to, right?"

Sullivan cast her tired-looking eyes downward. "That hasn't been officially confirmed, but we believe so."

Camille turned away from the detective and focused her attention on a pair of teenage girls standing on a lawn across the street. They looked sad and overwhelmed by everything happening around them. It was refreshing in a strange way. Teenagers never seemed sad or overwhelmed by anything these days that didn't involve their online social network.

"How long have you known her?" Detective Sullivan asked.

"Sixteen years," Camille answered, still looking at the girls. Judging by their similar physical appearance, they were probably sisters. Camille felt a pang of jealousy. She had lost her sister today.

"And when did you last see her?"

Camille redirected her attention to the detective. That's when she noticed the notepad. Aside from the badge, it was the main tool of the police detective's trade, used more frequently and much more effectively than a firearm ever would be. The sight of it made Camille tremble. "Can you first tell me what happened?"

"We're still in the process of establishing that. I'm sorry. I didn't catch your name."

The detective looked to be the same age as Camille, possibly a few years younger. Pretty young female cops had it rough on the street, from perps and colleagues alike, and Detective Sullivan was prettier than most. But behind her deep set hazel eyes was something very formidable. She may not have had the most imposing physical presence, but she clearly was no push over either.

"Camille Grisham," she answered and watched the detective scribble her name.

"Ms. Grisham, are you aware of any family she may have in the area? So far we haven't been able to establish a point of contact."

Julia's parents died in a plane crash when she was twenty-six. The only other family that she ever spoke of was her sister Nicole who lived in Castle Rock. Camille had only met her twice, and to hear Julia talk, the two of them weren't particularly close. Regardless of their relationship, the idea of Nicole not knowing made Camille feel sick.

"Her sister's name is Nicole Blair. All I know about her is that she's a veterinarian at the Douglas County Animal Hospital."

Sullivan nodded as she wrote. "That should be enough to find her."

Camille stood up and turned toward the house. From her new vantage point, she could see more of the activity happening inside. There were at least ten people in the living room, most of them men in plain clothes, walking around with flashlights, dusting the walls and windows, and holding items stored in zip lock baggies. A short man wearing an Animal Control jacket stood inside the doorway while another one sat on the front porch smoking a cigarette.

The investigator in Camille worried about the integrity of the scene with so many people operating in such a small area. But the investigator in her was mostly gone. All that was left was a devastated shell of a person who could only pray that the men in that house were working their asses off to find whoever did this.

"Ms. Grisham, when was the last time you saw Julia?"

Camille saw one of the investigators walk out of the house carrying a black plastic bag. Her breath caught as she tried to answer the detective's question.

"Ms. Grisham?"

Camille was silent as she watched the man put the large bag into the back of an unmarked white van.

"Ms. Grisham?" Detective Sullivan repeated in a voice that was losing its measure. "Can you tell me when you last saw the victim?"

"Yesterday," Camille finally answered.

"How long were you with her?"

"The entire day."

"And did you notice anything out of the ordinary in terms of her behavior?"

The investigator got inside the van and quickly drove away. Camille watched until it disappeared around a corner.

"Ms. Grisham?"

"No I didn't notice anything out of the ordinary in terms of her behavior." She turned her full attention back to the detective. "Look, I can appreciate that you have to ask these questions. But I need to know exactly what happened to her. And don't tell me that you're still in the midst of the investigation and haven't determined it yet, because I know better than that. The first responders knew within two minutes of being here exactly what happened, so I'm pretty sure you do too."

The detective's lips parted and for a moment she seemed to be at a loss for words. She blew a lock of curly brown hair from the corner of her eye and took in a deep breath. "Ms. Grisham I understand you're upset, but at this point I'm not really at liberty—"

"I don't think you have the slightest idea how upset I am right now." Camille's eyes began to sting again and she had to put her hands over them.

"Yes I do."

"Then at least give me the common courtesy of being honest."

Detective Sullivan rolled her eyes. "It's not about common courtesy. It's about maintaining the integrity of our investigation."

"I was an FBI agent for eight years, so I know all about maintaining the integrity of an investigation. And I know that you telling me how my best friend died will do absolutely *nothing* to compromise that integrity. For Christ's sake, you're a homicide detective. How stupid do we have to pretend to be?"

The detective's cheeks turned crimson and the muscles in her jaw nearly bulged through the skin. "The fact that you were an FBI agent means absolutely nothing to me right now. But your tone does. Do you want to try that again?"

As much as Camille hated to admit it, she never had the respect for local law enforcement that she should have. When she was brought into an investigation, it was usually because the locals had neither the resources nor the ability to complete the task on their own. Most cops don't take too kindly to having their cases taken away from them, especially by snobby D.C. types with fancy suits and inflated egos. And the working relationship Camille had with them reflected that territorial animosity. But she was no longer an agent and Detective Sullivan wasn't some subordinate she was forced to work with. The cocky attitude wasn't going to fly here.

"I'm sorry, detective. I was out of line," Camille said contritely. "It just feels like my entire life is flashing in front of my eyes, and when the flash is done, everything is going to permanently go black. Desperate doesn't begin to describe how that makes me feel."

Detective Sullivan didn't look the least bit prepared to accept the apology as she began flipping through her notepad. "The ME's initial report indicates that Ms. Leeds was shot with a high caliber weapon. Her two dogs were also killed, presumably by the same weapon, though that hasn't been confirmed. We don't have enough yet to fully establish a motive, but based on the point of forced entry and the condition of the house, it looks like a home invasion. Do you know what kind of vehicle she drove?"

"A Range Rover."

Sullivan nodded. "Officers located it this morning in an alley on the 3800 block of Gilpin. Does she know anyone in that area?"

"Not that I'm aware of."

"We're working on a couple of leads related to the car and its location, but we don't have anything solid as of yet."

Whether she was aware of it or not, Detective Sullivan was relaying information to Camille the same as she would a fellow officer. Terms like 'high caliber weapon' and 'point of forced entry' only mean something in law enforcement circles. Maybe the revelation of her FBI past had an effect after all. Or maybe the detective had a lot to learn when it came to talking to the average person about investigative matters. Either way, Camille was grateful for her sudden candor, even though it hurt like a punch to the stomach.

"We could really use your help in filling in some of the gaps, Ms. Grisham."

"I don't know how much I can offer," Camille said as she fought to maintain her balance on increasingly wobbly legs.

"I'll go back to my original question about her behavior. You said you didn't recognize anything out of the ordinary yesterday. What about the days prior?"

Camille shook her head. "Yesterday was the first time I'd seen her in almost two years. I just moved back here from the east coast. Today is my first full day home."

Something came over Detective Sullivan's face that looked like sadness. She quickly blinked and it went away. "Did you have phone conversations?"

"For the last month and a half we probably spoke on the phone every day."

"And during those conversations, did she ever indicate that something was wrong? Perhaps a bad fight with a boyfriend or a dispute with a neighbor?"

"Julia hasn't had a boyfriend in over a year, at least not one that I knew about." She paused to search her memory for anything else. "The only thing she complained about was work."

"What did she do?"

Camille got stuck on the word *did*. Julia was already being spoken of in the past tense and it made her want to scream again. "She's a lawyer."

"Criminal?"

"Corporate. Defending big companies against lawsuits, stuff like that."

The detective was scribbling notes at a furious pace. "And what was it that she most often complained about? Colleagues? Clients?"

"The first and only time I heard her complain about work was during the drive home from the airport yesterday. It wasn't anything specific. It just sounded to me like she was tired of being a lawyer."

"Are you sure there wasn't anything more to it?"

Camille hesitated. She had asked Julia the same question. Every instinct she had at the time told her that something wasn't right, and she pushed for answers. But the more she pushed, the further Julia retreated. In the past, the only time she put up a wall was when it came to talking about her relationships, especially the bad ones. Camille had wondered if that was the case here too. Even though the subject seemed to bother Julia to the point of not wanting to say a single word about it, she never gave even the slightest impression that it was anything approaching life and death status.

Camille cleared her throat and continued. "Julia isn't a complainer, not about work or anything else. So when she started talking the way she did, I sensed that it was her way of telling me there was something else bothering her."

"So what was bothering her?"

"She didn't say, but we were supposed to have dinner this evening to..." Camille's mouth started quivering and she had to stop.

Detective Sullivan immediately stopped writing and slipped her notepad into her jacket pocket. "We can stop for now. I know this is incredibly hard on you and there is probably still a lot to process. Trying to recall too much right now may even be counter-productive. With so much else on your mind, you might miss certain details of a conversation or an encounter that you otherwise wouldn't. If you'd like, we can resume this after you've had some time."

Camille nodded and was about to communicate her thanks when a male voice stopped her.

"Detective Sullivan."

Both Camille and the detective turned around to see a tall, stoutly-built man in an ill-fitting shirt and loosened tie standing at the crest of the hill staring down at them.

Detective Sullivan waved at him with a posture that was decidedly more rigid than before. "Detective Graham."

As he descended the hill, Camille could see a subtle smirk peeking out from under a thick, gray goatee, though she hoped she was reading that wrong.

"Is this the witness that Officer Davies was talking about?" he asked Sullivan without looking in Camille's direction.

"She's not a witness. She was a close friend of the victim," Sullivan corrected.

"People who are closest to the victim often make the best witnesses," Graham countered in a condescending tone. Then he turned to Camille. "Detective Walter Graham," he said as he stuck out a catcher's mitt of a hand.

Camille tentatively shook it. "Camille Grisham."

An instant gleam of recognition cut across Graham's face that Camille didn't like in the least. Such recognition meant he knew one of two things about her, neither of which she was ready to talk about.

"Paul Grisham's kid. I thought you looked familiar," he said with an affected smile that was almost comical in its insincerity. "I worked with your old man for a long time. Hell of a cop. I always hoped we could partner up on the detective beat one day, but he was smart enough to take the early pension. I bet his golf game is out of this world by now."

"I wouldn't really know," Camille muttered. She hadn't realized that both of her hands were balled up in tight fists until she felt the pain from her fingernails. Something about Detective Graham had immediately rubbed her the wrong way.

"And man, was he proud of you," Graham continued. "He had FBI banners and decals all over his cubicle. You would have thought he was the agent."

Camille responded with a tight half smile, then she looked at Sullivan.

The detective took the cue. "I was just wrapping up with Ms. Grisham. She was able to shed some light on the victim's state of mind during the final twenty-four hours before her death."

"So you were with her yesterday?" Graham asked Camille before his partner could continue.

"Yes. I already told Detective Sullivan that."

"I understand. But just for my own clarification. Approximately what time did you last speak with her?"

Camille sighed and shot another quick look to Sullivan. "She was at my house – my father's house – for most of the day and left about four p.m."

"And was that the last time you spoke? When she left your father's house?"

"Yes. Well, actually, she did call me later, but I missed the call."

Graham suddenly pulled out his own notepad. "And what time was that?"

Camille paused to search her memory. "If I had to guess, I'd say about six-thirty."

Graham wrote in his notepad then looked at Sullivan. This time there was little doubt about the smirk.

"Did she leave a message?" Sullivan chimed in, seemingly irritated that she hadn't gotten this information before now.

"No."

"Did you call her back?" Graham asked.

Camille took in a deep breath. She had conducted her fair share of interrogations, and this was beginning to feel a lot like one. "No. It had been a long day and I was getting tired. We were planning on meeting up tonight for dinner, and I figured that whatever it was could wait until then."

Graham nodded as he continued writing. "Was there something specific you were supposed to meet about?"

Sullivan cut in. "It's all in my notes, detective. If you want to review them we can go back—"

"Why would I want to review notes when I have the witness in front of me?" Graham asked curtly.

"Like I told your partner, Julia and I hadn't seen each other in a long time and we wanted to catch up."

Graham looked at Sullivan as if he expected her to fill in the blanks.

"The victim indicated that something was troubling her, though she didn't say what. She and Ms. Grisham were supposed to talk about it today," Sullivan reported.

"Is that correct?" Graham asked Camille.

Camille shook her head in disbelief that she was answering these questions again. Graham was the worst kind of cop: an arrogant know-it-all with no concept of how much of a hack he truly was. Idiots like him made her disdain for local police feel completely justified. "Just like it says in Detective Sullivan's notes."

Graham's face hardened.

"I was just about to give Ms. Grisham my card," Sullivan said to Graham. "I thought it would be best for her to let the smoke clear then have her come in so we could talk more about Julia and their scheduled dinner."

"Unfortunately we don't have the luxury of letting the smoke clear, Detective Sullivan," Graham said with a stiff glare that looked completely at home on his leathery, bloated face. Then he turned to Camille. "I know this is a very difficult time, and I'm truly sorry for your loss. But as Detective Sullivan may or may not have told you, we don't have much to work with right now. Any information we can get about Ms. Leeds, no matter how seemingly insignificant, will be extremely useful. Hell, you're a former federal agent. You know better than most what I'm talking about. So if it's not too much trouble, I'd like for you to come downtown with us so we can ask a few more questions, maybe get a written statement. We've done about all we can here anyway."

Camille looked at Detective Sullivan who promptly looked away. She was disappointed that Sullivan backed down, but she couldn't be upset with her. She may have had the makings of a solid detective, but it was obvious she was in no position to call the shots. Being a young female meant the deck was already somewhat stacked against her. And Graham made it very clear that he wasn't interested in making the road any easier.

But he was absolutely right about one thing. Time was not on their side. No matter the crime, the window for successfully solving it is always incredibly small. In most cases, the majority of useful evidence, witness statements, and anonymous tips are collected within the first forty-eight hours of the incident. After that, the trail begins to run cold. Even though she wanted nothing more than to crawl into the nearest hole and stay there, she knew she couldn't.

The fact remained that she was possibly the last person who Julia talked to. She may not have had a lot to give to the detectives, but right now it was probably a lot more than anyone else.

"I'm parked a few blocks over," she said to Sullivan.

"We'll drive you to your car then you can follow us from there," Graham answered.

Camille made her way under the yellow police line and back into the street. The two teenage sisters she noticed earlier were now standing beside their father. All three of them looked at Camille as she passed. The collective empathy in their faces almost made her cry again. She also thought about her own father. She would have to call him. He was probably awake by now, and if he wasn't already worried to death he soon would be. The words he spoke last night echoed in her mind: *"I've never worried more about you than I have for the last two months."*

Camille feared that before this was all over, the last two months were going to seem to him like a perfect day on the golf course.

CHAPTER 10
MORE QUESTIONS

Camille sat in a conference room inside the downtown Criminal Investigations Division, while Detectives Graham and Sullivan worked feverishly at their computers, most likely logging witness statements and crime scene evidence. At least that's what Camille's experience told her they should be doing. Before escorting her inside, Graham made the token offer of a Krispy Kreme doughnut and a cup of coffee. Camille declined both. All she wanted was to give her statement and get the hell out of here as fast as she could.

She called her father while she waited. He had seen the news report but didn't make the connection to Julia. When Camille made the connection for him, he was quiet for a long time. If the news had made him emotional, he would rather put the phone down and walk away than let Camille hear him cry. To him, sadness was an entirely private matter, not to be shared with anyone else in the world, including those closest to him. It was a complete sense of detachment that masqueraded as cast-iron toughness, and it allowed Paul to survive the streets for over two decades without a single scratch – to either his body or his psyche. The trait was passed on to Camille, and for a time she wore it with pride. Then she encountered a mass murderer who rudely informed her that she wasn't made of nearly the same stuff as her father.

After what felt like an hour of silence, Paul told Camille that he would meet her as soon as he could arrange for a ride. He didn't seem the least bit upset that she had taken his.

Graham and Sullivan finally made their way into the conference room some twenty minutes after Camille's phone conversation ended. They were each holding a cup of coffee and a manila folder. Sullivan was smiling as she took a seat in the chair nearest Camille. Camille didn't smile back.

When Graham sat down on the other side of the table, he immediately opened his folder and began sifting through the contents inside. "Sorry for the wait," he said without looking up. "Paperwork is one ugly bitch."

Sullivan shifted uncomfortably in her chair. "We've contacted Julia's sister in Castle Rock," she said as she opened her folder and pulled out a blank witness statement form. "She's on her way to meet the coroner as we speak. Once she establishes a positive ID, we can release Julia's name and more information about the crime to the public."

"Then we pray that the tips start rolling in," Graham continued. "A case like this lives or dies on the number of snitches who come out of the woodwork and how loud they're willing to sing."

Camille nodded then turned to Sullivan. "How is Nicole doing?"

"She slept in this morning and hadn't watched the news, so she had no idea. Those kinds of phone calls are the worst part of what we do." Sullivan cast her eyes down and the same look of sadness came over her that Camille noticed earlier. This time she didn't blink it away so quickly.

"Detective Sullivan has a witness statement for you to fill out," Graham said to Camille without a hint of the emotion evident on Sullivan's face.

On cue, Sullivan slid the paper across the table.

"But before you do that, I have a couple of questions," Graham continued.

"I have a couple of questions too," Camille interrupted. "Actually I have just one. Do you have any idea who did this?"

Graham and Sullivan looked at each other.

"No we don't," Graham answered.

"Not yet anyway," Sullivan interjected. "We only have a couple of leads so far, and they're slim at best. But we're working them the best we can."

"So was it a home invasion?" Camille asked.

"That's certainly a possibility," Graham answered. "All of the trademarks of a home invasion are there, but in cases like this we always have to pursue other angles so as not to prematurely rule anything else out."

"Which is why we wanted to bring you in for some follow up, Ms. Grisham," Sullivan continued. "The sooner we can get a complete picture of Julia Leeds and what was happening in her life prior to last night, the sooner our investigation can take shape."

"Of course I want to help in whatever way I can," Camille said. "But I honestly don't know much more beyond what I've already told you. I wish I would have pushed Julia harder for answers, but I didn't want to make a bigger deal out of it than it was." Camille felt her eyes begin to swell and reached for a nearby box of tissue.

"Why do you think she was so unwilling to talk? Was she normally a secretive person?" Graham inquired.

"No. Not with me anyway."

"But do you think there were aspects of her life that she could have kept hidden from you?"

"I can't sit here and say that she told me every single thing happening in her life, but she didn't keep things hidden either, especially the big things."

"Like relationships?"

"I knew about most of them."

"But not all."

Camille sensed Graham was going somewhere specific with this line of questioning and she braced herself. "I lived in Washington D.C., detective. I saw Julia once every couple of years, and we only got to talk on the phone a few times a month. There's no way I'm going to know everything."

Graham put up a hand. "I certainly understand that, Camille. I'm not suggesting you should. But you mentioned that a couple of months prior to you returning here, you talked to her almost every day."

Camille nodded.

"So that would have given you more opportunities to talk about things like relationships."

"Detective Sullivan and I have already had this conversation. Julia wasn't involved with anyone romantically."

"How do you know that for sure?"

"Because that's the kind of thing girls talk about," Camille answered with a sarcastic half smile. Out of the corner of her eye she saw Sullivan once again shift nervously in her chair.

Graham bit the corner of his lip as he pulled an eight by ten photo out of the manila folder and passed it to Camille. "Do you recognize this car?"

Camille took the photo and eyed it closely. The burgundy Range Rover she had ridden in twenty-four hours before was barely recognizable. All of the windows, including the windshield, had been smashed out, the trunk and hood were open, and all four wheels were gone. It was balanced tenuously on a pile of cinder blocks and wedged in between a dumpster and an abandoned washing machine. "It's Julia's," she answered as she slid the photo back across the table.

"That's correct. It was found by patrol officers in an alley approximately seven miles from the victim's home. On the street adjacent to the alley, the officers spotted a gray Chevy Impala. That vehicle happened to match the description of a car seen by one of the victim's neighbors around twelve-thirty this morning. The neighbor was awakened by the sound of loud music outside his house. When he looked out the window, he saw the Impala parked along the curb two houses down. That would put it directly in front of the victim's home."

Camille felt her stomach tighten as Graham continued.

"The neighbor watched from his window while the car idled on the curb with its lights on and windows down. According to his statement, the car sat for approximately two minutes before driving away. The neighbor then reported hearing the music again while the car drove off."

"So you think this car was somehow involved?" Camille asked.

Sullivan chimed in. "The neighbor claimed he had never seen that particular vehicle in the area before, so it raised some suspicion. But we had nothing to go on except a light-colored Chevy blasting rap music from its radio. That could have described literally thousands of cars in the city. Then we found a vehicle with the exact same description parked on the street less than 200 feet from where Julia's Range Rover was found."

"And that's where it gets interesting," Graham continued. He pulled out another piece of paper from the folder and began reading from it. "Officers ran the plates from the Impala, and it came back as being registered to a Steven Clemmons. When officers interviewed him, he claimed not to have left his house since arriving from work last evening, though there were apparently no witnesses to corroborate that. Officers then asked him where he worked. Turns out he's a mail clerk at the law firm of Brown, Wallace, and Epstein."

"When you told me that Julia was a lawyer it set off all kinds of alarm bells," Sullivan added. "So I did a little research and came up with something very interesting."

Camille felt the bottom of her queasy stomach completely drop out. "I already know, Detective Sullivan. Julia was a partner at the same firm."

Graham's face widened with a smile that Camille could only describe as hideous. "If that's not a crazy coincidence, I don't know what is."

"So are you saying that he was merely visiting Julia the night she was killed? Or are you saying he's the one who actually killed her?"

"There are theories being discussed, but so far there's no evidence to support them," Sullivan said. "If we could establish a link between Julia and Clemmons aside from the fact that they worked in the same building, it would at least give us more ammunition to approach Clemmons with. We have detectives at the firm right now interviewing Julia's colleagues and we'll see if that bears anything. But you were a close friend, Ms. Grisham. You've had conversations with her that her colleagues probably would not have had. I know it's hard to remember everything, especially given your current state of mind, but if you can think of anything that Julia may have mentioned, even something in passing that may have hinted at personal issues with a colleague or anyone else for that matter, it would really help."

Camille dabbed at the corner of her eye with a tissue. "I wish I could. I've replayed every conversation I've had with her for the past few weeks. Every single one. And I can't come up with anything aside from what I've already told you."

"It's okay, Camille. We don't want to tread the same ground here," Graham said almost dismissively as he closed the manila folder. "I just thought that hearing this new information would spark something. It's likely that the victim's colleagues can better speak to the matter anyway, considering they saw both her and Clemmons every day."

"But we do want to thank you for coming in and talking," Sullivan added. "I know how difficult it was to do so."

Camille nodded as she threw her damp tissue into the wastebasket. She almost felt compelled to return Sullivan's smile, but Graham's presence wouldn't allow it.

Sullivan pulled a pen from her breast pocket and handed it to Camille. "My card is attached to the witness statement. If you think of anything else, don't hesitate to call. We'll be sure to keep you in the loop regarding any developments in the case."

"I appreciate that," Camille said, her emotion-battered voice barely registering above a whisper.

Sullivan and Graham stood up at the same time. Sullivan extended her hand to Camille, Graham headed straight for the door.

"Take all the time you need with that statement," Graham said. "You're basically just writing down everything you told us. Of course, being a former FBI agent, I'm sure you know those things like the back of your hand. By the way, I'm sorry things ended with the Bureau the way they did. But I know from my experience with your old man that you Grishams are a feisty breed. I'm sure you'll be busting serial killers again in no time."

Even though Graham's words sounded complimentary, the sneer on his fat face left little doubt about the real intent behind them.

Screw this loser straight to hell, Camille thought, fighting like crazy to keep the words from actually coming out of her mouth.

"Detective Sullivan and I have a briefing to attend, so when you're finished you can give your statement to the officer outside. He'll make sure that it gets to one of us."

"I'll do that," Camille said, giving Graham the finger under the table.

"Goodbye, Ms. Grisham," Sullivan said as she walked out of the room. "And thank you again." The look in her eyes made Camille think that she was on the verge of apologizing, but she kept walking, then closed the door behind her.

Camille sat at the table staring at the blank statement. After she wrote her name and date of birth, she couldn't seem to get much further. Her mind swirled with images of Julia, lines of dialogue from their conversations, and questions of how different things may have been if she had only taken Julia's phone call last night.

Even though her heart was overwhelmed with grief and sadness, she knew that she somehow had the capacity to handle it. The one feeling Camille could not handle was guilt. She had already experienced enough of that to last two lifetimes. But she couldn't stop wondering why Julia had called. Did she suddenly get the urge to talk about what had been bothering her? Was she fearful about something? Did she simply want to hear Camille's voice again? The sad fact was that she would never know because she couldn't take five measly minutes to call back.

More than the three people that she allowed to die in Daniel Sykes' basement, more than the shame of running away from the only life she ever knew, that one missed phone call would haunt Camille for the rest of her life - a life that seemed to be losing more of its meaning by the second.

Her right hand began to tremble and she had to cup it with her left to stop the shaking. After a few deep breaths she eventually steadied it. It wasn't until she lifted the pen to continue writing that she realized she had ripped the statement into about twenty pieces.

CHAPTER 11
A SOFT PLACE TO LAND

Paul Grisham waited for his daughter inside the lobby of the DPD Administration Building where he had worked for the better part of ten years. When he talked to Camille she was preparing to be interviewed by two detectives, one of whom he had the displeasure of knowing quite well. Walter Graham was far and away the biggest jackass the department had to offer; a sexist, bigoted hack whose connections in the political realm far exceeded his effectiveness as a cop. And if Camille could see through him as quickly as he thought she would, Paul knew the chances of the interview going smoothly were not particularly good.

He couldn't remember a time when he was more desperate to be by her side.

The news he received this morning was devastating beyond comprehension. Through her sixteen-year friendship with Camille, Paul had come to love Julia like she was his own daughter. But the personal loss he felt was insignificant compared to what Camille was experiencing. There wasn't another person alive whom she was closer to than Julia, himself included. The two months prior to Camille's arrival home had been absolute hell. If it wasn't for Julia, Camille not only would have been completely consumed by that hell, but she may never have made it back home at all.

Now, with Julia no longer there to help cushion her fall, Paul feared for Camille. She may have been tough as nails, but she had also dealt with more pain and loss than any one person should ever have to endure.

Last night, when he was still giddy with happiness over his daughter being home and hopeful that she had taken her first steps on the road back to normal, Paul urged Camille to keep her thoughts squarely on the future. The past was the past, and even though things didn't end with the Bureau the way she would have wanted, life would go on, and hers was still young enough not to be defined by one tragic incident.

Now the future frightened him. He had no way to tell her that it would be okay; that she would emerge on the other side of this as a better, stronger person, because the very real possibility existed that she wouldn't.

He could do his best to convince her otherwise, but Paul never once lied to his daughter about anything, and he wasn't about to start now. All he could do was promise to be there for her; to help soften her fall as Julia did. He knew it wouldn't be the same, but he was prepared to try nonetheless.

The instant he saw Camille emerge from the lobby elevator, he ran to her. She looked as if she wanted to run too, but her legs could barely carry her beyond the elevator door. When he reached Camille, he took her in his arms and pulled her head into his chest. She sobbed, but otherwise didn't move. When he released her and looked into her eyes, he saw nothing. Though they made eye contact, she seemed to be looking through him at something else that wasn't actually there. Sixty-one years of life had done nothing to prepare him for the overwhelming sense of dread he felt at that moment. He did everything in his power not to let Camille see that dread. He had serious doubts that he succeeded.

"Come on sweetheart," he said with a gentle smile as he kissed her on the forehead. "Let's get you home."

CHAPTER 12

GOOD SOLIDER

Lieutenant Owen Hitchcock shook his head as he flipped through the medical examiner's summary of evidence.

"This is very grim," he said, not taking his eyes off the report.

Graham and Sullivan sat across from Hitchcock's desk in silence, neither of them eager to offer a reply.

Hitchcock took off his glasses and pinched the bridge of his nose. "So where are we at?" he asked no one in particular.

Graham cleared his throat and began reading from his own copy of the summary. "An autopsy is being performed as we speak. According to the report from the medical examiner on scene, the victim was shot four times. Double tap entry just above the sternum, one in the abdomen, and one through the left hand – probably defensive. There were also two ligature marks on her body: one on the left side of her neck measuring approximately four inches, and one around her right wrist. The ME has no explanation for them as of yet."

"Does that mean she was shot and strangled?" Hitchcock asked, his narrow eyes burrowing into Graham. Owen Hitchcock was a slight man who always seemed thinner than he had been the day before. Today his Oxford shirt collar fit too loosely around his neck. But what he lacked in size, he more than made up for in presence.

"We don't know," Graham responded.

"That level of violence certainly isn't common in home invasion cases," Sullivan offered.

"Nothing about this is common," Hitchcock responded. "Shooting the victim four times at close range is bad enough. Strangling her on top of it is complete overkill."

"Crime of passion," Graham said as if it were a statement of fact.

"But there's no evidence of a sexual assault," Sullivan countered.

"Which is the other baffling thing," Hitchcock added. "Right now we're operating on two theories. The first is that this was some random home invasion. The second is that the victim knew her assailant and the robbery became a secondary event."

"Stephen Clemmons," Graham said.

"Unfortunately his connection to the victim is purely circumstantial at this point," Sullivan responded.

Graham shot her a look that would have likely killed the average person where they stood. "You're talking to me about circumstantial? My God, Chloe. Are you a homicide detective or a prosecutor?"

"Mock me if you want to, Walter. But you know what I'm saying is true."

"At any rate, those are the two theories we're working with," Hitchcock interjected. "From the pictures I've seen, Julia Leeds was a very attractive woman. She was alone. More times than not, particularly in a home invasion scenario where the perpetrators go so far as to kill the victim, there is some sort of sexual assault involved."

"I agree," Graham said. "But maybe the assailant didn't have time. In terms of the crime of passion angle, I've seen plenty of instances where no sex assault took place. Those acts are usually based on rage, not power or sexual gratification."

Sullivan immediately responded. "The only issue I have with that theory is the lack of physical evidence. If this were a crime of passion, if Julia did know her assailant, wouldn't there have been some kind of confrontation? Some sign of a struggle? Where are the clumps of hair or traces of skin under her fingernails?"

Graham shook his head. "Who says she even had time to put up a fight?"

"And what about the dogs?" she added. "They were both shot downstairs. One in the kitchen near the sliding door where the assailant entered the house, and one in the living room near the staircase. You would think she would have been roused from her sleep either by their barking or the gunshots."

"The dogs were Dalmatians, so they probably always barked," Graham asserted. "And as far as the gunshots are concerned, it's likely the perp used a suppressor." He paused, looking at both Sullivan and Hitchcock with the same irritated expression. "I don't really understand where you're going with all of this."

"That's the point, Walter. None of us understand a goddamn thing about what happened here," Hitchcock said. "Believe me, I want this Clemmons angle to pan out more than anyone, but right now I'm just not seeing the connection."

Graham's brow furrowed. "Lieutenant, the victim's car was found on the same block where Clemmons lives. His own car matches the description given by her neighbor to a tee. Clemmons and the victim worked in the same law firm. I don't know how much more of a connection you need?"

"Has he ever been fingerprinted?" Hitchcock asked in a measured voice.

Sullivan flipped through her report. "Yes he has. He was arrested as a juvenile for breaking into a car. The charge against him was reduced to a misdemeanor and he never served any time, but he was fingerprinted nonetheless."

"And do his prints match any found at the crime scene?"

"So far no fingerprints have been recovered except for those belonging to the victim. No skin, hair, or fibers either."

Hitchcock sighed as he began reading from the evidence summary again. "It says here the victim was found in the bathroom, yet there were spatter patterns on the bed. Was she moved to the bathroom after she was shot? If so why? That would be an awful lot of trouble to go to for a simple home invasion. There's also the matter of the dogs. The fact that they were shot in two different locations in the house lends credence to Walt's theory that the assailant used a silencer. But how many common burglars, or jilted lovers for that matter, use a silencer? Has ballistics determined the caliber of the gun used?"

Sullivan flipped through a few more pages of the report. "Five bullet fragments were recovered, all belonging to a Remington .45 ACP hollow point."

"You're kidding me," Hitchcock said, his mouth hanging open. "That's military grade."

"How many meth-heads or law firm mail clerks do you know who carry around an MK23?" Sullivan quipped.

Graham laughed. "So now we're speculating that this was some sort of special-forces assassination? Is that how desperate we're getting?"

"Of course not," Hitchcock replied. "But this wasn't some strung out junkie looking to pawn a television either. This person was patient, they scouted well ahead, and they knew they had time. My guess, evidence notwithstanding, is that there was only one person. The more people involved in something like this, the messier the scene gets. This scene wasn't messy. We know that there were at least eight shots fired, two in each dog and four in Julia Leeds. Yet there wasn't a single shell casing found anywhere. The perp knew how to clean up after himself."

"But the house was completely ransacked," Sullivan said. "Not only was her car stolen, but it was evident that several large items were taken out of the house. Burglary was an obvious motive." She took a deep breath and rubbed her tired eyes. "I don't know, Lieutenant. Something just isn't adding up."

"What about the neighbor? The one who saw the Impala and discovered the victim?"

"His name is Dale Rooney," Sullivan said. "He's lived in the neighborhood for twenty-three years. Former bank manager, retired with a wife and no children. So far his statements are consistent and he otherwise checks out clean. He was understandably shaken when we talked to him. We'll give him a day or so before following up."

Hitchcock nodded then turned to Graham. "What are you thinking?"

"I guess I just don't understand why you're so quick to rule out Clemmons? Everything you're saying, one man, uncommon weapon, pre-planning of the crime, only supports my theory about him."

"Because it's just that Walt, a theory."

"According to the officers who talked to him this morning, he doesn't have an alibi for his whereabouts last night."

"Neither would I if I were in his position," Hitchcock said with a limp smile. "Look, I've been at this a long time, and I've been in too many meetings where we were convinced of a suspect's guilt regardless of what the evidence told us. Guess what the outcomes were when most of those cases went to grand juries. The system doesn't give a damn about hunches."

Graham buried his head in the palm of his hands. "So what are we supposed to do, Hitch? Give this cock-sucker a free pass? You and I both know there's a lot more to this than coincidence."

Hitchcock chewed nervously on the plastic tip of his glasses. "What have we managed to gather from the victim's car?"

Sullivan answered. "There were two sets of prints in the Range Rover, one belonging to Julia Leeds, one belonging to her friend

Camille Grisham. Julia gave her a ride home from the airport yesterday."

"I've read your notes on her," Hitchcock said to Sullivan. Then he blew out a loud sigh. "Do you know who she is?"

"She told me that she used to be an FBI agent. I also know that her father was in the department."

"That's right. But it's the first bit of information that should have us the most concerned," Hitchcock warned. "Not only was Camille Grisham an FBI agent, she was also a very high profile one. She was all over the news when that Circle Killer business broke."

Sullivan gasped, the recognition instantly coming to her. "That was her?"

"Yes it was. And once the media gets wind that she not only knew the victim but was possibly the last person to talk to her before she was killed, the scrutiny involved in this case is going to go through the roof."

"Let's not get too crazy about this yet," Graham cautioned. "She doesn't seem to know much in regard to the victim. It's not like the Circle Killer situation where she was in the goddamn house when he shot those girls. There isn't a whole lot she can say about this case, aside from the fact that she knew the victim."

"But that won't stop the vultures from circling," Hitchcock countered.

"Fine, we'll get a judge to sign off on some kind of fake gag order, force her to keep her mouth shut."

Sullivan looked at Graham with disgust. "Don't be an ass, Walter."

"Maybe you should watch how you talk–"

"This is not the time," Hitchcock interrupted. "We've got serious issues here. The department is a few minutes away from issuing a statement regarding Julia Leeds and the preliminary details of this case. Once that happens, people are going to freak out. She was a prominent lawyer, with ties to some of the most powerful people in this state. Young, beautiful lawyers with powerful friends aren't supposed to be killed in cold blood in their own homes. People will demand answers, and we had damn well better have them. You think you're feeling pressure now, just wait twelve hours."

Sullivan felt a sudden surge of adrenaline race through her body. She gripped her knees to keep her hands from shaking.

"You two are my leads on this, and I wouldn't trust anyone to guide us through it more than you," Hitchcock continued. "But we can't waste any time. We need to be thorough, but we also need to be fast. This can't wind up as one of those unsolved mysteries that people are still speculating about five years from now. We need an arrest, plain and simple. So brass tacks, how far away are we from getting one?"

"If we focus our attention on Clemmons, we may end up being a lot closer than you think," Graham declared.

"Do you agree with that assessment, Chloe?"

Sullivan didn't know what to think, but now was not the time to say so. She had learned from her short stint as Graham's partner that it was best to take his lead most of the time, whether she agreed with him or not. He had eighteen years as a homicide detective. She had nine months. Still, she wasn't sure if she was on board with this. From the moment Stephen Clemmons' name was mentioned, Graham had already concluded that they had found their man. But there was nothing in Clemmons' history that suggested violence, particularly violence of this magnitude. The only problem for him was that a vigilant neighbor saw a gray Chevy Impala that looked an awful lot like Clemmons' on his street close to the time Julia was killed. And because the car was playing rap music, and Clemmons fit the profile of a typical rap music fan, the case was clearly open and shut.

Unfortunately, it wasn't open and shut, not in Sullivan's mind at least. The fact that he and Julia Leeds worked for the same law firm certainly raised questions, and the discovery of the Range

Rover so close to his house was alarming. But if Clemmons was so careful about covering his tracks in Julia's house, why would he make the bone-headed mistake of parking her stolen car less than a block away from his own house and leaving it there for the police to find? The simple answer is that he wouldn't make that mistake. Unfortunately, Graham wasn't interested in hearing that, and judging by the way Lieutenant Hitchcock was now talking, he wasn't interested in hearing it either. So Detective Sullivan did what rookies in this department were supposed to do. She played along.

"We don't have a choice but to pursue our leads as thoroughly as we can," she said through pursed lips.

"I'll take that as a yes," Hitchcock said as he closed the evidence summary, put on his glasses, and straightened the tie around his skinny neck. "With that being the case, I'll leave you guys to it. Know that you'll have the full resources of the department behind you, including additional detectives. If you need anything else from me, all you have to do is ask. Someone's ass is bound to end up in a sling over this one, but it won't be any of ours. Understood?"

"Absolutely," Graham answered as he stood up, looked at Sullivan and nodded.

"Understood," Sullivan repeated like the good soldier that she was.

"Great. Now go nail that bastard. I don't care if it's Stephen Clemmons, Leroy the crack-head or Satan himself. You just nail his ass."

"You got it boss," Graham said with the wide-eyed look of an athlete amped up by his coach's halftime speech.

Sullivan walked out of Hitchcock's office without saying another word. From behind her, she heard Graham's voice.

"Hey Chloe. You and I need to talk about a few things."

Sullivan turned to him with a flat expression. "What things?"

"Later," was all he said. Then he turned and walked in the other direction.

She assumed he was getting to work on the one and only lead that he planned to follow. She would be getting to work too. There were a million other possibilities out there besides the thirty-four-year-old mail clerk with a solid employment record and no real criminal history. Someone had to pursue them.

Sullivan may have been a good soldier, but she finally decided that it was time to stop playing along.

CHAPTER 13

BLOOD ON MY HANDS

Julia's identity was officially revealed during the nine P.M. newscast, as were details about where she worked and the extensive connections she had in the legal and political community. But aside from the rampant speculation that foul play was involved, information regarding how she died was still being withheld, as were any possible motives behind her death.

The televised image of the crime scene that used to be Julia's house had been a constant throughout the day, and Camille had not been able to pull herself away from it since arriving home from her meeting with Detectives Sullivan and Graham.

Her father sat beside her on the couch the entire time, leaving only for the occasional bathroom or kitchen break. They didn't speak much. Mostly he just looked at her; sometimes with a reassuring smile, sometimes with a sad glance. But never once did he try to make sense of the situation or offer a comforting word. He was wise enough to know that there is no such thing as a comforting word on the day your daughter's best friend is murdered.

When the newscast moved on to a story about the city's latest budget crisis, he turned off the television. "I'm pretty sure you haven't eaten today. Do you want me to whip something up?" he asked as he gently squeezed her hand.

"No thank you," she answered stoically, her vacant eyes staring at nothing.

Paul got up from the couch and stood over Camille, his hand still holding hers. "I'm going to grab a cup of coffee then. Let me know if you change your mind."

Camille nodded, her expression unchanged.

Paul stood for a long time before finally letting go of her hand. By the time she summoned the will to look up he was already in the kitchen.

As she sat alone in the cold silence of the living room, the shock and overwhelming sadness of the day slowly gave way to a numb detachment that left her feeling as if she were floating above her own body, looking down at a person she no longer recognized. The result was a malaise that was becoming increasingly debilitating, and she worried that if she sat much longer it would eventually paralyze her.

So with every ounce of strength she could muster, Camille stood up from the couch, walked upstairs and into her bedroom. Fighting against the gravitational pull of her bed, she turned her attention to the two suitcases that she had yet to unpack. There wasn't much inside: a few standard-issue suits from her Bureau days, a handful of dresses that her hectic work schedule rarely afforded her time to wear, and the eight pairs of True Religion jeans that were her only real vice in life. But the unpacking would at least occupy her for a few minutes.

She hadn't been able to stop thinking about Graham and Sullivan, and how much, or how little, they actually knew about Julia's murder. She didn't know the first thing about Stephen Clemmons, and hoped that they were right in their suspicion of him. But Graham's thinly veiled assertion that Julia was having a secret relationship with him could not have been more off-base. The day Julia Leeds even entertained the thought of dating a mail clerk would mark the official end of the world. And even if she did date him, she would never hide it from Camille, even if she saw fit to hide it from the rest of the world. Camille had no doubt that Julia was keeping something from her yesterday, but it had absolutely nothing to do with Stephen Clemmons.

As she hung her clothes in the empty closet, Camille was troubled by something else. Why would Clemmons steal Julia's car, as Graham had suggested, and dump it less than a block from his own house? He wouldn't, unless he wanted every police officer in the city pounding on his door. Camille had dealt with every station of criminal imaginable, and not a single one of them was ever that stupid.

She wondered if Detective Sullivan felt the same way. Clemmons seemed to be Graham's crusade, and Sullivan didn't look anything like a wholly devoted follower. Camille hoped that she was as good a cop as she appeared to be. She also hoped that the young detective had the will to dig her heels in when she needed to; that she had learned to trust instincts that were more reliable than she probably realized. Camille may have lost a lot of things in the last two months, but her instincts were fully intact. And those instincts were telling her that something about Graham was not right. She knew it from the moment she met him, and nothing in the subsequent hour that she spent with him dissuaded her of that notion. But there was nothing she could do about Graham or Sullivan except leave them to their jobs and hope that the next time she saw them, they would be delivering the head of Julia's killer to her doorstep.

When Camille finished hanging the clothes from her first suitcase, she turned her attention to the second. There were mostly shoes in this one, along with a few other miscellaneous items that Camille didn't want to leave in the D.C. storage unit that housed most everything else she owned.

She took a step toward the suitcase but stopped. The feeling of weightlessness that had gripped her for most of the day suddenly returned and her legs buckled. Before she could steady herself, she stumbled backward into the closet, her fall partially broken by the suitcase she had just unpacked. She tried to pick herself up but the floor rose beneath her, sending her shoulder first into the wall. A searing pain shot through her torso and she covered her mouth to stifle her cries. Struggling to move legs that felt like cement, she pushed off her elbows to position herself upright against the closet wall. She hadn't noticed the blood on her fingers until she used them to wipe the tears rolling down her cheek. She was unsure where the blood came from until she put her hand over her mouth again. When she took it away, it was covered with a fresh layer of crimson. When she fell into the wall, she must have bitten into her lip with enough force to split it open. It was only when she realized this that the pain actually hit her.

In the dark of the closet, she saw flashes of light. Red and blue flares. White hot strobes. The dim yellow of filtered sunlight. When she pressed her palm against the closet wall in an attempt to push herself up, she felt not a smooth surface, but the jagged edges of cobblestone. The wall pulsated with the sounds of screaming — persistent, pleading, distant screaming. She had heard those screams many times before, just as often as she had felt the jagged edges of that cobblestone and seen the flashing lights. The screams came from the two University of Pennsylvania students who were held captive for three weeks inside Daniel Sykes' dank cobblestone cellar; the same cobblestone cellar where she cradled the bleeding head of Agent Andrew Sheridan seconds before he died. Now she found herself inside that cellar again. And like before her hands were covered in blood. But this time it wasn't Agent Sheridan's or even her own.

When Julia's pale, battered face suddenly appeared against the backdrop of flashing light, Camille again raised her hand to cover her mouth. Unlike before, she couldn't stifle the noise that came out of it. In an instant, another figure appeared in front of her. Convinced the massive shadow hovering over her was Daniel

Sykes, she retreated deeper into the closet, screaming as loudly as the limited air in her lungs would allow.

Large hands reached for her and she weakly attempted to push them away. "Camille calm down. It's me."

The voice barely registered above the volume of her screams.

"Camille, stop it. Stop it!"

The hands that she initially fought off grabbed her by the shoulders and shook.

"It's me, Camille. You're okay. I promise you're okay."

The recognition of her father's voice instantly stopped her. She watched with blurry eyes as he stood up and pulled the cord that hung from the ceiling. The closet suddenly filled with light, momentarily blinding her. When she opened her eyes and saw the startled expression on her father's face, she finally understood how bad things had gotten.

Though she passed the FBI's psych evals with flying colors, Camille had dealt with panic attacks of one degree or another since college. They intensified after her mother's cancer diagnosis, and by the time she and Agent Sheridan found themselves in the basement of the serial killer whom they had been tracking for three years, the attacks were unbearable in their intensity and inescapable in their regularity. Following the Sykes encounter and the mental trauma that followed, the attacks were occasionally accompanied by repetitive sounds and images. She refused to call them hallucinations, but acknowledged that they were not real. The red and blue flashes, she came to realize, represented the patrol car emergency lights that greeted her when she was pulled out of Sykes' basement. The dim yellow represented the muted sunlight that filtered in through Sykes' blackened basement windows – sunlight she was convinced she would never see again. And the screams belonged to Candace McPherson and Jessica Bailey, the two coeds that Sykes held in his basement and subsequently killed.

Though these visions had been increasingly intense in the last two months, tonight's episode was the worst. The visions felt real, from the jagged cobblestone on her fingers to the sight of Julia's blood-caked blond hair. For the longest of moments, Camille actually believed that Daniel Sykes was standing over her, and it wasn't until her father nearly shook the life out of her that she realized he wasn't.

"Put this on your lip. It's bleeding like crazy."

Camille felt a cold dampness on her mouth as her father put a wet washcloth over it. She wasn't even aware that he had left to get one.

"I'm so sorry dad," she said as she lowered the washcloth.

Paul immediately put it back over her mouth. "Best not to talk right now. You don't want that cut opening up again."

Camille agreed that it was best not to talk. She didn't know what to say anyway. Paul was aware of her anxiety problem, but not the full extent of it. Now he was. She knew there would come a time when she would have to tell him everything.

"It's okay, baby," he whispered as he sat beside her on the closet floor, his arms cradling her like the wounded child that she was. "I completely understand."

Fortunately, that time wasn't now.

CHAPTER 14

A TIME TO MOURN

Camille wore the same black dress to Julia's funeral that she had worn to Andrew Sheridan's seven weeks earlier.

When a federal agent is killed in the line of duty, the scale of the service is grand, the list of mourners is long and distinguished, and the remembrances are usually tales of bravery, sacrifice, and honor. Agent Sheridan's service was no different. Camille could still hear *Taps* as if the bagpipes were being played next to her ear. She could smell the gunpowder as if the last round of the twenty-one gun salute had just been fired. And she could clearly see the stars and stripes of the American flag that had been handed to Agent Sheridan's distraught widow as her husband of fifteen short years was being lowered into the ground.

Camille had nothing to say that day aside from the hollow words of condolence she had given to Mrs. Sheridan. She was asked to speak, to offer the service of over four hundred attendees some unknown anecdote on the man whose needless death they had come to mourn. But all she could remember about her partner of six-and-a-half-years was the dull black of his eight-ball hemorrhaged eyes and the way the entire left side of his face went slack as he tried to speak his last words. Andrew Sheridan was a hero in every sense of the word. It was he who led the charge into

Daniel Sykes' house without police back up when he found the school ID of Jessica Bailey in Sykes' abandoned car. It was he who discovered Sykes' cellar and the two girls trapped inside of it. And it was he who lost his life because his partner was rendered helpless by a panic attack upon discovery of the four other bodies in that cellar that were in various stages of decomposition. That last fact certainly qualified as an unknown anecdote. No one within the Bureau or Agent Sheridan's family was aware of the full extent of Camille's role in his death. And she had no intention of sharing it, at his funeral service or anywhere else.

Julia's service was a much more modest affair. Including family, friends, and the well-dressed, silver-haired men who more than likely headed her law firm, Camille counted roughly sixty people. Julia's family occupied the first two rows of the church. Camille and her father sat directly behind them. She immediately recognized Nicole Blair, who, aside from her short cropped brunette hair, was a spitting image of Julia. She sat stone faced in between her husband and two adolescent sons. Camille didn't know anyone else.

The service program was white with pink roses embroidered throughout. Above Julia's bright face were the words *In Loving Memory of Julia Leeds: a devoted sister, aunt, and friend.* Camille's eyes watered as she read the order of service. When she got to the *Remembrances* section, she nearly lost her breath. Much like it had been with Agent Sheridan, Camille knew that she would probably be looked upon to eulogize her friend. Though she didn't know most of the people in attendance, based upon the number of hugs and condolences she received when she arrived, most of them knew her. But as was the case with Agent Sheridan, Camille had neither the desire nor the courage to offer a proper testimonial. There was plenty she could say about Julia. She had enough warm stories and heartfelt memories to take up five memorial services. But there wasn't anything warm about the story she had to tell right now. And the only memories she could summon were her own feelings of loss and failure.

No one wanted to hear that Camille had lost two of the people closest to her in the world in less than eight weeks, and that in both instances, she blamed herself for the loss. Julia's death may not have been her fault directly, but in the three days since, Camille still had not forgiven herself for not taking Julia's phone call or pressing her harder for answers when it was obvious that she needed some sort of help.

Anyone with even a basic understanding of the situation would tell Camille that what happened to Julia was not her fault. But they would be wrong. Camille would never be able to explain to them why they were. She just knew it. Just like she knew that she could not stand before them now and offer a final tribute to a life that should never have been taken. Her empty words would do no justice to either Julia's life or her memory.

The service began with the Lord's Prayer and a hymn sung by a young woman identified as a member of the church's youth choir. Following an extended moment of silence that was punctuated by the sobs and sniffles of the mournful, the church pastor approached the podium – a large red bible in his hands and a look of heavy somberness on his face.

"May the Lord's everlasting grace be bestowed upon us as we gather to remember a remarkable young woman."

The picture hanging above the closed casket happened to be one of Camille's favorites. It showed Julia holding her two dogs when they were puppies. Her smile was radiant; a snapshot of happiness that Camille could now only pray was genuine.

After instructing the attendees to bow their heads for yet another prayer, the pastor opened his Bible and began reading a verse from the book of *Ecclesiastes*.

"There is a time for everything, and a season for every activity under Heaven. A time to be born and a time to die. A time to plant and a time to uproot. A time to kill and a time to heal. A time to tear down and a time to build. A time to weep and a time to laugh. A time to mourn and a time to dance."

There was indeed a time for everything. There would perhaps come a time when Camille would heal. A time when she would build. And even a time when she would laugh. But right now, for this and every other moment in the foreseeable future, there was only time to mourn.

Beyond her own sense of irreplaceable loss, Camille mourned for a world that would never get to know the Julia that she knew: the generous spirit, the loyal friend, the charismatic charmer.

The remembrances from family and friends were plentiful. Some were sad, some were reflective, and some were humorous. All of them were fitting.

When the service concluded and Julia's ivory casket was being wheeled out of the church, Camille held tight to her father's hand. He had been quiet for most of the service, his posture rigid and his jaw clenched. Despite his unwavering exterior, Camille knew that every muscle in his body was being charged with the task of keeping his frayed emotions in check.

"How are you holding up, dad?" It was the first time since this whole ordeal began that Camille had asked the question.

"Doing okay, I guess," he replied. Then he squeezed her hand tighter. "And you?"

Camille watched as the casket was wheeled outside and presumably into the back of a waiting hearse. She turned back to Paul, but could not find the words to reply.

The two were silent as they left the church.

When they reached the parking lot they were greeted by a woman and a teenage girl who said they were Julia's aunt and cousin. They all hugged as if they had known each other for years. "Julia talked about you often," the woman who introduced herself as Meredith told Camille. "It's a shame that when I finally get to meet you it's under these circumstances."

Camille nodded her agreement.

"Will we see you at the gravesite?" Meredith asked. "The procession will be leaving in about twenty minutes."

"We'll be there," Paul answered.

Meredith smiled. "Okay. Oh, and before I forget. Nicole was talking about you earlier. I think she wanted to say a couple of things. Would you mind waiting here while I go find her?"

"Of course not," Camille replied, although the sudden surge of anxiety swelling in her chest said otherwise. She hadn't yet spoken with Julia's sister, but had seen her in numerous interviews since Julia's death; each one of them a tearful plea from a woman desperate to find out who killed the last remaining member of her immediate family. It was extraordinarily difficult to watch, and Camille dreaded the inevitable day when those tearful eyes would be focused on her. That day had now come.

"Hi Camille," Nicole Blair said as she approached with extended arms.

They embraced with a force that both surprised and comforted Camille. "I'm so sorry, Nicole."

Nicole responded by squeezing tighter.

They held each other for several more seconds before Camille finally stepped back. "This is my father Paul. Dad, this is Julia's sister Nicole."

Neither of them hesitated in hugging the other.

"I'm so sorry for your loss, Nicole. But you gave her a beautiful tribute."

"Thank you, Mr. Grisham. I'm glad you could come." She turned back to Camille. "You guys are more than welcome to ride with us to the cemetery if you'd like. I'll be sure the driver gets you back here afterward."

"I appreciate it, but I think we'll be okay to drive ourselves," Camille said, not feeling the least bit comfortable with the idea of riding in the car reserved for Julia's family.

Nicole looked disappointed but nodded her understanding. "Okay. Do you mind then if we talk for a minute before we leave?"

"Of course not."

A long silence followed and Paul picked up on the cue. "I'll wait for you in the car, honey. Nicole, we'll see you at the cemetery."

Camille smiled at her father's trademark deftness.

"Nice to meet you, Mr. Grisham," Nicole said after another hug.

Camille waited until Paul was out of sight before speaking. "What did you want to talk about?"

Nicole took a deep breath and held it in, exhaling only after she was ready to speak. "The person who killed my sister."

Camille's body stiffened with tension. "What have the police told you?"

"Not as much as I would like. They keep asking if Julia was romantically involved with anyone. Whenever I tell them I'm not sure, they start throwing names at me as if that's supposed to jog my memory. I don't know if she was seeing anyone or not. She certainly never brought anyone around to meet us. I've repeatedly told them that but it doesn't seem good enough."

"Do you remember any of the names they mentioned?"

"No. Was there one that I should have remembered?"

Camille considered mentioning Stephen Clemmons but quickly thought better of it. "No. I was just curious."

"Did they ask you the same questions?"

"Yes. But my answer was the same as yours. If Julia was seeing anyone she didn't tell me about it. And we normally talked openly about those things."

Nicole's eyes briefly lost their focus, as if she was distracted by a far away thought. "My question is why are they asking about Julia's boyfriends when everyone seems to think it was a robbery?"

"It's standard in any type of homicide investigation to learn as much about the victim's life and the people in it, as possible so as to rule out all other motives, including personal ones."

Nicole looked at her with confused eyes. "So you're saying there's a possibility this was something personal? Like some kind of domestic thing?"

Camille was beginning to feel smothered by the weight of Nicole's questions. "I don't know."

"Neither do the police apparently. What sense does it make that her entire house would be ransacked and most everything she owned stolen if she was murdered by someone she knew?"

"Maybe it was purposefully done to make it appear that robbery was the motive," Camille said, regretting it the instant she did.

Something in Nicole's delicate face faltered and she looked as if she wanted to cry. "Is that what the police told you?"

"No."

"But that's what you think happened."

"I can't say right now, Nicole. The truth is that no one can."

"Except for the monster that killed her. And it seems to me that the police aren't any closer now to figuring out who that is than the day it happened."

Camille was trying her best to stay level-headed. "I've been on the other side of plenty of investigations like this, and unfortunately a resolution always takes more time than we'd like."

"So as someone who has been a part of these kinds of investigations, what does your gut tell you about this one?"

"I don't think I'm in the best position to offer any kind of analysis."

"I understand that you are as emotionally invested in this situation as any of us are. But the fact is that I trust your opinion right now a hell of a lot more than I trust those detectives."

A quiet desperation was building in Nicole's voice that frightened Camille. She could feel what was coming next and wanted nothing more than to walk away.

"Nicole, I don't think you should–"

"Help us find him Camille," Nicole interrupted.

106

"I'm not… I don't do that anymore."

"I understand that. And I'm truly sorry for everything that happened to you with that Circle Killer case. I know you don't have a badge anymore, but I'm sure you still have resources. The police are saying all the right things in the media, but it's obvious they don't have the first clue about what happened here. If they had anything remotely solid, I wouldn't be asking this of you. But we both know that they don't have anything. Just like we both know that you're twenty times more capable than anyone that department has to offer."

"I'm not a private investigator. I'd need a license for that."

"Screw a license. This is Julia we're talking about!"

The raw anger in Nicole's voice shocked Camille and rendered her speechless.

"I'm sorry," Nicole said with immediate contrition. "I didn't mean to yell."

Under normal circumstances, Camille's temper would have gotten the better of her and Nicole would have found herself cowering on the asphalt. But these were not normal circumstances. "It's okay."

"It's just that I know you of all people understand my level of frustration."

"I do."

"Then you know why I'm asking for your help."

Camille's head was starting to feel light. "As difficult as it is, we have to let the police do their job. I wish I could do more, Nicole, but I can't." She braced herself for another desperate plea, but was instead met with a look of solemn resignation.

"I'm sorry to hear that. I really am."

Camille opened her mouth to speak, but Nicole's embrace stopped her. As they stood in close silence, she wanted nothing more than to tell Nicole that she was right in her doubts about the police and their investigation. She wanted to tell her that she could do a better job than any of them, and that she owed it to Julia to take up the cause — badge or no badge. She wanted to tell Nicole that her sister's death would not be added to the long list of cold-case crimes that people would still be speculating about in ten years. She wanted to tell Nicole that she could be the courageous crusader who was willing to give up her own life if it meant finding out who ended Julia's.

But she knew that none of it was true.

"I'll see you at the cemetery," Nicole finally said. Then she turned and walked away.

Camille's eyes followed her until she met her husband and sons at the family car and they all piled inside.

"I'll see you there," she said to no one at all.

CHAPTER 15

EMPATHY

Sullivan was sitting at her desk looking over an evidence summary that continued to baffle her when an irate Graham walked into the office.

"I understand what you're saying, okay? And for the fifth time, I'm telling you I'll take care of it," he barked into his cell phone. He rolled his eyes as he listened to a lengthy response. "Yes I know how to get in touch with him. I'll call you back when I do." With that, Graham hung up the phone and stuffed it inside his jacket pocket.

Sullivan couldn't help but stare at his display. Graham made an entrance better than anyone else she had ever known, though there was nothing admirable about the way he did it.

"What was that all about?" she inquired.

Graham sat at his desk without looking at her. "Just keeping my ears to the ground. I have a couple of CI's who live in Clemmons' neighborhood and I've been trying to get them on the horn for hours. The homies are never around when you need them."

It was the third time this week that he had made Sullivan visibly cringe. So far that was a record. "Any developments on Clemmons?"

Graham looked up from his computer with an irritated glare. "Not yet. You didn't think we were going to arrest him this afternoon, did you?"

Sullivan shrugged. "We basically told the lieutenant that he was the guy, so yeah, I'm expecting something to come down the pike real soon."

Graham hissed in between his teeth and turned back to his computer. "I do forget sometimes that you're a rookie."

Sullivan immediately thought *what the hell does that mean*? She opened her mouth to give voice to the thought, then changed her mind. Instead she picked up the revised evidence summary that had just been put on her desk.

"You were out, so I'm assuming you haven't read this," she said as she held up the report.

Graham looked up from his computer. He could hardly hide his disinterest. "You're right, I haven't."

"Forensics did a second sweep of the crime scene this afternoon. It came up as clean as the first. No prints aside from Julia's. They also confirmed that each dog was shot twice at relatively close range, and definitely with the same gun."

"We already knew that," Graham sighed.

Sullivan continued like she didn't hear him. "They also checked the dog's teeth, on the chance that one of them got close enough to the perp to take a bite. There was no evidence to indicate that they had."

"Fantastic. Anything else?"

"The house was equipped with a security system, but it had apparently malfunctioned."

Graham looked up from his computer. "Why do you say that?"

"When the guys from the lab initially looked at it, they assumed that Julia hadn't set it that evening. But when they called the security company to confirm, their log showed that she had actually armed the system at ten fifty-six P.M., and that it went offline at approximately one seventeen A.M. The company reported no technical issues on their end. From what they saw they could only conclude that she disarmed it herself."

Graham said nothing as he continued to stare straight ahead.

"That would totally line up with the theory that Julia knew her assailant and disarmed it to let him in," Sullivan continued. "The only problem with that theory is the forced entry."

"No one ever said she let him in, Chloe," Graham sniffed.

"Still, isn't it strange that the security system magically goes offline what was probably moments before the break-in? I sure hope our perp went out and bought a lotto ticket after he was finished, because he was quite possibly the luckiest bastard in the world that night."

"Or maybe Leeds disarmed the system herself," Graham countered like he actually believed it.

"Walt, who disarms their alarm system at one seventeen in the morning, then goes back to bed?"

Graham let out a hard sigh and pushed his chair away from his desk. "How in the hell would I know? We can sit and speculate about it all day, but we're not home security technicians, we're homicide detectives. Now, do you want to inspect faulty burglar alarms or do you want to solve a murder?"

Sullivan was silent for a long moment. Then she put the evidence summary down on her desk. "I think you know the answer to that."

Graham stood up from his desk and walked over to hers. "Then maybe you'd like to join me in the conference room. Dale Rooney will be here any minute."

This would be their first opportunity to speak at length with the lone witness who reported seeing the car that matched Clemmons' on the night of Julia's murder. He was the only glue that held the Clemmons theory in place, and Sullivan was curious to see how well his recollection would hold up under her questioning. She only hoped she would get the chance to probe as deeply as she wanted to. Graham had a way of taking control of situations, and Sullivan had neither the clout nor the will to wrestle that control away from him.

She walked some distance behind him as they made their way to the conference room. "By the way, Julia Leeds's funeral was today."

"I know," Graham answered without looking back. "I'm surprised you didn't go."

Sullivan was perplexed by the comment. "Why would you say that?"

"I figured the lieutenant would want you there as a representative of the department that the family would be comfortable with."

Suddenly she wasn't so perplexed. "You mean because I'm a woman."

"I mean because of your empathetic nature." Graham stopped mid-stride and turned to her. "If you have any designs on making it beyond the rookie stage in this unit, you'd better get over this 'I'm a woman' trip ASAP. Nobody's looking to hold you back around here, but you damn sure better believe that nobody's gonna hold your hand either. If you want to keep making distinctions between yourself and everybody else because of some hang up you have, then that's your prerogative. Just don't be surprised when we finally start agreeing with you."

The speech sounded canned, and Sullivan couldn't help but wonder if he had kept it on reserve until the right opportunity presented itself. She couldn't get beyond the word *we*, and knew his saying it was no accident. But it ultimately didn't matter if the speech was rehearsed or spontaneous. It was obvious that Graham was the one with the hang up.

"Walter, do us both a favor and keep the focus on Rooney."

Graham smirked as he continued his walk to the conference room. "You got it, boss."

When they arrived, a young officer was standing outside the door with a middle-aged couple. After mouthing something to the pair, the officer walked over to Sullivan and Graham.

"Mr. and Mrs. Rooney just arrived," he said to Graham.

"Perfect timing," Graham answered, looking back at Sullivan. "Shall we get this proverbial show on the road?"

Sullivan nodded. "Thank you, Officer Davies."

"You're welcome, detective. Just come grab me when you're done. I'll be happy to escort them out."

Sullivan patted the officer on the back as he walked away.

"Is it me or does he look scared shitless?" Graham whispered as they approached Dale Rooney.

"That man has got the fate of an entire murder investigation resting in his hands. Wouldn't you be scared shitless?"

Sullivan suddenly felt a knot in her stomach and had only one thought to explain it: Graham may have been on to something with that whole empathetic nature thing.

CHAPTER 16

LEADING THE WITNESS

Dale Rooney sat with his wife Maggie at one end of the conference table while Detectives Graham and Sullivan sat at the other. Sullivan had offered coffee to the group, but only Dale accepted. His hands shook as he took the Styrofoam cup.

"Thank you again for coming in, Mr. and Mrs. Rooney," Graham began. "We shouldn't take up much of your time here. We just want to ask a few questions and show you a couple of photographs."

What photographs? Sullivan thought. They hadn't discussed showing any prior to the meeting.

"Okay," Dale replied as he took a gulp from his cup. "Just so you know, it was pretty dark out that night."

Dale's wife put her hand on his knee. "They know. Just tell them what you can."

"That's right, Mr. Rooney. Even the smallest details help," Sullivan added.

Dale stiffened in his chair. He was a short, round man with hooded brown eyes and a thick, well-kept beard. His horn-rimmed glasses and tweed jacket looked like something an Oxford economics professor would wear. But the prestigious air created by his attire was completely betrayed by his nervous demeanor.

"Where should I begin?" Dale asked.

"At the beginning," Sullivan answered.

Dale downed his remaining coffee like it was a shot of whiskey. He cast a glance at his wife, a slender redhead who, like Dale, seemed overdressed for the occasion. Then he turned to Graham.

"Well, I'd fallen asleep on the couch that night. I'm not sure what time it was when I drifted off, but when I woke up it was around twelve-thirty. At first I thought the music was coming from the television. But when I hit the mute button and the music was still there, I had a pretty good idea of what I was dealing with."

"Which was?" Sullivan asked.

"Some obnoxious jerk outside playing his car stereo too loud."

"And is that a common occurrence in the neighborhood?" Graham asked.

"Too common for my taste," Dale sniffed.

"What happened next?" Sullivan asked.

"Given the kind of music it was – rap, hip-hop, whatever you call it – my senses were on high alert, so I initially thought about calling the police."

"Completely understandable," Graham offered with an affected nod.

Sullivan rolled her eyes, hoping that no one noticed. "Please continue."

"I knew I at least needed to have some idea of what was out there before I called, so I went to the window. That was when I got my first look at the car."

"The gray Impala," Graham said.

"Correct."

"But Mr. Rooney, according to your statement, you couldn't be positive what color the Impala was," Sullivan countered, reading from Dale's written statement. "The only thing you knew for sure was that it was, quote, light."

Dale shifted in his chair. "As I recall it now, the car was definitely gray."

"And you're one hundred percent certain of that?"

"Yes," Dale answered without hesitation.

Sullivan tapped her pen against the table. "And according to your statement, you didn't get a good look at the license plate."

"Unfortunately not. The car was some distance away, and as I said, it was pretty dark. I went to retrieve a pair of binoculars in hopes that I could see it better. But before I could get to them the car was gone."

"How dark was it outside?" Sullivan asked.

"The street light was out in front of the house where the car was parked."

"That would be Julia Leeds's house," Graham said.

Dale cast his eyes downward. "Yes."

Sullivan wanted to continue her line of questioning regarding the color of the car and Dale's insistence that it was gray, despite his limited visibility and conflicting witness statement. But Graham's next move took the wind completely out of her sails.

"Mr. Rooney, I'm going to show you a few photographs. Just tell me if anything here looks familiar."

Dale shifted in his chair again, this time with visible nervousness. "Okay."

Graham opened up a manila folder and spread the contents out in front of him. There were four eight-by-ten photographs, all of them turned down. He flipped the first photo and slid it across the table.

Dale took the photo and held it up to his face as if he were analyzing an x-ray slide. "It looks a lot like the car I saw that night."

Graham flipped over the next two photos. They too were of a Chevy Impala. The first photo was taken from the left front at a ninety-degree angle and the second was taken from the rear. From the time stamp on the bottom of the photos, Sullivan knew they had come from the evidence lab, and were most likely shot by a CSI tech in front of Clemmons' house. She felt uneasy.

"This definitely looks like the car," Dale asserted as he looked at the other two photos. "As a matter of fact, I distinctly remember the red section on the right rear where it looked like part of the bumper was replaced. Absolutely sure of it."

Graham turned to Sullivan with a look of satisfaction that felt completely inappropriate.

"Okay, Mr. Rooney. I have one more photograph to show you. This one I want you to take your time with." Graham paused before turning the photo, building the suspense in the room to exaggerated heights. "Have you ever seen this person?"

Sullivan audibly gasped when she saw the photo. By the time Graham slid it across the table she was already out of her chair. "Detective, may I have a word with you?"

Graham's eyes were wide with confusion as he looked up at her. "Excuse me?"

"I need to talk to you outside."

Dale Rooney and his wife sat in nervous silence as Graham stood up. "We'll just be a moment folks," he said with a nonchalant smile. "As I said, Mr. Rooney, take your time with that photo."

Dale held it close to his face as the detectives walked into the hallway.

"What the hell is that?" Sullivan said before the conference room door closed behind them.

If Graham was surprised by Sullivan's outburst, he didn't show it. "I have no idea what you're talking about."

"The photograph of Stephen Clemmons."

"Listen—"

"Don't you think that was something we should have discussed beforehand? The pictures of the car are one thing. But a blow up of Clemmons' driver's license photo? That's so far over the top I don't even know where to begin."

"The only thing that's over the top is you pulling me out here in the middle of a witness interview," Graham snapped.

Sullivan shook her head. "If we tried to present any portion of this interview as evidence, Clemmons would have every constitutional lawyer in the country wanting to take up his cause. How could you not think about that?"

"Just calm down, Chloe."

"How am I supposed to calm down when you're compromising the entire investigation?"

"Because I'm not compromising the investigation."

"How do you figure that?"

"It's really simple. The car that Dale Rooney identified as being in front of Julia's house belongs to Stephen Clemmons. Is it at least plausible to assume that?"

"It's plausible, yes."

"And if we're operating on the theory that Leeds and Clemmons knew each other, perhaps even had something of a relationship – and right now that's the prevailing theory – then it stands to reason that he could have visited her house prior to the murder."

Sullivan was quiet as she let Graham's line of reasoning sink in.

"That means there is at least a possibility that Rooney has seen him before, particularly if he is as in tuned to the neighborhood as we think he is."

Sullivan wanted to disagree, but she couldn't. "I suppose so."

"Fantastic. Now can we stop dicking around out here? I really don't want to keep those people in here all day." Graham didn't wait for a response before opening the conference room door and walking inside.

Sullivan took her seat without saying anything. Her head was swirling with a mix of thoughts that she couldn't wrangle in. Despite Graham's logical explanation for showing Clemmons' photo, something about the tactic felt wrong.

"Sorry about that," Graham said to the couple as he sat down. "Just some procedural mumbo-jumbo. No big deal."

Dale's wife looked at Sullivan as if she wanted confirmation. Sullivan could only force a smile.

"Have you had a chance to look at the photo?" Graham asked.

"Yes," Dale replied without taking his eyes off of it. Then he looked at Sullivan. "Is this the man you think murdered Julia Leeds?"

Sullivan crossed her arms and looked at Graham to answer.

He didn't hesitate. "We can't say that as of yet, but he's someone we're interested in. I wanted to show you the photo in the event you may have seen him around your neighborhood at any point prior to Julia's murder."

Dale held up the picture in front of his wife. "Maggie?"

She gave the photo a quick glance. "He doesn't look familiar."

Dale placed the photo on the table and slid it back to Graham. "I mean, he could have been the person in the Impala, but I couldn't swear to that. And I would certainly remember if I'd seen him in the neighborhood."

Of course you would, Sullivan thought. "Did you get a good look inside the car, Mr. Rooney?"

"Not a good one. Again—"

"It was dark."

Dale appeared irritated by Sullivan's interruption. "Correct."

"So in fairness, how could you even speculate as to who was in the car, or how many of them there were for that matter?"

Dale pulled at his shirt collar. "I'm not trying to speculate. I just figured that by you showing me the photo," he paused to clear his throat. "I just figured he was someone important in all of this. Look, I didn't know Julia Leeds that well, but there isn't anyone alive who wants to catch this maniac more than I do. I can't even begin to tell you how it felt to walk up to her house and see…"

Maggie grabbed his arm and squeezed. "It's okay."

"We understand you've been through an awful lot, Mr. Rooney. You and your wife," Graham said. "You've been nothing but helpful."

Dale took off his glasses and rubbed both eyes. "We'll continue to do whatever we can to help, Detective Graham." The emotion in his eyes was offset by the sudden conviction in his voice. "If I have to keep looking at that photo, I will. If I need to look at more photos, I'll do that too."

Graham opened his mouth to reply, but was interrupted by Maggie.

"Should we be worried about him? The man in the photo?" she asked. "If he's capable of doing something like this, who's to say we're not in danger because we're talking to you?"

"You're not in danger." Sullivan's answer was almost dismissive, even though she knew the question was perfectly legitimate.

"I agree," Graham interjected. "You shouldn't feel the least bit uncomfortable. We have multiple detectives involved in the investigation, and we're monitoring every aspect of it as closely as possible."

"Including him?" Maggie asked.

"We're monitoring every aspect of the investigation," Graham reiterated.

"So what should my wife and I do in the meantime?" Dale asked.

"Just hang tight for now," Graham advised. "I may be calling on you again depending on where the process takes us."

Dale blew out a loud breath. "Understood. For now, is it okay if I look at that photo again? I just need to be sure there isn't something about him that I missed."

Sullivan looked at Graham as he took the photo out of the folder and slid it across the table. Graham did not look back.

*****

After more time with the photo and an extensive question and answer session regarding the early morning walk that led Dale to Julia Leeds's front door, the interview was finally over. As the Rooneys left, Graham went to great lengths to reassure them that Julia's killer would be caught, in large part because of Dale's invaluable testimony. Sullivan knew that his reassurance was hollow at best, and she added it to the growing list of thoughtless tactical errors he had made.

After Graham finished shaking hands with them he sat back down and watched from his chair as they walked out of the room. Surprised that he had not led the couple out, Sullivan took it upon herself to do so. But before she could leave the room, Graham stopped her.

"Detective Sullivan, can you stay for a moment? Officer Davies can escort Mr. and Mrs. Rooney out."

"Of course," Sullivan replied as the couple continued on without her.

"Could you close the door please?"

Sullivan did so and took a seat in the nearest chair.

"I've been meaning to have this conversation since our briefing in the lieutenant's office," Graham said. "But I thought it was something that could wait. Now I know it can't."

Sullivan suddenly felt nervous. "What's on your mind?"

"Your attitude."

"My attitude?"

"You know exactly what I'm talking about, Chloe. Just don't ever do it again."

"Do what?"

"Undermine me."

Sullivan's mouth flew open with shock. "Undermine you? What are you talking about?"

"In Lieutenant Hitchcock's office. You basically made me look like an idiot in there. And you tried to do it just now when you pulled me outside at the most crucial part of the interview. Do you have any idea how bad that made us look?"

Sullivan moved her lips to speak, but failed to produce any words.

"I don't have to tell you how long I've been doing this," he continued. "So I think I know a thing or two about conducting a murder investigation."

"I never suggested you didn't."

"But you certainly make it seem like I don't when it comes to Clemmons."

"Again, I never suggested that. There are just some things that don't add up."

"This isn't *CSI*, Chloe. Things rarely add up. But we work with what we have until the job gets done."

Now she was getting angry. Sullivan tolerated a lot from him, most of it because she had to. But the one thing she wasn't going to allow Graham to do was patronize her. "Stop right there, Walter. I know how to work the job, okay? I may be the newbie here, but I put in my beat time just like everybody else. I've seen plenty of crime scenes, and plenty of home invasions. I can spend five minutes in a house that's just been hit and give you the exact MO the perps used, down to the model of the sledgehammer they busted down the back door with. And nine out of ten times I'd be right. So when I tell you that the Leeds scene is unlike any I've ever seen – home invasion or domestic crime – that's not just some wild theory I'm trying to talk myself through, that's based on years of picking these scenes apart inch by inch."

Graham sat back in his chair and folded his arms. "That was a hell of a speech. I'm impressed, really. But it was completely unnecessary. I've been around you long enough to know that you're more than capable out there. If I had even the slightest doubt about that, you and I would have stopped riding together a long time ago. The point of this conversation is to stress how important it is that the two of us are on the same page going forward."

This time it was Sullivan who sat back in her chair and folded her arms.

Graham got the cue to keep talking. "I realize there's always room for divergent opinions when it comes to conducting an investigation. And a lot of times that can be a good thing. But this one is different, Chloe. Hitch was right when he said the scrutiny on the entire department is going to be through the roof. We have zero room to screw up. That's why we have to keep our focus tight. We don't have the luxury of speculating why the perp used a particular gun, or how he was able to shoot both dogs without either one of them taking a chunk out of his ass. We have to work with what we've got. This case is three days old, and do you know how many legitimate tips we've gotten in that time?" He made a zero shape with his fingers.

"I know," Sullivan said, already feeling like she was going to end up on the losing end of this argument.

"For a crime this high profile that's almost unheard of. By now the number of tips should have been in the hundreds. And of those, at least five would have held up as genuine leads. So the fact that we have nothing should tell you how up against it we are." He paused to emphasize the point. "Hitch says he's bringing in even more detectives to help, but ultimately this falls on you and me, Chloe. We're the leads, which means we set the direction of this investigation."

"I understand all of that, Walter. But the photo of Clemmons? What did you hope to achieve by showing it to Rooney? Aside from planting a seed that wouldn't otherwise be there?"

"I'm sorry if my tactics don't match up to your time-tested ethics. But sometimes you can only play the hand you've been dealt. And right now all we have is Clemmons. I don't think what I did was questionable in the least, and if you do then you obviously have a lot more to learn about how this process works."

There he was patronizing her again. She decided to let it go this time and keep the focus where it should be. "And it didn't worry you that Rooney took so much time looking at that photo *after* he said he didn't recognize Clemmons? It was like he was trying to convince himself that he did."

"In my mind he was only being thorough. Where is the problem in that?"

Sullivan shook her head. "The whole thing just seems wrong, Walt.

"What the hell is it with you and Clemmons?" he barked. "Just because he's a mail clerk you don't think he's smart enough to pull off something like this? Can mail clerks not pick up shell casings or commit a murder without leaving behind fingerprints? It doesn't take a freaking master's degree to be a smart criminal."

"From day one what have you always told me is the most important thing that a detective can have? Instincts they can trust. Well I've always trusted my instincts. And right now they're telling me that Clemmons is not who we want."

"What else do you have aside from instincts to tell you that?" Graham asked.

"The victim's car, for starters. If Clemmons was so methodical in leaving nothing behind at the crime scene, why would he steal it and park it a half a block away from his own house, in a place it was guaranteed to draw attention to itself?"

"Because he was arrogant enough to think that it couldn't be traced back to him? Because he really is that stupid? Who the hell knows? It's pure speculation either way, Chloe. And speculation isn't enough."

Sullivan struggled to find a response.

"Do you know what I have to tell me he did it?" Graham continued. "His car at the crime scene. When I put that together with where the victim's car was found, that's all I need to go after this guy with both guns."

Sullivan sat back in her chair, massaging her pulsating forehead. Now she really felt like she was losing this argument. "So what's the bottom line, Walt?"

"The bottom line is that despite what your instincts say, the evidence says that Clemmons is the guy. I'm going after him and I need you fully on board with that."

"And what if something else comes–"

"Right now there isn't anything else. There is only Clemmons. If we're going to have a problem working together on this, I suggest you put in for a case transfer right now."

Sullivan was stunned. She never imagined he would take it that far. "Are you kidding me?"

"Believe me Chlo', it's not what I want. But I also don't want this investigation compromised because your head is someplace else. I can't have you half-in on this."

Sullivan pushed her chair away from the table and stood up. "Fine."

"Fine as in you want to be transferred? Or fine as in you want to actually be my partner on this?"

"I'm your partner, Walter."

Graham looked at her with wary eyes. "You're certain about that?"

"Yes." There was nothing else she could say.

Graham stood up, then inexplicably extended his hand. "Glad to know we're finally on the same page. We're a much more effective team that way."

Sullivan shook his hand without saying anything.

"I think it's time we have our first face to face with Clemmons," Graham said. "The officers who initially questioned him told him to stand by for follow up, so he should be expecting our visit."

"It's been three days. If he really is the guy, aren't you worried he's on his way to Mexico by now?"

"We've had two details assigned to his house since this all happened. Aside from a couple of quick trips to his car, he hasn't left his house. I'm not expecting to get a lot out of this first go-round, unless Clemmons decides to do us a favor and confess. We'll just consider this one a quick meet and greet. Sound good?"

Sullivan nodded, then followed as Graham made his way out of the conference room. She was actually looking forward to meeting Clemmons, to see for herself if her instincts were as honed as she thought they were. And if they weren't? If Graham was right all along? Then that would be fine too. It would only prove Graham's point that she still had a lot to learn.

But while it may have been true that she had a lot to learn in general, when it came to Clemmons, Sullivan's instincts were not ready to concede just yet.

CHAPTER 17

SECOND THOUGHTS

Despite his wife's repeated attempts to engage him in conversation, Dale was quiet for most of the car ride home. The image of the man in the photograph, and what he had possibly done to Julia Leeds, kept playing repeatedly in his mind. When Detective Graham showed him the photo, he wasn't surprised by how the suspect looked. In fact, he expected it. What did surprise him was the venomous hatred that washed over him the instant he saw the man's face. He knew he was looking into the eyes of a killer, and even though his face was two dimensional, Dale could feel those cold-blooded eyes looking back at him. He didn't know the first thing about the police or how they conducted murder investigations, but he did know that Detective Graham showing him that photograph was no accident. He didn't come right out and say this was the man who murdered Julia Leeds, but he didn't have to. Everyone in the room, Graham in particular, seemed to know it.

Dale had told the truth when he said that it was too dark to see inside the car. But he also told the truth when he promised the detective that he would do whatever was necessary to help him find Julia's killer. He knew right now that he was the only one who could do so. He was the only one who heard the music that night, the only one who saw the Impala, the only one who found Julia Leeds's open door and the utter destruction that took place on the other side of it. And he was the only one who saw the picture of the man police were sure was responsible for all of it.

It was true that Dale didn't recognize him, and multiple looks at his photograph did nothing to change that. But if he really was Julia's killer, Dale knew he couldn't afford not to remember something. Even if that something had never actually occurred.

He felt surprised and uncomfortable with the thoughts that were formulating in his mind and knew that if he gave voice to them, even to his wife, he would immediately know how crazy he sounded and would never be able to act on them.

But he had to act on them, not for his own satisfaction, but for Julia Leeds.

For the first time in his life, his actions could have a significant impact on the world outside of his own. For the first time in his life, he wouldn't have to retreat into the cocoon of his own thoughts in order to feel significant. For the first time in his life, people would actually listen to him.

He knew right then that if Detective Graham were to call on him again, he wouldn't hesitate to remember exactly what he needed to in order for some measure of justice to finally be served in a world that he had long since checked out of.

As Dale stared at the road in front of him, he suddenly felt Maggie's hand grip his knee. When he glanced at her, she was smiling. He hadn't seen her smile like that in a long time. Not at him anyway. At that moment, there were no unspoken barriers between them, no yipping Pomeranian to distract them, no thoughts of a different life without her. There was only Dale, his wife, and a stirring in his chest he never thought he would feel again.

"I'm incredibly proud of the way you handled yourself in there," Maggie said, her grip tightening.

Not as proud as you're going to be, Dale thought with an ever-widening smile.

CHAPTER 18

SEEDS OF DOUBT

The ride to Stephen Clemmons' house was quiet. The only time Graham spoke was when he answered a call on his cell phone. The call was brief and his answers were short: "Yes." "No." "That shouldn't be a problem, sir." "No progress yet." "I'm headed there now."

When his call was finished and Sullivan asked him who it was, Graham's answer to her was just as succinct. "Hitchcock checking in."

She thought it was odd that he wouldn't offer any more details about his conversation with the lieutenant. Anything that may have been said was of as much consequence to her as it was to Graham. She also didn't like the line "*I'm headed there now*," as if she was stuck in the middle of a manicure. But she decided to leave it be.

When they turned onto the thirty eight hundred block of Gilpin Street, Graham picked up his two-way radio. "Two-five, this is Detective Graham. Copy?"

A voice came over the radio. "Copy, this is two-five."

"Detective Sullivan and I are en route and should be there momentarily. Is the bird still hiding in his nest?"

"Roger that," the voice answered with a slight chuckle. "Quiet as a tomb in there."

"Very good. If you guys want to take off, we've got it from here."

"Roger that. See you on the other side. Good luck in there."

"Thanks." As he put down the radio he pointed to a duplex on the corner. "There it is," he said to Sullivan.

She saw the now infamous gray Chevy Impala parked in front and another question immediately popped into her head. Why would Clemmons park it on the corner knowing he lived on such a busy street? There would be plenty of room to park it in the alley. She pushed the thought into the back of her mind. Speculation, as Graham called it, wasn't going to get her anywhere right now.

Graham pulled up to the curb across the street. "I have a couple of specific questions in mind, so let me take the lead, at least to start."

Sullivan knew it couldn't have been any other way. "No problem," she said as she pushed the car door open.

Seeing no doorbell, Graham banged on the door, much harder than he needed to in Sullivan's opinion, but it was effective, because Clemmons opened it right away. Perhaps he had been waiting for them after all.

"Stephen Clemmons?" Graham asked the man standing in the doorway.

"That's me," he said with eyes that Sullivan could only describe as terrified. "You must be the detective I was told to wait for."

"That's correct. I'm Walter Graham, this here is Detective Sullivan. We came to ask you a few questions about Julia Leeds."

Clemmons stood quietly at the door. He was a tall, pudgy man with sagging cheeks that resembled a Basset Hound's. It made him look sad even when he probably wasn't. He wore a Community College of Denver sweatshirt and a pair of wrinkled khakis. There was nothing about him that said murderer or even petty thief. But Sullivan had already known that. She threw a quick glance in Graham's direction to get a read on his expression. It was rigid, bordering on hostile.

"May we come in Mr. Clemmons?" Graham asked as he took a step toward the door.

Clemmons' index finger twitched as he held on to the door. He quickly brought the hand down and curled it up into a loose fist. Then he stepped aside. "Sure."

Graham walked through the doorway with Sullivan right behind him. She nodded at Clemmons as she walked past. He didn't nod back.

The three of them stood in the middle of the living room. The ramshackle condition of the exterior gave no indication of the near immaculate condition of the interior. Clemmons didn't have much space to work with, but he made the most of what he had. They stood next to a beige couch lined with burgundy throw pillows, a glass coffee table with several textbooks neatly stacked in the corner, a bookshelf filled with many more books, and several healthy-looking plants hanging from the ceiling. The small flat-screen TV was tuned to ESPN.

Sullivan suddenly felt as if she had no business in this house, and was glad that Graham had declared himself the lead.

Never one to waste time, Graham pulled out his notepad and pen and got right to it. "I know that officers were here a few days ago, but if you don't mind I'd like to ask you a few follow up questions."

Clemmons swallowed hard. "Like I told them, I'll cooperate as much as I can."

"We appreciate that, Mr. Clemmons. I'm going to start by quickly summarizing the information you gave to the officers, and all you have to tell me is whether or not my summary is correct. Okay?"

Clemmons made eye contact with Sullivan for the first time. She managed to hold his anxious gaze even though every part of her wanted to look away.

"Yeah, okay," he said as he turned back to Graham. "But before we do that, I've been watching the news about Julia. They're saying someone saw a gray Impala outside her house before she was murdered. Is that right?"

"I haven't seen that particular news report, so I can't speak on it," Graham answered flatly.

Clemmons swallowed again. "They also said that there weren't any suspects yet. Can you speak on that?"

Graham clenched his jaw as he looked down at his notepad. "We'll get to that, Mr. Clemmons. Right now I just need you to answer yes or no. According to the officer's notes, you arrived home from work at approximately five forty-five Thursday evening and didn't leave your house for the rest of the night, is that right?"

Clemmons looked at Sullivan again, then went back to Graham. "Yes."

"And you live here by yourself, so there is no one to corroborate that."

"That's right, I live here by myself."

"You also told them that you hadn't driven anywhere near the three hundred block of Monroe Street at any point that you could remember."

"I don't have any reason to ever get out that way."

"You work for the same law firm as the victim, correct?"

"Yes."

"But according to you, the two of you didn't know each other."

"That's right, we didn't."

At that last answer, Clemmons visibly stiffened. Sullivan was sure Graham had noticed it too.

"You never once spoke to her?" Graham pressed.

"I deliver mail to almost eighty lawyers every day. It's hard to keep track of who I speak to and who I don't."

"So it's possible you did?"

So what if he did! Where is the smoking gun in that? Sullivan thought, but she remained expressionless.

"I guess it's possible," he answered hesitantly.

Graham flipped through a few more pages of his notepad. "Mr. Clemmons, do you know a man by the name of Matthew Westerly?"

Clemmons nodded. "He's a lawyer at the firm."

"Actually the two of you are friends. He reported to our detectives that you've gone out for beers after work together on several occasions."

"That's right."

"Well, according to Mr. Westerly, you did know Julia Leeds. In fact, he recalled one outing over beers when you told him of a mail delivery to her office that became an extended conversation about your plans to become a paralegal. He said you couldn't stop talking about how beautiful she was and how you couldn't believe that she had taken so much time to talk to you." Graham paused for effect as he always did. "Does any of that ring a bell, Mr. Clemmons?"

Sullivan looked down at Clemmons' finger and noticed that it had started twitching again.

"I do remember that now," Clemmons said as he looked at his Nike running shoes. "It happened so long ago I guess it just slipped my mind."

"Mr. Westerly said it was less than two months ago."

Clemmons' right leg began to move the same way as his finger did, and Sullivan was suddenly worried that it would give out from under him.

"I don't know. Maybe I was confused by the officer's question. It was a lot to take in and I had just woken up when they came. I apologize for getting confused."

"That's quite all right," Graham said with his trademark look of satisfaction.

It wasn't a good moment for Clemmons, but Graham was still far from making his case in Sullivan's mind.

Graham pushed on. "And regarding the Range Rover; the one that was found in an alley across the street from here. You claimed that you had no knowledge of it being there."

"That's right, I didn't."

"You seem like the type of person who would have his finger on the pulse of this neighborhood. Had you heard any chatter about the Range Rover? Noticed any increased activity since its discovery?"

"I mostly keep to myself here, so it's rare that I have my finger on the pulse of anything when it comes to this neighborhood, detective."

Graham stopped writing and looked at Sullivan, who had to fight to conceal her smile.

"That being the case, you didn't notice anything out of the ordinary?" Graham asked with a hint of irritation.

"Ordinary seems to change around here from one day to the next. But as far as that night, no I didn't notice anything."

"What about the following morning?" Sullivan asked.

Clemmons hesitated.

"Mr. Clemmons?"

"I didn't notice anything."

Of all the questions he was asked, this was the one that seemed to make him the most uncomfortable, and for the first time, he failed to make eye contact with either Graham or Sullivan.

"Are you sure?" Sullivan asked, picking up on his shifting mood.

Clemmons attempted to smile. "Unless you count the two detectives who have been parked down the street for most of the week as out of the ordinary, then I would have to say that I'm sure."

This time Clemmons maintained his eye contact with Sullivan.

"Do you own a gun, Mr. Clemmons?"

He turned to Graham with an incredulous stare. "No."

Sullivan looked at Graham with a similar stare, completely thrown by the question. Graham glanced back at her impassively.

"Look detectives, I've cooperated with you just like I said I would. But I've already answered these questions, and if I'm being honest, I don't understand why I have to answer them in the first place. I may have misspoken about Julia Leeds earlier, but that one conversation is the only contact I've ever really had with her. I've never been to her house. I didn't even know where she lived until I saw it on the news. And I sure as hell didn't kill her."

"No one is saying you killed her, Mr. Clemmons," Sullivan said in the most reassuring voice she could offer. "We're simply here because–"

Graham interrupted. "When I asked if you knew Julia Leeds, you told me flat out that you didn't. When I asked if you had so much as said hello to her, you couldn't recall. But then when I tell you about Mr. Westerly's assertion that you talked to her extensively, it suddenly all comes back to you? I'm just wondering what other important details you're forgetting?"

With eyes that looked like they were beginning to water, Clemmons looked directly at Sullivan. "I didn't kill anybody, period. You want to check my house? You want to take my fingerprints? You want to give me a lie detector test? Do what you have to do. I really don't care."

I know you didn't kill anybody, Mr. Clemmons. "None of that will be necessary, sir," Sullivan said.

"Thank you for your time, Mr. Clemmons," Graham said as he pulled a card out from the back of his notepad. Then, as if it were an afterthought, he added: "By the way, do you have one of those loud, hip-hop stereo systems in your car? The kind you can hear coming a mile away?"

Clemmons responded to Graham with an angry smirk. "All of us black folk in the hood have them, detective. I figured you would have had that profile down by now."

Sullivan suddenly felt embarrassed and wanted nothing more than to leave.

"Indeed," Graham said as he reopened his notepad. "I only ask because the witnesses who reported seeing the gray Impala in front of Julia Leeds's house the night of her murder also reported hearing loud music coming from that car before it drove away."

Sullivan heard the word *witnesses* and knew it wasn't a matter of Graham misspeaking. He was purposefully misleading Clemmons.

Clemmons shrugged. "How am I supposed to respond to that? There are a lot of cars that have loud stereos."

"I suppose that is a pretty standard feature of gray Impalas," Graham said without a hint of sarcasm.

Clemmons shrugged again but was otherwise quiet.

"Are there any questions you have of us, Mr. Clemmons?" Sullivan asked in a quick attempt to shift the focus.

"You mean aside from the obvious?"

"And what is the obvious?" Graham sniffed.

Sullivan knew what the obvious was, and couldn't believe that Graham was going to make Clemmons say it.

"Did you really come here to ask me questions? Or to tell me that I'm a suspect?"

Graham looked at Sullivan. She hesitated before looking back.

"We're working a lot of different angles right now," was the best she could come up with.

Clemmons didn't blink. "No offense, Detective Sullivan, but it's a really simple question."

"I'm afraid that's not something we can talk about right now," Graham said matter-of-factly. "We're still in the information-gathering stage with a lot more witnesses to talk to."

Another untruth.

"Did they all see me at Julia Leeds's house too?"

The room fell into silence.

Rather than answer a question he knew he couldn't, Graham headed for the door.

"Thank you again for your time, Mr. Clemmons. You were very cooperative and we appreciate it," Sullivan said.

"Yes we do," Graham added, handing Sullivan his card as he walked out the door. "Should anything else jog your memory, don't hesitate to call me."

Sullivan gave Clemmons the card and followed him to the door. Before she walked out, she extended her hand.

Much to her surprise, Clemmons was quick to shake it. "I know this has been a really difficult few days for you," she offered. "Hang in there." She looked at the coffee table filled with textbooks. "Best of luck with school too."

Even though Sullivan knew she did little to ease his mind, she was still moved when he said "Thank you."

By the time Sullivan stepped onto the porch, Graham was standing in front of Clemmons' car with a small digital camera in hand. As she walked toward her partner, she turned back to see Clemmons standing on the lawn. He looked afraid, and he should have been. Graham's over-zealousness was beginning to frighten her too.

"What are you doing?" she asked when they were out of earshot.

"Just getting a couple of pictures."

"What for? The CSI techs already took care of that."

"Clemmons doesn't know that. This is only for show. I'm just trying to rattle him a little bit. We need to remind him that he's not out of the woods just because we're leaving without arresting him." Graham raised the camera and started taking pictures again. "If his car wasn't there, then he's got nothing to worry about, right?"

"Just like you were trying to rattle him with that nonsense about multiple witnesses?"

"It's called scare tactics, Chloe."

Sullivan shook her head and walked away. "It's also incredibly reckless."

"Why are you getting so bent out of shape?" he asked from a few paces behind her. "All I'm doing is planting a few seeds of doubt in the guy's mind, letting him think we know more than we actually do. Did you see how he almost shit his pants when I told him what Westerly said? He didn't think we'd find out about that. I'm telling you, there's more to this. And the longer we can keep him on edge, the more likely he'll crack when the time finally comes."

Sullivan stopped. "But that's what you don't get, Walter. He won't crack because he didn't do it."

Graham rolled his eyes. "Didn't we just have a long conversation about this? I was under the impression that we saw eye to eye on the importance of being unified."

"He didn't do it. If I was fifty-one percent sure of it before we came here then I'm one-hundred percent sure now. I'm sorry we can't see eye to eye on this, but you are so barking up the wrong tree with Clemmons it's not even funny."

"You're right, Chloe. It's not funny at all." He walked past her and headed straight for the car without saying another word.

The more Sullivan fought him, the tougher things were going to get for her, and not just with this investigation, but with every investigation she would conduct with him going forward. Her chances of having a future working relationship with Graham were dying by the second, and she was the one digging the grave. Once he branded her as being difficult, her chances of having a solid working relationship with any detective in the unit were slim.

But right now she couldn't be swayed by fear. Right now she could only be swayed by the truth. Unfortunately, the truth of this case was getting murkier with each passing moment. As was her perception of Graham. In the dozen or so cases they had worked together, she had never seen him this short-sided in his pursuit of a suspect. Even with all the evidence to the contrary, he was absolutely hell-bent on making Clemmons something that he clearly was not.

The longer Graham persisted, the more she began to wonder if his motives were something beyond the justice he took an oath to pursue. She began to wonder if his motives were somehow personal.

She had nothing to support that suspicion other than a gut-feeling. But it was the same gut-feeling that told her Julia Leeds wasn't killed for her flat screen television. It was the same gut feeling that told her that Julia's car being found here, a block away from the suspicious Impala that happened to belong to one of her co-workers, was entirely too convenient. It was the same gut-feeling that was telling her that Graham was already formulating the reasons for his impending recommendation that she be dismissed from the Leeds case.

More times than not, her gut was right. She had no reason to doubt it now. There was more here, and she would figure it out, even if she had to do it on her own.

Based on the hostile glare that Graham gave her as they drove away from Clemmons' house, Sullivan could not shake the feeling that she was already on her own.

CHAPTER 19

A PAWN ON A BOARD OF KINGS

Stephen Clemmons sat on his couch staring at the cover of a textbook he had been studying every night for the past three months: *Advanced Case Studies in Criminal Justice*.

After two years of night classes, he was a semester and a half away from completing his Associates degree in Paralegal Studies. It had been a long journey from where he started, and there were more than a few missteps along the way. But Stephen knew that he was ultimately doing it the right way, which was a lot more than he could say for anyone else he knew.

He had put in an application five different times before finally landing the mail clerk job at Brown, Wallace, and Epstein. Most people don't view being a mail clerk as anything to be particularly proud of. But as far as Stephen was concerned, it was the perfect job. The pay may have been minimal, the work may have been tedious, and his tiny basement cubicle may not have provided the most scenic view, but he got to watch some of the best lawyers in the country up close on a daily basis. Just being in their presence was an educational experience that far exceeded anything he had learned in the classroom. He even got to know a few of the attorneys personally. One of them, a third-year associate who graduated from Harvard, invited him out for beers on a routine basis. Though Stephen had absolutely nothing in common with him or his group of well-bred, well-paid friends, he was perfectly content to sit back and listen to their stories of courtroom battles and boardroom takeovers, dreaming of the day when he was in the position to tell a few stories of his own. At thirty-four-years-old, he had gotten a much later start than any of them, but as his mail room supervisor said after Stephen told her about his law school aspirations, *it's not where you start, it's where you finish.*

After years of hard work, after years of nearly everyone he knew telling him that he was wasting his time, Stephen could finally see the finish line. Stories about CEOs who slowly climbed their way out of the mail room and kept climbing until they reached the top floor are so commonplace that they are almost cliché. But Stephen was still inspired by them. He may not have had designs on climbing all the way to the senior partner penthouse suite, but he was well on his way to making it out of the basement and into a room with a much brighter view.

Then a junior partner who worked in his firm was murdered, and it was as if everything he had worked so hard for instantaneously blew up in his face.

He had just finished getting ready for work that morning when the doorbell rang. Stephen was startled when he looked through the peephole to see two uniformed officers standing on his front porch. After inviting themselves in, the officers proceeded to ask him a series of rapid-fire questions about his car, where he had been the night before, if he was aware of a vandalized Range Rover in the alley across the street, where he worked, how long he had worked there, and if he knew a woman named Julia Leeds.

The questions came so fast he was barely able to process them. He told the officers as calmly as he could that the car was indeed his, that he had been up most of the night studying for a midterm, and that he knew nothing about a vandalized Range Rover. Lastly, he told them that he didn't know Julia Leeds.

Stephen wasn't sure why he lied about her, other than his survival instincts telling him that he should. When you live in this neighborhood and the cops show up at your door for any reason, survival trumps everything, including the truth. But in this instance, he had nothing to hide. He and Julia may have worked in the same office, but they were far from being friends. They had only had one conversation in the entire time he had been there. If pressed, it was entirely likely that she wouldn't have remembered it at all. But he knew exactly who she was. The fact that the police were now mentioning her name in reference to questions about his car and his whereabouts made him nervous enough to justify that particular omission.

When they finally informed him that they were investigating a homicide, Stephen's nervousness turned into outright fear.

Before the officers left, they informed him it would be best not to go into work because detectives would probably need to talk to him again before the day was over. Stephen called into work, telling his supervisor he was sick. That wasn't a lie. He threw up twenty minutes after the officers left.

The detectives that the officers spoke of did not show up until today. But when they left, as had happened after the officer's initial visit, Stephen felt like throwing up.

The revelation of his conversation with Matthew Westerly, his third-year associate beer buddy, definitely made him nervous. Even though he knew there was nothing more to the story, his initial withholding of it made it a bigger deal than it should have been. Now it looked like he had something to hide. He was also nervous about Detective Graham's claim of multiple witnesses that still needed to be talked to. Who exactly were these witnesses and what did they see?

Why the police would show up on his doorstep, let alone suspect him of anything, was beyond his ability to comprehend. He couldn't remember the last time he was anywhere near the area where Julia lived. He certainly wasn't there the night she was killed.

But it was obvious the police didn't believe him. The only question in his mind now was why.

He began to wonder if he was being targeted because he worked with Julia. Whether he personally knew her or not, the fact that police would show up at his house to ask him about the murder of a person he happened to work in the same building with seemed entirely too crazy to be coincidental. The very real possibility that it wasn't coincidental led to a whole other series of questions that he was not at all prepared to deal with.

It didn't take much imagination to figure out what all of this would mean for him. To even be mentioned in connection with something so horrible effectively meant that everything he had worked for could instantly be taken away. There certainly wouldn't be a future at Brown and Wallace. And that was the best case scenario.

Stephen may not have known much about the world as a whole, but he did have a firm understanding of his place in it. It didn't matter that he was completely innocent. Being black and under suspicion was as good as being guilty. And no amount of evidence to the contrary, short of a full confession by the real killer, would ever change that verdict.

He thought of the hundred or so lawyers who worked at the firm and wondered if any one of them would ever consider defending him if it came down to that. Probably not even his Harvard-educated beer buddy, Stephen solemnly concluded, especially now that the police had gotten to him. If there was a fight to be waged, he would have to take it on all by himself.

After the detectives finally drove away, Stephen walked to his car. He had anxiously watched as Detective Graham took pictures of it while his partner looked on. Even though they were out of earshot, it appeared that they were having a disagreement of some sort. Not that it mattered. Detective Sullivan may have seemed more sympathetic than her partner, but at the end of the day they played for the same team.

He wondered if Detective Graham had gotten any pictures of the car's interior, the same car interior that had been vandalized the night of Julia's murder.

Steven first noticed it after the officers left his house Friday morning. As much as he knew he needed to heed their instructions to stay close, sitting around the house only made him anxious and he desperately needed to get some fresh air. Despite the fact that both he and the car had been branded as "suspicious", Stephen decided there would be no harm in taking it out for a quick drive around the neighborhood.

The problem came when he put his key in the driver's side lock. No matter how hard he turned, the door wouldn't open. He took the key out and inserted it again. It still wouldn't open. So he went to the passenger's side. When he put the key in that lock it turned and the door opened as it was supposed to.

He breathed a sigh of relief and ducked inside. But what he saw as he slid into the passenger's seat nearly made his heart stop.

The ignition housing had been completely ripped open, exposing the red and green wires underneath, and a large screwdriver was jammed inside the starter.

When Stephen was a teenager, he ran with a crowd that he probably shouldn't have, and a few times they convinced him to tag along while they broke into cars and stole the stereos inside. On one occasion, they decided that taking the stereo wasn't enough and thought it would be a lot more fun to steal the actual car. Monte Collins, the leader and most experienced criminal of the group, ripped open the starter, crossed a couple of wires, and used a screwdriver to start the ignition. He did it all in fewer than ninety seconds.

What Stephen saw now didn't look nearly as professional as what Monte had done. But when he turned the screwdriver and heard the engine roar to life, he knew it was just as effective.

He had felt sick yet again. A horribly surreal day had instantly taken a turn into the otherworldly. When the cops first showed up,

Stephen felt like he was living out an episode of *Law & Order*. But things like this don't even happen in television shows. Now he felt like he was living a game of chess where he was the only pawn on a board filled with kings.

There was simply no way to win.

Standing here three days later looking at the screwdriver that someone had used to steal his car, a thought suddenly came to him. He may have been home studying the night that Julia Leeds was killed, but his car was exactly where Detective Graham said it was. And even though the proof that someone else had driven it there was right here for the entire world to see, short of that full confession he prayed would soon come, who in the hell was going to believe him?

If the Denver police department had anything to say about it, the answer would be no one.

After a few minutes spent looking for the gray Crown Victoria that had been a constant presence on his street since Friday, Stephen had gone back inside, sat down on the couch, and looked at his textbook. He'd had the silly notion that a bit of studying might serve to take his mind off of everything. But he never opened it.

And after what happened today, he figured there would never be another reason to open it again.

CHAPTER 20

LOOSE ENDS

The Leeds job had been executed to absolute perfection.

It was a bold declaration, but one that the man hired to carry out the job was fully prepared to make. Even by his own exceedingly high standards, perfection was rare. In this case however, he struggled to find another word to adequately describe the outcome.

The growing number of media outlets reporting on the story had already come to the collective conclusion that Julia Leeds was the victim of a home invasion gone horribly wrong. Based on the information these news outlets, and thus the rest of the public, were privy to, the conclusion was a sound one.

But as was usually the case, there was a great deal of the story that the media wasn't privy to. And as hard as they may eventually try, Joseph Solomon went to great lengths to ensure that neither they, nor anyone else, would ever be privy to more.

From the time he began his surveillance of Julia Leeds nearly three weeks ago, Solomon knew the operation would be fairly straightforward. Julia was a creature of habit, never once deviating from the daily routine of taking her dogs out for a six A.M. run, leaving for work at eight, and arriving back home some twelve hours later. There were no dinner dates, no visitors, no late night telephone conversations. This predictability made her the easiest target imaginable. And aside from the minor hassle of disarming her security system and dealing with her two behemoth guard dogs, everything went exactly as he had drawn it up.

Staging a burglary scene to look authentic, particularly when the motive is something else entirely, is a process that requires more meticulous planning than one realizes.

'*The devil is in the details,*' a man Solomon would loosely consider a mentor once told him. '*A cop's natural inclination is to dig. Never give them a reason to dig any further than the surface.*'

Home invasions were usually poorly planned and even more poorly executed. Robbers kicked down doors, left fingerprints, and ransacked the house until they found what they wanted, and if they were of the ruthless, drug-crazed variety, they killed anyone they saw without a moment's hesitation.

When a first responder entered a scene and saw any of these trademarks, he knew exactly what he was dealing with. The suspects would be profiled by the time the incident was called in to detectives, and those suspects usually resembled the meth freak or crack addict who routinely occupied the backseat of the cop's patrol car.

Solomon, however, was no out of control meth freak. He was focused, highly organized, and very skilled. But the scene he left behind could not reflect any of that. The scene had to look chaotic, violent, and rushed, all without a single trace of himself left behind. It was a tall order to be sure. Fortunately, he had an abundance of experience to draw from.

He was particularly proud of the Leeds scene. It took him nearly two hours to make his way through each room, but by the time he was finished, every drawer in the house had been emptied, every closet had been rummaged through, the mattresses in the two spare bedrooms had been flipped, and most importantly, every item that a burglar would even consider taking had been removed from the house.

He ended up leaving all of it in the same alley where Julia's Range Rover was ultimately found. He had chosen that alley specifically. The lowlifes who occupied it could smell stolen merch a thousand miles away, even at three-thirty in the morning, so Solomon felt confident that nothing would be left behind.

But there was another reason why he chose that alley. It was in direct proximity to the home of one Stephen Clemmons, the man whose car was seen near the crime scene a short time before Julia's death. Solomon knew it had been seen because he was behind the wheel when he spotted Julia's neighbor staring out his window at it.

Clemmons came gift-wrapped to Solomon, courtesy of the man who had hired him for the job. As part of the lengthy dossier he provided on Julia, he included a list of every employee at Brown, Wallace, and Epstein, along with their position within the firm, their home addresses and telephone numbers. The sheer amount of detail in the document was staggering; something only a high-level insider within the firm would have access to. But Solomon thought it would ultimately be useless, until he saw Clemmons' highlighted address with the word '*Diversion*' written next to it. He knew exactly what that word meant.

Even though the diversion had been executed as smoothly as the rest of the operation, Solomon realized, with the benefit of hindsight, that stealing Clemmons' car, driving it back to Julia's, and doing everything he could to call attention to it while he was there was a really bad idea. He had never taken a chance like that before. And with good reason. There were a million ways the plan could have gone wrong. He could have been pulled over, Clemmons could have seen him steal the car or realized it was gone before it could be brought back, one of Julia's neighbors could have immediately called the police, or worse yet, the car could have gone unnoticed altogether.

There was also the matter of involving a second person in the operation. Solomon preferred to work alone, but the logistics of stealing Clemmons' car and Julia's car and driving them both to the same location would have been impossible to navigate by himself. The man he entrusted with the task of driving the Range Rover had as large a stake in the outcome as anyone else. But Solomon had serious concerns about his ability to improvise should any aspect of the operation break down.

Fortunately, none of the worst case scenarios that he envisioned actually came to fruition. Solomon took the Impala without incident and brought it back three hours later. With the car parked safely in front of Clemmons' house, he saw no need to conceal the hotwire job.

The neighbor two houses down from Julia's, no doubt roused by the music Solomon made sure was loud enough for the entire block to hear, saw the car first from his living room window, then from the front porch. And best of all, when Solomon drove through the Gilpin neighborhood a few hours later to make sure that Julia's Range Rover was where it was supposed to be, he saw a patrol car parked directly in front of Clemmons' house.

Tough luck for the lowly mail clerk that he made such a sensible scapegoat.

If investigators had done even a fraction of their due diligence, they would have discovered early on that Clemmons and Julia worked for the same law firm. It didn't matter that they most likely never knew each other. Once the police began feeling the heat that this case was sure to generate, they would start making things up; connecting dots that were never meant to be connected. He knew all-too-well how the game operated. In this case, he even had a hand in writing the playbook.

"Perfection," he uttered to himself with a smile that only accentuated the sharpness of his chiseled jaw line. "I should charge those idiots double."

But before he started demanding more money, Solomon knew he first had to complete the job he was originally paid to do. The logistical phase of the operation was over. Now it was time to recover the information that made the operation necessary in the first place.

Before he proceeded to destroy Julia's house, Solomon removed two computers from her home office: a clunky Gateway desktop and a Sony VAIO notebook. He also scoured the house for all of the portable computer disks he could find. He came upon a box of CD-ROMs, several flash drives, even three floppy disks. He also looked for homemade DVDs; even though he was assured that she would never have such a thing lying around. She didn't.

Solomon had strict instructions to recover her computer and every piece of data associated with it. But he was not told what information would be on that computer or the associated disks. There was mention of a possible SD video card or Windows movie file, which provided one obvious clue. But aside from that, his employer was intentionally vague. Compartmentalization at its finest.

Ultimately, it didn't matter what Solomon knew and what he didn't. The directive was simple. It also seemed silly in a way. All of this effort for a couple of computers and a handful of flash disks. But Solomon learned long ago that the 'whys' never mattered.

Still, he couldn't help but be curious.

Sitting in his apartment bedroom with the five P.M. newscast turned down, Solomon set up the desktop computer on his bed and powered it on. A green indicator light blinked, then something inside the CPU tower made a sharp grinding sound. After five agonizing minutes, the monitor displayed a Windows XP symbol and the computer came to life. But that life seemed to be hanging on by the thinnest of threads.

The lone file on the desktop was a Microsoft Word document titled '*Copper Mountain info 11-29-09*'. Solomon clicked on the file but it took at least forty-five seconds to open. During that time the sharp grinding noise inside the CPU returned, convincing Solomon that it was on the verge of exploding. Instead, it moved mind-numbingly slow through every other document that Solomon tried to open. Fortunately there weren't many. An Excel spreadsheet titled '*Julia's Budget Dec '08*', a picture folder with seven photos of Julia's dogs, the same ones he shot and killed before proceeding to Julia's bedroom, and a PDF file that simply refused to open were all that he found. After a thorough check of the hard drive, including hidden and temporary folders, he determined there was nothing else of value on the computer.

Next he inserted each of the floppy disks. This was probably the only computer in existence that still had the drive to support them, but it didn't matter. Every one of the disks was empty. When he inserted one of the CD-ROMs, he immediately received a DRIVE NOT SUPPORTED message. He received the same message when he inserted one of the flash disks. After another forty seconds of grinding and barking, Solomon officially declared the computer worthless and wondered why Julia ever wasted her time with it.

The second computer seemed more her style. The Sony VAIO looked brand new, and probably cost way more money than any computer should. He eagerly hit the laptop's power button and sat back in anticipation of the flurry of files he was sure would be there.

But there were no files. There wasn't even a start up message. He saw nothing more than a blue screen with a blinking gray cursor in the top left corner. When Solomon pressed the enter button, the screen went black and the computer shut off. When he hit the power button again, the computer failed to respond altogether.

Solomon pounded his fist against the keyboard and tossed the computer aside. The VAIO was one of the most expensive laptops on the market. It shouldn't have just stop working, not unless it was hit with a Trojan horse or something equally fatal. But why would Julia allow herself to have two inoperable computers? She undoubtedly brought work home almost every night, and it would be impossible to do that work without a computer. Something wasn't adding up.

THE STRATEGIST

Eager to get at least some idea of the information on the disks, Solomon pulled out his own Apple MacBook. He turned it on and breathed a sigh of relief when the desktop immediately came up.

He started with the CD-ROMs. There were fifty-two in all. Every one of them was blank. Same with the eight flash disks.

Solomon bit down hard on his lip. There was not a single piece of data on either of the computers or any of the disks. A million thoughts simultaneously ran through his head. All of them led to bad outcomes. Foremost in his mind was the idea that he had somehow misunderstood his directive. *'Get her computer and any disks that you can find.'* There wasn't much ambiguity there.

That only left the possibility that Julia either never had the information to begin with, or she got rid of it before he or anyone else could get to it. Either possibility presented a major problem.

The final exchange between Solomon and his employer was scheduled to take place in two days. Solomon was to deliver the computer data in exchange for the rest of his fee. But that exchange would now have to be put on hold. There would be no way to gauge his employer's reaction to this delay. But Solomon knew how he personally felt about it - pissed off.

More than anything else in the world, he hated loose ends. It was particularly bad when the failure had nothing to do with him, as was the case now.

Solomon was not a private investigator, which meant that he had no intention of digging any deeper for those files than he already had. But that still didn't change the fact that the job was now unfinished, and unless Julia was killed over two worthless computers and a bunch of empty data disks, his employer would expect more.

Solomon had survived this long in the worlds he operated in because of two things: skill and instincts. Neither one had ever failed him. Solomon's instincts were talking to him loud and clear right now. They were telling him that this simple little job was far from over. If someone other than his employer had the disks,

153

Solomon knew it would be his job to find them. And once he did, that someone would most certainly have to die. It wasn't a scenario he was particularly fond of, but one that his vast experience told him was inevitable.

He immediately thought about the other woman in this equation. It was the same woman who Julia picked up from the airport the morning of her murder. The same woman whose house Julia had been in most of that day. The same woman who showed up at Julia's house after her murder in hysterics. The same woman who recently left the FBI because she stood by while her partner was executed by a third-rate serial killer.

When Solomon followed Julia to the airport, after a sharp deviation from her morning routine that included a thirty minute stop at the First Western Bank, he assumed she had taken the day off to pick up a family member or some male suitor that he knew nothing about.

When he saw Julia walk back to her car some forty minutes after they'd arrived, nothing in Solomon's wildest imagination could have prepared him for who he saw walking behind her.

Camille Grisham looked much younger in person than she did on television. While her physical stature was formidable, her facial features were delicate, with no sign of the hard-edge that was portrayed by her FBI friends during various interviews and special reports. Her dark wavy hair was pulled back tightly, revealing a rich, pretty face that seemed more at home on a magazine cover than in some crime lab. But her eyes were tired and somber. No surprise if all the news reports that Solomon had heard about her were true.

He had felt an uncomfortable thump in his chest as Julia lifted the FBI agent's suitcases into the back of her Range Rover. As the two stood outside of the car talking, the agent glanced over both shoulders, as if she sensed someone was watching her. The action unnerved Solomon more than he cared to admit, and he fought the urge to lower his head out of sight.

"Keep it together," he had whispered to himself.

He followed them to a house that was only a few blocks from the bar he had met his employer in only a few nights earlier. Solomon was instantly reminded of how small the world really was.

He watched the house for a long time. As the minutes turned into hours, any hope he may have had that Julia and the agent were merely acquaintances slowly evaporated. How close they actually were was something Solomon didn't know. But he had to assume they were close enough to discuss the private, personal matters of their lives. That left open the very real possibility that the agent knew things pertaining to his employer, things that Solomon himself may not even know. People like Camille Grisham are trained to connect dots that the average person, even the average cop, would never even consider. No matter how well-staged a crime scene was, her first instinct would be to dig deeper. And if she had any inkling of the circle that Julia Leeds was a part of, that would be the first place she would dig.

Thinking about all of this made his mind leap to conclusions that frightened him, and he knew he had to pull it together. Maybe the agent knew everything. Maybe she knew nothing. Either way, Solomon still had a job to do. The disks would be found, no matter who had them. And if finding them meant ending the nightmare that had become Camille Grisham's life, then so be it.

As he pulled out his cell phone to make the call he absolutely dreaded making, Solomon was reminded of a basic truth that he had briefly, and foolishly, allowed himself to forget.

There is no such thing as perfection.

CHAPTER 21

THE ENVELOPE

Camille had barely spoken a word in the day and a half since Julia's funeral. Following her incident in the closet, she began taking the anti-anxiety pills that were prescribed to her after Agent Sheridan's death. The results were not what she had hoped for. Though they succeeded in keeping her calm, the after effects left her with a feeling of complete physical disconnect, not only from herself, but from the entire world around her.

She wanted to tell her father everything she was feeling, but she knew it would only give him another reason to worry, and Camille had already given him enough reasons to worry. Her withdrawal from the world had also, by extension, been a withdrawal from him. He had tried his best to stay engaged, to regularly check in on her, to give her an ear that was all too willing to listen. But she kept quiet; content to lock herself in her bedroom while the world around her slowly transformed into one that she no longer recognized.

Her cell phone rang a lot during that time. She knew they were mostly calls of condolence, though she never answered a single one. People certainly meant well, but there wasn't anything they could say to make her feel better. The fact of the matter was that she didn't want to feel better. She didn't want the world to return to normal or find a way to heal her shattered psyche. In Camille's mind, she deserved nothing more than to spend the rest of her life in the purgatory of her childhood bedroom, and until her father physically put her out on the street, she had no intention of being anywhere else.

Then she received the call that changed everything.

Much as she had done with every other call to her cell phone, she let it go directly to voicemail rather than answer it. She had listened to and deleted twenty-two other messages before she finally came upon it. It had been left nearly three hours prior.

"Good morning, Camille. My name is Laurence Pine and I'm an attorney with Pine, Goldwin and Associates," the message said. "I oversaw Julia Leeds's estate and we've just completed the reading of her will. There were items left to you by Julia, and we can arrange to have you come to our office so our clerk can process those items for you. But there was something else that Julia left for you, something that wasn't an official part of her will. I'd prefer to meet with you personally regarding this, so I'm calling to see if you are available sometime today. I'll leave my schedule open in the event that you are. My direct line is 303-" Camille didn't wait for the rest of the number. She simply hit the 'redial' button.

After a brief conversation with the attorney and an agreed upon meeting time, Camille was showered and dressed in twenty minutes.

When she went downstairs, her father was in the kitchen. The look of surprise on his face was palpable. "Are you headed out?" he asked as he stood over a grilled cheese sandwich cooking on the stove.

"For a little while. I just talked to Julia's attorney. Her estate reading was today and apparently something was left for me that he wants to talk about."

"Are you sure that's something you can handle right now?"

"No. But I need to go anyway."

Paul turned off the stove. "Well give me a minute. I'll drive you."

"You don't have to do that, dad. I'll be okay. I need to be back in the world by myself at some point."

"Are you sure this is the right situation to do that?"

Camille shook her head. "There won't be any such thing as the right situation."

Paul nodded his agreement then turned back to his grilled cheese.

"It sure smells good," Camille said as she attempted a smile.

"Made with entirely too much butter, just the way you like it. I'd be happy to grill one up for you before you leave."

"Maybe later."

"And you're positive you're okay to drive?" he asked, now barely able to contain the anxious father that had been bottled up in him for days.

"Positive," she answered, forcing her smile even wider. "I promise I won't be gone long."

"Okay. Just make sure you're safe out there. And call me if you need to, for any reason at all."

Camille almost rolled her eyes at the comment but held back. The sudden, unexpected death of someone you know makes you worry that much more for everyone else you know. Camille couldn't fault Paul for being nervous about her being anywhere out of his sight.

"I will." She leaned in to kiss him on the cheek then walked out. "I love you," she said over her shoulder as she opened the front door.

"I love you too, bunny!" he yelled back.

He hadn't called her bunny since she was ten-years-old. It had always given her the biggest smile when she heard it.

She was thankful he couldn't see her reaction now.

THE STRATEGIST

*****

The offices of Pine, Goldwin and Associates were located on the eighteen floor of the Wells Fargo Building, better known to those familiar with the Denver skyline as the 'cash register'. Camille sat alone in a spacious, softly lit lobby adorned with marble sculptures of half-clothed women playing harps and Spartan warriors dressed in battle gear, while the young receptionist left to inform Mr. Pine of her arrival. Mozart's *The Marriage of Figaro* was playing softly on the receptionist's desktop radio. Next to that sat a tray of handmade pastries and an ice bucket filled with bottles of water and orange juice. If nothing else, Laurence Pine knew how to create a welcoming environment. Unfortunately, the warm atmosphere did little to calm her frayed nerves.

The receptionist returned no later than thirty seconds after she left, the man Camille assumed to be Laurence Pine walking beside her.

"I'm so glad you could make it, Camille," he said with a broad smile as he extended a hand to her.

He was a tall, good-looking man who was much younger than Camille expected. Despite the tension of the moment, his smile unexpectedly disarmed her. She rose to shake his hand.

"It's nice to meet you, Mr. Pine."

"No formalities needed here. Laurence will do just fine."

"Laurence it is," Camille said with a smile that had quietly infiltrated her face. She allowed the warm feeling to linger a moment longer than it should have before she buried it in a serious demeanor.

The instant Pine saw the look, his smile faded. "Can I offer you something?" he asked, pointing to the tray on the receptionist's desk.

"No thank you."

"Okay. Then if you'd like to follow me, my office is right down the hall."

Pine's office was large, offering a clean view of Rocky Mountains that were sprinkled white with the season's first snowfall.

"Please have a seat," he said, pointing to a leather swivel chair that faced his desk.

As Camille sat, she watched Pine walk to a file cabinet adjacent to his desk. After unlocking and opening one of the drawers, he emerged with a large brown envelope in hand.

"Before we start, I should probably tell you a little about my relationship with Julia," Pine said as he sat down. "First off, we've known each other for well over a decade. We were actually in the same graduating class at Yale. She had originally recruited me when she came back to Denver to work for Brown, Wallace, and Epstein. I took her up on it, but after a year at the firm I got sick of the political in-fighting and decided to start up my own shop instead. Julia and I remained good friends throughout the years and I've been her personal attorney for almost six. She spoke of you often. In fact, the last time I talked to her was on the morning she was to pick you up from the airport. She couldn't have been more excited you were coming. We hadn't talked for a while and had made tentative plans to get together for lunch. Of course I had no way of knowing that would be the last time I would…" His voice trailed off as he chewed on the tip of his fingernail.

"I'm sorry," Camille said, looking at a once strong, confident face that was now contorted with emotion.

Pine cleared his throat in an obvious effort to compose himself. "It's been difficult on everyone who knew her. And there were a lot of people around here who knew her. But no one knew her as well as you. I'm aware of the circumstances of your return here and the hell that you've been through since. I can sit here and say that I have some idea of how you feel. But the reality is I don't. All I can say is I'm sorry."

"Thank you," Camille answered in a broken voice.

The two sat in prolonged silence, each seeming to process the gravity of the moment in their own way. After a few moments, Pine spoke.

"I guess I should get to why I actually called you here. As I mentioned, Julia and I met last Thursday morning. She had originally told me that the purpose of the meeting was to modify her existing will. But when she got here I discovered that she actually wanted to draft a second one. I told her that in all the years I've been doing this, I've never heard of anyone wanting a second will in addition to the one they already had. Typical Julia, she smiled at me and said 'Larry my man, there's a first time for everything.'"

Camille laughed. Typical Julia indeed.

Pine continued. "She went on to tell me that it wasn't an official will and had nothing to do with the division of her assets. All she said was that it was something to be handled by me and only me in the event of her death. Nothing to notarize or otherwise document. Just my word that I would do with it what she asked me to do. I laughed when I took the envelope, not knowing what it was and never once thinking to ask. Obviously I wasn't laughing the next morning."

Camille edged forward in her chair as Pine held up the envelope.

"As per her instructions, I didn't open it until after the reading of her will was complete. I found two items inside – a handwritten letter addressed to me and a smaller envelope. The letter was short, and didn't say anything about the contents of the envelope."

With that, Pine handed Camille the large mailer. She reached inside and pulled out the small, unmarked envelope. The lightweight paper suddenly felt like an eighty-pound weight in her hand and she let it drop to the desk.

"Did the note say anything else?"

"Only that it was to be given to you immediately."

Camille's chest felt heavy. "How did she seem to you that day?"

Pine briefly searched his memory before answering. "Fine. Happy. Couldn't stop talking about how excited she was to see you."

"Did she seem off in any other way, like she was worried about anything?"

"If she was, she didn't show it. When she gave me the envelope she was pretty nonchalant, like she was making a conscious effort to downplay the importance of her request. Of course I knew better. Julia never did anything nonchalantly." Pine paused to reflect further. "I know what you're getting at with the question, and the timing of her visit is something I've been wracking my brain over. She wasn't nervous, she wasn't flustered. She was nothing more than her usual boisterous, charming-as-hell self. I personally think the fact that she died less than a day later was one of those instances of the universe swift-kicking us in the ass with a not-so-gentle reminder that nothing in this life, not even the air we breathe, belongs to us."

Diverting her damp eyes away from Pine, Camille looked at the envelope. But she was suddenly afraid to touch it. Whatever was inside would serve as the last contact Julia would ever make with her. After this, there would be nothing else. The finality of it made Camille want to run away, to tell Laurence Pine to keep it for another five, ten, twenty years, or perhaps to never give it to her at all. At least then there would be a chapter of their relationship that would always remain open; one last meeting left strictly to the imagination, free to be constantly molded by any mood – happy, sad, or otherwise – that Camille saw fit.

But she couldn't run away. Not from this.

She picked it up and looked at Pine; his anxious face mirroring hers. She closed her eyes, took a quiet breath, and tore the envelope open. A large silver key fell out and landed in her lap. She left it there while she pulled out the note. Julia's handwriting was immediately evident, so perfect that it could have been generated by a printing press. When she looked at the note closer, the first two words immediately caught her eye, and seeing them made every cell in her body scream out in agonizing pain.

'*Dear Cam*'

CHAPTER 22

A FINAL PLEA

With eyes that had already begun to swell, Camille thanked Pine and quickly left his office. She felt bad about the abrupt exit, but knew that if she had stayed any longer, Pine would have been stuck in the uncomfortable position of trying to console someone who was beyond consoling. Aside from not wanting to disrupt his day in such a fashion, there was no way she could allow herself to be that vulnerable with someone she had just met, no matter how positive her first impression of him was.

So she waited until she got to her car before reading the rest of the note. But when she got there she was once again hesitant. In an effort to stall, she took the key out of her pocket and studied it closely. It was unlike any she had ever seen, with a large ring and two small grooves on either end of a long, thin cylinder. The thought of what such a key might open unnerved her, and she suddenly questioned her desire to know. But she quickly pushed the thought aside. After taking a series of deep, measured breaths, she slowly unfolded the paper and continued reading.

Dear Cam,
I wrote this note fully intending that you
would never have to read it. Sounds kinda

dumb, right? It does to me too. Writing a
note to someone that you never want that
person to see. But in this case, it's true.
I never wanted you to read it. Because
if you are, it means only one thing. And
right now that's a scenario I can't bear
to imagine. But it is one that I'm
obviously very fearful of.

I guess 'sorry' isn't the appropriate word to
use, even though it's the first one that comes
to mind. I'm sorry I put you in this position.
I'm sorry I wasn't as forthright with you
as I should have been. I'm sorry I'm
not there to fight a battle that is entirely
mine to fight. I'm sorry I'm not there to say
thank you for being the only reason I've
been able to make it this far.

Camille began to sob so loudly that she worried people walking down the street would hear and come rushing up to her car. She buried her head in her hands in an effort to muffle the noise. It didn't work. Five long minutes passed before she could calm down long enough to continue reading.

A series of events have occurred over the past
six years that have led to this point; events that
I wasn't able to explain to you in detail — either
because I didn't have time to, or more likely
because I was afraid to. I can't go into great
detail here, otherwise this letter would turn into
a novel, and we both know I'm not the world's
greatest writer!

But the key I left is for a safe deposit box that I
opened in your name. Inside that box is a flash
disk. You'll find everything you need there. I'm
sorry to say you won't be happy when you learn
what's on it, especially when you discover my
personal role in everything. But it was important
to tell you the entire truth; not only of the
situation that led to this, but also of
my unfortunate part in it. All I can say
is I hope you will eventually forgive
me. I understand there are bigger
things at stake than your forgiveness.
But I hope that when the smoke clears,
and with your involvement I'm confident
it will, forgiveness is a place you can
eventually get to.

The last thing I'll say is that the people
who did this to me are very recognizable.
And they're also very, very dangerous.
The things they are involved in go deeper
than even I understand. But their agenda
is clear. And it needs to be stopped. I said
earlier that I'm sorry I put you in this
position, and I am. This is something I
should have done myself. But I was too
afraid. And with good reason. But you're
better than me. Stronger than me. Braver
than me. You always have been.
That's why I'm trusting you to do what
I couldn't. But please be careful doing it.
When you're finished with them, make it
a point to nail their asses right to the wall!
Tough talk from a wimp, right?

The safe deposit box is located at the
First Western Bank on 17th and Broadway.
Get there as soon as you possibly can.
Once you see what's inside, you'll
understand my sense of urgency.

I love you so much Cam! And again,
I'm sorry.
~Jules

The letter was so overwhelming that Camille didn't even attempt to process the words or what they meant. There would be plenty of time for that. Instead she chose to focus on the clear- cut instructions Julia had given her. *Get there as soon as you possibly can. Once you see what's inside, you'll understand my sense of urgency.*

But it wasn't urgency that made Camille peel out of her parking spot, speed through two red lights, and sprint mindlessly past everyone between her and the First Western Bank lobby.

It was anger.

CHAPTER 23

BOX 682F

Screw you, Julia. Why didn't you tell me? I could have helped you. I would have done anything to help you. Sixteen years and all I have left of you is this goddamn note and a safe deposit box key? After everything that's happened? Why didn't you just tell me? You selfish bitch.

Camille's gasp echoed through the crowded bank. For the first time in her life, she genuinely hated herself. She knew those thoughts came from a place of anger and sadness and loss. But she never should have given voice to them. *I'm so sorry. I swear I didn't mean any of it.*

She was on the verge of breaking down and knew that she needed to get whatever was inside that box and leave as soon as possible.

After a couple of minutes, a heavy set man in a seersucker suit approached her. "Ms. Grisham? My name is Raphael. I was told you're here to open your safe deposit box."

"Yes."

Raphael consulted the piece of paper in his hand. "I see you are a co-signer on the box along with Julia Leeds."

Camille nodded.

"Very good. If I can just see your ID, we can get you back there."

Camille showed him her driver's license, shaking with anticipation as she did.

"Thank you," he said as he glanced at it and handed it back. "Right this way please."

He led Camille past a row of tellers and executive offices into a long, narrow corridor that ended at a set of double doors.

"And you have the key?" Raphael asked over his shoulder as he continued walking.

Camille pulled the key out of her pocket and held it up. "Yes."

Once they reached the doors, Raphael punched in a code on a keypad above the door handle. A green light flashed and he pulled the handle.

"Right this way."

They entered a large room that housed rows of safe deposit boxes as far as her eye could see. People stored all manner of valuables here: family heirlooms, expensive jewelry, and in Julia's case, terrible secrets.

"Ms. Leeds was here just last week putting items in the box." He paused as if waiting for a response. When Camille said nothing, he continued. "She'd been a customer of the bank for a long time, and a lot of us knew her quite well. Needless to say we were all devastated when we heard the news."

Camille could only nod.

"Julia actually mentioned you a couple of times during that visit," Raphael continued. "She said that after she finished she would be picking you up from the airport. Called you her bestie." He said 'bestie' with the knowing smile of someone who had a lot of experience using the term. "She also said that you would likely be picking up the items in the box because most of them belonged to you."

This was of course news to Camille, but she played along. "I just didn't think I would be picking them up this soon."

The man's face took on a solemn expression. He was silent as they stopped in front of a box labeled 682 F. He fished in his coat pocket until he pulled out a key that looked exactly like the one Camille had.

"May I have your key please?"

Camille handed it to him and watched as he inserted it into a narrow slot. He then took his key and inserted it in the slot below. He turned both, opened the door and pulled out a short metal box. He set it on a table in front of them.

"Here you are, Ms. Grisham. If you have any questions or concerns I'll be right over there." He pointed to a chair and desk near the door they came through. His smile had returned.

"Thanks for your help, Raphael," Camille answered, countering his smile with one of her own. *Good soul,* she thought about him, not really knowing why. The only thing she did know was that good souls were in very short supply these days.

He walked to his desk and sat down, leaving Camille alone with the box.

She stared at it for a long time. Since reading the letter she could think of nothing else except opening it. But suddenly she was afraid to. Her mind was flooded with so many possibilities that she hadn't even tried to conceive of what could be inside. Now that she actually stood in front of it, her mind drifted to very dark places. Whatever was in here stood as a final testament to Julia's life; something so valuable that it needed to live on even if she didn't. Opening this box would bring a finality to Julia's life that Camille had managed to keep at a distance up to this point.

But there was something else that made her afraid; a thought she hadn't been able to shake ever since she read the note.

Julia knew this was going to happen.

She knew it when she picked Camille up from the airport. She knew it when she insisted her problems could wait, even though Camille knew otherwise. She knew it when she called Camille for the last time.

Julia's reluctance to talk made even less sense than it did before. If she was concerned enough to go through all of this trouble with the safe deposit box and the envelope, why didn't she say anything? Of anyone she knew, Camille would have been in the best position to help her; not by retrieving some information from a safe deposit box after she was dead, but by going after whoever was trying to hurt her while she was alive. The Circle Killer and the psychological trauma he caused be damned. Camille would have faced down ten Daniel Sykes' if that's what it took to protect her best friend.

But she wouldn't get that chance now. Julia was dead. And Camille was left with the now all too familiar feeling of knowing that she could have done something to prevent it. Her sadness once again turned to anger.

Knowing she now had no choice but to stifle that anger, Camille held her breath as she reached for the latch.

Five... four... three... two... one ...

Then she closed her eyes, slowly exhaled, and lifted the lid.

CHAPTER 24

INSURANCE POLICY

The first thing Camille saw was a legal-sized piece of paper folded into quarters. She took it out of the box and unfolded it, immediately recognizing Julia's handwriting again. There were three short paragraphs of text followed by a long list of bulleted items. Unsure that she could trust her reaction, Camille resisted the urge to read more closely.

She set the paper on the table and turned back to the box. The only other item inside was a sealed envelope that looked a lot like the one Julia had left with Laurence Pine. She picked it up and felt something hard and rectangular-shaped inside.

Not feeling ready to open the envelope, she set it next to the paper, closed the box and called for Raphael.

"All finished?" he asked as he quickly approached.

"All finished."

He nodded, then opened the box. "Will you be leaving anything else behind?"

"I don't think so."

"Are you sure? Ms. Leeds pre-paid for six months, so if you need more time…"

"I'm positive. But thank you."

"No problem," Raphael said as he closed the box and slid it back into its wall slot. "If you're ready, please follow me."

Once Camille got back to her car she felt safe enough to open the envelope. Inside was the flash disk that Julia spoke of in the original note. She immediately put it inside her jacket pocket, then unfolded the paper.

Julia's handwriting covered nearly every inch of the page, including the margins, which was uncharacteristically sloppy for her. The script also didn't have the refined edge that Julia's writing normally had. It looked rushed, almost as if she couldn't write fast enough to keep pace with her thoughts.

The words '*Insurance Policy*' were written in large block letters at the top of the paper. Below that, Camille saw her name again, followed by a succinctly-written list of facts that didn't make much sense.

> *You can contact my personal lawyer Laurence Pine*
> *in regard to the Excel file 'Schumann-Springwell'*
> *He'll know what to do with it.*

> *I forgot to include the name of the investment manager*
> *for the Colorado PERA account. Nicolas Jacoby. He*
> *works for the Schumann Investment Group.*
> *'Some of these files are self-explanatory, while some you*
> *won't be able to make heads or tails out of. What you*
> *can't figure out, the Securities and Exchange Commission*
> *can. Don't hesitate to get them involved if you have to.'*

And then there was the paragraph that most got Camille's attention.

> *Even though it's the last thing I want you to*
> *see, please make sure you watch the movie file first.*
> *Very painful and embarrassing, but it's also very*

*important. You may recognize the man in the
video, but if you don't, all you have to do is turn
to the political section of any Colorado newspaper.
He did this to me Camille. I may not have direct
proof to substantiate that, but I'm telling you he did.*

Camille couldn't read any further. Her stomach turned and she thought she was going to be sick. She took a long pull from a half-empty water bottle that was sitting in the cup holder, not knowing or caring how long it had been sitting there. After opening the window and taking in a couple of deep breaths, she felt better.

Then she felt the weight of the flash disk in her pocket and her stomach suddenly felt queasy again.

There was probably more on that disk than she could even imagine, and Julia had entrusted her to keep it safe. But it didn't matter what kind of information was stored on it, the fact that Julia died over what amounted to a two inch piece of plastic was overwhelming in its absurdity. And no matter what she saw in the movie file, no matter who the man was in it, no matter the physical or emotional risk to herself, Camille simply could not let that pass.

'He did this to me, Camille.'

Powered by a sudden surge of adrenaline, Camille started the car and sped away. All she could think about now was getting to a computer. Though her father had a perfectly capable PC in his office, Camille would have to use her own. She may eventually call on him to help, but she knew that what she was about to see required absolute privacy. Julia had entrusted her with this disk above everyone else, even her own family. Camille had to honor that, even if it meant that her father could never see what was on it.

When she got home, she walked into the living room and saw him sitting in front of the television. He greeted her with a thin smile.

"Sorry, I haven't been able to turn it off."

Camille took off her coat and sat down next to him. "You don't have anything to apologize for." She glanced at the television and saw that it was tuned to CNN Headline News. "Have you heard anything else?"

"The bastards are already sensationalizing it with a tagline: 'Beautiful young lawyer gunned down in home invasion.'" He shook his head. "They're also saying that the department is looking at a person of interest in the case, but they aren't giving a name."

"Smells like BS to me," Camille said as the newscast abruptly transitioned to a report on the disappearance of honey bees.

Paul turned off the television. "When you were talking to the detectives, did they mention anything about having a suspect in mind?"

"They did. A mail clerk at Julia's firm."

"And what do you think about that?"

"Not much."

"As in you don't buy him as a suspect?"

"As in I'd bet my life that he had nothing to do with it."

Paul's eyes widened. "And did you tell them that?"

"I'm not in the FBI anymore, dad. Why would they care what I think?"

Paul's expression flattened. "What did you think about the detectives?"

"Graham's an asshole."

Paul chuckled. "You certainly read that one correctly."

"He talked about how he wished he had the chance to work with you on the detective beat because you were such a great cop. No one can dispute that you were a great cop, but it didn't sound the least bit sincere coming from him."

Paul leaned back on the couch and briefly reflected. "I could tell you stories about Walter Graham. He's not nearly as well-liked in the department as he thinks he is."

"If I had to wager a guess, I'd say there was some dirt somewhere in his past."

One side of Paul's mouth curled up in a tight smile. "Like I said, I could tell you some stories. But we'll save those for another time."

"His partner seems pretty solid."

"What's his name?"

"*Her* name is Chloe Sullivan."

Paul blushed. "I'm familiar with her. She was a beat cop when I was around. Good one too. Nice to know she made her way up."

"She reminds me of myself," Camille said, finally giving voice to something she had thought from the moment she met Sullivan.

Paul put a hand on his daughter's knee. "If she's anything like you, then the monster who did this doesn't stand a chance."

Camille tried to imagine the face of the man in the video she had yet to watch.

He did this to me, Camille.

"Let's hope you're right."

Paul stood up. "So did all that driving help you work up an appetite? I can get that grilled cheese ready for you in five minutes."

"I grabbed a Quarter Pounder on the way home," Camille said. Another simple but necessary lie. As much as her father's presence comforted her, she couldn't afford to spend another second down here.

"Can I make you a cup of tea or something?"

"More than anything I just need to lay down. I don't know if I'll even be able to sleep right now, but I need to try."

"Okay. If you need a little help, I have some Tylenol P.M. in the medicine cabinet."

Camille didn't have the heart to tell him that she had something twice as strong tucked away in her nightstand. "Thanks."

"Not a problem. If you're going to be sleep, I may just head out for a while. As hard as it's been to concentrate on anything else but you, there are actually a few errands I need to run. But only if you're sure you'll be okay here by yourself."

I actually prefer it was what she wanted to say to him. "I promise I'll be fine," was what she said instead.

"Then I'll get out of your hair for a while." He kissed her on the forehead, took the car keys that Camille set down on the coffee table, and left.

She waited until she heard him get in his car and drive away before she rushed upstairs to her bedroom. She couldn't get there fast enough.

CHAPTER 25

MY FINAL NIGHT WITH ELLIOTT

Camille hadn't used her laptop since unpacking it the night she arrived. There were no flights or hotel rooms to book, no Facebook status to update, and she had stopped checking her email account weeks ago, so she hadn't expected to get any real use out of it aside from an occasional game of Solitaire. Nothing in her darkest imagination could have prepared her for how wrong she would be.

Before inserting the disk, Camille unfolded the paper that was included in the safe deposit box and laid it out in front of her. When she glanced at it she saw the words 'mayor' and 'senate race', but like most every other word on the page, they meant nothing to her.

After another few moments of needless stalling, she finally picked up the disk.

Let go of the fear and just do it.

She closed her eyes as she slid it into the USB port.

Within seconds a window opened up displaying at least one hundred file folders. Each one was titled and dated: '*7th Congressional Re-Districting*', '*Precinct Judges NW Denver*', and so on. She clicked on a folder titled '*Den County Clerk & Recorder Stats*' and saw more Excel documents than she cared to count.

It didn't matter what kind of instructions Julia had written down, Camille knew that most of this stuff was too far above her pay-grade to ever figure out. She hadn't had much experience with the Bureau's White Collar Crimes Division and knew absolutely nothing about congressional districts and precinct judges. But Julia was fully aware of that. Yet she left her responsible for the information anyway. Despite her current inability to decode what she was seeing, Camille knew there was something here worth decoding. And judging by the sheer number of files on the disk, it was something big.

She continued scrolling through folders with titles that required a *Representative Government 101* glossary to understand. Then, halfway down the page, she came across a Windows Movie file that stopped her cold. Unlike the rest of the files, the title was simple and straightforward. No glossary needed.

'MY FINAL NIGHT WITH ELLIOTT'

She re-read the note. *"Even though it's the last thing I want you to see, make sure you watch the movie file first. Very painful and embarrassing, but it's also very important."*

Her hand trembled as she double-clicked the file.

The first thing she saw was a grainy shot from high above a bed. Seeing it had immediately confirmed Camille's worst fears. She was tempted to turn it off right then, but knew she had to keep watching, no matter what.

After a few seconds, a lean, middle-aged man wearing only a towel entered the frame. He was talking over his shoulder as he rubbed something on his chest and arms.

"I mean it, Jules. You keep doing that and you're going to have a hard time getting rid of me."

"Empty promises," Camille heard a female voice say off-camera. Despite its muted quality, she knew the voice all too well.

"Okay, let's switch places for a day and we'll see how you deal with the complicated hell that is my life," the man answered.

"Your life is only as complicated as you make it, Elliott."

"And you don't think you have anything to do with that?"

Julia finally came into the camera's view. She was completely naked and drying her hair with a towel. Camille instinctively looked away.

"I take no responsibility for the hell that is your life," she said lightly. "All I ever ask is to be more a part of that life. Hell or not."

When Camille looked at the screen again, Julia was sitting on the bed still drying her hair. The man stood over her.

"I don't think it would be nearly as hellish if you were in it more."

Julia stopped drying her hair and looked up at him. "Make it happen then."

"You don't think I'm trying?"

"All I know is that after you leave here you're going home to a woman who thinks you still love her. Beyond that, I don't know what you're doing."

He sighed. "I told you I'm working on it."

Camille had to avert her eyes again, feeling embarrassed by what she was seeing. The woman in the video was definitely Julia, but aside from the way she looked, Camille recognized nothing about her. She spoke in a desperate, pleading tone that Camille had never heard before. She was the worst possible cliché – the jaded other woman who clung to the delusional hope of a future that would never be. She hated to even think of the word 'pathetic' in regard to Julia, but that is exactly what she was. And it was sad beyond description.

"Actions, Elliott."

He smiled. "I prefer it when you call me Richmond," he said as he moved closer to her. "Somehow you manage to make that name sound incredibly sexy."

Even though the camera was some distance away, Camille could see the smile forming on Julia's face. "Is that right, Richmond?" She emphasized his name in such a way that left little doubt as to what was coming next.

A gentle pull on his towel caused it to fall to the floor. For a moment, Julia sat motionless, staring at his erect penis. When she took it in her hands, Camille got up and walked away. She felt like crying but didn't allow herself to. She knew the tears would be not of sadness but of angry judgment. And the last thing she could allow herself to do was stand in judgment. This video obviously existed for reasons far beyond what she was seeing right now, and no matter how Camille may have felt about it, she had to keep watching.

When she walked back to the computer, Julia and the man she called Elliott had switched positions and he was now the one sitting on the bed while Julia stood over him, one leg straddling his waist.

Camille looked at the time meter on the bottom of the screen and saw there were fifty-eight minutes remaining in the video. As Julia brought her other leg up and lowered herself onto Elliott's lap, Camille hit the fast forward button and looked away.

She periodically checked the screen while rapidly moving images flashed in front of her. The fact that she had seen Julia in such an intimate and personal circumstance was surreal. In sixteen years, Camille thought she knew everything there was to know about her. But she was beginning to think that she never really knew Julia at all. The woman she knew would have never put herself in a circumstance like this. The woman she knew would have never slept with a married man. And she would certainly never beg for his affection. If you know a person long enough, you eventually see all sides of them – even the sides they desperately try to hide. Julia went to great lengths to keep this side of herself hidden from Camille for as long as she could. But even she knew it couldn't stay hidden forever.

When the video finally reached a point when Julia and Elliott were no longer in bed, Camille pressed 'play'. The camera held the shot of an empty bed with the two of them nowhere to be found. After a couple of minutes, Camille hit fast forward again, advancing through another ten minutes of video time before a fully clothed Julia finally appeared in the bedroom. By the time Camille pressed 'play', Julia was already in mid-sentence.

"That's always the way it goes! You get your rocks off here then run home and put on your fucking family man suit!"

"Whatever!" Camille heard Elliott shout from off camera.

"Yeah whatever, Elliott! Whatever! I wonder if that's what she'd say if she ever found out. Do you think she would be so nonchalant about it?"

As taken aback as Camille was by what she saw earlier in the video, Julia's angry display was absolutely shocking. She had witnessed Julia raise her voice only a few times, and never to this level. Her eyes were wild and she looked as if she were ready to throw a punch. Camille feared she would do just that when Elliott finally entered the bedroom.

"I don't suggest you talk like that," he answered. Even though his tone was measured, there was an unmistakable menace behind it.

Julia didn't seem the least bit fazed. "Oh really? Give me one good reason why I shouldn't call her right now?"

"Because you would ruin a lot of lives, starting with your own."

"Is that supposed to be a threat?"

Elliott approached her until he was only a few inches from her face. Julia didn't give an inch of ground.

"The way I'm reading this conversation, you're the one making threats." He started to bring his hand up, but when Julia brushed by him and sat on the bed, he lowered it.

"I haven't started making threats yet, *Richmond*." The emphasis on his name wasn't nearly as sexy this time.

There was a brief moment of silence as Julia sat on the bed and Elliott stood in the corner looking at the wall. Both appeared emotionally spent. Then Elliott began looking around the room. "Let me guess, you're recording this."

Julia stood up. "Seriously? What kind of stupid question is that?" she asked in the high-pitched voice that Camille knew she only used when she was lying. "The video camera is downstairs hooked up to my TV if you want to go check." Julia didn't bat an eyelash, even though she practically spoke into the camera as she said it.

"Don't act like you're suddenly above doing it."

"If I recall, anytime there was ever a video, it was because you asked for it. Why on earth would I want to record myself having sex with an asshole?"

Elliott stopped looking around the room and turned his focus back to her. "I don't think you would have had a problem with it half an hour ago."

"Funny how quickly things change, isn't it?"

Elliott leaned against the dresser and cast his eyes downward, apparently satisfied with Julia's answer about the camera. She had obviously concealed it well, because he had looked directly into it at least three different times.

"So maybe you should tell me what I'm supposed to do?" he asked.

"Tell the truth for once in your life, Elliott. Just tell the truth."

"Christ, Julia! What am I not telling the truth about?" It was the first time he had raised his voice. Camille recoiled as much as Julia had appeared to. "You know I'm married! You know I have children! You know the public position I'm in! I've never hidden a single thing from you!"

"You've hidden a lot from your wife though. Haven't you?"

"Do not mention her again. You've said enough already. Do you understand? Keep her name out of your mouth." Camille felt tense as he approached Julia again.

"You mean her full name – Mayor Sonya Janice Richmond?" Julia said with a sneer. "I certainly wouldn't want to piss off a mayor, especially one who is less than two months away from becoming a United States Senator. I doubt you would either. What do you think would piss her off more? You fucking me or you fucking the voters of this state in order to get her to Washington?"

Camille felt like she was watching a movie and the woman on screen was an actress doing a terrible impersonation of her friend. Nothing about it seemed real.

But the next thing Camille saw reminded her of just how horribly real this was.

Elliott grabbed Julia by the arm and pulled her close. "So you want me to threaten you? Is that it?"

"Let go." Julia's back was to the camera now, but Camille could still sense the fear on her face.

"You're going down a road that you really don't want to go down, Julia. I suggest you back off." Elliott let go of her arm and she staggered backward.

Julia sniffled and dabbed at the corner of her eye. "You've been so concerned about not hurting your wife and children. Did you ever once stop to think about the consequences of hurting me? Or constantly lying to me? Or putting your goddamn hands on me?"

Elliott was silent.

"You obviously know what your wife can do," she continued. "But you should be just as worried about what I can do."

Elliott crossed his arms. "And what exactly can you do?"

Camille felt short of breath. This was no longer a video she was watching on a computer. This was Julia's life unraveling in front of her eyes. She found herself praying that Julia would not answer the question and simply walk away.

"You probably should have thought about that before you asked me to be in your videos. You *definitely* should have thought about it before you started talking to me about Springwell Technologies."

"Do you honestly think you can—"

Julia put her hands up. "Just don't take me for granted, Elliott. And I'm not talking about from a relationship standpoint, because you've clearly shown me that you don't give a damn about that. I'm talking about you thinking that I'm just going to allow you to hurt me time and time again without ever striking back at you. I have plenty of ways I can strike back at you."

Elliott shook his head. "All of this because I'm not going home to tell my wife of twenty-six years that I'm leaving her? You're sadder, and a hell of a lot more delusional, than I thought."

"Delusional?"

"Yes delusional. I don't think you have any idea what you're saying right now. Because if you really stopped to think about it, you would realize just how detrimental it could be and you would immediately stop talking."

"Sorry to disappoint you, but I have a *lot* more to say. You've made it abundantly clear that I have no future with you aside from a weekly blow job. As much as that kills me, I'm a big girl and I'll eventually get over it. But knowing now that you think so little of me, what incentive could I possibly have to keep protecting you?"

Julia's words hung in the air for a long time, almost as if Elliott didn't know how to respond. As he walked up to Julia and put a finger in her face, Camille knew that he had found that response.

"You know what your incentive is? Actually living long enough to get over it. Maybe it's just me, but I couldn't possibly think of a better reason to keep your mouth shut. Could you?"

Camille gasped at the exact same moment as Julia did.

"So you're threatening my life now?"

"You're threatening mine."

"Unless you're prepared to act on that threat right this instant, you're going to regret you ever said it. Trust me. Now do yourself a huge favor and get the hell out of my house. And pray you don't see yourself on the ten o'clock news tonight." She pointed at the bedroom door with a fully extended arm.

Elliott slowly backed away from her and made his way out of the room. "There will definitely be regrets at the end of this, but they won't be mine."

"Keep walking, dipshit!"

"Trust me!" Elliott shouted off-camera.

Julia stood frozen in the middle of the room while the sound of fading footsteps gave way to a door being slammed and the subsequent sound of barking dogs. After a few moments, she turned toward the camera, then stared directly into it. "I wonder if anybody else who happens to see this would take him as seriously as I do?" She shrugged her shoulders and turned away. "I guess we'll see." She started to walk out of the room then glanced back at the camera. "For the record, I wasn't serious. But he doesn't have to know that, does he?"

After that, the monitor went black.

Camille sat motionless in front of the computer, staring at the screen long after there was nothing left to see. There was so much to process in that hour-long video that she didn't even know where to begin. But she did know one thing right away: everything Julia had written on that paper suddenly made perfect sense, none of it more so than the line that Camille had not been able to get out of her head ever since she first read it.

'He *did this to me.*'

And now Camille knew exactly who *he* was. He was the husband of Sonya Richmond, the mayor of the city. Camille read about her when she picked up the Post at the airport. She had learned that Mayor Richmond was currently in the middle of a U.S. Senate campaign against the state's Attorney General, a man whose name she didn't pay attention to. In fact, the story as a whole meant nothing to her when she first read it.

But now it meant a whole lot, not only because the mayor's husband was sleeping with her best friend, but also because the mayor's husband quite possibly murdered her best friend. Though she had no direct proof of that yet, the video she just watched provided some pretty damning evidence.

It was now up to her to do with that evidence what Julia couldn't.

But how? There was no smoking gun. Short of that, anything she took to the police, including this video, would be viewed as strictly circumstantial. Even if there was enough evidence in Julia's files to connect Elliott Richmond to some kind of political or financial wrongdoing, there is nothing that ties him directly to her murder. Camille could give a damn about his political life. Richmond deserved to hang, not spend fifteen years in a country club with prison bars.

There was also the small matter of Richmond being the mayor's husband. Camille could very well find someone in the department willing to listen to her, but there would be two hundred others ready to laugh her and her video right out of the station.

From what she read in the article, Mayor Richmond was a popular incumbent; a two-term Democrat who also happened to be a former state judge and city council member. Her law and order background undoubtedly garnered respect with the police who called her boss. It also meant that Camille would need a lot more than this video and a few Excel spreadsheets to convince anyone in the DPD that the husband of this popular mayor was capable of murder.

Unsure of her next move, Camille decided to find out more about Elliott Richmond. A Google search yielded endless references to him as Denver's 'First Man'. As Camille dug deeper, she learned that he had been his wife's senior political strategist since she took office, and was currently managing her senate campaign. Prior to his wife's election as mayor, he was a Senior Vice-President for Guaranty Bank & Trust, as well as a board member of the Schumann Investment Group, a high profile financial investment firm. Various websites also touted his philanthropic efforts – one even pushing for his appointment as the next superintendent of the Denver public school district, based on his "unparalleled dedication to the educational advancement of the city's children."

Camille looked hard, but there was not a single word about Elliott Richmond the philandering murderer. That news story had yet to break.

If Camille had her way, it would very soon.

But she had to proceed with caution. There were still too many unknowns, including how Julia came upon the files in the first place. Neither the video nor Julia's copious notes provided any clues. The last thing Camille wanted to do was make this information public without understanding the full extent of what she was making public.

Then there was the video itself and the inherent issues that came with releasing it. The fact of the matter was that none of it made Julia look good, and Camille feared that the further it went, the more likely it would be that Julia the victim would morph into Julia the villain; portrayed as some bitter, conniving home-wrecker who made videotapes with the men she slept with in order to blackmail them. Camille could never let that perception take hold.

As much as she wanted to honor Julia's privacy, she knew she needed to bring someone else into this. Her father was the smartest cop she had ever known, and if anyone would know how to work through this, it would be him. But he was too close to the situation to be of any objective use. The same went for Julia's sister.

That left only one viable option.

Though she still had questions about Detective Sullivan, one thing Camille couldn't deny was her desire to solve this case. Unfortunately, she wasn't sure if she could say the same about Graham, and that made her nervous. In reality, she wasn't sure if she could trust either of them as far as she could throw them. But right now she didn't have much choice.

She kept her thoughts on Sullivan as she searched the house for her card. Despite a rocky first impression, Camille felt a connection with her almost immediately. It was the kind of connection that could only exist between cops who were cut from the same cloth, though she speculated that Sullivan was made of much tougher stuff than she ever was.

When the detective answered on the first ring, Camille could only pray that her speculation was true.

CHAPTER 26
OPPOSING FORCES

For the second time in a week, Camille found herself in the detective bureau's conference room. When she walked in behind Sullivan and Graham she noticed a small camera hanging from the ceiling just above the door. She hadn't noticed it before, then she realized that was probably by design. This conference room most likely doubled as an interrogation room. Camille had seen more than her share of those, but she never had the full experience of sitting in the other chair until today. She didn't like the feeling one bit.

This time around, Graham didn't offer any doughnuts, though Sullivan did offer a Diet Coke from the vending machine, which Camille accepted. She opened the can and took a couple of sips, waiting for one of them to say something.

"Thank you for contacting us," Sullivan began. "How have you been holding up through everything?"

Even though Sullivan's question seemed to come from a place of genuine concern, Camille could only answer with a shrug.

Sullivan communicated her understanding with a nod, then looked at Graham.

"So I understand you have some new information regarding Julia," he said flatly. There was no manila folder in front of him now, nor did he pull out his notepad. If Camille didn't know any better, she would think he was completely disinterested.

She pushed the thought out of her mind and unzipped the messenger bag she brought with her. From it she pulled out her own manila folder and set it down on the table.

"It's hard to even know where to start," she said as she opened the folder.

Sullivan eyed it closely. "Just start from the beginning."

Camille took a long breath, giving herself time to find the right words. "This morning I got a phone call from Julia's lawyer following the reading of her will. Apparently she had left some things for me and I needed to go to his office to claim them. When I got there I learned that she had also left something that was not an official part of the will, but was only to be opened by me in the event of her…" Camille couldn't even finish the sentence in her mind.

Sullivan leaned forward in her chair as Camille took the envelope out of the folder. "What was it?" she asked.

Camille explained Julia's instructions, the note, the safe deposit box key, and the fact that Julia had given them to her lawyer less than twenty-four hours before her murder.

Sullivan looked at Graham, who had noticeably perked up, then asked Camille: "What did the note say?"

Camille pulled it out of the folder. Even though Graham was sitting right next to her, she slid it across the table to Sullivan.

She eyed it closely. "You're positive this is her handwriting?"

"Absolutely."

When Sullivan finished reading, she let out an audible sigh and passed the note to Graham.

"What did she mean when she said 'I never wanted you to read it. Because if you are, it means only one thing'?" Sullivan asked.

Camille hesitated. The words were in her head but she was afraid to give voice to them. "Do you want me to be completely honest?" It was a silly thing to say and she knew it. She was merely stalling again.

"Obviously we do," Graham said as he looked up from the note.

"I think she knew something was going to happen to her."

"Like what?" Sullivan asked.

Camille pressed her palms against the edge of the table. "Like she was going to be killed."

The two detectives shifted in their chairs at the same time. Sullivan looked at Graham with concerned eyes, while Graham appeared to roll his.

Sullivan leaned forward even further. "Say that again?"

"I think she knew this was going to happen to her, or at least she was worried enough about it to leave this note as an insurance policy."

"Insurance against what?"

"Hold on a second. I'm confused," Graham cut in. "The first time we met you said that Julia was hesitant to talk to you. Yet she writes you this mysterious note? Which she just happens to leave with her lawyer less than a day before she's found dead? That seems very coincidental, and frankly very strange. It would seem to me that if she genuinely feared for her life, she wouldn't hesitate to tell you or the police. Instead she chooses to tell you after the fact through some cryptic note that she didn't even give to you directly. Call me crazy, but something about that just doesn't wash."

As much as Camille loathed Graham right now, she couldn't deny the logic of his argument. The unfortunate reality was that she had thought many of the same things.

"I can't pretend to know what Julia was thinking, Detective Graham," she said. "All I have is what she wrote down. And her words are pretty clear."

Graham sat back in his chair, a look of frustration overwhelming his face.

"What about the safe deposit box?" Sullivan asked in her usual calm tone.

"That's the main reason I'm here." Camille pulled the second note from the folder. This time she gave it to Graham.

He began reading. "What is this?" he asked with a glazed expression. "I can't make heads or tails of any of it."

"The set of instructions I was telling you about."

"Instructions for what?"

"For the computer disk."

"What computer disk?" Sullivan asked.

"The only two items in the safe deposit box were those instructions and a flash disk. The bullet items on that list are in reference to certain files on the disk."

Graham looked at the note more closely.

"What kind of files were on the disk?" Sullivan asked as she craned her neck to see what Graham was looking at.

"Hundreds of Excel spreadsheets with tables, graphs, voter demographic information, things like that. Lots of Word documents that looked like internal memoranda items. The letterheads were from the Schumann Investment Group and Springwell Technologies."

"Do either of those companies mean anything to you?" Sullivan asked.

"I've never heard of either one."

"So why did she leave the disk with you?" Graham asked.

"I asked myself the same question. It didn't make much sense, even with the instructions she left." Camille paused to gather herself. This was the part she was dreading from the moment she decided to make the call to Sullivan. "But there was another file on the disk. A movie file. Once I saw that, everything else began to make sense."

"The same movie file that Julia mentions in the note?" Sullivan asked. Then she started reading. "Even though it's the last thing I want you to see, make sure you watch the movie file first. Very painful and embarrassing, but it's also very important."

Camille swallowed hard. "Yes."

Graham jumped in. "But wait, what does the rest of this mean?" He also read from the note. "You may recognize the man in the video, but if you don't, all you have to do is turn to the political section of any Colorado newspaper. He did this to me, Camille."

Camille looked at Graham, then back at Sullivan. Both of their faces carried the same bewildered expression. She knew she couldn't skate around this any longer. "On the disk, there was a video file of Julia with a man. For the first half of the video, they were having... they were intimate. During the second half, they were arguing."

"About what?" Sullivan asked.

"At first it was about their relationship. Julia wasn't happy with how it was going and she let him know that. But then it escalated. They both started yelling and there were... threats."

"What kinds of threats?" Graham asked.

"The man is married, and Julia threatened to tell his wife about the affair they were having. He told her she would regret it if she did. There was a lot of back and forth between them. It got pretty scary."

"Okay, let's back up a minute," Sullivan said. "You're saying that Julia was involved in a relationship?"

"Apparently so."

"Do you know the man in the video?" Graham asked.

"I'd never seen him before."

"So she kept him a secret from you."

Graham had insinuated as much during their first go-around here. She didn't want to give him the satisfaction of knowing he was right, but she had to. "Yes she did."

"How did the video end?" Sullivan asked.

"It ended with him threatening to kill her if she didn't keep quiet about their relationship."

Sullivan pulled out her notepad. "Did he say that explicitly, that he would kill her?"

"He didn't say it explicitly, but anyone watching the video would know exactly what he meant."

"Why don't you let us see the video so we can judge for ourselves," Graham said with eyes that registered considerably more interest than before.

"I can't do that."

"What do you mean you can't do that?"

Camille looked Graham square in his eye. "Because I'm not positive that I can trust you with it."

Graham looked back at Camille with disgust. "You can't trust us? Are you kidding me? If you can't trust us then why did you come here?"

Camille looked at Sullivan. Her expression was much more measured. "I came here because I think the man in that video is the one who killed Julia."

Graham got up from his chair, and for a second Camille thought he was going to storm out of the room. Instead he buried his face in both hands and began rubbing his forehead. "Am I in the Twilight Zone or something?" he said to Sullivan.

"Ms. Grisham, why do you think he killed her?" Sullivan calmly asked.

"Look at the second note, the paragraph where she talks about the man in the video. What does the last line of that paragraph say?"

Sullivan read it, then took a moment before she repeated the line out loud. "It says 'He did this to me.'"

"That could mean anything," Graham barked. "Nowhere in this note does it say 'he threatened to kill me' or even 'I'm afraid of him'. If she had written that, then we could possibly draw a different conclusion. But if all you have is 'he did this', then I'd have to say that you don't really have anything. Not without the context of the video anyway; the video you don't trust us with."

"There's a very good reason why I don't trust you or anyone else with it."

"Do tell," Graham said sarcastically.

"Because of the man in the video."

"Who is he, Camille?" It was the first time that Sullivan had displayed frustration.

The cards were basically on the table now. Time to go all in. "Elliott Richmond."

Graham's face could not have dropped any faster.

"Elliott Richmond, as in Sonya Richmond's husband?" Sullivan asked with a look that went beyond dumbfounded.

Camille nodded.

"Oh my God."

Graham began pacing. "You have to be mistaken about that."

"I'm not," Camille said firmly.

"Yes you are," Graham said just as firmly.

This was exactly the reaction that Camille expected from Graham. But it didn't stop the anger from swelling in her chest.

"Camille, you realize what you're saying, right?" Sullivan said.

"I'm saying that the mayor's husband killed my best friend," Camille answered without a moment's hesitation.

Graham stopped pacing. "Well, if this isn't the biggest crock of shit I've ever heard."

Sullivan put her hands up. "Okay, let's all just keep calm. We have to talk through this rationally."

"Seems to me that rationality has gone right out the window," Graham said as he sat down. "You've just made one of the most outrageous claims that I've ever heard in all my years of law enforcement. It's an insult to Mr. Richmond, to the mayor, and to the citizens of this city who voted for her. And now you're going to insult Detective Sullivan and me by telling us that we're not trustworthy enough to see the video that you base these claims on?

Right now I don't care that you're Paul Grisham's kid or that you washed out of the FBI, I have half a mind to escort you the hell out of here right now."

"Detective Graham, that's enough." Sullivan angrily responded.

Camille sat stone-faced, her eyes burning into Graham's. "At least now I know my lack of trust is justified."

"Camille, what could we do to make you comfortable enough to–"

Graham interrupted his partner. "Enough of the games. If we think you're withholding evidence vital to our investigation I can get on the phone and have a search warrant within ten minutes. And if you still want to be cute I can have you arrested for obstruction of justice."

Camille tried to keep calm, but her resolve was cracking. "You're a bigger hack than I thought, Detective Graham. These little *Law & Order*-style scare tactics might work on the average nineteen-year-old car thief you bring in here, but I've forgotten more law than you can ever hope to know. You can't arrest me for anything. And the idea of you even trying to get a search warrant is flat-out ridiculous." She turned to Sullivan. "You asked me what you could do to make me comfortable enough to give you the video. The answer right now is nothing."

"So what are we supposed to do?" Sullivan asked incredulously. "Just act like you never came in here? Act like you never mentioned Elliott Richmond's name in connection to Julia's death? Once something like that is out of the bag it doesn't exactly go back in."

"Detective Graham would tell you that's exactly what you should do. According to him, it's an insult to Elliott Richmond and the city of Denver that I would even suggest him capable of something like this. So why go forward? We don't want Julia's murder to insult anyone."

Graham looked at Camille with venomous eyes. "Watch it."

"You should just go back to pursuing mail clerks and Chevy Impalas that play that scary ghetto music. I'm sure arresting Stephen Clemmons wouldn't be the least bit insulting to the citizens of this fine city." Camille began collecting the papers she had spread on the table.

"Those documents are potential evidence," Sullivan said.

Camille shook her head as she put the last piece in the folder. "No they're not. It's just paper, Detective Sullivan. The real evidence is probably being fabricated as we speak."

Graham's hand curled up into a tight fist and he looked like he wanted to pound it against the table. "What the hell is that supposed to mean?"

Camille put the folder in her messenger bag and stood up. "It doesn't mean anything, Detective Graham. Just like my coming here didn't mean anything."

"You're wrong about that," Sullivan declared. "Just like you're wrong when you say you can't trust us with the video. All we're interested in is finding Julia's killer. And I personally don't care if it's Elliott Richmond or the mayor or the goddamn Duchess of York."

"It's good that that's your personal opinion, Detective Sullivan. And I really do believe you feel that way. I'm just worried that yours is the minority opinion." She turned to Graham. He looked like he wanted to hit her.

"Let us see the video so we can do our job," he said in between clenched teeth.

Camille took a deep breath and turned to Sullivan. "I want your personal word that you meant what you said."

"You mean about going after Elliott Richmond? You have my personal word that if there's hard evidence to suggest he did this, I'll go after him with everything I have."

Camille knew she was just naïve enough to mean it.

She turned to Graham. "What about you? Are you more concerned about insulting the mayor? Or finding Julia's actual killer?"

Graham stared at her for what felt like a long time. She could see the wheels churning in his mind, struggling to come up with an answer that sounded better than the truth he actually felt.

"There's only one thing that's being insulted right now. This right here," he said as he unclipped the badge from his waist and held it out in front of him. "You're insulting mine, you're insulting Detective Sullivan's. Most importantly, you're insulting everything it stands for. I can't speak for my partner, but I personally don't appreciate being insulted. So you keep your goddamn disk and everything on it. Unless you have a video of a crime taking place, which it doesn't sound like you do, then it's of no use anyway. So don't trust us with it. That's fine. But don't you dare question my integrity." Graham punctuated his speech with a scowl that was intended to be menacing but instead came across as overly rehearsed. "And as far as finding Julia's actual killer, we already have."

Camille looked at Sullivan with wide eyes. "What does that mean?"

Sullivan looked almost embarrassed as she reported the news. "An arrest warrant has been issued for Stephen Clemmons. Officers are en route to his house as we speak."

Camille couldn't believe what she had just heard. "An arrest warrant? Based on what?"

Graham was quick to answer. "Based on eyewitness testimony that puts his car in front of Julia's house the night she was killed, as well as her car being found near his home, and the fact that they knew each other, despite his initial denial of that fact. It's called hard evidence, something that holds up in court a lot better than some fucking sex tape."

Camille held Graham's hard stare, even though every cell in her body was breaking down simultaneously.

"Can we at least talk about this, Camille?" Sullivan asked.

"Apparently there's nothing left to talk about," Camille answered as she slung her messenger bag over her shoulder. "I appreciate your help, detectives."

With that, she walked out of the conference room and out of the Criminal Investigation Unit, confident that she wouldn't be back for a third round of questioning. She was right to assume that she couldn't trust Graham. It was clear that he wasn't the least bit interested in pursuing any lead other than the complete dead-end that was Stephen Clemmons. And no matter how good Detective Sullivan's intentions were, as long as she continued to answer to him, she couldn't be trusted either.

As it stood, she wasn't sure if anyone could be trusted. Not even herself.

But it was looking more and more like she only had herself to rely on. And if Camille were being honest, she would admit that that was a hell of a lot riskier than blindly giving that disk to Graham, the mayor, or even Elliott Richmond himself.

CHAPTER 27

LOOKING BACK/ PUSHING FORWARD

Camille had actually met the Circle Killer three months before he murdered her partner and effectively changed her life forever. Daniel Sykes was part of a search and rescue operation involving an Alexandria, Virginia woman named Sherrie Creswell who had gone missing two weeks earlier.

In the beginning, there was nothing to distinguish Sykes from the other eighty or so volunteers who showed up for the three-day effort. In fact, there was nothing distinguishable about him at all. He was of average height and weight, with average brown hair, average brown eyes and an average handshake. Camille's first impression of him was neither good nor bad. He was simply there. In hindsight, she realized that he was everything her extensive profile suggested he would be. But that was the problem with pegging the Circle Killer as an average-looking thirty to forty-year-old white male. The pool was quite large.

Camille didn't think much of it when Sykes began asking questions. As far as she could tell, he was nothing more than a nervous local who had a wife and children of his own to protect. She had always found that volunteers who were also family men were the most enthusiastic about helping. They helped not only because they were concerned about the missing, they also helped out of a sense of obligation to their own families and their safety. Their search for the missing was also a search for the abductor. So when Sykes cornered Camille on the second day out and began asking a series of pointed questions about the victim and any leads the FBI may have concerning her possible abductor, Camille answered him the same way she would answer any other invested member of the community.

What she didn't learn until much later was that Sykes was not a member of the community at all. During an appearance on *Nightline* shortly after Sykes' arrest and subsequent confession, his estranged wife claimed that he had never spent any significant time there. But he was there long enough to rape and murder Sherrie Creswell and dump her mutilated body into a ravine one hundred and fifty miles away from the search area he so dutifully helped Camille comb through.

She had completely forgotten about the encounter in Alexandria until Sykes reminded her of it during their third and final interrogation session.

"Of all the risks I ever took, approaching you was definitely the riskiest," he had said to her from across a bolted down steel table that he was handcuffed and shackled to. "Truth be told, I thought you were going to arrest me the moment you saw me. I suppose if one took the time to psychoanalyze me, they'd probably get me to admit that I actually wanted to get caught at that point. Funny how that works, huh? Wanting to get caught. Anyway, when I saw you, you had this look in your eye, and I said to myself, 'Yep Dan, she's the one to do it. Talk to her, she'll peg you in two seconds flat.' But it didn't quite work out that way. I guess I watch too many movies. You guys aren't nearly as smart as you're portrayed in the movies."

At that point, the encounter in Alexandria instantly came back to her; every sickening detail of it.

The fact that she had spent two and a half days rubbing shoulders with the very killer she had spent the previous three years trying to capture was difficult enough to swallow. The fact that he managed to kill six more people after their meeting was entirely too much to handle, and it made her understand for the first time in her life what genuine self-loathing felt like. Prior to that, the word 'suicide' had never even entered her vocabulary.

Two weeks after her last interrogation of Sykes, an interrogation that abruptly ended after he personally thanked her for giving him the time to meet those two lovely co-eds who would turn out to be his last, and most satisfying victims, the word suicide became much more than a part of her vocabulary.

It became the only feasible solution.

One morning after her customary six A.M. cup of coffee, she filled her bathtub to shoulder level, opened up the straight-edged razor she had bought the night before, and pressed hard against her left wrist. When she saw the first trickle of blood, she promptly stopped. She may have been a coward, but she wasn't a selfish coward. The thought of leaving the people she loved the most in the world, namely her father and Julia, made her sad in a way she didn't think was possible, as did the thought of spending the rest of eternity apologizing to her mother.

So Camille drained the bathtub, wrapped the razor in three inches of duct tape and put it in the trash, then she called her father and Julia to tell them she would be leaving the Bureau and coming home.

But she was hanging on by the thinnest of threads; clinging to the fallacy that a change in scenery would bring about a change in fortune. Daniel Sykes and all the terrible memories he created existed in a world that Camille knew she could no longer be a part of. And she naively thought that if she ran far enough, she would eventually be able to escape that world.

What she realized during her taxi ride home from police headquarters was that she hadn't run far enough. Her memories of the world she tried to flee were dangerously fresh, the self-loathing born from her failure in Alexandria was still there, and with Julia's death, her desire to reclaim even a basic sense of trust in herself had all but been obliterated.

For the second time in as many months, someone extraordinarily close to her had been murdered. And for the second time, Camille blamed herself.

She let Agent Sheridan go into Sykes' house without backup because the discovery of a freshly severed head in his backyard had nearly made her faint. She heard the first gunshot in the house, but could not get her wobbly legs to move fast enough to prevent the next eight. Six of those gunshots killed the two teenagers Sykes had held captive in his basement. Three of them killed Agent Sheridan.

Now the despair of losing her partner was replaced with the despair of losing her best friend; and all she wanted to do was unwrap that razor and use it the way she originally intended to.

But self-loathing was a craving she no longer had the time to indulge. Julia didn't expect her to feel sorry for herself. Julia expected her to fight.

So Camille was left with a choice: continue to run until she found the safe hiding place that had thus far eluded her, or trust herself enough to finally stand up and fight. She already knew what choice she would have to make, even before she saw Detectives Graham and Sullivan. She tried to tell herself that asking them for help was the right thing to do, but she realized now that the act was merely a way of buying time until she could summon the courage to do what Julia ultimately expected her to do.

As the taxi dropped her off in front of her father's house, she began to understand that it wasn't about summoning courage. It was about pushing forward whether the courage was there or not. Elliott Richmond was responsible for Julia's murder. And so far, Camille was the only person alive willing to believe that. It also made her the only person capable of actually doing something about it.

And she was capable, despite the memories that continued to haunt her, despite the demons that refused to stop whispering *failure* in her ear.

Now was the time that she would finally stand up and fight. She still wasn't sure if she trusted herself not to fall again. But it didn't matter. Avenging Julia's death would be all the motivation she would ever need to pick herself back up.

The pity parade is over, she thought as she saw her father standing in the driveway.

Suddenly, Daniel Sykes' face began to fade and the demons whispering in her ear were barely audible. Camille wasn't sure how long she could keep them at bay, but right now she didn't care.

It just felt good to finally stop running.

CHAPTER 28

COMPLICATIONS

Walter Graham sat at his desk in silence. He hadn't spoken a word to Sullivan since their meeting with Camille ended. It wasn't that he didn't have anything to say, he simply didn't want to say the wrong thing. Camille had thrown him a curve ball the likes of which he could never have imagined, and in his mind he had already whiffed at it several times. He was confident that Sullivan hadn't seen his frayed nerves in the conference room. But he wasn't sure how much longer he could keep them hidden.

When Sullivan emerged from the bathroom and proceeded to make a bee-line for his desk, he knew he would have to keep up appearances a little while longer.

"It's been half an hour, Walter. Are you planning on talking about what just happened? Or are we going to pretend that Camille Grisham was never here?"

"I'm not pretending that she wasn't here. I just don't think anything she said is particularly worth talking about."

A look of disbelief flooded Sullivan's face. "Nothing worth talking about? You've got to be kidding."

"She's an emotional wreck, Chloe. Her best friend was just murdered and she's grasping at anything she can to find out who killed her. Look, she even said so herself, she has no direct evidence that Elliott Richmond had anything to do with Julia Leeds aside from an affair. Granted that's not a good thing to do when you're married, but the last time I checked, infidelity is not a capital offense. Nor does it lead to murder. There's no evidence that ties him to Julia's house. In fact, if you watched the news, you would have seen that Richmond and the mayor were attending a fundraiser in Aspen that day and decided to stay the night. I'd say that puts him pretty damn far from the crime scene." Graham had actually rehearsed this speech in his mind for the better part of twenty minutes. He was quite pleased with the way he executed it.

Sullivan didn't seem as impressed. "Why would you go on that rant in the end anyway? She was this close to giving us the disk, then you start in with that nonsense about the badge. It's no wonder she walked out."

"Nice to know you thought it was nonsense." Graham's face turned red as he ran his hand across his goatee. "Anyway, she wasn't giving us anything. Camille Grisham's whole spiel was complete bullshit. I don't understand how you can't see that."

"Walter, we have a responsibility to the victim and her family to conduct as thorough an investigation as possible; and that includes listening to Camille Grisham's bullshit."

"Are you lecturing me now?"

"Of course not. All I'm saying is that you should have given her at least some benefit of the doubt. As impossible as it is to believe, there could possibly be something to it, something that could lead us in another direction. We need a break, Walt, because you and I both know, Impala or no Impala, what we have on Stephen Clemmons right now is less than adequate. Yes we've arrested him, and the public will probably think they can sleep better tonight. But a grand jury would laugh if we presented our current case to them. At this point we don't have a choice but to continue to investigate whatever comes up, no matter how crazy it seems. Otherwise, we'll never solve this thing."

All Graham wanted her to do now was leave. And he was willing to say whatever he had to in order for that to happen. "I don't know, Chloe. It really sounds like you're lecturing me, and frankly I don't appreciate it."

"Maybe you need a lecture at this point."

"Maybe I do. But not from you."

Sullivan shook her head and walked back to her desk. Graham thought he heard her say 'asshole' under her breath as she sat down. *If she's lucky, one day she'll find the courage to tell me that to my face,* he thought to himself as he turned back to his computer.

But his mind was far from work. Graham had been preoccupied with his cell phone and an important call that had yet to come. He made a phone call of his own five minutes after Camille Grisham left their office, and the voicemail he left was urgent; so urgent that he expected an immediate callback. But it hadn't come. And the longer he was made to wait, the more the armor that protected his increasingly fragile psyche began to crack.

Just as he was about to check his phone to make sure it was still working, it began to vibrate. His mind scrambled in fifty different directions as he picked it up and rushed away from his desk and into the stairwell. He didn't care how it looked. He didn't care about the panic that had surely risen in his face. He only cared about the reaction he would get to the unfortunate news he was about to deliver. If he knew the man on the other end of the phone as well as he thought he did, the term 'nuclear explosion' would only begin to describe it.

Graham tried to catch his breath as he pressed 'talk', but he couldn't. He proceeded anyway.

"There might be complications, sir. Significant ones."

CHAPTER 29

PLAN A

"Boy, I never know whether you're coming or going," Paul said as Camille climbed out of the taxi. "Here I am thinking you're in bed and instead you pull up behind me in the driveway. Have you always been this impossible to keep up with?"

Camille shrugged as she walked toward him. "You should know the answer to that is a resounding yes, considering you raised me to be that way."

Paul smiled. He always looked so prideful when he smiled at her, like the words 'nice work dad' were always in the forefront of his mind. "Where have you been?"

Camille stopped a few feet in front of him, fearful of how fast the smile would go away once she told him. "I went to see Graham and Sullivan."

His smile went away faster than she thought it would. "Honey, why didn't you call me? I could have taken you. Was there some movement in the investigation?"

Camille looked down at her New Balance sneakers, knowing that she was going to be getting a lot of use out of them soon. "They're arresting Stephen Clemmons."

Paul's look of concern was quickly replaced with one of confusion. "So why were you there?"

"I called them."

"Why?"

Camille looked down at her shoes again, silently ordering them to keep her firmly planted where she was. "Because I discovered some information about Julia that I thought they might find useful."

"And?"

"I realized it wasn't useful to them at all."

Paul put a hand up. "Okay, now I'm thoroughly confused. Did this information have to do with Clemmons?"

"No."

"What then?"

With fingers that suddenly felt numb, Camille reached into her coat pocket and pulled out the disk.

Paul squinted as he looked at it. "What's this?"

Camille walked a few steps closer. "Something that you may not be at all prepared to handle."

"I don't like the way that sounds."

"You shouldn't."

"Scale from one to ten, ten being unbearable."

Camille didn't blink. "Twenty-five."

Paul's square jaw suddenly went slack.

She wrapped her arm tightly around his. "Let's go into your office. I have something to show you."

Once inside, Camille took a seat in front of the computer while her father stood anxiously over her shoulder. She slid the disk into the USB port and quickly found the video file. Before she opened it, she looked up.

"Okay dad, this is going to sound really weird, but I need you to turn away from the monitor for a few minutes."

"You're kidding, right?"

"No I'm not." Her look was dead serious, and Paul responded accordingly.

She fast-forwarded through the first forty-five minutes of the video until she reached the point where Julia appeared in the bedroom fully dressed, then she paused it.

"You can turn around now."

He did so with a nervous smile firmly planted on his face. When he saw what was on the monitor, the smile went away. "What's this?"

"A video of Julia."

"I can see that. But what else am I looking at here?"

"I can't tell you the whole story right now. I just need you to watch."

Paul nodded and took a seat next to Camille as she pressed 'play'. He sat motionlessly as the scene between Julia and Elliott Richmond played out in front of him. He bucked slightly when Richmond approached Julia with his finger pointed in her face. But other than that, he didn't make a sound.

When the video finally ended, Paul turned to Camille with damp eyes. "Where did this come from?"

"Julia," Camille answered as evenly as she could.

Paul shook his head. His stare was distant and confused.

"Maybe I should explain now."

"That would be a good idea."

Camille proceeded to tell him everything, from her visit with the lawyer, to the safe deposit box, to the hundreds of documents on the disk, to her theory about Richmond.

As she had expected, he was rendered speechless.

"I know it's a lot to take in."

Paul blew out a loud breath. "When you said twenty-five out of a one to ten scale, you weren't kidding."

"I'm sorry, but I had to show you."

"I'm glad you did. I take it the part you didn't show me involved the two of them..."

"Yes."

Paul nodded. "And you showed this to Graham and Sullivan?"

"I only told them about it."

"What was their reaction when they found out Elliott Richmond was involved?"

"Lots of barking, most of it done by Graham."

"Meaning he didn't believe you?"

"I'm sure he believed me. He just didn't care."

Paul looked genuinely shocked. "I know the guy is a major-league prick, but how could he not care?"

"Because Richmond's wife is his boss. And apparently no one in this city named Richmond is capable of doing anything the least bit questionable."

"We all know that's not true."

"Graham doesn't."

Paul stood up and began pacing. "Can I see that letter again?" He stopped only long enough for Camille to hand it to him. Once he began reading, the pacing picked up. "You showed this to them and they had no reaction to it?"

Camille shook her head. "For all Graham knew I wrote it myself."

Paul sat down. "I have to admit that even I'm having a hard time processing this. You realize that Elliott Richmond is the most politically-connected man in the entire state, right?"

"He's also one of the most popular. Powerful campaign strategist, generous philanthropist, seven-handicap. I know all of that. And I'm not the least bit moved."

"And you really think he was involved in Julia's murder?"

"I don't think he was involved in her murder. He was directly responsible for it. It's right there in black and white, dad."

Paul read Julia's words out loud. "He did this to me."

"Even if I didn't actually witness him threatening her, which I did, those words would be enough."

Paul put the note on the desk and took a deep breath. "Your conviction is certainly enough for me."

Camille felt a wave of relief wash over her. "I'm happy to hear you say that."

"I've always trusted your instincts, Camille. They're a cop's instincts. And despite what you may think, you still have them."

Camille shrugged, not sure if she was ready to accept that. But something inside was speaking to her, and the more she listened, the more she connected to the old Camille Grisham. She couldn't deny how emboldened it made her feel. "All I know is that I personally plan to string him up for what he did. I don't care how well-connected he is."

A hint of concern returned to Paul's face. "I can appreciate the sentiment, believe me. But are you sure that's something you even want to think about right now? Things are happening at a lightning pace here. And frankly I'm worried that it's already been too much for you to deal with. If you try to take on this thing with Richmond by yourself, it could be enough to completely break you down. And I won't let that happen."

"It's already happened, dad."

"I won't let it get any worse."

"As much as you may want to, you can't protect me from this. I don't need protecting. It was Julia who needed it. And I didn't do it. I have to make up for that."

"You don't get to blame yourself, Camille."

"The only thing I'm blaming myself for now is wasting time going to Graham and Sullivan when I should have gone after Richmond right away."

"Okay, let's slow down here. How exactly would you have gone after Richmond?"

"I don't know. I suppose I could have started with his wife. She's pretty accessible these days."

Paul's chuckle was betrayed by the look of abject horror on his face. "Goddamn it, I think you're actually serious."

"Of course I'm serious. Considering everything I just showed you, why wouldn't I be?"

"Because there is a smarter way to go about it."

Camille wasn't interested in being smart, but she respected him enough to remain quiet while he continued.

"You still have a few contacts in the Denver field office, right? You could show the video to them. I realize that Julia's murder is technically out of the Bureau's jurisdiction, but they could certainly put some pressure on the department to broaden their scope, especially if they have documented proof that Elliott Richmond is involved in large-scale fraud."

Camille sighed. "My contacts in the field office are loose at best. Besides, in cases like this, Bureau may as well stand for Bureaucracy. The higher up the food chain this goes, the more bogged down in the process it becomes. Graham and Sullivan's investigation is moving along at an insanely fast rate. They've had Clemmons targeted from day one and apparently they now have enough to arrest him. Graham especially seems hell-bent on making Clemmons the guy, to the point where he would probably manufacture evidence against him if he had to. If he's officially charged, that means the feds case against Richmond would be more about corporate malfeasance than Julia's murder. From there the process could drag on for months, maybe longer. In the meantime, Richmond gets more time to mount a defense, and considering his financial means, I'm sure it would be a very effective one. By the time the trial of yet another corrupt politician finally begins, Julia's murder will be forgotten about altogether."

Paul shook his head. "So I'm assuming that was a very detailed way of telling me that going to the FBI is out of the question."

"For now, yes."

Paul threw up his hands as if to surrender. "Okay Camille, I'll bite. What's your plan?"

"In her note, Julia instructed me to forward a number of the Excel documents to her personal lawyer. She said he would know what to do with them. When we're done here I'm going to call him to set up a meeting."

Paul nodded. "That sounds reasonable enough. What then?"

Camille smiled, though given the heavy weight of the moment she wasn't sure how appropriate it was. "Well, since a phone call to the mayor is officially off the table, I suppose I'll have to think about it."

Paul leaned across the desk and grabbed Camille's hand. "Look, I know what you're feeling right now. Three years into the job, a good friend was killed off-duty because he walked into a 7-Eleven at the wrong time of night. Tore up the entire department. When we talked behind closed doors, it wasn't about arresting the asshole who did it; it was about digging a hole in the ground and throwing him in it. So I know how intoxicating revenge can be. But with time we collectively got a hold of ourselves and right now Officer Albright's killer is alive and rotting in a Cañon City prison cell. Sometimes the process needs a kick in the ass. And in this particular case, it does. If you have to be the one to do that, then so be it. But it has to be done within the framework of the system, Camille. Sometimes the process may be slower than we'd like, but we still have to allow that process to work itself out. We took an oath to do it that way."

"With all due respect to everything you just said, we both know that if the process is allowed to work itself out the way it usually does, Elliott Richmond is going to walk away free and clear. Like you said, he's the most politically-connected man in the entire state, which also means he's one of the most closely-protected. No one in their right mind is brave enough to even insinuate that he could do something like this, even with the existence of that video. Detective Graham already expressed his level of personal offense at my suggestion. Besides, I gave up the badge, which means I also gave up the oath associated with it."

Paul moved his hand away from Camille's and stood up. It was the first time she saw anger in his face. "I can't tell you what to do, and I obviously can't tie you to that chair, so I'm going to ask that you just consider what I'm saying. You can't take this on right now, not because Richmond is too formidable, but because the emotion of this situation is. You've been riding this adrenaline wave all week, you've barely sat still, and I'm sure you haven't eaten. When you come down from this, you're going to come down hard, and I don't want you out there on some wild-eyed crusade when that happens. I'm not against you on any of this. All I ask is that you give yourself time. This has been one of the worst weeks of my life, so I can only imagine how bad it's been for you. Don't make the situation worse by doing something that's fueled by anger. Please. For me."

Camille stood up and approached him with her arms extended. She couldn't help but be moved by his words. "I'll do anything for you, dad. You know that." She felt warm as he wrapped his arms around her.

But she also felt guilty, because for as much as his advice made perfect sense, she had no intention of taking it. Despite her empty promises, she would be visiting Mayor Richmond's campaign headquarters as planned. The directions were already plugged into her cell phone. All she needed to do was to get to her father's car again. She had hoped the trip would be made with his blessing. Now all Camille could do was hope that he would eventually forgive her.

When Paul looked into her eyes, the overwhelming sense of relief on his face was punctuated by that familiar look of pride. It almost made her cry.

"Thank you, sweetheart."

"You're welcome, dad."

CHAPTER 30

DIRT

The fact that Elliott Richmond lived his life in a perpetual state of nervousness came as a surprise to few who knew him. As the campaign strategist for the leading candidate in one of the country's most scrutinized senate races, Elliott's sole responsibility was to ensure that nothing derailed the freight train that was destined to lead him to Washington D.C. Right now, that train was running full steam ahead, and the track in front of him looked smooth and swift. His candidate was comfortably ahead in every poll, the list of campaign donors was swelling, and many of the country's most powerful politicians, the Vice-President of the United States included, were on board with enthusiastic endorsements.

But even with all of this good fortune, Elliott rarely experienced a restful night of sleep. His mind was constantly filled with questions: questions about money, questions about the next interview or debate, questions about his opponent's ability to dig up dirt that wasn't buried far enough beneath the surface.

Most political candidates have something from their past that can be used against them if their opposition has the resources to uncover it and the will to use it. Elliott certainly had enough on Robert Haney to ruin his chances should the Attorney General's fledgling campaign ever pick up enough momentum to become a genuine threat. But so far that hadn't happened, which meant that Haney's three year extra-marital affair with his communications director could stay comfortably hidden from his wife and the rest of the world.

What was ironic to Elliott was that his own candidate didn't have a speck of dirt that anyone could use against her. As career politicians went, Sonya Richmond's past was as blemish-free as they came. Four years as a state judge, six years on the Denver City Council, one term as a representative in the Colorado legislature, and two terms as Denver's current mayor were all conducted with nothing but the utmost integrity and commitment to the citizens she served. Because of that, she was as popular as any public figure in the state. Before she even hinted at running for the senate, local pundits predicted a landslide victory, irrespective of her opponent.

Elliott should have never spent a single night worrying about the veracity of his candidate's record or her chances for victory in November. But he did worry about his candidate's chances, because there was a blemish in her past, a glaring one that threatened to not only derail the freight train, but destroy it altogether.

She married him.

Sonya may not have had any dirt that could come back to haunt her, but Elliott had plenty. He was covered in it. And the more he tried to wipe it away, the more layers he uncovered.

The first and most important layer was Julia Leeds. In the eighteen months that he'd had sex with her, Elliott never had even the slightest indication that she was as unstable as she ultimately turned out to be. Only a woman afflicted with severe mental problems could believe that anything she had to offer – emotionally, financially, or sexually – would ever be enough to make him abandon a life he had spent the better part of thirty years systematically building.

But Julia believed that he would. And when Elliott informed her of just how delusional she was, she threatened to destroy that systematically-built life piece by piece.

Even if they were made in the heat of a particularly vicious argument, how was he not supposed to take those threats seriously? How was he not supposed to think that Julia was capable of destroying not only his life, but his wife's? She had the means to do it. And when he abruptly ended their affair, she had the motivation. The one thing Elliott could not allow her was the time.

Enter the second layer. Joseph Solomon, a man who came highly recommended by someone Elliott trusted a great deal, was hired to handle the Julia Leeds problem before it had a chance to escalate. But two days ago, Elliott received a phone call from that trusted person informing him that Solomon had not fully solved the problem. He received a second phone call from that same person no less than thirty minutes ago, this one more urgent than the first. As a result, Elliott now had a third layer to contend with; a layer that was potentially more dangerous than the first two combined.

According to the message, Walter Graham, the lead detective in Julia's murder investigation, was nearly hysterical with panic. Elliott knew a great many people in the Denver Police Department, but few had a sensibility more amenable to his efforts than Graham. He had first met the detective over a decade ago. Back then he was a take-no-shit cowboy who intimidated people simply by the way he wore his badge. He was also a well-respected veteran of the force, with an arrest record second to none. Most importantly, he was a highly corruptible cop with a firm grasp of how to conduct, and ultimately manipulate, a murder investigation. According to the stories he'd heard, little had changed about the detective in that decade.

In spite of the inherent risk that came with involving too many people in this already risky scenario, Elliott had no concerns when it came to Walter Graham; a man whose exceedingly checkered past managed to disappear not only from his Internal Affairs file, but from the headlines of every newspaper in the state, only because of Elliott's influence. But those files could reappear as quickly and easily as they had gone missing. And even though Graham knew nothing about the operation he was participating in beyond his role in it, he did know that much. *Scratch my back and I won't stab yours.* Elliott hadn't spoken two words to Graham in the decade since they'd first met. But he still considered the detective to be the perfect ally.

Then came the phone call that changed everything.

According to Elliot's source, Graham had just conducted an interview with Julia's best friend. This friend claimed to have an incriminating video of Elliott and Julia in a heated argument. Elliott assumed it was the very same video that Julia had sent him a five minute excerpt of three weeks earlier. In the subject line of the email that she had attached the clip to, Julia wrote the eight words that virtually assured her death: 'Next time I send it to your wife.'

Graham had apparently done his best to get the disk, but failed. After apologizing profusely, he swore to do anything he needed to do to fix the situation. Though Elliott was not privy to the actual conversation being reported to him, the take-no-shit cowboy had seemingly turned into a sniveling teenager who called to tell his father that he accidentally wrecked the family minivan. His disappointment in the detective couldn't have been more profound.

But the fear that resulted from the phone call was much worse. Julia's best friend, he was informed, was also a former FBI agent. And if she really did have the video, as well as any of the other documents that Julia had in her possession, the chances were quite good that she would know exactly what she was looking at. She would also know exactly what to do with it.

As he fretted over the possibilities, Elliott picked up the wastebasket that sat next to his desk and put it in his lap. He had a feeling he was going to throw up and didn't want to ruin the suit that he had to wear to the Denver Chamber of Commerce luncheon he was scheduled to attend in an hour. His wife was already there, along with every other person who formed the exceedingly powerful political circle that he would do anything to remain a part of.

For now, his prominent standing in that circle was safe. Two days ago, he had assumed it was iron-clad. But the nightmare that started two months ago in Julia's bedroom and had seemingly ended four nights ago was far from over. And if he didn't discover a solution to his current crisis and discover it very fast, that prominent standing may vanish altogether.

As Elliott cradled the wastebasket, convinced the contents of his queasy stomach would soon fill it, he was nearly startled out of his chair by the buzz of his office intercom.

Fighting to recapture the breath that had suddenly left his body, he picked up the receiver.

"What is it, Sarah?"

"Sorry to bother you, Elliott. But someone is here to see you."

Elliott put the wastebasket down, straightened his tie, and held a compact mirror up to a youthful, sun-bleached face that was currently offset by deep frown lines. "Who is it?"

"A new donor," Sarah answered enthusiastically.

Elliott's frown lines instantly disappeared, as did the queasiness in his stomach. Money had a way of doing that. "I'll be right there."

He got up from his desk, put on his expensive suit coat, and walked out into the lobby of his wife's campaign headquarters. The thousand mega-watt smile that he had long used to charm the wealthy into pulling out their checkbooks was on full display.

The moment he entered the lobby and saw who was really there waiting for him, the smile went away.

CHAPTER 31

FULL CIRCLE

Solomon couldn't help but smile when he saw the look of utter astonishment on Elliott Richmond's face. He was used to inspiring that look in people. But the sense of raw power it infused him with never got old.

He had only met Richmond twice. Both meetings were brief and to the point. But in those few moments he gained more insight into the man respectfully referred to as 'The Strategist' than most people, even the ones closest to him, would learn in a lifetime. The nickname was well-deserved. Richmond was as thoughtful and organized a plotter as Solomon had ever met. But there was nothing at all respectful about him.

The girl who escorted him through Mayor Richmond's campaign headquarters wore the same astonished look as her boss. But hers was inspired by something else. At first Solomon had suspected, with as little vanity as possible, that it had something to do with his looks. But the way she introduced him to Richmond let him know that it probably had a lot more to do with her perception of his wallet size.

"Hey there," she chirped with a fresh-out-of-college kind of enthusiasm when Richmond entered the lobby. "This is the brand new donor I was telling you about. He also calls himself the mayor's most enthusiastic supporter." Solomon had thrown in that little tidbit for good measure. "Elliott Richmond, meet Solomon Gates."

A rather ridiculous pseudonym, Solomon had concluded the instant he came up with it. But pseudonyms, ridiculous or not, were an indispensable part of his life.

"Mr. Gates. It's a pleasure to meet you," Richmond said with a bogus smile as he shook Solomon's hand.

Solomon squeezed hard and immediately felt the smaller man's hand buckle under the strength of his grip. "It's a pleasure to meet you too, Mr. Richmond. Sarah wasn't kidding when she said that I'm your wife's most enthusiastic supporter. She's gotten my vote in every election since she first ran for city council. But now that the stakes are a bit higher, I figured it was time to finally put my money where my vote is."

"That's awfully generous of you," Richmond said as he rubbed his hand. "When you're running a campaign as big as this one, you can never have enough enthusiastic supporters."

After a moment of silence that bordered on awkward, Sarah extended her hand to Solomon. "Well, I guess I'll leave you two alone. Mr. Gates, it was really nice meeting you."

Solomon took the girl's hand and squeezed gently. "The pleasure was mine, Sarah. Hopefully we'll see each other again." Her breath caught slightly as she pulled her hand away and walked out of the lobby.

Once Sarah was out of sight, Richmond abandoned the fake smile, looked at Solomon and shook his head. "So is it finally safe to end the *Amos and Andy* routine?"

"I thought it was kind of fun," Solomon countered. "Imagine me as the fine, upstanding patriot whose willing to put his hard earned millions behind the one politician he believes will finally do some good in this God-forsaken world. I should consider taking up acting."

"The world's first contract-killer to ever win an Oscar. Inspiring."

Solomon's half-smile quickly disappeared. "Do you have an office?"

Richmond nodded then turned around and started walking. Solomon followed in silence until they reached an isolated corner in the back of the building.

"Come in and have a seat," Richmond directed as he opened the office door and pointed to the high back leather chair in front of his massive mahogany desk.

Solomon waited for Richmond to situate himself behind the desk before sitting. "Judging by that slack-faced look of yours, I can only assume you're surprised to see me."

"Surprised is one word. Mortified is another. Why would you even consider coming here?"

"I understand that I'm violating the whole chain of command thing. But considering the current situation, the breach was necessary."

Richmond took a long breath. "I'm fully aware of the current situation. But showing up here was not the way to handle it. If anybody recognized you—"

"So you know about the disks?"

"Yes I do."

"Then I can safely assume that this operation wasn't about retrieving two inoperable computers and a box full of blank media? Because that's exactly what I got."

"Of course it wasn't about that," Richmond answered. "There was supposed to be specific, highly sensitive information on those disks."

"But there wasn't, unless you count her ski itinerary as highly sensitive."

Richmond shook his head and mumbled under his breath. "This is such a nightmare."

"Where is the information I was supposed to retrieve?"

Richmond wrung his hands then set them down hard on the desk. "I just finished a rather disheartening phone call with your boss. Did he send you here?"

"I haven't spoken to him yet. I found my way here all on my own."

"So you don't know."

Solomon had only been here two minutes, and he was already getting angry. "Not until you tell me."

"Someone else has the disks."

Of course, Solomon thought, surprised by his own lack of surprise. "Who?"

Richmond put a hand over his mouth, as if to stifle the words that were about to come out of it. "An FBI agent."

Solomon's blood instantly ran cold. Afraid that Richmond would see the fear in his icy blue eyes, he cast them away. "You can't be serious."

"She's a former FBI agent, not that that makes it any better."

"Of course it doesn't. Just tell me how it happened."

"I really assumed you would be in the loop with all of this."

"I'm not always as available as my bosses would like. So why don't you do me a favor and bring me up to speed."

"I'll have to tell them to keep better tabs on you," Richmond said flatly. "At any rate, this former FBI agent also happens to be Julia's best friend. They spent that entire last day together and the agent was most likely the last person to talk to Julia before she was killed."

Solomon's chest suddenly felt heavy.

Richmond continued. "So to answer your question, she probably got the disk directly from the source."

Solomon tried to regulate his breathing, but his lungs felt as if someone were sitting on them. The agent Richmond spoke of could only be Camille Grisham, the same Camille Grisham he allowed Julia to spend the entire day with without intervening. They never should have made it home from the airport. Of course, he wasn't prepared to tell Richmond that. "I'm assuming she told someone in the DPD about it."

Richmond nodded. "The two detectives assigned to the case. She told them that it contained, among other things, an incriminating video of me that essentially proves that I killed Julia."

Solomon always figured it was something like that, but he still couldn't hide the look of mild surprise on his face. "And what was their reaction?"

"Fortunately she didn't get much traction with it. Not yet anyway."

"If we're lucky she won't get any more with the Clemmons angle playing out the way it is."

"I understand an arrest is imminent."

"He's already in custody."

"You should be proud of yourself," Richmond said with a strained smile.

"I don't deserve any pats on the back yet. There's too much left on the table."

Richmond nodded. "Indeed there is."

After a prolonged silence, Solomon asked: "What about the video? Is it as bad as the agent said it is?"

"It's worse."

Solomon leaned back in his chair. "Do you mind telling me what's on it?"

"I mind."

Solomon smiled. "Fair enough."

"The only thing you need to concern yourself with is how we're going to get it back."

"You mean how I'm going to get it back."

Richmond nodded. "There's an extra payout when you do."

"So you're negotiating with me directly now? My boss will be disappointed that he wasn't invited to the table."

"Wasn't that the point of you coming here? To avoid the red tape of a middleman?"

"That middleman is pretty goddamn important."

"Not nearly as important as I am. Get me that disk and you can name your price."

Right now, that didn't help Solomon feel any better. Even though he knew it would come down to this, he wasn't eager to plan yet another operation, especially one involving an FBI agent. But he tried to temper his lack of enthusiasm with a healthy dose of gratitude. If it indeed was Camille Grisham who had the disk, finding her would be easy. Not only did he know what she looked like, he also knew where she lived. If need be, he could walk out the door, track down the agent, and do whatever he had to do until he got the disk. If he was lucky, he would be able to pick up his payment tomorrow as originally scheduled. Then he remembered that there was no such thing as luck when it came to his job.

"I'll be at the pickup location tomorrow at eleven a.m. as planned," Solomon proclaimed as he stood up. "We can negotiate my additional fee later."

Richmond looked confused. "What are you talking about?"

"I'm going to get your disk back."

"How?"

"Eleven A.M."

The confusion in Richmond's eyes was quickly replaced with awe. "If you say so."

"I'll drop the disk in the same bin I pick up the money from. I don't want to see anyone else there, so you need to arrange to have it picked up after I'm gone. If I see something I don't like, the whole thing is off and the disk goes in a trash bin somewhere."

"Understood," Richmond answered. Then he stood up and extended his hand.

Solomon had to think before finally shaking it. He had made lots of deals with lots of devils before, but never the same one twice. "Okay," he said as he took Richmond's hand. His grip was much lighter this time. "Now why don't you escort your big donor out to the lobby? It's good for appearances."

Richmond nodded in agreement. "After you."

As they exited the office and walked down the short corridor that led to the lobby, Solomon was suddenly curious to see more. He knew it was somewhat irregular, but he was never one to deny his curiosities. He turned to Richmond. "You know, I've never actually seen how one of these big-time campaigns actually works. Why don't you give me a quick tour before I go?"

Richmond seemed slightly annoyed by the request. He obviously thought it was irregular too. But at this point why would he say no? He pointed at a door to the left of the lobby. "Right through there."

Solomon opened the door and was immediately taken by what he saw. The headquarters itself was located in what could kindly be called a questionable neighborhood, nestled between what looked like a group home for wayward teenagers on one side and a housing project on the other. He had read in the paper that the site was chosen specifically to appease the large pool of Latino voters who lived in the area. Whatever the motives, the location left a lot to be desired.

But inside, the setup was extremely well put together. It was spacious, with dozens of phone banks occupied with volunteers and cubicles filled with young, energetic staff members. Everyone seemed to be frantically making copies of things. It was as upbeat an atmosphere as Solomon had ever been in. The mayor was far ahead in the polls, and the attitudes of the staff and volunteers reflected that. There were piles of yard signs waiting to be handed out, balloons with 'Richmond for U.S. Senate' hanging from the ceiling, and a poster-sized dart board with Attorney General Robert Haney's smiling face on it. On a radio somewhere close by, U2's *Beautiful Day* was playing.

Solomon wasn't quite ready to share that sentiment, but he could say the day was definitely starting to look up. He turned to Richmond, who was understandably beaming with pride. "The Strategist has done quite well for himself," he said with a smile.

Richmond smiled back. "Thank you, Mr. Gates."

Solomon took in the scene one last time then turned to leave. He had pressing business to attend to. Richmond followed.

"So, you still haven't told me how you plan to get this done," Richmond said in a low tone. "I haven't told you anything about this agent. How will you even know where to start?"

Solomon stopped him before they entered the lobby door. "I have ways, Mr. Richmond. It won't be difficult."

Richmond nodded, then opened the door to the lobby. The first person they saw was Richmond's assistant Sarah. She looked slightly flustered, but relieved to see them. "Oh, there you are Elliott. I was worried that you'd left for the Chamber luncheon already."

Richmond looked at his Rolex. "Not for another twenty minutes. What's up?"

Sarah smiled. "It looks like this is our lucky day. Someone else just came in who is apparently very interested in giving to the campaign."

"Another donor, I hope?"

"I wasn't able to get a sense of that. But she did say that she had access to resources that the campaign would be interested in. I'm thinking she belongs to some sort of organization, like the NAACP or something."

Richmond looked at Solomon. "Well, we can never take the African-American vote for granted, can we?" Then he looked at Sarah. "Is she in the lobby?"

"Yep. She's standing by the entrance."

"Well let's go say hello, make her feel at home."

Sarah turned toward the lobby while Richmond and Solomon followed. Richmond saw the woman first. "Hello there," he said in what was probably his standard ass-kissing voice. "Welcome to our little operation."

By the time Solomon looked up to see that the woman getting her ass kissed was Camille Grisham, Richmond was already shaking her hand.

He instinctively reached for his gun, but stopped short of pulling it out. Even though the move was subtle, it was enough to get her attention. When she glanced at him, the smile that she was putting on for Richmond went away.

She knew. Somehow, she knew.

"And this is Solomon Gates," Sarah said as she put a hand on Solomon's elbow. "He's another one of our supporters."

Camille nodded, though she didn't extend her hand. "Naomi Stephens. Pleasure."

Naomi Stephens? Today was certainly the day for aliases. "Likewise," Solomon answered as he tried to fake his way through a smile. The agent didn't even bother trying. "Well Elliott, I have to run," he said, squeezing Richmond's shoulder. "I'm sure we'll catch up again very soon."

"You can count on it, Mr. Gates," Richmond answered confidently.

Solomon looked back at Camille. The look in her eye hadn't changed. It was obvious that Richmond didn't know who she was, and he wanted to warn him. But there was no reasonable way to do that. So he silently wished him luck and walked out the door.

"Have a good day Solomon," Camille Grisham called out. Her tone was flat and lifeless. And it scared the hell out of him.

"You do the same, Naomi," he said, trying to match her tone. Unlike him, she didn't look the least bit afraid.

But she soon would be.

CHAPTER 32
ANOTHER ENTHUSIASTIC SUPPORTER

The Elliott Richmond that Camille stood less than two feet away from looked nothing like the monster she saw on the video. In real life he didn't have nearly the same physical stature that his on camera behavior would have suggested. Camille would even go so far as to call him unimpressive. He looked and acted more like a used car salesman than the wealthy, politically-connected murderer that he actually was.

Solomon Gates, on the other hand, was formidable in the way she expected Elliott Richmond to be. Standing well over six feet, with a stature befitting the average Roman gladiator, Gates was a darkly handsome man, with a thick mane of black hair and an angular, sharply-chiseled face. His presence cast a shadow over all of them that made her leery. Something about him also felt familiar. In the case of most people, familiar is good. In his case, it was not.

Whatever her feelings about Gates, she couldn't let them distract her from the real reason she was here.

"So Naomi, Sarah tells me that you're a member of an organization?" Richmond asked with an inflated smile.

The nice girl who escorted her in was still standing nearby, half listening to the conversation. Camille would have to maintain some semblance of decorum as long as she was around. So she ground her teeth, clenched her jaw, and manufactured a smile that matched Richmond's in its absurdity. "An organization? Not exactly. Let's just say I represent an influential block of people who are tired of the same old business as usual." She had once heard that line in a movie.

"I would say that you and I already have something rather significant in common. The status quo is something we can no longer tolerate. Mayor Richmond is determined to change things. With like-minded people like you on board, that change is going to come faster than people realize."

Camille continued to play along as Sarah suddenly became distracted by her cell phone. "I believe the mayor can change a lot of things, Mr. Richmond. That's why I'm here."

Richmond put a hand on her shoulder. "Please, I insist you call me Elliott." Camille had to resist the urge to snatch his measly paw off her shoulder and bend it ninety degrees backward.

The first thought that entered her mind was what could Julia have possibly seen in him. The second thought was how easy it would be to beat the living crap out of him if she had to. She didn't anticipate it coming down to that. But then again, the meeting had just gotten started.

"Fair enough, Elliott," she answered with the last ounce of levity she could muster.

When Sarah was finally finished with her phone call, she walked over to Camille and Richmond. "That was the mayor. I didn't want to interrupt your meeting so I went ahead and took the call for you."

"That's perfectly okay. What did she need?"

"She wanted to let you know that she is going to be about twenty minutes late to the Chamber luncheon. The Five Points town hall meeting ran long and she hit a snarl in traffic."

Richmond sighed. "I guess we could have predicted that one, huh? Thanks for letting me know."

She smiled. "You're welcome. Nice to meet you, Naomi."

Camille returned her smile. "Nice to meet you too." She suddenly felt afraid for Sarah. She obviously had no idea who she was working for, and if he hadn't already tried to have his way with her, he was certainly thinking about it. Camille wanted to warn her, just like she wanted to warn everyone here.

"We'll be sure to hold things down while you're gone," Sarah said as she walked out of the lobby.

"I have no doubt you will," Richmond answered, his eyes lingering on the girl until she disappeared behind the door. After she was gone he put his hand back on Camille's shoulder. "The Chamber of Commerce is honoring the mayor with an award this afternoon and as usual she's running late. She jokes that when she's elected to the senate she's going to be late to the swearing-in and they're going to take her seat away before she even gets the chance to sit in it."

With no one left to put on a show for, Camille didn't even attempt to smile. "I take it you're the punctual one in the family?"

Richmond shrugged. "I may only be slightly better about it than she is. Speaking of which, I'm afraid I'm going to have to cut this short. If I don't get going I may not make it at all."

"I can appreciate that you're busy, Elliott. I happen to be kind of busy myself. In fact, this has probably been the longest, most emotionally hellish week of my entire life. And when you've had the life I've had, that's really saying something. To be honest, I'm lucky to have made it here at all. If I'm not careful, I may have a complete nervous breakdown right here in this office. So for both our sakes, I'll be as quick as I can." Camille maintained a steady measure in her voice that made Richmond visibly nervous. That was the whole idea.

"I'm not sure I follow."

"Do we really have to discuss this out here?"

Richmond slowly backpedaled his way toward the lobby door. "I don't know what you're referring to. But as I said, I'm running late, and I don't think I really have time to—"

"Because my best friend was murdered a week ago," Camille interrupted, her voice losing its measure. "And I'd rather not talk about the specifics of it in this very public room. When you hear what I have to say, you're not going to want to talk here either."

Camille's words stopped Richmond cold. "What on earth are you talking about?"

Camille said nothing as she pulled out a silver flash disk and tossed it to him. He fumbled trying to catch it and it fell to the ground.

"Don't worry if you broke that one. I have copies."

Richmond looked at her with pitiful eyes as he bent down to pick up the disk. Camille wanted to bask in the sight of this pathetic man in his tailored suit crouching on the ground like the dog that he was, but she suddenly felt light-headed. This nightmare of a day was starting to catch up to her, just like her father warned it would.

"What is this?" Richmond asked as he held up the disk.

"Almost a thousand Excel and Word documents related to the Schumann Investment Group and Springwell Technologies. Do either of those names ring a bell? From what I'm beginning to learn, you're pretty familiar with both. There's also a PowerPoint presentation for the Schumann Board of Directors detailing a number of risky investments that Schumann entered into, using the retirement income of state employees as collateral. There are three other PowerPoints which detail income losses as a result of collapsed stock prices and a plan for affected board members to recoup their losses. Once again, at the expense of state employees. And then there's the interesting bit about Springwell Technologies and the online voting project that they were spearheading. Funny that you would have an involvement in something like that, considering your wife is dependent on those very votes to win her senate seat. Personally, I don't know anything about this stuff, so most of it is Greek to me. But I do recognize criminal activity when I see it. And what I saw in those documents looked pretty damn criminal." Camille had to pause to stop herself from shaking. "But the best part is the video."

Richmond's face suddenly turned to stone. "That's enough."

"So you know what I'm talking about? I'm glad I don't have to explain any further.

"I said that's eno—"

"Did you honestly think you could say the things that you said on that video and actually get away with it? You had to know that it was eventually going to come out. Did Julia tell you she was going to make it public? Is that why you did it?" Camille was talking much louder than she needed to, but at this point she didn't care if anyone heard.

"For God sake, keep your voice down," Richmond said in an angry whisper.

"If it's really that much of a concern, maybe we should find someplace more private to talk this out."

"I have an even better idea. Get the hell out of here before I have you thrown out."

Richmond took a step toward Camille, and her mind instantly flashed back to an image of him doing the same thing to Julia. If his finger came anywhere near her face, she was fully prepared to break it.

"If you need a cop to escort me out, you should consider calling Detective Walter Graham in homicide. He's pretty busy with Julia's case, but I'm sure he'd drop everything and rush right over if you asked him to. Thinks the world of you. When I took this disk to him, he got so angry I thought he was going to shoot me on the spot. We should all have someone in the world who thinks that highly of us. Makes me think the two of you are buddies or something. Anyway, it's fortunate for me that Graham isn't the only cop in town. Something tells me they won't all react as strongly as he did."

Richmond nodded as his face suddenly lit up with recognition. "I personally think Naomi is a much prettier name than Camille. You should really think about having it changed."

"I don't think my father would be too happy about that, considering he was the one who named me. You know how stubborn cops can be."

"They're a lot like former FBI agents. They don't always know when to quit." Richmond smirked. "But in your case, I guess you did."

Camille felt her hand curl up in a tight fist. "Enough with the bullshit banter, Elliott. I came here to ask you a very simple question."

Richmond's posture became rigid. "What question is that?"

"Are you going to do the right thing?"

A hint of a smile came across his face. "Is this on the record or off?"

"This isn't a newspaper interview," Camille answered briskly. "Besides, I already have you on video. I don't need you on tape too."

"Right. Well, as I said in that video you keep referring to, I don't take kindly to being threatened."

"Believe me, I know. You usually kill people who threaten you. But I figured I had nothing to lose, so why not take the chance?"

"You really are funny, Camille. Or should I say Agent Grisham. But I didn't kill Julia. I may have done other things that I shouldn't have. But I didn't kill her."

Camille shook her head. "I'm going to ask you one more time. Are you going to do the right thing? So far your answer seems to be no. I want to give you the opportunity to reevaluate that before I leave."

"Maybe you should reevaluate what's going to happen *after* you leave."

Camille opened her mouth to respond, but the look in Richmond's eyes stopped her. She caught her first glimpse of the monster. It was a fleeting appearance, but the resulting chill that came over her lingered. She did her best to push it back. "I know exactly what's going to happen after I leave."

"Do tell."

"Since you've made it clear that you're not going to do the right thing, and since both of us are so pressed for time, I'm only going to say one more thing." She reached into her pocket, pulled out another flash disk, and threw it to Richmond. This time he caught it cleanly. "That one is for your wife. Give her my regards."

Without saying another word, Camille stormed out of the lobby and through the front door.

Her primary purpose in coming here was to rattle Richmond. She knew he wouldn't tearfully confess or explode with self-righteous rage. Guilty people rarely did either. What they do is exactly what he did: keep calm until the storm appeared to pass. Richmond kept cool as long as he could, but with Camille's last words to him, he was well aware that the storm had yet to pass. That meant he was undoubtedly plotting his next move.

But so was Camille.

The plan was less than ideal, and the results could be worse than anything she had currently imagined. But Elliott Richmond had forced her hand, as had Detective Graham before him. She had only one card left to play, and despite the devastation that could be left in its wake, she had to play it.

With her method of execution firmly in mind, Camille pulled out her cell phone. Laurence Pine answered on the second ring. "This is Laurence."

"This is Camille Grisham. Are you available to meet?"

Pine hesitated before answering. "Sure. Is something wrong?"

"Very much so."

"What is it?"

She took a breath and held it in. "I was hoping you could tell me."

CHAPTER 33

END IN SIGHT

Solomon had considered shooting Camille Grisham the second she walked out of Richmond's office. She was well within range of his PSG-1 automatic rifle, and he could have easily gotten off two clean rounds before she even realized that she was hit by the first. But that was the riskiest of propositions, even in a neighborhood where drive-by shootings were a weekly occurrence. So he waited until she drove away.

As he had done with Julia Leeds so many times before, Solomon followed at what he considered to be a safe distance. But unlike Julia, there would be no on-going surveillance. There would be no planning. There would be no waiting.

Camille showing up at Richmond's campaign headquarters only confirmed what Solomon already knew: she not only had the disk but had every intention of releasing the information on it. And since going to the police didn't work, she came to Richmond in the hopes of blackmailing him into some made-for-TV confession.

Solomon didn't know him very well, but he was convinced that Richmond would not have folded, even under that kind of pressure. That meant Camille would have to resort to something else. He couldn't even wager a guess as to what that something else would be. But he also knew it didn't matter. The end was close. By noon tomorrow, Camille Grisham would be dead, the disk and any copies she had would be in Richmond's possession, the mayor would still be firmly ahead in the polls, and Solomon would find himself considerably richer.

But there was a lot to do between now and then. Not only did he have to wait for the right opportunity to move on the agent, but he had to do it in such a way that wouldn't bring suspicion on Richmond, and ultimately himself. That would take patience and planning, and unfortunately he didn't have the luxury of either. He would have to improvise.

When Camille pulled up to a meter in front of the Wells Fargo building, the same building he had trailed her best friend to less than a week earlier, Solomon decided not to follow. Because he hadn't gotten to Camille sooner, he realized that certain wheels had already been set in motion and he was probably too late to stop them. For all he knew she could have been on her way to the attorney general's office with the disk in her hand and the destruction of Richmond's life in her heart. It was a chance he had to take. Solomon may have been hell-bent on finishing the job, but he wasn't willing to do so at the expense of his own well-being. He knew that making a move now would be based more on impulse than common sense. In Solomon's experience, acting on impulse led to mistakes. Mistakes led to being caught.

So he let her go, secure in the knowledge that he would see her again very soon. It ultimately didn't matter who she talked to in the interim or what she told them. If Solomon had his way, and he was confident he would, Camille wouldn't live long enough to see the outcome.

CHAPTER 34

FILLING THE GAPS

Laurence Pine's assistant stood up the instant she saw Camille approaching her desk. "Mr. Pine is waiting for you," she said with an appropriate sense of urgency. "Right this way."

Camille nodded and followed her through the same marble-floored corridor that had first led her to Pine's office suite only a few hours earlier.

His office door was ajar. Through the sliver of an opening, Camille could see him seated behind his desk scrolling through an electronic tablet. Though Camille didn't know him well enough to distinguish one mood from another, she guessed that he was on edge. After a gentle knock on the door, the receptionist peeked inside.

"Excuse me, Mr. Pine. Camille Grisham is here."

Pine stood up and had walked around his desk before Camille could even step through the door. "Please come in," he said as he clipped the top button of his suit jacket. Instead of the handshake that Camille was expecting, he pulled out the chair in front of his desk. "Have a seat."

"Will there be anything else?" Pine's young receptionist then asked.

"No calls please. Regardless of who it is," Pine directed.

She nodded, flashed a quick smile and quietly let herself out.

Camille waited until she heard the door close before speaking. "Thank you for accommodating me on such short notice."

Pine slipped on a pair of horn-rimmed glasses over eyes that had already worn the strain of a long day. "The call sounded rather urgent. And considering the circumstances surrounding our first meeting, I wasn't about to make you wait."

"I really appreciate that, because this can't wait."

Pine leaned forward in his chair. "I'm all ears."

"I need to know about Julia's professional life."

"What would you like to know specifically?"

"Anything you can tell me about what she did at Brown, Wallace, and Epstein, in particular any connection that either she or her firm had to the Schumann Investment Group, Springwell Technologies or Elliott Richmond."

Pine seemed to be at an immediate loss for words.

"Mr. Pine?"

He took off his glasses and set them down on his desk. "May I ask why you want to know?"

"The key that Julia left for me was for a safe deposit box. Inside that box was a flash disk as well as a corresponding list of written instructions. She mentioned your name in reference to an Excel spreadsheet titled 'Schumann-Springwell'. She said that you would know what to do with it."

"Did you open the spreadsheet?"

"It was filled with percentages, financial figures, and pie charts that meant absolutely nothing to me. Same with the other nine hundred or so files that were on the disk."

"Nine hundred? Jesus, what was she planning on doing with all of that?"

"That's what I came here to find out."

"I'm sorry that you came all the way back here in search of answers, Ms. Grisham. But I'm afraid I don't know nearly as much as you think I do."

Camille reached into her coat pocket, pulled out Julia's note, and handed it to Pine.

After reaching for his glasses, he unfolded the note and began silently reading. It wasn't long before he started shaking his head. "My God," he muttered without looking up.

"Now do you understand why I came here?"

Once Pine finished the note, he handed it back to Camille. He was still shaking his head. "What does all of this mean?"

"I already told you, I'm not familiar with–"

"Not the files. The fact that she went through the trouble of transferring them to a disk and locking that disk in a safe deposit box less than a day before she was murdered. If I had asked myself that question before now, I would have assumed that it was a crazy coincidence. But now…"

"Coincidence is officially off the table," Camille declared.

Pine swallowed hard.

"I know you were her personal lawyer. But you also said that the two of you were good friends. I'm sure she confided in you, especially about things related to a profession you were both in. Anything you can offer will help." Camille could feel the desperation growing in her voice, despite a concerted effort to maintain her composure. "Please."

Pine sat back in his chair, his eyes drifting to the majestic view outside the office window. "I need to preface this by saying that she never discussed the specifics of her work with the Schumann Investment Group or Springwell Technologies. The confidentiality agreement she was most certainly made to sign was part of the reason. My own survival instinct was the other."

"What do you mean?"

"I rarely asked Julia about the details of her work because she was involved in things I wanted to know nothing about. The less I knew, the less I had to lie about if such a time ever came. Plausible deniability. It's the standard-bearer for our profession."

"Why don't you just tell me what you do know, beginning with her work for Elliott Richmond."

"The story begins and ends with her work for Elliott Richmond. Julia had been with Brown, Wallace, and Epstein for a total of ten years. Eight of those years were spent as an associate. The partners always felt like she had the potential, but her inability to land money-making clients held her back. It got to the point two years ago where she feared the firm would let her go altogether. Then she landed the account that changed everything."

"Schumann Investment Group," Camille said.

Pine nodded. "During that time Schumann was exploring the possibility of branching out into the home mortgage market, and Julia was brought in to do some side consulting work. Apparently they were so impressed with that work that they hired her on as full-time counsel. It was a major coup for Brown and Wallace, and they rewarded Julia with a junior partnership six months later."

Camille smiled as she remembered the phone call she received from Julia about her promotion. Saddened that she wasn't able to celebrate the momentous occasion with her best friend, Julia decided that she would bring the celebration to her. Camille called her bluff, then had to recant eight hours later when Julia called her again, this time from Dulles Airport. That four-day celebration turned out to be the last extended time that Camille would ever spend with her.

Pine continued. "Things seemed to be good for a while, then Julia began dropping subtle hints that issues were starting to arise."

"What kinds of issues?"

"Complaints about the people she worked for. Before Schumann, the only thing Julia ever complained about in relation to her job was not making enough money. But she knew that was a function of her lack of rainmaking ability and took full responsibility for it. Her gripes were never personal though. She respected the firm and everyone associated with it. Once Elliott Richmond came on the scene, things changed. All I heard about was how difficult he could be to work with, how unethical the Schumann management was as a whole, and how she wished she had never accepted the junior partner position."

Camille nodded. "That was the same thing she said to me. When I told her she should just leave and go do something else, she told me that it was too late. I could never get her to elaborate on exactly what that meant."

Pine chuckled nervously. "The explanation she gave me was that by signing the contract with Schumann and accepting junior partnership, she had essentially sold her soul to the devil. She enjoyed the spoils, but they came with a price."

"Which was?"

"Blind loyalty to the firm and her client. Julia had an inquisitive nature. If she didn't understand something, she'd ask questions until she got the answer she needed. If she didn't like something, she spoke up about it. When you're an up-and-coming associate, that kind of mentality is seen as a positive. But once you reach a certain level, asking too many questions can be seen as rocking the boat, upsetting the balance. You're encouraged to toe the line, to maintain the status quo. There is simply too much at stake to do otherwise. But it wasn't in Julia's nature to adhere to that kind of philosophy. So when she came across certain aspects of Schumann's business practices that she deemed questionable, she took her concerns to the partners at her firm. But she was met with nothing but resistance – essentially told that Brown and Wallace's bottom lines were more important than her, quote, theories. In a nutshell, she was told to shut up and play along, or risk getting moved along – right out of the firm."

"What did she discover about Schumann's business practices that had her so concerned?"

"She didn't offer a ton of specifics, and I didn't ask. But what she did tell me was that Schumann was, in legal terms, a subsidiary of a larger company that was unknown to the general public. In real world terms, Schumann was nothing more than a public front for the work that this other company was actually doing behind the scenes."

"And what is the name of this company?"

Pine hesitated before answering. "Horis and Roth Limited."

Camille shrugged her shoulders.

"No one else seems to be familiar with them either," Pine responded. "I did some research of my own and couldn't come up with anything. But Julia was apparently very familiar with them. According to her, Horis and Roth, under Elliott Richmond's directive, was secretly financing a project that was publicly sponsored by the Denver County Clerk and Recorder's office. Julia referred to it as the Ace Project. It sought to incorporate social media into the voting process by allowing people to cast votes through text message, email, and Facebook-style social media. Similar projects had been implemented in other states with varying degrees of success. But Colorado's would be the largest such project to date, and with the current senate race projected to bring out the largest non-presidential year turnout in the history of the state, it would be the perfect test case. Julia didn't go into any specifics about her role, if any, in the project, the connection between Horis and Roth and Springwell Technologies, or the role that the Denver County Clerk played in the project. But she did tell me that there came a point where she no longer wanted anything to do with it."

"And she told her partners at the firm all of this?"

"According to her, she told them everything. But as I said, she was completely stonewalled. Before her death, Julia was seriously contemplating leaving the firm, even though doing so would be career suicide. Brown and Wallace's reach is very far, and given the circumstances of her departure, she would be hard-pressed to find a comparable firm willing to take her on, even as a bargain-basement Associate. She knew this, and that's why she expressed so much regret about signing on as partner. Once you're inside a circle like that, it's very difficult to get out of it."

"The existence of the disk meant that she was trying," Camille insisted.

"I'd say she was too. Unfortunately, someone made sure she didn't succeed."

Camille shook Elliott Richmond's face out of her mind. "Even though you didn't want to talk about the specifics of Julia's work, I'm sure you formed your own opinions as to what was going on."

"In my opinion, uninformed as it may be, I think this whole thing centers on Elliott Richmond, his ties to Horis and Roth, and his influence over the Springwell project. He certainly had the pull to manipulate it in any fashion he saw fit. And everyone knows he had the motivation to do so. I think that Julia and Richmond were closer than she let on, and through her insider status she learned things about the project and its ultimate intent. She may have gone along for the sake of getting along at first, but Julia's moral compass eventually steered her back in the right direction. Unfortunately, her moral code meant nothing to the people she was dealing with."

"And it got her killed."

Pine cringed at Camille's blunt statement. "You're saying the two are connected?"

Camille handed the note back to Pine. "Julia said it herself."

Pine scanned the note again, his eyes stopping on the sentence Camille hoped they would. "He did this to me Camille," he read out loud. "You think the 'he' is Elliott Richmond?"

"Knowing what you now know, don't you?"

Pine responded by pinching the bridge of his nose.

"Personally Mr. Pine, I'm one hundred percent certain of it."

"But what about Stephen Clemmons, the man the police just arrested? According to everything I've read they seem fairly certain that he's the guy."

"And I'm certain that he's not."

Pine was silent for a long time before responding. "If you're right about any of this, the fallout is going to be catastrophic."

"From my perspective, the fallout has already been catastrophic."

Pine nodded his agreement. "What else can I do to help?"

"You've already done a lot and I really appreciate it," Camille said with a thin smile. "What I'd really like to do now is speak with someone at Springwell Technologies. I'm not exactly sure how that's going to happen, but I need to try."

"Unfortunately I don't have any personal connections at Springwell. But Julia did mention the name of a programmer there once or twice. I believe his name is Andy. She only mentioned him in passing, so I couldn't tell you anything else about him."

It may not have been much, but at least Camille had a name. At this point it was the best that she could hope for. "I'll see what I can do to fill in the gaps."

Pine nodded once again, the weight of the conversation causing his broad shoulders to slump. Camille empathized with him. She also envied him. He knew things about Julia that she never did; things that Julia intentionally hid from her. It made her wonder, for the briefest of moments, if the two of them were truly as close as Camille had assumed. Camille would tell her anything, and she had – from the full story of what happened in Sykes' basement, to her near suicide attempt. She did so without a moment's hesitation because she was confident there wasn't another person in the world she could trust more. Now Camille couldn't help but question whether the feeling was mutual. She had tried to push the thought out of her mind as she had done with everything else, but it lingered. And even when all the other questions were answered, when time lessened the sting of grief and the guilt of inaction, she feared that it would continue to do so.

But looking at Pine, she couldn't help but appreciate him for being the sounding board that Julia needed. Camille could tell that he was a man of integrity who had wanted nothing but the best for her friend. More than anything he had done, Pine provided Camille with a much needed reminder that for all the grief she felt, she didn't have anything close to a monopoly on it.

"If there is anything else I can do to help, all you have to do is ask," he said. Then he retrieved a business card from his desk. "I'm not sure where you're going with this," he said as he wrote on the back of it. "But I'm sure it's somewhere very specific. Whatever happens, would you please keep me in the loop?"

When Camille took the card the first thing she noticed was Pine's handwritten personal cell number. "I absolutely will," she answered, meaning every word of it.

CHAPTER 35

THE ARCHITECT

The offices of Springwell Technologies were located on the second floor of a converted Tudor-style mansion that it shared with an architecture firm and a personal injury law practice. With nothing else aside from pop-culture stereotypes to draw from, Camille imagined that she would walk into an office space filled with underage Bill Gates wannabes drinking Red Bull by the gallon while they worked on complicated computer programs, played video games, and endlessly debated the true meaning behind the *Lost* series finale.

What she saw instead was a sterile gray work space with few frills and even fewer people. The only noise she heard as she walked through the glass door was the occasional clatter of fingers striking a keyboard and the office's lone copy machine churning out pages that no one seemed to be in a particular hurry to collect. In fact, it wasn't until Camille called out that she saw anyone at all.

"Hello? Is there anyone here who can help me?"

At that, a middle-aged man with a mess of curly red hair better suited on a ten-year-old peeked at her from the top of his cubicle partition. "Are you lost?" he asked in the slow drawl of someone either in desperate need of caffeine or fresh off a long hit of marijuana.

Even though Camille needed a laugh and this burnout provided ample material, she kept her composure. "Is this Springwell Technologies?"

"The one and only," he said as he stood up. He wore a black tee-shirt with the iconic Rolling Stones tongue and lips logo on the front.

Upon seeing it, Camille whispered: "I guess the stereotypes are true."

"What was that?" the man she had already given the name 'Shaggy' asked obliviously.

"I'm sorry. I said I'm looking for Andy," Camille answered, praying like mad that she wasn't already talking to him.

"Andy," Shaggy repeated, appearing to confuse himself in the process. "You mean Andy Rosario?"

I mean Andy Griffith you flaming moron. "Is there more than one?"

"Actually up until a month ago there were three. Recessions are a bitch, right? Rosie was the only Andy who survived it."

Rosie? Camille looked hard at Shaggy's cubicle, half expecting Rod Serling to emerge from it with his trademark cigarette in hand and that knowing half-smile on his face. "Then that's the Andy I'm here to see."

"As you can tell, this is our busy season. With all these people in here it may take a while to find him." When Shaggy laughed, Camille knew right away that a lack of caffeine was not to blame. "Just joking of course."

"Of course."

"He's actually got his own office in the back, which explains why he survived the purging of the Andys as we called it." He paused in an awkward attempt to let Camille share in the joke. Her stone-faced silence quickly got him back on track. "Can I ask who's here to see him?"

"Camille Grisham from Horis and Roth Limited."

The little remaining levity on Shaggy's face went away immediately. "I see. Andy has been on a conference call for the past hour. Let me run back and see if he's finished."

And run Shaggy did. The drastic sobering of his demeanor told Camille one very important thing: the phantom company known as Horis and Roth Limited was very real, and obviously very important. Andy Rosario's harried emergence from his office no less than ten seconds after he was summoned all but confirmed it.

"Good afternoon," he said with the polished smile of a door-to-door vacuum salesman.

"You must be Andy Rosario," she said, matching his affected tone.

"I am. And your name?"

She extended her hand. "Camille Grisham."

Dressed professionally in a white Oxford shirt and khaki slacks, Andy reminded her of a young Antonio Banderas with a hint of the accent and none of the charm. When he took her hand she recoiled with genuine fear that he would kiss it. Fortunately he spared himself the indignity. "It's nice to meet you. Ramsey tells me you're with Horis and Roth?"

You mean Shaggy? "Yes."

Andy kept his smile even as he tried to swallow the lump in his throat. "What brings you by, Ms. Grisham?"

Camille looked at Shaggy whose tongue was practically wagging as he hung on their every word. "May we speak in your office, Mr. Rosario?"

Andy looked toward his office like he was momentarily distracted by something in it, then he turned back to her. "If it's all the same, why don't we talk in the courtyard instead?"

Camille was thrown by the request but did not let her face communicate it. "If you'd feel more comfortable there."

"I would."

"Then by all means lead the way."

252

The two sat on adjacent benches in the small, neatly landscaped backyard of the mansion. The dark, cloudy skies that had been a constant in the week that Camille had been here finally gave way to sun and late summer temperatures, allowing the colorful array of annuals around them one last chance to bloom.

"Aside from the beautiful scenery, is there a specific reason why we're out here?" Camille asked.

Andy sat forward with his elbows on his knees. He clasped his hands together to prevent them from shaking. "Less ears out here. No one who has visited from your company has ever felt comfortable having a meeting in there. I wanted to respect your need for privacy."

Camille nodded like she knew exactly what he was talking about. "I appreciate that." Then after a short silence: "So you know why I'm here."

Andy rested his back against the bench and crossed his legs. "Actually I don't. I figured that after Mr. Richmond terminated our contract and made us sign those amended confidentiality agreements, our association was over."

Camille's mind was suddenly lost in a scramble, but she was intent on keeping up appearances. "Let's just say I'm here for a quick follow up, like an exit interview." She silently cursed herself for not coming up with something better.

"An exit interview?" Andy clearly wasn't buying it either.

Camille decided it best not to belabor the point. "Am I the only executive from Horis and Roth that you've had contact with since your contract was terminated?"

"As far as I know, yes."

"And when was the last time you spoke with Mr. Richmond?"

Andy paused to search his memory. "Four or five months ago I guess. He came into the office to personally beta-test the program. We had to clear everybody out before he came. Called more attention to himself than he needed to if you ask me. But he was happy with the results. The next conversation I had with someone from Horis and Roth was with one of Mr. Richmond's liaisons over the phone. The guy didn't even tell me his name. Two weeks later a lawyer shows up telling me that the project has been terminated. Then he hands me a briefcase full of documents to sign. But I'm sure you know this already."

"I'm simply interested in hearing things from your perspective, Mr. Rosario."

Andy sighed loudly. "If you're here to see if I or any of my remaining staff have violated our confidentiality agreements, I promise you we haven't. I can't speak for the majority of the staff that had to be let go after our contract was taken away. But I'm sure they're understandably disgruntled, so who knows if they've talked to anyone or not."

"I'm not interested in confidentiality agreements."

Andy's eyes narrowed with confusion. "Then what exactly are you interested in?"

Camille took a deep breath, fully aware that it was time to end the game of charades. "The specifics of your work on the project."

"Okay, now I'm really confused. Why would you need me to talk specifics about a project that your company is no longer interested in?"

"Because I'm not actually with Horis and Roth."

Andy's eyes widened. "What are you talking abou-"

"I need you to listen to me very carefully. I know all about the Ace Project and what its publicly-stated goals were. I also know it was Horis and Roth Limited, not the city of Denver that actually financed the project. The vast majority of the public is completely unaware that Horis and Roth Limited even exists, let alone that Elliott Richmond, the mayor's husband, is its chairman and CEO. Now I'm assuming there's a very good reason why the company has kept its operations secret from the public. How they've managed to do so is another story. I don't expect you to tell me that. What I do expect you to tell me is how this fledgling technology firm of yours with no significant track record managed to make a deal with such a company?"

Andy's face stiffened and his chest swelled. False bravado. "Maybe you should start by telling me who you are and why you have the right to come into my place of business and ask these kinds of questions?"

Camille sighed. She really didn't want to fight with this guy, even though his resistance was warranted. She would have to dig deep to find the tact necessary to keep the conversation constructive. "Before I tell you who I am, please know that I'm not interested in getting you or your company in any kind of trouble. I respect the fact that you signed a confidentiality agreement, and in most cases I'm in favor of honoring such an agreement. But something very bad happened to someone very close to me, and it happened, in my opinion, because of her knowledge of this project."

The hard edges in Andy's face suddenly softened. "Who are you talking about?"

"Do you know Julia Leeds?"

His eyes lit up with instant recognition. "Of course. Her name has been all over the news."

"Did you know her before she was all over the news?"

Camille's question was met with silence.

"Andy?"

"She was in here a couple of times."

"Did Elliott Richmond ever accompany her?"

"Once. Her second trip I believe. But I really can't talk about what she did while she was here or even why she was here. If anyone from Horis and Roth even knew that I was talking to you…"

"To hell with the confidentiality agreement, Andy. She was murdered. Do you understand that? A man who had nothing to do with that murder is about to be charged with it, while the person responsible, the person you're trying to protect with your confidentiality agreement, is going to get away with it!"

So much for tact.

Andy's mouth quivered. "Are you with the police?"

"No."

"Then what's your interest in this?"

Camille took a deep breath. "Julia accumulated a series of documents shortly before her death that detailed Elliott Richmond's work on the Ace Project; work that Julia had serious misgivings about. She had collected this information with the intent of making it public. When she was murdered, the documents came into my possession with the specific request that I carry out what she couldn't. And I intend to do exactly that. But first I need to know everything there is to know about the project. As I've said, my issue is not with you or your company. Even though I'm not currently in law enforcement, I know a lot of people who are. So if the fear of violating your agreement is all that is holding you back, don't worry about that. If it ever comes down to it, I'll make sure you're protected."

"Will you and your law enforcement friends also be there to make sure I don't end up like Julia Leeds?"

The genuine fear in Andy's voice stopped Camille cold. It wasn't until then that she fully realized what she was asking this young man to do. The story that he had to tell was of vital interest to her, but the admission would not only put his business at risk, it would put his life at risk. Camille knew she hadn't been as sensitive to that as she needed to be.

"I realize that you don't know me from a hole in the wall. But on my life I will do everything I can to make sure nothing happens to you."

Andy buried his face in his hands and kept it there for a long time. Camille sat in silence, understanding what the moment meant for him. Though there was no way to know which direction his thoughts would take him, she feared that he would ask her to leave;

convinced that discovering the truth about who ended Julia's life was not worth the risk to his own. The longer he sat there, the greater her fear became. It all but evaporated when he lifted his head and looked resolutely into her eyes.

"The fact that Horis and Roth was a company that none of us had ever heard of was a major red flag, as was the fact that the mayor's husband was spearheading the project," Andy began. "But it was the biggest contract our company had ever signed, and the potential payout beyond the contract's expiration was entirely too much to pass up. Plus, this was ground-breaking stuff they were talking about. Integrating the voting process with social media. It seemed like a no-brainer, especially because these politicians are always talking about how much they value the young vote. Yet no one else had taken this radical a step. We would have been the first. And if the project was successful, it would have been the model for every other state in the country. Needless to say we couldn't have been more excited."

"So what led to your contract with Horis and Roth being terminated?"

Andy shrugged. "Good question. It came completely out of the blue. Like I said, Mr. Richmond seemed happy with the way the project was coming together and anytime he didn't like something we were always open to his changes. But then there came a point when the communication between he and I broke down. I put in numerous calls to his assistant but she would always claim that he was unavailable. I even called Brown, Wallace, and Epstein in the hopes of at least reaching Julia Leeds. But I didn't have any luck with her either. Then we started experiencing problems with the program itself. There were databases that I created that I suddenly no longer had access to. We found out later that all of the encryption codes had been changed from a remote location, which essentially took away our programming and editing ability. That was when I really started to question what Elliott Richmond's true motives were." Andy paused to take a drink from a bottle of water.

It trembled in his hand. "There were certain details about the project that we were never told about, and we were okay with that. But when they began restricting our access, it felt like they were hiding much bigger things."

"And what do you think they were hiding?"

"I started thinking about things logically and asked myself why would the campaign manager of the city's mayor and current U.S. Senate candidate be interested in financing a new technology that promised to revolutionize the way people voted? And why would he choose to keep his involvement in the project a secret? Well, the obvious conflict of interest is the answer to the second question. As far as the first, the only reasoning that made sense was that Elliott Richmond wanted to create this technology so he could manipulate it. And what reason would a man whose wife is in the middle of a major election have to manipulate such technology?"

Andy's silence indicated that he had thrown the question back at Camille. Fortunately she already knew the answer. "Rigging that election."

"Yep. And this is the perfect avenue through which to attempt such a thing. A brand new technology, little regulation, especially considering that he'd probably bought off the entire Clerk and Recorder's office, and not a single hanging Chad for anyone to analyze."

"Were you able to find any proof to support that?"

"Had I not been frozen out of almost every file connected to the project I probably could have collected something."

"Did you communicate your suspicion to anyone else?"

"Not to anyone here. But I had some questions for the good folks at Horis and Roth. Unfortunately, I only got as far as Elliott Richmond's unnamed liaison. Two weeks later, our contract was a vapor trail in the clouds. One month after that, a staff of twenty-eight dwindled to five. It completely decimated us. And since we haven't been offered a single contract since, who knows how long the rest of us will last."

"I'm truly sorry about that," Camille offered, genuinely meaning it.

"There are a lot of smart people here, so I'm sure everyone will land on their feet. Still sucks the way it all went down though. I guess that's the price you pay for making a deal with the devil, huh?"

Camille nodded.

"You know, I didn't recognize you at first," Andy said, breaking the silence that had momentarily settled over them. "I really did think you were an executive from Horis and Roth, albeit a casually dressed one." His smile was genuine for the first time. "But as soon as you mentioned Julia Leeds and your connection to law enforcement, it all came together. I suppose it helped that you actually told me your name. Felt like a major-league idiot that I didn't pick up on it sooner."

Camille couldn't help but feel uncomfortable. "Frankly, I'm surprised you didn't run in the other direction."

"It was actually the only reason I opened up." After a long pause he added: "I am sorry about Julia."

"Thank you."

"You mentioned before that you thought her death was connected to this project, and by extension, to Elliott Richmond."

"That's right."

"Did she say that in the documents you mentioned? The ones she intended to make public?"

"I really can't get into the specifics of it. All I can tell you for now is that you've been very helpful to me."

Andy took a deep breath. "And that part about you protecting me should it come down to that?"

"I meant it, Andy."

"Something tells me it's going to come down to that."

Camille agreed, though she couldn't bring herself to say it.

"As far as I'm concerned, Springwell Technologies doesn't have anything to hide," Andy confidently declared. "So if I have to tell this story again, I will. Should I expect the police to show up at our door after you leave?"

"Let's just say that for now I'm an army of one."

Andy extended his hand. "In that case, I only have one thing to say, and I mean this with a little bit of concern and a whole lot of sincerity. Good luck."

Camille shook his hand, satisfied that she had gotten everything she came here for. Now that she had, she knew what her next move had to be. She also knew that it was Elliott Richmond, not her, who would need a healthy dose of good luck.

.

CHAPTER 36

COUNSEL FOR THE DEFENSE

The sight of Stephen Clemmons in handcuffs was as surreal as anything that Detective Sullivan had seen in her short law enforcement career. But judging by the looks of satisfaction on the faces of Graham and the three others who were assembled for Clemmons' first interrogation as an official suspect, hers was the minority opinion.

The three men, all of whom would be watching the question and answer session from an adjacent room via closed-circuit monitor, were Lieutenant Hitchcock, Commander Oliver Brandt, and Denver PD Chief P.J Connolly. Hitchcock was the only one of the three who had done any actual leg work on the case. His stake in this interview was personal. Brandt and Connolly, on the other hand, were merely figureheads whose presence was meant to give the proceedings more weight and legitimacy than they actually deserved. In Sullivan's mind they had no business being here. She was probably alone in that opinion as well.

The five of them huddled outside the interview room while Clemmons waited by himself inside. "I'm assuming he's retained counsel?" Chief Connolly asked the group. A transplant from Philadelphia where he served as the city's police commissioner for eleven years, Connolly's three years as Denver's top cop had been defined by his constant struggle to gain the confidence of the rank and file. Everything from his six-foot-five, two hundred and sixty pound frame, to the baritone voice that was peppered with his native Boston accent, screamed east coast bluster; and his abrasive, unapproachable style rubbed most in the department the wrong way. Even Detective Graham felt uncomfortable in his company. But he was Mayor Richmond's most prized appointee, and as long as he stayed securely tucked inside her hip pocket, it didn't matter one bit that ninety-five percent of his subordinates despised him.

"From what I understand he has. We're just not sure who it is or where the hell they are," Graham offered.

Sullivan noticed that his normally tight short sleeve pastel shirts were a little roomier these days, while the circles around his pale blue eyes were a little bit darker. Graham was never one to take care of himself with exercise or a proper diet, so she doubted his emaciated appearance had anything to do with a sudden lifestyle change. The Leeds case had affected him more than he cared to admit. The pressure for a swift resolution was unrelenting, and from the beginning, Graham seemed intent on shouldering the responsibility for that resolution all by himself. Now that the resolution he so enthusiastically lobbied for appeared imminent, Graham looked like a man who, physically at least, had nothing left to give.

"Rumor has it that one of the attorneys at Brown, Wallace, and Epstein is representing him," Hitchcock said, the bags under his eyes even more pronounced than Graham's.

"You've got to be kidding me," Commander Brandt cried.

Aside from his high profile position as the Chief's right hand and his rock-solid reputation as a tactical planner, Sullivan knew very little about Brandt. His day to day responsibilities centered on the SWAT and gang units and he rarely interacted personally with the detectives in homicide. Were it not for Lieutenant Hitchcock briefing him prior to this meeting, Sullivan felt confident that Brandt wouldn't have even known her name.

"As I said, that's the rumor," Hitchcock reiterated.

"I guess we'll find out, if the douche bag ever shows," Graham said with a sneer.

Almost on cue, a good-looking kid with a long, purposeful stride and a perfectly tailored pin-striped suit approached them. He couldn't have been any older than thirty, but as he met the collective stares of the city's police chief and his four cohorts, he displayed the self-assurance of a man who was infinitely more battle-tested. He bypassed everyone, including the Chief, and extended his hand to Graham.

"Detective Graham, I believe we've met before. I'm Matthew Westerly from Brown, Wallace, and Epstein. You questioned me last week about Stephen Clemmons' association with Julia Leeds."

Graham's sneer went away as he shook the attorney's hand. "I do remember you, Mr. Westerly. As a matter of fact, I was meaning to call you to say thanks. You're statement was quite helpful in getting us to this point." The sarcasm in his voice was thick.

"I'm glad you think so. But as far as I can tell, it's that kind of circumstantial testimony that your case against Mr. Clemmons is predicated on. And if that truly is all you have, then his time in custody will be a lot shorter than you've led the public to believe."

"Our evidence is far from circumstantial, Mr. Westerly," Commander Brandt chided.

Sullivan shook her head. What the hell did he know about Clemmons or the evidence against him? "I'm Detective Sullivan," she said as she extended her hand to Westerly. "This is Commander Oliver Brandt and DPD Chief P.J. Connolly."

"In case you were wondering," a seemingly offended Connolly barked.

"I know who you all are," Westerly responded to the group, though his eyes were still locked on Graham.

"Then why don't you extend us the same courtesy, Mr. Westerly?" Sullivan asked in a polite tone she hoped would bring some measure back to the conversation.

"I've been retained as Mr. Clemmons' legal counsel."

Though Sullivan knew as much the instant she saw him, the look of astonishment on her face was difficult to mask. It was a look shared by the others in the group, most especially Graham. Sullivan could see the wheels turning in his mind as he tried to formulate a response. But it didn't matter what Graham said, because he knew the same thing all of them did: Matthew Westerly's presence was also a proclamation by Brown, Wallace, and Epstein of their belief in Stephen Clemmons' innocence. And that meant the case against him suddenly got a lot weaker.

"Now, as nice as this little meet and greet has been, I suspect my client is sitting in that interview room all by himself, and I'd like to spend a few moments with him before the interview."

Graham nodded at Connolly, Brandt and Hitchcock, and the three men made their way to the room where they were set up to watch Clemmons. Connolly glared at Westerly as he walked past, but the attorney, still eager to prove his mettle, didn't flinch.

"Right this way." Sullivan pointed to the closed door in front of them.

Westerly was the first to enter the room, with Graham and Sullivan close behind. Graham was halfway through the door before Westerly's outstretched arm stopped him.

"I need to be alone with my client, please. And make sure they mute the audio feed until we're done."

Graham said nothing as he backed up enough to allow Westerly to close the door.

The rush of adrenaline created by Westerly's arrival suddenly ebbed and Sullivan felt the need to sit. Graham, meanwhile, paced in front of the door with the pent-up energy of a boxer confined to his corner in the anxious final seconds before the bell sounded.

"How are you doing Walt?" Sullivan asked, already knowing the answer.

Graham shook his head. "These scumbags have the audacity to represent the man who murdered a partner in their own firm? What a joke."

But it wasn't a joke. The impenetrable armor that was the case against Stephen Clemmons just showed its first major crack. And Sullivan knew, just as she had always known, that there were many more cracks still to be exposed.

I told you so was the only thing she could think to say in response. But she wisely concluded that frosty silence was much more appropriate to the situation

.

CHAPTER 37

FORCING THE ISSUE

Westerly's apparent strategy had been to put the two detectives on the defensive as quickly as he could. Thirty minutes into the interrogation, it became painfully obvious to everyone involved that his strategy was working.

"I apologize if I'm a little slow on the uptake," Westerly said as he combed through his notes with a feigned look of confusion. "But I'm trying my best to understand this. Your witness is awakened in the middle of the night by loud music, looks outside his window, and supposedly sees my client's car in front of Julia Leeds's house. The car idles there for upwards of two minutes with music blaring, before it finally drives off. Now, aside from the fact that the witness, according to his own initial statement, didn't get a good enough look at the car to accurately describe the color, he also couldn't provide a license plate number or a description of the driver. Am I right so far?"

Graham seethed, but was otherwise quiet.

"You're correct," Sullivan reluctantly answered for him. Her cell phone buzzed inside her jacket pocket. She quickly silenced it.

"So did it ever strike either of you as odd that Mr. Clemmons would drive to the victim's house, theoretically to kill her, and then announce his arrival to the entire neighborhood with this loud music before he could even accomplish his objective?"

"It certainly struck me as odd," Graham sharply responded. "Stupid actually. But in my line of work I see people do stupid things on a daily basis. Maybe your client can better explain it."

Clemmons rolled his eyes. "I can't explain it since I wasn't there."

"There you go, detective. My client wasn't there."

"Give me a break. I could have my witness here within the hour. Let's see what happens when he gets a look at your client in person."

Westerly smiled. "You do that, Detective Graham. While you're at it, tell your witness to bring the video of Mr. Clemmons entering Julia's house, because absent that, a grand jury will laugh you right out of the courtroom."

Clemmons leaned in toward Westerly. "Did you tell them about the starter?"

"The what?" Sullivan asked.

"Detective Graham, I understand that you took pictures of my client's car after you and Detective Sullivan visited his house."

"That's right, as did the CSI techs the day of Julia's murder."

"Did you take pictures of the interior?"

Graham hesitated before answering. "Not that I recall. Why?"

"Because on the morning after Julia's murder, shortly after patrol officers from the DPD visited his house for the first time, my client came out to his car to discover that the ignition housing had been busted and a screwdriver inserted in the starter. It hadn't been that way when he came home from work the previous evening."

Sullivan's eyes narrowed. "Are you telling us your car was stolen, Mr. Clemmons?"

Clemmons looked at her with the same pleading expression he gave her as she left his house. "It had to have been. No other explanation."

Sullivan turned to Graham. "Was there any mention of this in the evidence summary?"

Graham laughed. "So you're telling us that someone stole your car while you were sleeping? And this person's joyriding expedition just happened to take them to Julia Leeds's house the night she was killed? Is that the official defense?" He looked at Westerly, then at Sullivan. "Why am I the only one laughing at this?"

"Because the rest of us understand that it isn't a laughing matter," Westerly said.

Graham rubbed his temples, his laughter giving way to frustration. "Someone steals your car, makes a stop at the victim's house less than two hours before the medical examiner speculates she was murdered, then parks the car back in front of your house the next morning without you having any knowledge that it was gone. Yeah, I'd say that's a real laugh riot."

"Before you impounded the car, did you dust the interior for prints?" Westerly asked with a sigh.

"Standard procedure," Sullivan answered. "The only driver's side prints that came up belonged to Mr. Clemmons." She was prepared to continue when the vibration of her cell phone stopped her. This time she pulled it out of her pocket and checked the number. Her breath caught when she saw the name Camille Grisham flash across the screen.

"Why didn't you mention any of this when we first talked?" Graham asked Clemmons.

Sullivan held her breath as she waited for a voicemail notification. There wasn't one.

"Would you have believed me if I did?" Clemmons shot back.

Graham leaned back in his chair and smirked.

Clemmons nodded. "That's why I didn't tell you."

"It would have been in your best interest to do so," Sullivan said, putting her cell phone back in her pocket. "It isn't up to you to determine what useful evidence is and what it isn't. Had you told us right away, we would have had more time to pursue any relevant leads related to your car, provided there were any."

Graham rolled his eyes. "Please, Chloe. You and I both know there weren't."

"And that closed-minded attitude has been your problem, detective," Westerly charged.

"And stupid conspiracy theories have been yours, counselor."

Sullivan raised her hand and was preparing to make a plea for calm when her cell phone vibrated for a third time. When she saw Camille's name yet again, she could no longer ignore it. "I'm sorry, Walt. I have to take this."

Graham's eyes grew wide. "Right now? Who is it?"

Sullivan left Graham's question hanging in the air and silently excused herself from the room.

She hit the redial button as soon as she stepped outside. Camille answered on the first ring.

"Detective Sullivan?"

"Yes, it's me."

"I'm glad you called back. I apologize for blowing up your cell phone, but I had to reach you."

"Well that's pretty obvious. I had to walk out of an interview with Stephen Clemmons and his attorney, so this had better be important."

Sullivan could hear Camille's breathing deepen.

"It is, even more so now that I know where you just were. We both know that you're holding the wrong man in custody. You may not have believed in my theory about Richmond, but I'm telling you he is the one responsible, and I have more proof now than when I last saw you."

Camille was wrong to think that she didn't believe her. "Explain what you mean by proof."

Camille hesitated. "Granted, I haven't uncovered a smoking gun yet. But I've certainly discovered more of what may have motivated him to do it. And his extramarital affair with her was only part of it."

"What was the other part of it?"

"Have you ever heard of Horis and Roth Limited?"

"No."

"Neither has most of the public. But it is a rather large investment capital firm that is headed by someone you have heard of."

"Elliott Richmond," Sullivan said without having to think about it.

"Exactly. The Schumann Investment Group, the company that Julia referenced in her letter, is merely a public front for Horis and Roth. Schumann, i.e. Horis and Roth, was Julia's largest client. Through her work with the firm, and ultimately Elliott Richmond, she got involved in a project that was publicly initiated by the Denver Clerk and Recorder's office, but was privately financed by Richmond. It involved the use of email, fax, and social media as a way for people to cast votes in the upcoming election. It wouldn't take a rocket scientist to figure out what Richmond's true motives were in helping to develop such technology. When Julia figured out those motives, she planned to make as much of it public as she could. That explains why she complained so vehemently about work but refused to go into specific details. She was scared out of her mind, Detective Sullivan. And now that I understand what she was up against, I completely understand why."

Sullivan's mind suddenly felt overloaded and she had to take a moment to let it clear. "How did you come upon all of this?"

"That's not really important right now. What is important is what I've done with it."

Sullivan felt a knot in her stomach. She didn't know where this was going, but she knew she wasn't going to like it. "And what did you do with it?"

"Since my trip to the detective bureau was largely ineffective, the only other option I had was to go directly to the source."

"Please tell me you don't mean Elliott Richmond."

"That's exactly who I mean."

The knot in Sullivan's stomach rose into her chest. "What did you do?"

"I merely paid a visit to his wife's campaign headquarters, the same as any other citizen has the right to do."

"You aren't any other citizen, Camille. What were you thinking?"

"I needed him to know who I was and what I knew about him. All I did was talk, nothing more. But it wasn't as productive as I would have liked."

"You mean you didn't frighten him into a confession," Sullivan scoffed.

"I wasn't naïve enough to think that would happen. But I was hoping to at least rattle him a little bit. Unfortunately I didn't have much luck with that either. So I figured I needed to force the issue."

"Force the issue?"

Camille's prolonged silence frightened Sullivan more than anything she could have actually said. When Camille finally did speak, she only said seven words, but those words managed to render everything else – Clemmons' interrogation, Matthew Westerly, the cracks in Graham's iron-clad case – totally irrelevant.

"I sent a package to the mayor."

CHAPTER 38

GRACE UNDER FIRE

If one word came to define Sonya Richmond's existence, it would be balance. During the course of a typical eighteen-hour workday, she was forced to wear many different hats. Sometimes she needed to switch those hats at a moment's notice; sometimes she needed to wear five of them at once. For a woman who earned the media nickname 'Grace' because of her uncanny ability to stay level-headed even under the most intense situations, the juggling act was easy.

But there were days when the mayor's grace was severely tested. And today was proving to be the toughest test of all.

It began with a contentious town hall meeting in Denver's Five Points Neighborhood, a historically African-American subdivision whose social and economic make up had undergone a radical, and unwelcomed, transformation due to its recent gentrification. Residents who called the Five Points home for decades were now being squeezed out in droves because of increased property taxes and greedy land developers who believed that multi-unit lofts and trendy coffee shops were worth more to the neighborhood than the homes those proud people raised their children in. The residents who attended the town hall were mostly black, over sixty, and fed up with a city and a mayor they felt had systematically disenfranchised them. When Sonya was sworn in, she took the oath to represent everyone. And for the most part she upheld that oath. But that didn't mean she could solve everyone's problems in the fashion they needed her to. Despite the daily toll of life as a sitting mayor and active U.S. Senate candidate, Sonya wore the stress well. She easily looked ten years younger than her actual age of fifty-two, and the smile that many had called the softest, most disarming they had ever seen was always on display, always ready to diffuse any situation, always employed with the intent of winning over even her most ardent critics – and she had plenty of those. But when the Five Points residents began throwing words at her like 'racist' and 'corrupt' and 'hypocrite', she knew there wouldn't be a smile in the world pretty enough to win them over.

Things weren't much better at the Denver Chamber of Commerce Business Awards luncheon she attended a couple of hours later. In addition to the opportunity to spread the message of her campaign to yet another audience, she was slated to receive a special recognition for her long-standing commitment to small business development. Her husband Elliott was supposed to present her with the honor, but when the time came, Elliott was nowhere to be found. Sonya's communications director was forced to fill in at the last minute. When Elliott showed up some forty-five minutes after she received the award, he had no explanation and seemingly felt no remorse. His demeanor was as cold and distant as Sonya had ever seen it. She would have actually been worried about him had she not been so upset. Elliott's mood could change on a dime, and in their twenty-six years of marriage, Sonya had come to know those moods and what could trigger them better than she knew her own. But there was no accounting for his attitude today. Her first fear was that it was campaign related. But beyond his repeated assurances that it wasn't, she was left with no other explanation.

So she let it go, as she had done so many times before. Sonya was never one to shy away from a political battle, whether it was with the city council, the local unions, or the state attorney general who doubled as her senate campaign opponent. But the personal battles were always difficult to handle. As a career manager, Elliott was an invaluable partner and highly trusted advisor. As a father, he was demanding, yet deeply committed. As a husband, he was physically and emotionally vacant. Sonya was well aware of the reasons why. There had been other women throughout their marriage. He had admitted to a couple of them, wrongly assuming that all the others were a secret.

Julia Leeds was one he hadn't admitted to, but Sonya knew about their relationship almost from the moment it began, though the extent of that relationship didn't become clear to her until this evening.

Now, as she sat in her home office, still reeling from the video image of Julia engaging her husband in the most intimate ways imaginable, Sonya was hit with the bleak realization that the personal battle she was about to embark on would be by far the most difficult of her life.

The flash disk had been delivered to her office at the City and County Building via courier a couple of hours earlier, along with a note explaining its contents: *Summary of Schumann Investment Group 2013 Board of Directors meeting ~ Attention Sonya Richmond*. The disk was passed on to Sonya by her assistant after assurances that it had been thoroughly scanned for viruses and other potential malware.

As a significant stakeholder in Schumann Investments, she was used to receiving such summaries on a regular basis, so she thought nothing of it as she put the disk in her briefcase and brought it home.

With her two children at soccer and field-hockey practice, and Elliott unaccounted for since they left the Chamber luncheon, Sonya had decided to squeeze in a few fundraising calls before her future United States Senator hat would need to be replaced with the mother/chef/tutor hat that she did her best to wear with pride every night.

It was during a break between calls that she took out the disk for what she thought would be a quick once-over. Sonya knew how wrong her thought was the instant she inserted the disk. There were hundreds of files pertaining to the Schumann Investment Group, Brown, Wallace, and Epstein, Springwell Technologies, and the Denver Clerk and Recorder's office. But it was the movie file that immediately caught her attention. The title of the file: '*My Final Night with Elliott*' conjured up the worst fears imaginable. And within seconds of opening the file, Sonya's worst fears were confirmed.

Beyond the primal devastation that came from watching her husband having sex with another woman, a woman who was now dead, what bothered Sonya the most were the words the two of them exchanged afterward. Even though their words were filled with venom, and in Julia's case, hatred, there was also passion behind them that had long been absent in Sonya's own marriage. Watching the argument infused her with a feeling of jealousy that both enraged and mystified her. But it was the last words that Elliott spoke before he walked out of Julia's bedroom that truly frightened her. "*There will definitely be regrets at the end of all this, but they won't be mine.*"

The attention that Julia Leeds's murder received bordered on excessive, and though no one in the media was aware of her business connections to Elliott, Sonya was still forced to answer questions regarding the investigation. Based on the regular updates she had received from Police Chief Connolly, she knew that they had a suspect in mind almost from the beginning, and as of today that suspect was in custody. With her mind focused on issues infinitely more important than who killed Julia Leeds, she accepted the direction of the department's investigation and publicly praised Chief Connolly for a job well done. But Sonya had always found it odd that Elliott had never once spoken about Julia's murder, even though she was his firm's lead counsel. As such, she would be as intimately involved in his business dealings as anyone else, and her loss undoubtedly had a tremendous impact on him. Yet, her death was seemingly nothing more than a news story to him, and any news story that didn't directly involve the campaign was of no consequence.

Guilt about the affair was the reason Sonya came up with to explain this. But after seeing the video and viewing a number of the other documents on the disk – documents about a project that only she, Elliott, and a few select others were supposed to know about – Sonya began to suspect something else altogether. The thought took her mind to very dark places. But the most terrifying thing of all was that none of what she suspected surprised her in the least. Elliott was a powerful man capable of great good. But his need for power was insatiable, and as he had shown Sonya in a variety of ways over the years, should anything arise that he perceived to be a threat to his power, he would abandon everything, including his own morals, in order to neutralize that threat.

Based on what she just saw, Julia Leeds was a threat. And Elliott neutralized her.

The disk and its contents were the obvious reason why. What wasn't obvious was where the disk came from, if Elliott knew of its continued existence, or how it ended up in her hands. There was no note aside from the Board of Directors cover. If it was sent to her, it was no doubt sent to her opponent, and probably every media outlet in the city. And if that were the case, she would be powerless to stop it. The only option she had was to employ a spin control campaign the likes of which the world had never seen. She had the resources to do so. All she needed to do now was summon the will. She was on the cusp of achieving something that she had worked her entire professional life for, but the existence of this disk promised to destroy not only her senate campaign, but her entire life. She was not about to let that happen, either to herself or her children. If she and Elliott still had one thing in common, it was that insatiable need for power, and the ability to abandon everything – including your spouse of twenty-six years – in order to preserve it.

She had considered calling his cell phone, but ultimately thought it a useless gesture. Nothing he could say would change the situation or make her feel any better about it. Instead, she put the disk back in her briefcase and made another phone call. Just as she finished the ten-minute conversation, she heard a key in the front door, followed by the sounds of random teenage chatter.

"Hey you two," she said with a manufactured smile as her daughter Miranda and son Owen stood in the office doorway.

"Mom, would you please tell your child that I'm just as capable of driving us home as she is? You and dad got that car for both of us," a newly licensed Owen told his mother.

Miranda, eighteen and clearly above it all, rolled her eyes at her younger brother. "It's bad enough that I have to wait for you forty minutes after my practice ends. Now you want me to let you drive so we can both end up wrapped around a telephone pole? You are beyond clueless."

"Unbelievable. Mom—"

Sonya cut off her son's protest before it could start. "I'm a politician, which means I've mastered the art of compromise. So why don't you guys get changed, I'll start dinner, and we'll come up with a solution that works for the both of you."

Miranda sighed while Owen hoisted his muddy soccer cleats on his shoulder. They mumbled insults to each other as they walked out of the office.

A typical night in the Richmond household had suddenly become far from typical. But her children couldn't know that. And right now, neither could Elliott. Fortunately, the mom hat that she changed into this time every night fit as snugly as ever.

The faithful, understanding, overly-tolerant wife hat, however, would be a much different story.

.

CHAPTER 39

OFFICER DAVIES

Detective Graham could not help but feel good about himself, despite Matthew Westerly, his ties to Brown, Wallace, and Epstein, and his enthusiastic, yet misguided, belief in his client's innocence. He knew in the end that it didn't matter what Matthew Westerly thought. The entire police department stood behind Graham's assertion that Clemmons was guilty. And that belief was all that the public would need to ultimately convict him, circumstantial evidence and all. Stephen Clemmons was a nobody, a black nobody at that. Matthew Westerly couldn't find a jury anywhere who would take his client's side, even if the senior partners at his grand old law firm selected them personally.

As he made the short walk from his desk to Commander Brandt's office, the same Commander Brandt he had made a frantic phone call to only a short time earlier, Graham tried to convince himself that he wasn't looking for a pat on the back. But he knew that he was deserving of one. He had steered the investigation exactly as the commander had asked, never once revealing even a hint of his objective to his partner, the lieutenant, or anyone else. Even with the curveball that was Camille Grisham, Graham kept his head, and his focus. And because of that, the public would rest easier thinking that Julia Leeds' murderer was behind bars, the mayor would commend him for a job well done, and someone with a vast amount of power would owe him a very big favor.

Before today, Graham had no idea who that someone was. When he was initially approached by Commander Brandt, he was told first and foremost not to ask any questions. So he didn't. As a member of the Army Rangers, he was well versed in the standards of protocol and chain of command: you do your job and only your job, you never question orders, and you never worry about the larger meaning of it all. And Graham didn't worry. Commander Brandt ensured that he was well-compensated for his efforts. His retirement nest egg was considerably larger, and his spotty personnel file was suddenly blemish-free. All he needed to say was a silent 'thank you' to the man he now knew to be ultimately responsible, and not give him, Julia Leeds, or Camille Grisham's computer disk another thought.

The door to Commander Brandt's office was ajar, and inside he could see Brandt and what looked like a uniformed officer huddled in quiet conversation. When Graham knocked on the door, the two men quickly separated and Brandt rushed toward him. He yanked the door open, greeting Graham with a look he could only describe as irritated.

"Can I help you?" he asked, as if Graham were a door to door salesman who had interrupted his dinner.

Graham was taken aback by his tone and at first didn't know how to reply.

The commander's round, pale face was suddenly infused with red. "What do you want, detective? I'm in the middle of a meeting."

The uniformed officer, who Graham now recognized as Patrick Davies, stared at him with the same irritated look as Brandt.

"I need to talk to you," Graham finally said. "It's about the Clemmons interview."

"It's not a good time, Walter."

"How can it not be a good time, sir?" Graham asked with genuine confusion.

"Because there are much more important things going on right now."

"Are you kidding me? What could possibly be more important to anyone in this department than Stephen Clemmons?"

Brandt shook his head as he looked back at Davies.

"What the hell does he have to do with anything?" Graham asked, pointing at the officer.

Davies' hard stare didn't waver.

"As I said, we have other business to attend to right now. If you want you can schedule a meeting with me sometime this evening or tomorrow morning. "

Now Graham was the one who was irritated. "Schedule a meeting with you? Look, if you're still upset about that Camille Grisham thing, I don't think it's anything we need to worry about any—"

Brandt sighed as he pushed the door closed. "Goodbye Walter."

Graham put a hand up to stop the door. "Goddamn it, Oliver. You can't just dismiss me like that. After everything I've done, I deserve a few minutes."

Before Brandt could even respond, Officer Davies rushed to the door and slammed it in Graham's face.

The detective was too stunned to move. From behind the door, he heard voices, though he couldn't hear what they were saying. Had it been anyone other than Commander Brandt, he would have stormed the office door and demanded answers. But doing so would probably cost him a lot more than his badge. So he waited. In less than a minute, the door swung open, and Officer Davies blew past Graham like he wasn't even there. Graham immediately turned to give chase, but a heavy hand stopped him.

"Don't think about it, Walter."

Graham's eyes burned with a fury that he did nothing to suppress. "Who does that cocksucker think he is?"

Brandt simply stared at him.

Graham fought the urge to punch him in the face. "You're just going to let him get away with doing that to me?"

"At this point I'm not particularly worried about it."

"Did I just step into Bizarro World or something? What the hell is this all about?"

"Something that doesn't involve you."

"Now all of a sudden things don't involve me? Stephen Clemmons is sitting in that holding cell right now because of me. I get that done and now I'm not of any use to you anymore?"

Brandt's doughy face suddenly contorted with anger. "I suggest you watch yourself, Walter. What's happening now is of no concern to you whatsoever. I don't know how many different ways I have to tell you that."

"But it's of concern to Officer Davies?"

Brandt walked back into his office. "I don't have time to sooth your hurt feelings, detective. As I said before, if you want to talk another time, email a meeting request." With that, Brandt closed the door.

Graham was in the process of raising his hand to pound on it when a voice stopped him.

"What's going on Walter?"

Graham turned to see Detective Sullivan approaching. He couldn't help but roll his eyes.

"What were you and the commander talking about?"

"Nothing," he mumbled.

"Well, I need to talk to you."

"About what?"

"Camille Grisham."

"I don't need to hear one word about Camille Grisham."

"It's important, Walter."

"No it is not." Graham tried to walk past her but she stopped him. "Take your hand off me, Chloe."

She promptly complied. The concern in her eyes was palpable, but Graham couldn't worry about explaining. He walked away without saying another word. At that moment he couldn't have cared less about Camille Grisham or his soon-to-be ex-partner. He had one objective and one objective only: find Officer Patrick Davies and put him in his place.

CHAPTER 40

FAR AND AWAY

Sullivan's first thought was to go to Lieutenant Hitchcock's office to voice her concerns about Graham's behavior. But the word *rat* kept echoing in her mind. She knew she wasn't a rat. She was simply worried about her partner. Sadly, Graham wouldn't see it that way. "*It always starts out with worry,*" she could hear him say. "*But it ends with you selling me out to Internal Affairs. It's touching how concerned you rats can be.*" Sullivan tried to shake Graham's voice out of her head as she raised her hand to knock on Hitchcock's door. The lieutenant never hesitated to tell her that his door was always open should she ever need him. But she suddenly realized that this meeting would mark the first time that she would actually be inside his office by herself. Every other time she had been there, it had been with Graham. Even during her first briefing the morning after she was promoted to detective, he was right by her side, whispering in her ear about the perils of working homicide, the tedious paperwork they'd routinely be bombarded with, and his enormously high expectations that she would 'beat the odds'. To this day she had no idea what odds she was supposed to beat, or if she had actually beat them.

With no one-on-one experience to draw from, it was impossible to know what Hitchcock's reaction would be to her.

The sad fact was that there wasn't a single person in the detective bureau with whom she felt comfortable enough to express her true fears about Graham. He had served with most of these guys since they were young beat cops. Even if Hitchcock shared Sullivan's concerns, his long-standing relationship with Graham meant that he would still give him the benefit of the doubt.

It was a benefit that Sullivan had yet to earn. Being the only girl in the old boy's club meant that she was already toeing a fine line. If she were to make the wrong kind of noise now, her career as a Denver homicide detective could be over before it had the chance to begin.

Standing outside Hitchcock's door, Sullivan understood for the first time just how alone she was. There were no friends. There were no after work venting sessions with the boys and a few beers. And ultimately there was no respect, at least not from Graham. She was on her own, and had been from the start.

It probably didn't help that there wasn't an ounce of blue blood running through her veins. Her father ran his own drywall business, her mother was a kindergarten school teacher, and her four brothers and sisters were all working the standard nine-to-five in one boring capacity or another. She was the first in her family who had ever considered becoming a cop. No one from the Boulder, Colorado suburb that she was born in had an interest in even seeing a gun, let alone carrying one. So the Sullivan family had a difficult time accepting Chloe's choice of profession. Ten years and three promotions later, they still did.

Press on, Chloe is what she would tell herself after every family get-together when the questions became too ridiculous and insulting to handle. *"Aren't you getting too old for this cop-thing, sweetheart? At some point you have to think about children." "Are you ever afraid that you're going to shoot yourself with that thing?"* Finding the courage to press on in the face of her resentment became more difficult each time she had to do it.

It would be difficult now too, but just like she had done so many times before, she found the courage.

Sullivan stepped away from Lieutenant Hitchcock's door. She didn't need him to intervene on her behalf. She needed to hash things out with Graham on her own. And she needed to do it right away.

After passing his empty desk, she made stops at Commander Brandt's office, the conference room, and the coffee lounge where he spent entirely too much of his day. But Graham was nowhere to be found. Confident that he had left the building, she rushed down the stairs and into the parking garage on the off-chance that she would run into him before he could drive away. When she saw him leaning against the open door of his car, she was relieved. But as she approached him, her stomach suddenly felt queasy. Unfortunately, it was a feeling she was growing accustomed to every time she saw him.

This time, however, it felt much worse.

Walking up behind him, Sullivan could see that his cell phone was pressed hard against his ear, but she didn't hear any conversation. Just as she was about to call out to him, a patrol car roared past them and out of the parking garage. When Graham saw it he shoved the phone in his coat pocket and turned around to get in his car, nearly running head-first into Sullivan as he did.

"Holy shit, Chloe. Are you trying to give me a heart attack?"

"Sorry Walt," she answered with as much calm as she could muster.

"Next time you decide to hover behind me, give a little warning."

"I didn't want to interrupt your phone call."

Graham mumbled something indecipherable and slid into the driver's seat.

"Who were you talking to?"

He started the car without answering.

"What the hell is your problem, Walter?"

Graham strapped on his seat belt, grabbed the door handle and looked up at her. "We're on opposite sides of this thing, Chloe. I only wish I had known that before I agreed to take you on in the first place."

Sullivan shook her head. "We aren't on opposite sides of anything."

He glared at her before pulling the door closed. She barely had a chance to back away before he peeled out of the parking space.

Sullivan suddenly felt frozen. She wanted to call someone, but she had no idea who to call. And even if she found someone, she wouldn't have anything substantial to tell them. Internal Affairs generally doesn't waste time investigating secretive asshole detectives who are rude to their partners.

So she did the only thing she could do.

She was in her car and out of the parking garage before she gave herself time to think about it. By the time she came to appreciate the depths of the risk she was taking, she had already caught up to Graham's car.

Of all the instincts that drove her since this investigation began, the instinct to follow him had been far and away the strongest. She gave no thought to where he would lead her. But Sullivan knew with every fabric of her being that she needed to be there.

CHAPTER 41

DÉJÀ VU

When Camille walked into the house some five hours after promising she wouldn't leave, she headed straight for her father's computer with the five blank flash disks she had picked up on her way back. Since she was only interested in copying the movie file, the transfers would only take a couple of minutes, and she was hopeful that she could make the copies and leave before he realized she had come home.

She had just inserted the first disk when she heard his voice.

"If you keep stealing my car, I may need to have you arrested," Paul said in a not so ironic voice.

"I had to go dad," Camille answered without turning around. She wanted to keep focused on her task, but she also didn't want to see the look on his face, a look that no doubt resembled disappointment. She heard his footsteps approaching.

"Do I even want to know what you did while you were out?"

"Probably not," she answered, still unable to look him in the eye. When the video was transferred onto the first disk, she inserted the second.

"And what do you plan on doing with that?" Paul asked.

"I'm taking it to the Denver field office. The special agent-in-charge is named Peter Willis. I plan on calling him in the morning."

"And the rest of the disks?"

Camille stared silently at the monitor. The floor creaked as Paul inched closer.

"I hope like hell you don't plan on confronting Richmond yourself."

Camille finally summoned the courage to turn around and look at him. The look of disappointment on his face was more profound than she could have imagined. "I'm afraid that ship has already sailed."

Paul bit down on his lip. "Christ, Camille. You promised me you wouldn't do that. What on earth were you thinking?"

"I wasn't thinking. If I had been, I would have realized from the beginning that Elliott was the wrong Richmond to go to."

"You're not even going to tell me that you—"

"I sent a copy of the video to her office."

The look of disappointment in Paul's face was suddenly replaced by something much darker. "You did what?"

"I sent it to her office," Camille calmly repeated. "But I have no way of knowing whether or not she actually got it. So to answer your question about what I'm doing with this disk, I'm on my way to deliver it to her personally. It's what I should have done in the first place."

"So it wasn't bad enough that you directly confronted Elliott Richmond. Now you're going to confront his wife? There simply aren't words to express how unbelievably foolish that is. What if her children see it?"

The shock on his face was offset by the resoluteness in hers. "That would be terrible, but it's not really my problem."

Paul walked to the computer, knelt down, and took the second disk out. "Then I guess I have to make it mine."

"What are you doing?"

"Stopping you from doing something really dangerous."

Camille's eyes burned with anger. "Give me that disk."

"Give me that one," he countered, pointing to the disk that Camille held in her hand.

"I can't just let this pass, no matter what you or anybody else has to say. One way or another Elliott Richmond is going to account for what he did. "

"Nobody is asking you to let it pass, honey. Just don't do it this way."

"Dad, we've already had this conversation."

"That's right, we have. And I'm hoping this time you'll actually listen to me."

Camille got up from the computer, still clutching the disk in her hand. "Keep the rest of them. I can make more copies whenever I need to."

She tried to walk out of the room but Paul grabbed her by the arm. She tried to break free but his grip was too strong.

"What are you doing? Let go of me."

Paul was silent as he took hold of her other arm.

Camille tried harder to pull away, but couldn't. She was about to push him in the chest when she looked into his face. What she saw made every muscle in her body go limp.

He was crying.

CHAPTER 42

BROKEN COMPASS

For the first time in recent memory, Graham was second-guessing himself. Knowing how problematic it would be to confront Davies inside police headquarters, he decided it best to wait until the officer left the building, which he did within five minutes of their encounter in Commander Brandt's office. After a lengthy wait in the parking garage, during which time he had to endure the indignity of yet another meaningless conversation with Detective Sullivan, Graham trailed Officer Davies' patrol car for over ten miles without giving it a second thought. But as he watched it pull up to the curb in front of Camille Grisham's house, he suddenly felt nervous.

The school of police work he came from was very old and the rules were very strict. The first rule was to do whatever you had to do to make it home to your family every night. The second rule was never to bring compassion with you when you walked the street. Compassion was born not only out of weakness, but out of a misguided sense that the world operated on a defined system of right and wrong. It was easy for men in ivory towers to philosophize about morality and justice. But in the world he operated in, morality was non-existent, and true justice only occurred when the accused lacked the means to buy their way out of it. The irony of the system was that there was no system. Life on the street was survival of the fittest; every man for himself and only himself. That was the credo Graham had lived by for nearly three decades, and it provided all the justification he needed for what he had done to Stephen Clemmons and countless others like him.

Clemmons was nothing more than a means to an end; a way to ensure Graham's continued survival. More importantly, he was an easy mark. Men like him were arrested every single day. Ninety-five percent of them claimed they were innocent. Clemmons was no different. And like the rest, his claim of innocence would register as less than a blip on the public's radar screen. Once they turned on their televisions and saw his picture with the caption 'suspect' underneath, they would feel confident that all was again right in their universe. In turn, they would fall all over themselves praising Graham and the department for providing the swift, sure justice that they demanded.

Stephen Clemmons was a gift.

Camille Grisham was something else entirely.

From the moment he met her outside of Julia Leeds's house, Graham saw something in Camille that worried him. Aside from the fact that she was a former FBI agent and the daughter of a cop he had the displeasure of knowing very well, there was a desperation in her eyes that was troublesome. It wasn't the kind of desperation that came from grief; it was the kind that came from an urgent need for answers. She wasn't the least bit concerned with being comforted or consoled. She wanted blood.

If Graham were thinking clearly, he would have warned Commander Brandt after that first meeting. By the time he and Sullivan interviewed Camille for the second time a few days later, it was too late.

Graham had not been aware of the 'who' behind Julia Leeds's murder until Camille showed up with a flash disk and a long list of pointed accusations. When he heard Elliott Richmond's name, he wasn't the least bit surprised. Richmond was one of the wealthiest, most well-respected men in the state. He was also the most morally bankrupt.

With his recent behavior, Graham was making a strong push for second place.

The work he did for Brandt didn't bother him, even with his knowledge of Elliot Richmond's involvement. His moral compass had been broken a long time ago, and it was entirely too late to fix it. What did bother Graham was the sudden uncertainty he felt as he sat in front of Camille Grisham's house. She may have been a potentially fatal thorn in his side, and her father may have been an uppity, self-righteous do-gooder who rubbed most everyone around him the wrong way with his idiotic idealism. But they were still cops, as was the man whom he had blindly followed here.

Graham knew little about Patrick Davies prior to this week, other than the fact that he was a young patrolman recently out of the academy with no significant track record of arrests, citations, or even traffic stops. Yet the talk around the campfire was that the top brass, from Chief Connolly and Commander Brandt on down, had him pegged as a rising star. He recalled Davies being at Julia Leeds' house during the initial investigation. In fact it was he who informed Detective Sullivan and himself of the potential witness on scene – the witness who turned out to be Camille Grisham. He also escorted Dale Rooney and his wife out of the homicide unit after their interview. Beyond that, Graham had no basis on which to form an opinion about the officer.

Until today.

He couldn't have begun to guess what Commander Brandt and Davies were meeting about, and he ultimately didn't care. All he knew was that he had never been more professionally or personally disrespected. The fact that Brandt allowed it to happen was disappointing in more ways than he could express. But he would deal with that disappointment another time. Right now his sights were set on sending a message to the rising star who had just made the biggest mistake of his young career.

THE STRATEGIST

There was one more rule of police work that Graham lived by: always protect the shield, and those who wore it, no matter what. But Graham no longer had the luxury of living by outdated codes of honor and loyalty. Just like morality and justice, those concepts were relative at best. For better or worse, his loyalty had been to the man who could end his career and his life with one call to Internal Affairs if he didn't do exactly what he was told. But with his actions today, Commander Brandt had proven that that loyalty only went one way. Graham had done what he was told, and after he collected the payout due him, he would have to seriously reconsider his role in the department, or if he would have a role at all.

But not before he dealt with Davies.

Survival of the fittest.

Graham pushed his nervousness aside as he got out of his car and walked toward Davies' parked cruiser.

Every man for himself and only himself.

He had become so focused on his own thoughts that he didn't realize Detective Sullivan had been walking behind him, shouting his name. When he finally did realize what he was seeing, he still didn't believe it.

CHAPTER 43
THE POINT OF NO RETURN

"Walter? Walter will you please answer me? What are you doing here?"

Sullivan had taken down Camille's address from the statement she had given last week. She took special note of it because she fully expected to make a trip here at some point in the near future, particularly after her revelation of the disk.

Even as she watched Graham get out of his car and walk toward the patrol cruiser parked in front of Camille's house, Sullivan still couldn't believe that she was here now.

"Hey!"

At that, Graham finally turned around. His eyes were vacant, like her presence hadn't fully registered with him.

"What are you doing, Walter?"

She initially allowed for the possibility that he was hit with the sudden realization that Camille's story was worth another listen. Even though it didn't make any sense that he would come alone, particularly after he had gone out of his way to completely discredit her and her story, she wanted to believe that he was still a good cop capable of doing good things.

But when her question was met with silence, she allowed for another possibility: he wasn't here to talk about the disk at all.

"It doesn't matter what you may be trying to do to me behind the scenes. As it stands right now I'm still your partner, and I deserve to know what's going on."

"Don't tell me what you deserve to know, Chloe," Graham finally answered, his eyes no longer empty. "This doesn't have anything to do with you."

"If you're here because of Camille Grisham, then it most certainly does."

Graham put his hands on his wide hips. "You've got some goddamn nerve following me. Who do you think you are? Oh wait, I'll tell you who you are, you're the last person on the planet I have to answer to. What's going on here is way above your pay-grade. So do yourself a favor and leave it alone. Okay?"

He turned away from her and continued walking.

Sullivan first had the feeling outside of Stephen Clemmons' house that something wasn't right with Graham. As she watched him now, she finally understood what that something was.

"Why have you been so secretive throughout this whole thing? The phone calls that you tell me nothing about, the long stretches of time when you disappear without anyone knowing where you are, the fact that I followed you to Camille Grisham's house and you won't even so much as acknowledge that we're here. Why don't you stop treating me like I'm an idiot and just admit that you have another agenda here."

"Do you realize what you're doing right now?"

"Why don't you tell me?"

"Digging your grave as a homicide detective."

"From where I'm standing it might be the other way around."

Graham's mouth curled up in a tight smile. "You have no idea how quickly I can end things for you."

"Is that a threat?"

"Threats are idle words made by people with no real power to back them up."

As she looked into Graham's eyes she saw an apprehension, perhaps even a sadness, that completely betrayed the hard bite of his words, and she felt an inexplicable pang of sympathy. "What's happened to make you act like this?"

"Like I said before, it's beyond your capacity to understand. Maybe after ten years of working this beat, you'll get it."

"I need to understand now."

Graham shook his head. "Not possible." Then he put his hands on his hips again, this time opening his suit jacket just wide enough to reveal the department-issued Glock Nine holstered under his arm.

"So you're going to shoot me now?" Sullivan roared, her sympathy instantly replaced with anger.

"Don't be ridiculous, Chloe. You're taking this entirely too far now."

But she wasn't. "I feel like I don't even know who you are anymore. How could I possibly know what you're capable of?"

Graham shrugged his shoulders. "I guess you don't. So maybe you should leave me the hell alone," he warned before continuing toward the patrol car.

Sullivan knew that this encounter would spell the end of a lot of things: her relationship with Graham, her work on the Leeds case, possibly her career as a detective. But she was determined not to let the encounter end with him winning.

"What is he doing here?" Sullivan asked, pointing at the parked patrol car.

Graham kept walking without saying a word.

"If you even sniff Camille Grisham's doorstep, I will go to Internal Affairs right this minute and do whatever I have to do to make sure you're brought up on charges of evidence tampering, witness intimidation, racial profiling, wearing that same god-awful suit three days a week, and any other goddamn thing I can dream up. I may be committing career suicide in the process, but I guarantee you'll be jumping off the bridge with me."

When Graham turned to her, he was biting hard on his lower lip, but it didn't stop the quivering. "You don't have the balls to do it."

Sullivan looked him dead in the eye. "They're a lot bigger than you think."

CHAPTER 44

COMPANY

Joseph Solomon, or the man otherwise known as Officer Patrick Davies, almost laughed as he watched the two homicide detectives arguing in the middle of the street. They looked like an old married couple who had finally had enough of each other's bullshit and decided to hash it out one last time for the entire neighborhood to see. But they weren't a married couple and this wasn't their neighborhood. In this neighborhood, they stuck out like the clueless morons they were.

The moment he saw Graham's Crown Victoria come around the corner, Solomon knew he had been followed. The arrival of the second detective, however, had completely thrown him. From what he knew of Graham and Sullivan, they always rode together, so the fact that they arrived separately was puzzling. But the confrontational scene that played out as they exited their cars was downright bizarre.

Solomon was parked too far away to hear their words, but the looks on their contorted faces more than told the story. Graham looked more irritated than upset, while Detective Sullivan argued as if her very existence depended on the outcome.

The spectacle was so distracting that Solomon hadn't even stopped to consider the potential danger to himself. But as Graham made a bee-line for his car, with Detective Sullivan trailing close behind, Solomon suddenly understood the danger all too well.

Resisting the urge to start the car, he sat upright in his seat and moved his eyes to his dashboard computer. When the pair got close enough, Sullivan's voice was the first one he heard. She was babbling something about Internal Affairs and witness tampering and sounded very serious about it.

"*You don't have the balls to do it*," was Graham's only response.

"*They're a lot bigger than you think*," was Sullivan's. Despite her obvious femininity, Solomon didn't doubt her declaration for a second. And based on the frown lines creasing Graham's face, neither did he. The detective was in serious trouble, and he knew it.

But now so was Solomon.

When he looked in his rear view mirror again, the pair stood directly behind his car.

"I'd like to see you try it, Chloe. I really would," Graham cried. Then he walked up to Solomon's window. "I need to talk to you, officer."

Solomon's first instinct was to reach for his gun, but he kept his hands steady. "Yes sir?" he asked in a voice that wasn't naturally his.

"Is there a reason you're parked in front of Camille Grisham's house."

"I wasn't aware I was in front of Camille Grisham's house, sir." Solomon managed to keep himself perfectly still despite every muscle in his body screaming in protest. "A call came in about potential shots fired in the area."

Sullivan seemed confused as she scanned the block. "And you were the only unit to respond?"

"When I got here I saw three teenagers on the corner back there. Turns out they were only shooting off firecrackers. I radioed it in to dispatch and they must have called off the other units before they could get here."

Sullivan's nod communicated her satisfaction with Solomon's story, while Graham's steely glare communicated a desire to fight.

"So why are you still here?" Graham asked accusingly.

"When I saw you and Detective Sullivan pull up, I thought maybe something else had happened and I wanted to stick around in case you needed backup."

Graham obviously knew that was a lie. The only thing left for Solomon to wonder was whether or not the detective would call him out on that lie; even though he would be exposing his own reasons for being here by doing so. Solomon had realized after the fact that it probably wasn't the smartest of moves to antagonize Graham the way he had, and Brandt gave him an earful about it before sending him to Camille Grisham's house to carry out his final directive. But the arrogant asshole had it coming. Graham thought that he could dismiss him because he assumed Solomon to be nothing more than another rookie patrol officer. The truth was that Graham knew absolutely nothing about him, nor did anyone else aside from Brandt and Elliott Richmond. Had Graham known just who it was he was trying to push around with the weight of his thirty meaningless years of seniority, he would have walked away just as quickly as he came. But he didn't know, and because of that, he trailed the young Officer Davies here with the intention of issuing some John Wayne-style retribution. What he also didn't know was that because of that decision, he was a few moments away from losing his life.

"Is that really what you thought, Officer Davies? Because if that were the case, if you were so concerned about our well-being, why haven't you moved your ass so much as a millimeter since we got here?"

"Seriously Walter?" Sullivan snapped.

Graham continued as if he didn't hear her. "Did Brandt send you out here? Is that why he didn't want to include me in your little meeting? Is that why you slammed Brandt's office door in my goddamned face?"

Sullivan grabbed Graham's shoulder in an attempt to push him away, but he held his ground.

"I'm right here, officer. Slam the door in my face now. Can you do it now that Brandt isn't here to step in front of you? Why don't you get out of the car and finish what you started. I'm right here."

"That's enough Walter! I mean it!" Detective Sullivan fumed with rage as she stared her partner down.

Graham looked at her with weary eyes. "Go fuck yourself, Chloe." Then he turned to Solomon. "You be sure to do the same."

Solomon said nothing as he suppressed a smile. Then he watched through his rear-view mirror as Graham turned around and walked back toward his car.

"I apologize, Officer Davies," Sullivan offered. "I promise he didn't mean any of that."

Solomon looked up at her and smiled. "No need to apologize for him, Detective Sullivan. Besides, I understand the stress he's feeling. The entire department has been under the gun with that Leeds case, but you and Graham have had it especially rough. Hopefully arresting Clemmons will finally put everyone's mind at ease. Congratulations on snagging him, by the way."

"Thank you," Sullivan answered with a nod, though her eyes seemed weighed down with doubt. She looked back at Graham who was continuing toward his car. Then she looked at Camille Grisham's house. "Carry on with what you were doing, officer. And stay safe out here." She tapped the roof of his car and walked away.

"You as well, detective," he muttered, doubtful that she heard it.

As Sullivan approached Camille's front door, Solomon knew he had a major problem. His window for retrieving the disk was getting smaller by the moment, and with him now being placed in front of Camille's house, the cover of anonymity he hoped to remain hidden under had been blown wide open.

Given everything that had just happened, he began to wonder if it wouldn't be best to cut his losses and bow out of the operation while he still could. The decision, should he opt to make it, would prove to be a life-changing one.

But that decision would ultimately have to wait.

For now there was a more pressing matter to attend to. As the Crown Victoria carrying Detective Graham slowly drove past, Solomon craned his neck to look at him. Graham returned the look with a scowl that was meant to intimidate him. It didn't.

Solomon waited until the detective turned the corner before pulling away from the curb to give chase.

After what was no doubt a long, lonely, unfulfilled life, Walter Graham was finally going to be put out of his misery.

CHAPTER 45

SECOND THOUGHTS

Camille sat in her father's office, completely unaware of the situation unfolding less than two hundred feet from her front door.

Paul had excused himself to the restroom ten minutes earlier and had yet to return. He was undoubtedly still emotional from their confrontation about the disk, but Camille suspected that he was just as upset at displaying that emotion in the first place.

Before now, she had given no real thought to what all of this was doing to him. Camille had completely let her emotions take over, with little regard for how reckless it was making her, or how terrified that reckless behavior would make her father. *Everyone has their limit* was what he had told her the first night she was home. And it seemed that between Julia's murder, Camille's crippling grief, the existence of the disk, and her intentions for it, Paul Grisham had finally met his. She suddenly worried for him. But she also knew that she had to keep moving forward, and that meant going through with her intention of visiting Mayor Richmond with disk in hand.

The more Camille thought about the idea, however, the more she questioned it. Even if the mayor received the disk directly, and she actually took the time to look at it, her first and only instinct would be to cover up the information on it. Despite the personal betrayal Sonya Richmond would feel, that betrayal would be incidental compared to the loss she would suffer should the public ever learn of the disk. She would undoubtedly do everything she could to ensure that such a loss never occurred. And she would most likely succeed.

Still, Camille knew she had to try.

Before her father left, he gave back the disk that he had taken away from her. He didn't say a word as he did so. After Camille finished copying the movie file onto it, she put it in her pocket along with the first one. She then sealed the original in an envelope and took it upstairs to her bedroom, where she hid it under a pile of socks in her nightstand drawer.

When Camille came back downstairs, her father was standing in the foyer. She paused as she reached the bottom step, unsure of what to say to him.

"So I take it you got all of your copies made?" he asked.

Camille nodded.

He cast his eyes downward and put a hand in his pocket. When Camille saw his hand again he was holding his car keys.

She resisted the urge to reach for them, quietly holding her ground instead.

Paul looked up, forced a smile, and set the keys on the table. "All I can say is I trust you to do the right thing."

When Camille took a step toward him, he walked away.

"Dad?"

He was silent as he walked into the kitchen.

Instead of going after him, Camille reached for the keys. But she hesitated to pick them up. Paul may have trusted her to do the right thing, but she suddenly didn't know what the right thing was. The plan was to show Sonya Richmond the disk with the intention of blackmailing her husband into a confession. But people like Sonya and Elliott Richmond weren't easily blackmailed, particularly when the blackmailer is little more than a has-been federal agent with no real power to do anything but talk. They had the means to not only cover up the disk, but to bury Camille right along with it. And they wouldn't hesitate to do so. Her father knew that. That was why he did everything he could to stop her. But he now knew that he couldn't. Setting those car keys on the table wasn't his way of giving his blessing; it was his way of admitting that he had given up.

As much as she wanted to say that it didn't matter whether or not he was in her corner, it did matter. And now that she was faced with the realization that he wasn't, she wondered if she should give up too. She picked up the car keys and held them tightly in her hand, hopeful that the answer would come to her. Instead she was frozen with indecision. She turned toward the front door, then the kitchen, then back again. With one breath she wanted to tell her father he was right, with the next she wanted to tell him she was leaving.

But before Camille could make a final decision, she was startled by a knock on the front door. Her father appeared in the living room immediately.

"Is someone at the door?" he asked Camille who was still frozen where she stood. A second series of knocks answered his question before she could. After looking through the peephole he quickly opened the door. "Can I help you?" he said to the person standing on the other side.

"Hello, sir. My name is Detective Chloe Sullivan. I'm here to see Camille Grisham. Is she available? It's rather urgent."

The sound of Detective Sullivan's voice instantly broke Camille's paralysis and she was at the door before her father could answer. "Detective Sullivan?"

A flash of relief came over Sullivan's haggard face. "Camille. I need you to come with me right away."

"Why? What's the matter?" Paul asked anxiously.

"I'm sorry," Sullivan said with a hint of embarrassment. "You must be Sergeant Grisham."

Paul nodded as he shook her hand. "Why does Camille need to come with you?"

Camille nudged past him and into the doorway.

"I don't have a lot of time to explain it right now, Camille," Sullivan said. "But I need you to bring the disk."

"So that idiot Graham can take another crack at it? No thanks," Paul barked.

"Dad, please."

"Detective Graham is no longer a factor in this investigation as far as I'm concerned," Sullivan asserted.

Camille's mouth flew open in shock. "What do you mean?"

"As I said, I don't have time to explain it. Just know that there are people in the department aside from me who would be willing to investigate your claims about Elliott Richmond if they were allowed to know the whole story. If you don't mind, I'd like you to come with me so we can talk to one."

"And who exactly would that be?" Camille asked warily.

"My lieutenant Owen Hitchcock."

Camille looked at her father. His eyes were lit up with recognition.

"I've known Owen for almost thirty years," he said. His tone let Camille know that this was a good thing.

She nodded her understanding then turned back to Sullivan. "And you promise, no Graham?"

"No Graham," Sullivan affirmed.

Paul put a hand on Camille's shoulder. "Do you want me to come with you?"

She desperately wanted him to come, but something stopped her from saying it. "I should be okay."

"Are you sure?"

Camille wasn't sure at all, but she nodded anyway.

Paul promptly stepped out of the doorway. Camille gripped his arm as she passed.

"We need the disk," Sullivan said as Camille met her on the porch.

Camille reached into her pocket and pulled out the copies. "Will two be enough?"

Sullivan nodded as she pushed back a thin smile. "Let's go."

CHAPTER 46

SUPPERSSOR

Graham had pulled out his cell phone to call Brandt the moment he got into his car, but after five minutes of driving he still could not bring himself to dial.

Sullivan had really screwed him over this time. There was no way to anticipate that she would go so far as to follow him, but he still wanted to kick himself for allowing her to tail him for over ten miles without having the first clue that she was there. The truth was that he'd had his head so far up his ass during this entire investigation that Sullivan could have driven next to him with her siren blaring and he wouldn't have even bothered to change lanes. He was now completely out of his depth, and because he had been too stubborn to admit that to himself, he was thoroughly outsmarted by a rookie charity case of a detective whose sole contribution to the department up to this point was filling the female quota. What was worse, she told him that she was going to report him to Internal Affairs if he didn't leave Camille Grisham's house, and he essentially let her get away with it. She threatened him and he cowered. And because he did, the inevitable shit-storm brought on by his confronting Davies would only be the beginning.

The irony was that very man he was deathly afraid to call was also the only man who could save him. Brandt could make Chloe

Sullivan go away forever with one phone call; the same as he had done to Julia Leeds; the same as he could do to Graham if he wasn't careful. The risk to himself was very real, but it was one he knew he had to take.

He had hesitated long enough. If he had any hope of salvaging this situation, the call had to be made. He may have screwed up in this particular instance, but he had scratched Brandt's back plenty enough to warrant a favor. Once he realized how much it would be in his own self-interest to do so, the commander would certainly honor Graham's request. The hard part was going to be asking.

He pulled into the parking lot of an elementary school that looked depressingly abandoned, and searched his phone for the contact O. BRANDT. Once he found it, he took the deepest breath of his life and hit 'talk'. The commander picked up after four long rings.

"This is Oliver," he said in a voice that was barely audible over the den of noise in the background.

"Graham. Can you talk, sir?"

"Hold on," he said. After a few seconds, the background noise subsided. "We're five minutes away from giving a press conference on Clemmons, so you'll have to make it quick."

Graham cleared his throat. "It's about your guy."

"What do you mean my guy?"

"You know exactly who I'm talking about. Officer Davies."

"What about him?" Brandt asked with a deep sigh.

"Why did I just run into him in front of Camille Grisham's house?"

Graham heard the commander's throat catch. "I have no idea why he was outside of Camille Grisham's house."

"Of course you do. You sent him there, and because you didn't want me to know that, you allowed that prick to slam a door in my face."

"Jesus, are you still crying over that? Look, I'm sorry it happened, okay? I already talked to him about it. What else do you want me to say?"

"You can start by answering my original question."

"The only reason why you would know that Davies was at Camille Grisham's house was because you were there yourself. So why don't you tell me what you were doing."

Graham fixed his stare on a row of swings on the school's playground. One of them swung freely even though there was no breeze to speak of. "Following him."

Brandt's chuckle was peppered with nervousness. "That figures. You know what your problem has always been? You have no idea when to quit."

"Maybe I could learn if you would just answer my question, commander."

"I already answered your question when I told you it was none of your business."

"But it is my business, and it always has been. The problem now is that I'm not the only one who feels that way."

"What do you mean?"

"Chloe was here too."

"Unbelievable. As if confronting Officer Davies wasn't stupid enough, you decided to complicate matters by bringing your partner along?"

"I didn't bring her anywhere. She followed me." He then told Brandt every cringe-worthy detail of the confrontation that ensued. Graham felt shame as he recounted the story. As he predicted, the commander was not happy.

"You threatened her *and* Officer Davies? Are you kidding me?"

Graham was silent as he continued watching the swings. When the one that was moving abruptly stopped, his heart skipped a beat.

"You have got to be the biggest goddamned idiot I've ever met," Brandt proclaimed, further rubbing salt in Graham's ever deepening wound.

His cheeks suddenly felt hot and he could feel his pulse quicken. If anyone else had called him a goddamned idiot, they'd be spitting the dirt out of their mouth with bloody saliva. But this was Oliver Brandt, which meant he could say anything he damn well please, no matter how emasculating, and Graham had to take it.

"I can't control her."

"Well you certainly need to learn how to. What exactly does she know?"

"About Clemmons? Nothing. She's been skeptical about him for the entire course of the investigation, but I planted enough doubt to keep her at bay. I'm fairly certain she's on board with Camille Grisham's story though."

"And what does she know about your issues with Davies?"

"I don't know. But it would be wise to assume that Chloe knows more than we think she does. And considering the fact that she threw the Internal Affairs card at me, you also need to assume that she will tell anybody who is willing to listen."

"Jesus Christ. How did you handle her?"

"I walked away. What was I supposed to do?"

"And you left her at Camille Grisham's house?"

Graham didn't have a response.

"I'll take your silence as confirmation of your stupidity," Brandt continued. "And because of that stupidity, we now have an unnecessarily complicated situation on our hands. Your partner is probably with Grisham as we speak, telling her God-knows-what. Meanwhile you're probably parked on the side of the road somewhere, crying to me about how sorry you are that you panicked. How am I supposed to take that, Walter?"

"I don't know, sir. Maybe you can start by helping me come up with a solution."

"For your screw up?"

Graham could feel something inside of him begin to break and he suddenly didn't care about Internal Affairs or the seven-year-old evidence tampering case against him that magically went away last week. He only cared about making Brandt sweat the same way he was. "You have my ass in a sling over this IA rap, but don't forget, commander, I have your ass too, should it ever come down to that."

Brandt chuckled again, but this time there was no nervousness behind it. "I really don't think you want to go there, detective."

"You're right, I don't. But this isn't going to be a case of the deckhand going down with the Titanic. If I don't get a lifeboat, everyone on the goddamn ship, the captain included, is going down with me. The only question is who Elliott Richmond would retaliate against first – you or me?"

Brandt was silent for a long time. "I'll give you one thing, you can come up with the world's most colorful threats. Unfortunately, I'm not the least bit moved by them. So I'll come up with a colorful threat of my own. Handle Detective Sullivan, or her ratting you out to Internal Affairs will be the least of your worries. And unlike you, I actually have the ability to back up what I say." He paused. "And don't ever let Elliott Richmond's name come out of your mouth again. Do I make myself clear?"

Brandt had made himself perfectly clear, but Graham wouldn't allow himself to admit it. He lowered the phone, closed his eyes, and indulged in the thought of showing up at the Clemmons press conference, walking up to Brandt as he stood behind Chief Connolly like the lap dog that he was, and shooting him point blank in between the eyes. The thought made him smile in a way that actually frightened him.

It was with this smile on his face that Graham first felt the searing pain explode in his neck and tear down the left side of his body. Simultaneous to that was the feeling of liquid warmth filling his throat and chest. He didn't actually gag until he saw the large splatter of bright red blood covering the front of his checkerboard dress shirt. His wife had picked out that awful shirt for him this morning, the same as she picked out his awful shirts every morning. She did it more out of habit than concern; she had stopped caring about him and his appearance a long time ago. He knew that she would be happy to not have to do it anymore.

As the rest of the world around him began to fade, the only sound he heard was Brandt's voice. He tried to lift the phone up to his ear, but his arm felt heavy. As the phone fell helplessly into his lap, he saw a shape appear in his blurred peripheral vision. It could have been a man. Graham hoped with the last thought he could summon that it was an angel. He knew he had done nothing in his life to warrant such a blessing, but he held on to the thought as tightly as he could.

If it's an angel, I'll see light.

Graham did see light. A flash from his periphery. It was orange and it was brief.

Then there was nothing.

CHAPTER 47

EXTRA LABOR

Solomon unscrewed the suppressor from his Heckler and Koch and carefully holstered the gun in the small of his back. Then he reached inside the car and took the cell phone out of Detective Graham's dead hand. The voice on the other end was speaking as if someone was still there to listen. When Solomon brought the phone up to his ear, he was nearly deafened by the yelling.

"I know you're there Walter! I can hear you breathing! I'm only asking you one more time! Do I make myself clear?"

Solomon recognized the pseudo-tough voice of Oliver Brandt immediately. He almost couldn't believe that he was hearing it. But with the way everything else had gone during the course of this job, it also made total sense.

"You make yourself perfectly clear, commander."

"Walter?" Brandt asked, raising his voice to an almost comical level of intensity.

"Detective Graham is currently unavailable to finish this conversation," Solomon answered sharply. "I'm taking over in his absence."

"What are you talking about?"

"The detective is dead."

Brandt was silent.

"Are you there commander?"

"Davies? Is that you?" This time Brandt's voice barely registered above a whisper.

"For the purposes of this conversation, Joseph Solomon will do just fine."

A shallow breath was the only response Commander Brandt could offer.

"Seeing as I had to kill your friend in a very public place, I'm going to make this really quick," Solomon continued. "The plan that I was sent here to carry out is officially out the window."

"Why?"

"Detective Graham followed me to Camille Grisham's house, apparently to confront me about what happened outside of your office. Unbeknownst to both of us, he brought Chloe Sullivan with him. The two of them get into it in the middle of the street and manage to pull me in before I can drive away. The whole time Graham is looking at me like he wants to break my skull open."

"I already know all of this."

"Then you also know why I had to kill him."

"You didn't have to kill him," Brandt cried, his once resonant voice beginning to crack. "There were a million other ways you could have handled the situation. Do you understand that he was a member of this department for over thirty years? You think Julia Leeds brought heat on us? Imagine what this is going to do. How could you be so unbelievably reckless?"

"He's dead, commander. The how's don't really matter at this point. What does matter is that I had the perfect beat on Camille until your gopher boy's stunt ruined it. By now I'm sure she's been visited by Detective Sullivan and they're both on their way to headquarters where someone not corrupted by Richmond's money is going to have another crack at that disk."

Solomon heard something that sounded like a moan escape Brandt's mouth when he tried to speak. "What exactly are you saying?"

"I'm saying there's nothing I can do for you now. I'm saying that any real chance you had of getting that disk back is gone."

"Bullshit. There has to be some way you can still get to her."

"I've already done more than what was agreed to before I started this job, Brandt. I just killed a cop for Christ's sake. As if that weren't enough, you're now asking me to hunt down another cop who is protecting the former FBI agent you also want dead? When you look at the scenario in its totality, I'm sure you can understand why it gives me pause, especially considering I've only gotten a fraction of the money owed to me."

"Don't talk to me about money. Just get that disk."

"There's no way that's going to happen, not with the heat that's already coming down on Richmond. It's just a matter of time before that heat trickles down to you. As far as I'm concerned, the job is finished. Give me what I'm owed and that will be the end of it."

"Damn it, that's not the end of it. I hired you to retrieve that disk. The disk is not retrieved, so as far as I'm concerned, the job is not finished."

"It's only unfinished if you don't give me my money."

"What is that supposed to mean?"

"I know things about you and this department; things you desperately want to keep from the rest of the world. And I have absolutely no fear of exposing you, Connolly, Elliott Richmond, and every single one of the so-called police officers that you've recruited to your unit. There is also the small matter of you being behind the wheel of Julia's Range Rover the night of her murder. Given how sloppy you seem to be with everything else in your life, I'm sure you managed to leave something behind that the crime scene techs could find should they be persuaded to look."

Brandt laughed. "It would be a lot easier to commit suicide."

Solomon hesitated before responding. "You're probably right. How about I catch your son Jackson's soccer match tonight instead? Of course you'll miss all the fun, just like you miss every other important event in his life, because you're too busy whoring yourself to the mayor's husband. But I'm sure your wife will understand. If you want, I can give her a message of condolence from you."

"You can threaten me all you want to, but don't you dare threaten my family."

"I don't give a damn about your family, as long as you pay me."

"What am I supposed to do about Camille Grisham?" Brandt asked after an extended silence.

"I don't care anymore."

"As long as you're a member of this department, you should care." Brandt was interrupted by chatter in the background. "Yes. I know. I'll be right there," he said in a muted voice. Then he spoke back into the phone. "I can't talk about this now. The press conference is about to start."

"My money," Solomon said again.

"We'll talk about it another time. I have to go."

Solomon smiled to keep himself from exploding. "How about I just see you after the press conference, Oliver? We'll settle it then. If the meeting doesn't go well, I won't even charge for the extra labor of killing you."

The other end of the phone was silent and Solomon assumed that Brandt had hung up. But he was certain the message had been delivered.

He took out a handkerchief and wiped down the phone, lest he leave behind a stray whisker from his ever-thickening five o'clock shadow. He tossed the phone next to Graham's dead body, took off his latex gloves and jogged across the parking lot to his cruiser.

His next stop would be DPD headquarters. As frightening as Solomon's threat may have sounded, Brandt probably didn't expect him to make good on it. But Solomon had every intention of making good on it. No matter how much he may have wanted to finish the Leeds job, the situation was too far gone, and Solomon getting his hands on the disk wasn't going to change that. If anything, going through with the plan would only make matters worse. He had never killed a cop before, and even though the uniform he wore was little more than an elaborate costume, it still felt like something of a betrayal. Now, if he wanted to get that disk, he would most likely have to kill three. That wasn't a chance he was willing to take for any amount of money. It would be far easier to make Brandt disappear, keep the fee that he had already collected, and call it even.

Of course, Solomon hoped it wouldn't come to that. Money or no money, all he wanted was for the entire ordeal to be over with. It had already been way more than he had bargained for, and if he wasn't careful it had the potential to get worse.

As he got into his cruiser, he looked in the rearview mirror and spotted a familiar black Crown Victoria driving down the street adjacent to the school.

When the car suddenly stopped in the middle of the street, Solomon took out his binoculars to get a closer look.

It was then that he realized things were about to get much worse.

CHAPTER 48

FLASHBACK

Camille had barely settled into the passenger's seat of Detective Sullivan's car when a sudden pull on the brakes almost sent her flying into the dashboard.

"Oh my God, what is it?" Camille frantically asked as she looked around for the animal or worse yet, the child that Sullivan had slammed on her brakes to avoid hitting. When she saw nothing, she settled back in her seat. "Why did we stop?"

Sullivan was quiet as they idled in the middle of the street.

"What are you looking at?"

"That car over there," Sullivan finally said. "It looks like Walter's."

Camille looked toward the school parking lot a few hundred feet away where she saw a car that looked exactly like the one they were in. She couldn't help but roll her eyes. "Fantastic."

"What is he doing?" Sullivan muttered.

"Maybe he's having engine trouble. Maybe he's found a date. Maybe he's hiding from the world. After the run-in you two just had, why do you even care?"

"Because something is wrong."

"Unfortunately we don't have a lot of time to worry about it. At least that was what you told me when you showed up at my house. I don't want to sound insensitive, but I personally couldn't care less what Detective Graham is–"

"Wait a second," Sullivan cut in, pointing to the DPD patrol car parked in the adjacent loading dock. "Is that Officer Davies?"

"I don't really see why it matters."

"It matters," Sullivan said as she put the car in reverse."

"What are you doing?"

Camille got her answer when Sullivan pulled into the school entrance.

"I'm sure Walt isn't going to be the least bit happy to see me again, but I have to be sure."

"Sure of what?"

Sullivan said nothing.

When they pulled up next to the Crown Victoria and saw Detective Graham slumped down in the driver's seat, the answer became horrifyingly clear.

"Oh my God," Sullivan shouted as she rushed out of the car.

Camille quickly followed. She could see the blood before she even made her way to the driver's side where Graham sat. Once she got there and could see the full scope of what had actually happened she felt sick to her stomach.

Sullivan reached inside the car and put two fingers up to Graham's neck. Camille couldn't tell whether she was checking for a pulse or attempting to stem the flow of blood from the gaping wound just below his jaw line. Both gestures seemed useless.

"Damn it, Walter. How did you let this happen?" Sullivan said, trying to choke back emotion. She cradled his neck for a moment longer, as if she still hoped he could offer a response. When he didn't, she lifted her head out of the car and pointed at Camille. Her hand was covered in blood. "My two-way is in the car! Can you bring it back here?"

Camille was frozen, just as she had been months earlier in Daniel Sykes' basement. She had been too late to save Agent Sheridan, but she had cradled him in her arms like there was still a chance. She had heard the girl's desperate cries for help. But she couldn't move. Even after she heard the first gunshot and one of the girl's cries had gone silent, Camille still could not bear to remove her hand from the wound in Agent Sheridan's forehead. The pressure from her grip had managed to stop the bleeding and she tried to convince herself that if he didn't lose anymore blood, he could be saved. But she was lying to herself and she knew it. The truth was that she was in the midst of a panic attack so severe that the only thing keeping her from disconnecting completely was the feeling of Sheridan's blood on her fingers. Sitting in the middle of that cold, dank dungeon that reeked of death and decay, hearing screams of pain and terror echo off the gray cobblestone walls, applying pressure to her dead partner's wound was the only tangible thing left in a situation that had become darkly surreal. And now that same panic was setting in again. Only this time, she didn't have anything tangible to hold onto.

"Camille!"

Sullivan's voice was little more than a distant echo, drowned out by those screams in the basement and the subsequent gunshots that silenced them forever.

"Camille!" Sullivan was shaking Camille's shoulders now. "I need to stay with him! Please get my radio from the car!"

Camille nodded then ran to Sullivan's car as fast as her numb legs would carry her. She found the radio in the compartment between the driver and passenger's seat. On her way back, she glanced over her shoulder. That was when she got her first good look at the patrol car that Sullivan had noticed earlier. The driver's side door was open, and Camille thought she could see someone looking in her direction through the open window. As she got closer to Sullivan and Graham, she looked over her shoulder again. This time she was positive she saw someone staring at her. He wore sunglasses that matched the dark tint of his uniform. And now he appeared to be holding something out of the window. It looked silver but it could have been black. It looked like a pair of binoculars, but it could have been a gun.

A gun?

Sullivan took the two-way radio and had begun her emergency relay before Camille could say anything.

"Code ten, code ten, officer down! West side parking lot of Braswell Elementary School! I repeat, officer down!" Panic rose with each word she spoke.

As Camille glanced over her shoulder at the patrol car, her panic rose as well. The driver's side door was still open, but she could no longer see the officer sitting inside. By the time she turned back to Sullivan, she felt the first sting just below her left shoulder blade. Before Camille could open her mouth to say the word 'help', she felt the second sting slide across her left cheek. She hadn't realized that she was shot until she heard two more rapid-fire pops. Then she saw Detective Sullivan crumble onto the asphalt.

CHAPTER 49

CUTTING LOSSES

So much for not killing anyone else, Solomon thought with a hint of regret as he threw his PSG-1 into the backseat of the squad car. He knew that Detective Sullivan had most likely been killed right away. The first shot caused her to fall forward; the second sent her crashing into the ground. Camille Grisham was another story. She barely moved after the first shot and staggered backward only a few feet after the second. She cupped the side of her face before finally falling to her knees. He couldn't be sure if either shot was clean enough to be anything more than superficial, so he approached the parking lot under the assumption that he still had work to do.

Before Solomon got the first shot off, he saw Sullivan talking into her two-way radio, which meant she was able to put in a call for help. He cursed himself for not moving in on them sooner, just like he'd been cursing himself for a lot of things lately. But it was too late to worry about that. Right now he had to focus on the task at hand, which was making sure no one in that parking lot was left alive.

He climbed into his cruiser and drove the short distance to a parking lot that was completely empty except for two Crown Victoria's and three law enforcement agents – two of whom

Solomon felt confident were dead. The third one would soon be dead too.

Given the events of the day, it was very likely that Camille would be carrying the disk, or at least a copy of it, with her. But at this point, Solomon wouldn't even bother to retrieve it. The cat had most certainly already been let out of the bag. The fact that Camille had a disk in the first place meant that Julia Leeds planned for such a scenario long before Solomon had gotten to her.

Throughout the entire ordeal, Elliott Richmond had operated under the false assumption that he was the smartest person in the room. He was the one with all the answers; the one pulling all the strings. But Julia Leeds had been a step ahead of him from day one. She knew exactly what Richmond was capable of, and she took steps to ensure that the world would know about it should he ever decide to act.

And now the world would know, which meant this entire episode of Solomon's life had been a complete waste of effort.

The more he thought about that fact, the more it angered him. He had done everything he was supposed to do. In the end, Richmond was the one who failed. Because of him, an easy job had deteriorated into an unmitigated disaster. Because of him, four people would end up dead. If Solomon felt that Elliott Richmond would do anything other than toe the line of absolute innocence once he was exposed, he wouldn't hesitate to make him the fifth. But Richmond was not a threat to him. Neither was Camille Grisham.

But he had to kill her just the same.

Solomon stopped a few feet from the car that Camille and Detective Sullivan had arrived in, got out of his own car, and listened. The only sound he heard was indecipherable chatter from Sullivan's open radio.

With his Heckler and Koch drawn, Solomon inched his way toward the back of Sullivan's Crown Victoria. From his current vantage point, he could see Graham slumped in the driver's seat of his own car a few feet away. Detective Sullivan, and presumably Camille Grisham, were somewhere on the other side.

Solomon heard a scrape against the asphalt. Then another. He crouched down behind the car and listened. When he heard nothing else, he quickly stood up, realizing that he had taken a defensive position that was based on fear and nothing more. When he first encountered Camille outside of Julia's house, then a second time in Mayor Richmond's campaign headquarters, Solomon had seen something in her that was very formidable; a dark presence that she obviously went to great lengths to contain. Elliott Richmond had probably not seen it until it was too late. But Solomon saw it right away, and it put him on notice. Camille may have no longer had the seal of the FBI behind her, but she was still dangerous. He knew from personal experience that true darkness could never be contained for long, and he'd shuddered at the thought of being in Camille's path when her efforts to contain the darkness within herself finally failed.

But he no longer had to worry about that. Camille was not standing at the other end of a dark alley waiting to draw her gun on him. She was most likely sitting a few feet away in a pool of blood waiting for him to finish her off. He was anxious to oblige.

When he walked around to the left side of the car, he saw Detective Sullivan lying motionlessly on her side. Her ivory blouse was stained red on the left side of her upper torso, as was her right leg just above the knee. The two-way radio was still tucked in her hand. Solomon kicked the radio, sending it hurling across the parking lot until it came to a rest in multiple pieces. The detective didn't move.

Seeing no need to further engage, Solomon moved to the front of her car, then to the right side. From there, he made his way to Graham's. The smell of copper was thick as he passed the open window where his body had already begun to decompose. Pellets of shattered glass crunched under his boots as he rounded the front of Graham's car, then up the other side. Solomon stopped there. His arm trembled before it involuntarily fell to his side, taking the gun down with it. It was as if the asphalt under his feet suddenly became quicksand and he was unable to prevent himself from being pulled under.

Camille Grisham was nowhere to be found.

CHAPTER 50

THE FOURTH INTERROGATION

Before she made her way into the backseat of Detective Graham's car, Camille had managed to pry the Glock out of his shoulder holster. Once inside the car, she crouched down in between the seats as far as she could; covering most of her body with his oversized trench coat. Then she listened. Aside from the chatter on Detective Sullivan's radio, she heard nothing, and for a time she thought the DPD officer, the man who had most likely shot them all, had left. Then she heard footsteps. She'd had a fleeting hope that it was a concerned passerby who could offer help. But passersby in this neighborhood were rarely concerned and they almost never helped. Her notion was confirmed when the footsteps stopped and she heard a thump that caused Sullivan's radio to go silent. Seconds later she heard it skidding across the asphalt. The officer had apparently come to finish what he'd started.

When Camille allowed herself a moment to think about where the officer came from or what his motives were, the name *Richmond* immediately came to mind. He had more than adequate resources to bring in a hired gun from within the police ranks to do something like this. And he clearly had the motivation.

But right now it didn't matter where the officer came from or what his motives were.

She had to find a way to stop him.

When she no longer heard his footsteps, she decided to make a move that would better allow her to key in on his position.

Though her gunshot wounds were superficial, the pain was searing, and she struggled to pull off Detective Graham's coat. The first thing she saw when she lifted her head was part of Graham's skull lying on the seat next to her. She wanted to retreat at the sight of it, but something inside the hard-as-nails, Quantico-trained, Special Agent-In-Charge-of-Ridding-the-World-of-Everything-Evil-and-Impure Grisham would simply not allow it. It was a side of herself that she never thought she would see again; and its timely appearance was most welcomed.

She sat Graham's gun down on the seat while she used her good arm to slowly push the door. The hinges squeaked loudly as it opened. "*Shit*," she grunted as she abruptly stopped to listen for any reaction to the noise. When she heard none, she continued pushing. The door opened the rest of the way without making a sound. With her left arm trailing uselessly behind her, Camille pulled herself across the back seat until she was out of the car.

Once her feet were under her, she reached back into the car to retrieve the gun, then gently closed the door, stopping short of the latch.

The only thing she saw in her immediate field of vision was the school playground some distance in front of her. Detective Sullivan's car was on the other side of Graham's, as was presumably Detective Sullivan. Camille's only thought was to get to her.

Until she heard footsteps.

They came from somewhere behind her. They were slow, they were cautious, and they were searching. She crouched down against the car, the gun held high in front of her. As the footsteps drew closer, Camille's index finger wrapped loosely around the trigger.

When the footsteps stopped, her grip tightened. He was on the other side of Graham's car, no more than a few feet away. And he was here for her.

Camille heard the faint scream of a siren somewhere in the distance. Then a second one. But the sound was of no comfort to her. It didn't matter if they arrived in five minutes or five seconds. The resolution to this situation was completely out of their hands.

It was squarely in hers.

Using every ounce of physical strength she had left, Camille lifted herself off the ground until her eyes were level with the car window. It was then that she saw him, standing directly in front of the window with his back to her. His arms were down at his sides and his broad shoulders appeared slumped. It was an unnerving sight, and for a moment, Camille was unsure of how to react. She slowly turned on her heels until her body was square to the window, then she pointed the gun through it, taking dead aim at his back. Presuming he was carrying a gun, she thought about taking a shoulder shot, disabling him enough so that he would drop it. But she couldn't see which hand he held the gun in. Then she thought about aiming higher, creating a disability that was much more permanent. But shooting someone in the back of the head would never pass the self-defense test, no matter how loosely the term was defined.

Finally she stood completely upright, extended the gun as far out in front of her as she could, and yelled. "Drop the weapon and raise your hands where I can see them!"

From her new vantage point she could only see the man from the shoulders up. But she saw enough to know that he hadn't budged an inch.

"I said put your hands where I can see them!" Camille staggered along the edge of the car until she could see his profile. When he turned his head to look at her, she gasped.

The young, red-faced officer she first saw in front of Julia's house looked both amused and disgusted as he shook his head at her. But it was Camille who felt disgusted when she was hit with the sudden realization that she had met the officer a second time – with Elliott Richmond only a few hours ago.

"Let me guess," he said with a pained half-smile. "You were in the car."

Camille kept her gun trained on him as she inched closer. She remembered he had called himself Solomon Gates. But Camille now knew that name was about as genuine as her use of Naomi Stephens had been. As she made her way around the car, she could see a gun dangling in his left hand. She extended hers further. "I said drop it, now!"

"You do a great impersonation of a cop. Has anyone ever told you that?"

The sirens were getting closer.

"So do you. Now shut up and drop the gun!"

He moved for the first time, subtly shifting his weight to his left side. His shoulder flinched slightly, and Camille instinctively knew that he was preparing to raise it. She fired her gun before he could. The shot landed square in the middle of his shoulder blade, the damage to his auxiliary nerve causing him to instantly drop the gun. He stumbled backward onto the hood of Sullivan's car, cradling the wound. Camille knew the pain of getting shot in the shoulder first hand. The payback felt good.

She ran toward him as quickly as her heavy legs would take her. When she was mere inches away, she aimed her gun directly at his head, holding it so close that the end of the barrel nearly touched him.

"You should have listened when I told you to drop it," she said, suddenly feeling every bit in control of the situation.

"I suppose I should have," he answered in between labored breaths. Blood was beginning to seep through the fingers that he held up to the wound, and the skin on his muscular face was already growing pale. "You've got me Agent Grisham. Dead to rights." He winced as he applied more pressure to his shoulder. "Is this the part of the interrogation where I spill my guts? Confess all the sordid little details?"

He was smug in spite of the situation and it infuriated her. Camille took another step toward him. Even though the barrel of her gun was now pressed firmly against his sweaty temple, he didn't give an inch of ground. "You can start by telling me your real name. I know it's not Solomon Gates, and Officer Davies doesn't ring particularly true either."

He smiled thinly. "Starting with the basic stuff. I like that. The only problem is those sirens approaching don't give either of us much time. You can ask fifty questions until they slap the handcuffs on you, or you can end this the right way."

"You're crazy. No one is slapping handcuffs on me."

"Look around. Two dead detectives. You holding a gun up to a police officer's head. You'll be lucky if they don't shoot you on sight."

"I didn't kill anyone, asshole. And you're not a real police officer. If they didn't realize that before, they certainly will now." Camille pressed the gun harder into the side of his head.

"Maybe. But maybe not. Why wait for them to arrive to find out? If the roles were reversed, I'd certainly kill you."

"Isn't that what Elliott Richmond sent you here to do in the first place?"

His smile broadened. "A gentleman never tells."

"Answer the question!"

"Were you always this aggressive an interrogator, Camille? I bet you were really tough, especially with that serial killer of yours. How long did it take to get a confession out of him? If you employed the gun-up-to-the-temple technique, I imagine it didn't take long at all."

Camille thought about Sykes and her three separate interrogations of him. He toyed with her every step of the way, offering only the tiniest kernel of information before later disavowing his testimony altogether. This went on for each emotionally draining four-hour session, until the third one, when he recounted their meeting in Alexandria, then followed that up by listing the names of four women and two teenage boys he killed in the interim. That was how the interrogation began. It was also the last thing Camille heard before she ran out of the room in tears, and ran away from the FBI in shame.

Right now another killer was trying to toy with her in the exact same way. But if this was an interrogation, it certainly was not going to end the way the last one did.

Without giving it a second thought, Camille took the gun away from his temple and put it under his chin, pushing up until his head went backwards. "Right now I don't care about Richmond, I don't care about the disk, and I don't care about you trying to kill me. I only want to know one thing. Were you the one who killed Julia?"

He gagged as Camille pressed the barrel deep into the soft flesh under his chin. She eased up enough to allow him to speak.

"We don't have time for this. My friends are almost here."

Camille could see the approaching lights out of the corner of her eye. She was distracted for no more than a millisecond, but that was all the time he needed. She felt the blow to her chest before she saw it coming. It wasn't hard, just enough to send her reeling backward a few steps. But it gave him the leverage he needed to grab her arm with one hand and bend her wrist back with the other, causing her to drop the gun. Even after being disabled by a gunshot, his strength was overwhelming. She bellowed in pain as he pressed down on her wound then kicked her in the ribs. This blow sent her careening onto the pavement, landing on her wounded arm. She let out another wail of pain. Then she saw him bend down to pick up his gun.

In an instant he was standing over her, staring straight into her eyes. His gun hung low on his side. Pain shot from Camille's arm to the rest of her body like streaks of lightning and she could barely keep her eyes open. But she kept focused on him. If she was going to die, she wasn't going to die a coward. She bit down hard on her bottom lip to stop it from quivering and lifted her head off the asphalt. She didn't flinch, even as he lifted his gun and pointed it at her face.

The sirens that were once barely a whisper in the distance had now become deafeningly loud. The man, whose real identity she would probably never know, looked at the approaching police cars, then looked back down at her. For the first time she saw something in his face that resembled fear. "You want to know if I killed your friend?" he asked in an almost solemn voice as his hand tightened around the gun. "Why don't you ask her yourself?"

Camille had just closed her eyes in anticipation of the impact when she heard a battered female voice shout: "Put it down now!"

Before Camille could open her eyes, she heard a gunshot.

When she looked up, she saw the officer writhing on the ground. He was cradling his hand underneath his chest. The gun he had tried to kill her with rested a few feet away from him.

Powered by a sudden adrenaline surge, Camille jumped to her feet. Instead of picking up the gun, she kicked it as far as she could. It came to a stop underneath the wheel of a police cruiser. There were at least ten of them, and double the number of uniforms, all of them looking at her with their guns drawn. Camille instinctively put her good arm up in surrender. She couldn't lift the second one at all.

"Are you all right, Chloe?" one of the patrol officers said. It wasn't until then that Camille realized the officers weren't actually looking at her.

When she turned around she saw Detective Sullivan on one knee, a few feet from the man who had shot her. Her blouse was covered in blood and her once pretty face looked gaunt. The gun she had just fired was still raised, as if she feared she would have to use it again.

Within seconds the officers swarmed in, one group rushing to Detective Sullivan's aid, the other descending on the man who murdered Camille's best friend. He hadn't admitted to it, but Camille knew; just like she knew who had hired him to do it.

This morning, those officers were confident that he was one of their own. They probably told jokes over coffee and bagels. Now he was powerless to offer resistance as they put handcuffs on his wrists and lifted him to his feet. Camille tried to get one last look at him as they passed, but the officers had him completely surrounded, like a group of Secret Service agents shielding the President. It had all happened so fast. One minute he was holding a gun to her head, the next he was being whisked away in the back of a police cargo van with six officers in tow.

She looked at the scene around her, and the almost indescribable level of destruction he had left in his wake. It was entirely too much to process. She dropped hard to one knee. She felt no pain. She felt no fear. She felt nothing.

Two paramedics sped past her pulling a stretcher. They stopped in front of Detective Sullivan and began the frenzied work of trying to save her life. It wasn't until Camille was pulled up and lifted onto a stretcher of her own that she realized anyone had even noticed her.

The back of the ambulance was cold and the faces hovering over her looked concerned. And all she could say before everything around her went black was: "Someone please call my father."

CHAPTER 51

A TIME TO HEAL

Camille checked herself out of the Rose Medical Center four days later, a full three days earlier than her doctors recommended. She knew it probably wasn't wise to disobey their orders, but she couldn't take the fanatical attention a moment longer.

There were dozens of visitors during those four days, most of whom were part of the jovial celebration in her honor less than two weeks before. But many of the visitors to her hospital room were unexpected, including Julia's sister Nicole, who visited on the second day. Even though she was clearly overwhelmed by her own grief and sense of loss, she sat at Camille's bedside for over three hours.

"I can't begin to tell you how grateful I am," she said. "Julia would be extremely proud of you."

Camille smiled despite the physical and emotional pain that was otherwise battering her existence. "I'm the one who's proud of her. You should be too. The only thing Julia wanted was to do the right thing. And in the end, she did. That makes her the only hero in this particular scenario."

After Camille was released from surgery to remove bullet fragments from her arm, Paul turned the disk over to Lieutenant

Hitchcock personally. The investigation of Elliott Richmond began immediately. The details of that investigation, as well as the contents of the disk, were leaked to the media, presumably by someone within the department, the very next day. Nicole heard those details, along with the rest of the country, and became immediately convinced that Richmond was her sister's killer.

"The people who did this to her are going to hang," Nicole insisted. "Without you that wouldn't have been possible. In my book, that makes you a hero too."

Camille wanted to protest Nicole's declaration, but decided it was best not to.

Based on the personal briefing she had received from Hitchcock, the man he had wrongly known as Officer Patrick Davies was cooperating fully in the investigation. Within hours of his arrest, Joseph Solomon had not only revealed his actual identity, but had confessed to the murder of Detective Graham, the attempted murders of Camille and Detective Sullivan, and revealed that he may have had 'involvement' in Julia's murder. But aside from the claim that his conspirators were high-level officials whom he would reveal only after he was guaranteed full immunity, he offered nothing more about himself or the specifics of his involvement.

A dozen fingerprint index checks came up with zero matches for Joseph Solomon, as did medical, DMV, and social security records. It was as if he never existed. Because of this, details about the shootings, and Solomon's role in them, were being withheld from the public as the department scrambled to not only find any tangible information on their suspect, but also to figure out how this man with no traceable history ended up in a DPD uniform. Whatever they eventually discovered, the public relations nightmare was going to be unavoidable.

The department may have had Solomon clean on one count of murder and two counts of attempted murder, but as far as establishing a firm connection between him, Elliott Richmond, and

Julia's murder, they were a million miles away from square one. And unless Solomon was willing to talk without the immunity that no judge in the free world would grant him, the chances of Elliott Richmond walking, at least in Camille's mind, were roughly one hundred percent. But she wasn't about to tell Julia's sister that. "I hope they hang too," was all she could bring herself to say.

Immediately following the media leak, a reporter from the Denver Post showed up at Camille's bedside, angling for the rights to an exclusive interview. Her father, and self-appointed watchdog, not-so-kindly escorted the reporter out of the room and into the elevator; with the promise of severe bodily injury should he ever return. He didn't. But several others attempted to follow in his footsteps. Not one of them ever got close enough to ask a single relevant question, but their numbers and persistence were enough to let Camille know the heights that the story had reached in a relatively short time. She had kept the television turned off for fear of seeing her name and face on the news yet again. Based on the number of media visits she received, this fear had become a stark reality, and she would have to face it head on very soon.

Camille discharged herself at nine a.m. She had just packed the last of her flowers and get-well cards for the trip home when one last visitor knocked on the hospital room door.

"That's probably the nurse coming to wheel you out," Paul said as he went to the door.

The man standing on the other side was not a nurse. He wore a modest suit and tie; his black shoes so polished they were almost too bright to look at.

"May I help you?" Paul asked in his newly perfected watchdog tone.

"Hello," the man said shyly as he extended his hand. "I'm sorry to bother you, but I was hoping to see Ms. Grisham. My name is Stephen Clemmons."

Paul didn't hesitate to take his hand. "Paul Grisham. Nice to meet you, young man." He smiled as he invited Clemmons inside.

When Camille met Stephen's gaze, a lump the size of an apple instantly formed in her throat and she thought she was going to cry.

This is the man who Detective Graham insisted had brutally killed my best friend? She realized at that moment that man's ability to become corrupted by power, greed, and pure hatred knew absolutely no bounds. If a fundamentally decent man like this was not protected from the destructive effects of that corruption, what man or woman in this world would be?

"It's a pleasure to meet you," Camille said with a slightly broken voice as she shook his hand.

"It's nice to meet you too. Looks like you're on your way out of here."

"Against my doctor's orders and my father's pleading. But I'm anxious to get home."

"I can't say that I blame you. Listen, I don't want to hold you up. I just stopped by to thank you for everything you've done in trying to help the police find out who did this. I only met Julia once, but I knew what a good person she was. Everyone at the firm did. She didn't deserve any of this."

Camille nodded. "Neither did you, Stephen."

Something tightened in Clemmons' face, but he softened it with a smile. "Thanks."

"So where do things stand? I read that you were released on bail."

"Yes. I still don't know who posted it though. All I was told was that I was free to leave. The grand jury hearing is in two weeks, but my attorney says that with all of the recent developments, we may not even make it to that before the charges are dropped altogether."

Camille hoped he was right, but as was the case with Nicole Blair, she did not want to give voice to her overwhelming doubt. "You have a lot of people in your corner, Stephen."

"Speaking of someone being in my corner, I recently visited Detective Sullivan."

Camille's eyes lit up. With her own stay in the hospital, she hadn't had the chance to visit Sullivan. Lieutenant Hitchcock reported that she had been in surgery for three hours to remove bullet fragments from her leg and abdomen. But aside from a ruptured spleen, there was no serious internal damage and she was expected to make a full recovery. Camille had passed along a message of thanks for Hitchcock to deliver to her, but she looked forward to doing it personally very soon.

"How is she?" Camille asked.

"She seemed good, considering the circumstances. There was a lot of family there at the time, little kids and stuff, so I didn't stay long. But I had to see her. When she and Detective Graham came to my house, Detective Sullivan was the only one who seemed willing to listen to me. If it wasn't for her, I think Detective Graham would have taken me out of there in handcuffs and shackles, or worse. I feel like she actually went to bat for me, and I wanted to thank her, and to tell her I was glad she was okay."

"She definitely went to bat for you, Stephen. And for good reason."

Stephen smiled, almost blushing with embarrassment. Then he continued. "Anyway, the reason I brought it up is because she told me that you were the one who deserved all the thanks. She said it was you who did all the fighting to make sure the truth came out. I know you went through a lot to get that truth out. So again, I just want to say thank you, not just for myself, but for everybody who knew Julia. From what the news says, this story could get a whole lot worse before it gets better. But I know justice will prevail in the end. I know it doesn't always happen that way. But in this case, I have to believe it."

Camille nodded. She felt like crying again, and this time she succumbed to the urge.

A wave of sadness washed over Stephen's plump face. "I'm sorry, Ms. Grisham. I didn't mean to upset you."

She quickly composed herself. "You didn't upset me at all. In fact, I couldn't be happier that we met. I'm so sorry about what happened to you. I can promise you that the people working this case now are right-minded, and they're just as eager to uncover the full truth of what happened to Julia as I am. So you keep thinking positively about this. If nothing else, you're inspiring me to do the same."

The sadness in Stephen's face was replaced with a light smile. "Positivity is pretty hard to come by these days, but it's all I have to get me through this."

"I understand from Detective Sullivan that you're in school?"

Clemmons nodded. "Paralegal studies."

"I hope you can continue that now."

"I plan to. Brown, Wallace, and Epstein offered me my old job back should the investigation turn out the way they assume it will."

"Do you think you'll go back?" Camille asked.

Clemmons briefly lost himself in thought, then shrugged. "I'm not sure yet. I'm not sure about a lot of things yet. I'm technically still a suspect. So until I find resolution there, nothing else really matters."

Camille nodded. "I completely understand. And you will find resolution."

"I sure hope you're right." After a quiet moment, Clemmons extended his hand. "It was wonderful meeting you, Ms. Grisham."

Camille stood up, gently pushed his hand away and hugged him instead. "It's Camille to you," she answered.

When they separated, Stephen lightly dabbed the corner of his eye. "Thank you, Camille."

"You're welcome."

"Take care of yourself Stephen," Paul offered as he walked Clemmons to the door.

"There are a lot of wounds to heal, Mr. Grisham. But I'm working on it. "

In that moment, Camille realized just how much the two of them had in common. The time for healing had indeed begun.

CHAPTER 52

FIFTEEN YEARS LATER

Dale Rooney felt like an irrelevant spectator as he first watched the reports of Stephen Clemmons' arrest, the widespread doubt about his guilt, and his subsequent release on bail. Never once did those news reports mention the importance of Dale's testimony. It seemed, in fact, that no one cared about Dale's testimony, not even the police. Since giving his last statement to Detectives Graham and Sullivan, Dale had waited by the phone night and day in anticipation of the phone call requesting the positive identification of Clemmons that he was fully prepared to give. But no such phone call came. When Dale put in multiple calls to Detective Graham's cell phone, none were answered. The star witness in the Julia Leeds murder investigation didn't feel like much of a star anymore.

He felt betrayed.

It was a feeling that only deepened as he watched the news reports of Detective Graham's murder and its possible connection to Julia Leeds. The man arrested for Graham's murder, as well as the shootings of Detective Sullivan and Camille Grisham was believed to be a police officer. As if that didn't shake Dale badly enough, the latest rumors were that this police officer had admitted to playing a role in Julia's murder, and had named Graham and several other high profile officials as co-conspirators. Once again, Dale waited for his name to be mentioned.

From the beginning, he felt justified in his actions because the police, and Detective Graham in particular, made him feel as if his eyewitness account was the key component to their investigation; the difference between a quick arrest and a twenty-year-old cold case. But if the reports about this officer were true, Dale wasn't helping the police department at all. He was being used by them.

As the details continued to emerge about the real story behind Julia's murder, Dale wondered how long it would be before Stephen Clemmons' innocence was confirmed, and the actual motivations behind his arrest were revealed. When the story is told years from now, and Clemmons is known only as the man who was set up by the police as a suspect in a murder he had nothing to do with, Dale had no doubt that his role as an all-too-willing accomplice in that setup would be highlighted. The only question that remained was would he be reviled like the others, or would he be given proper acknowledgment as the unwitting mark that he turned out to be? The best that Dale could hope for was that whenever the story was finally told, his apology to Clemmons, the one that he desperately looked forward to giving, would be front and center.

One thing was for certain, whenever the time did come for that story to be told, Dale Rooney would not be an easy man to find. The realtor had been hired, the 'for sale' sign had been put up in his yard, and the search for the life that should have been his fifteen years ago was thoroughly underway. This time when Dale mentioned his intentions to Maggie, she did not put up a fight. It seemed that something inexplicable had happened to them as a result of this otherwise horrific ordeal: Maggie noticed him again. When they spoke now, it wasn't about a past full of regrets or a present full of resentment and misunderstanding. It was about a future they planned to spend together. If nothing else positive came from this situation, and so far nothing else had, Maggie had developed a newfound respect for her husband. Dale, in turn, rediscovered the wife, lover, and best friend he had forgotten ever existed. Even though that rediscovery came with a cost that he would have to live with for the rest of his life, Dale knew he wouldn't change a thing.

With Trinket the Pomeranian yipping in her lap, Maggie pulled up a website filled with real estate listings. "So what exactly did you have in mind?"

Dale didn't hesitate in his response. "Someplace so far removed from civilization that even the world's most sophisticated GPS won't be able to find us."

Now if only he could find that German Shepard.

CHAPTER 53

WOLVES

There were eight people inside Mayor Sonya Richmond's office. Aside from the mayor, none of them were public figures. They could drive down any street, shop in any grocery store, or walk into any office building and blend in perfectly with any other ordinary person there.

But the people in this office were far from ordinary. They were part of an unseen conglomerate that powered the economic, political, media, and social machine for the state and points far beyond it. Theirs was a circle of influence so secret and so powerful that no one except for its members even knew of its existence. And today they assembled to discuss a matter of the gravest importance.

The circle was in danger of being compromised.

It seemed that one of their own had managed to get himself into a situation that he could not get out of, and instead of calling upon those members of the circle with the resources and expertise to help him, he decided to resolve the situation on his own. The result was not only a personal crisis for the member, but a professional crisis for his wife – herself a highly valued member of the circle.

With a firestorm brewing that involved large-scale financial and political wrongdoing, as well as rampant marital infidelity, the people in this room were charged with finding a swift resolution.

For Sonya Richmond, resolution didn't mean finding a way to save her marriage. It meant finding a way to cut herself loose from a man she had stopped loving years ago; a man whose only real value to her decreased exponentially with each new report that surfaced about his various misdeeds.

His behavior had always been a potential liability for her. Before now she had always found a way to manage it. But with the existence of the disk and its impending release to the public, he had finally created a situation that went beyond her ability to manage.

Even though she first learned of the disk days ago, Elliott had waited until the story broke on the ten P.M. news to tell her. She didn't act surprised, but she also refrained from telling him that she had already seen it. Instead she half-listened as he insisted that they could find a way through the situation as long as they stuck together. Sonya already knew there would be no getting through the situation together.

The election was two weeks away, and her twelve-point lead in the polls virtually assured that she would become the next United States Senator from the state of Colorado. Certain members of the circle had aspirations for her that were far greater, and with their help she would eventually get there too. But the senate was a necessary first step.

Now, one flash disk threatened to destroy everything. The fact that Elliott had such a gross inability to keep his dick in his pants was bad enough, but the fact that that shortcoming was on full display in a video that was dangerously close to becoming a part of the public record was something she simply could not tolerate. She had to act quickly to mitigate the damage. And holding a press conference where she tearfully stood by her man while he declared his innocence was simply not going to do.

The result was this meeting. The group discussed various scenarios for the better part of four hours before finally coming to a consensus. The ultimate decision was not an easy one to make, but Sonya knew it was the only one that could be made in the best interests of all involved, Elliott included.

She requested that the other members be present when she called him into her office. They agreed, with the stipulation that Sonya would be the only one to speak. The decision may have been a collective one, but the responsibility to hand it down was strictly hers.

Sonya understood, and with a heart that was surprisingly heavy, she summoned Elliott to the meeting.

He was silent as he entered. Meetings with this many members at once were rare. He knew everyone in this room, but had never met with all of them at the same time. He swallowed hard as he sat.

"Hello Elliott," Sonya said. Her tone was formal.

"Hi honey," he answered nervously, his eyes shifting from one member to the next. "What's going on?"

Sonya fanned a stack of papers on her desk. "We... I have to tell you something."

Elliott sat upright in his chair. He looked at the group again. Every one of them held his glance. "Okay."

Sonya sighed, then looked at her husband with an unwavering stare. "We have to feed you to the wolves."

Elliott chuckled. "Feed me to the wolves? What the hell does that mean?"

"It means that I can't stand by you on this."

Elliott's smile went away and he leaned forward in his chair. "What?"

"I have a news conference scheduled for two-thirty today. I'm basically going to look into the camera and tell the entire nation that I'm completely disassociating myself from you. Call it a pre-emptive strike."

347

Elliott's mouth quivered. "You can't do that. You're my wife. I didn't do what they're accusing me of. I didn't kill anybody. Why would you even say…"

"Elliott, please."

"Look Sonya, can we at least talk about this?"

"I'm sorry, but there's nothing to talk about. If the world thinks you murdered that girl, then I'm not going to say or do a single thing that dissuades them of that notion. You can swear up and down that you're not guilty of this. And at the end of it all, you might even convince some jury of that. In the meantime, you're going to drown, and I'm not about to drown with you."

Elliott's mouth no longer quivered. In fact, he didn't move at all. He simply stared at the Colorado state seal that was etched into the wall behind his wife.

"I'm as much of a victim in this whole thing as Julia Leeds is," she continued. "By the time I'm finished, the voters of this state will think I'm more of a victim. I know it's a terrible situation, Elliott. But what's going on here is much bigger than you. Sometimes sacrifices have to be made for the greater good. If you truly believe in what we're doing, you'll understand why the sacrifice has to be you."

Elliott shook his head and looked at the group of stoic men sitting in front of him. "So that's it? You're not even going to try to make this better?"

Not a single one of them flinched.

Elliott turned back to his wife. "Anything that I did, I did it for you. For us. For our future."

"I wish I could believe that. I really do. But the reality is that you were only trying to save your own ass. If you were really thinking about me, you would have ended the affair and that bullshit Ace Project a long time ago."

Elliott buried his face in his hands. "What about our children?"

"Considering everything that you're accused of, they'll be better off without you," she answered with a coldness that was not entirely consistent with how she felt. But right now it didn't matter how she felt. All that mattered was that the circle would remain unbroken.

Once she took her rightful place in the senate and began the journey to even bigger and better things, she would look back on this meeting and realize how correct her decision was.

But for the time being, it left a hole in Sonya's heart so big, she wondered if anything she ever achieved would fill it again.

CHAPTER 54

FORGING A NEW BOND

The press conference was being carried live by every major news network in the country, and as Camille sat next to Chloe Sullivan's hospital bed, she hung on every single word. Mayor Richmond began by addressing the shootings of Camille and Detectives Sullivan and Graham and assured the public that the man arrested for those shootings would be prosecuted to the fullest extent of the law. But she never once mentioned Joseph Solomon's name, his affiliation with the Denver police department, or his involvement in Julia's murder. She did, however, go to great lengths to assure the voters of the state that her campaign was being run with the upmost honesty and integrity, and challenged anyone to argue otherwise. Every time she used the word honesty - and Camille's latest count had the number at thirty-five - Mayor Richmond looked directly into the camera; her earnestness so practiced that it almost looked authentic. When she spoke of her husband, however, the mayor did not look into the camera once.

She chose to address the charges against him by not addressing them at all. Camille hadn't expected a mea culpa, but she did expect the mayor to vehemently refute the accusations of voter fraud and financial malfeasance. Instead she vowed a full commitment to her campaign and its supporters while due process was allowed to play itself out.

"I cannot let the alleged actions of my husband, whether they are true or not, destroy a campaign that I've fought so vigorously to win. I expect that Elliott will fight these charges to the best of his ability, but I do not condone his actions, nor can I stand by him as he mounts a defense. My family has been embarrassed, I have been personally devastated, and the citizens whose lives have been most affected by these accusations have been betrayed. I will maintain the transparency that you've grown accustomed to during the remainder of this campaign, but I ask that you please respect my privacy, as well as that of my two children, when it comes to these very personal matters. Thank you." Before Mayor Richmond could take a step away from the podium, she was bombarded with a series of rapid-fire questions.

A young man in a black suit stepped up to the microphone. "I'm sorry ladies and gentlemen, but the mayor will not be taking questions at this time."

The inquiries continued, however. One question stood above the others and immediately commanded the attention of the room. "Mayor Richmond, what about the accusations that your husband was romantically involved with Julia Leeds? And the assertions that she was murdered because of it?"

Mayor Richmond made her way back to the microphone over the feeble protests of the kid in the suit. "I'm aware of those accusations, but seeing as I have no knowledge of this supposed disk that the media is talking about, I have no comment except that I fully expect the criminal justice system to run its course. The truth will come out one way or another, and I will do everything in my power to ensure that the right person is prosecuted for Julia Leeds's murder, whoever that person turns out to be."

Another barrage of questions followed. "What do you say to the members of Julia's family who claim that you know more than you're leading us to believe?"

Mayor Richmond took a deep breath and looked into the camera one last time. "First and foremost, I offer my deepest condolences for their indescribable loss. Second, I want to see the person or persons who killed her brought to justice just as much as anyone else does. While the accusations against Elliott are shocking, I cannot let personal feelings deter me from discovering the truth. And discovering the truth is exactly what I plan to do."

She made her way off the podium under the continuous flare of camera bulbs and a torrent of questions that would never be answered.

When the press conference was over, Detective Sullivan looked at Camille and shook her head. "So much for standing by your man."

"I've never seen anything quite like that," Camille said.

"Does she honestly think that she can hold one press conference where she throws her husband under the bus then go back to business as usual?"

"That's exactly what she thinks."

"Then she's crazier than I thought."

"I think she knows full well what she will be able to get away with and what she won't. And she knows she's going to get away with this."

"Even if she has to destroy her family in the process?"

"Her husband already beat her to the punch on that one. She's simply putting the final nail in the coffin."

A solemn look suddenly came over Sullivan's face. "I'm so sorry, Camille."

"Sorry for what?"

"Sorry that your best friend was killed. Sorry about the resistance you got from Graham when you confronted us with the truth of what happened. Sorry for all the time that was wasted because of it. Mostly I'm sorry that I didn't stand up for you sooner."

Camille's chest felt heavy. "I appreciate all of that, Detective Sullivan. But you don't have anything to be sorry for. I've dealt with enough sorrow and regret to last three lifetimes, and I know it never leads to anything healthy or productive. It only eats at you until there is nothing left. I don't want that to happen to you in any way, shape, or form. Understood?"

"Loud and clear," Sullivan answered with a mild look of surprise. "Thank you for understanding."

"I understand much more than you realize."

"I imagine you do." Sullivan strained as she propped herself up in bed.

Camille saw her struggling and stood up to help.

"Thank you," Sullivan said with a sigh as she settled in. "I swear if I don't get out of this bed soon I'm going to strangle somebody."

Camille smiled. "Just don't let it be me."

Sullivan smiled back. "Don't worry. You're safe."

The detective was due to be released from the hospital in the morning. The surgeries to remove her spleen and the bullet fragments in her upper thigh and torso were successful, and physically she was expected to recover. The emotional recovery, as Camille knew all too well, would be another story.

"So what's the plan once you get out of here?" Camille asked.

"Conventional wisdom says I should take some time to recover, go on an extended vacation somewhere. But I don't know if the quiet would be a blessing or a curse at this point. Every time I close my eyes I see Graham. I can hear his voice as if he's standing next to me. I need to keep my mind active. And if the only way I can do that is by getting back on the street, then that's what I have to do."

Paul, who had been sitting quietly in the corner, interjected for the first time. "I know from personal experience how easy it is to think that way. But I also know that if you don't take some time for yourself right now, you're going to regret it down the road. At the very least you want to talk to someone."

"As long as they're not affiliated with the department," Sullivan said.

"Why do you say that?" Paul asked.

"Because after everything that's happened, I don't know who I can trust there and who I can't. I'm sure there are worse things that can happen to a police officer than getting shot and nearly killed by a fellow police officer, but I don't know what those things are."

"He wasn't a fellow officer," Camille reminded her. "He was nothing more than a contract killer who wore a costume."

"And that makes it so much worse, Camille. The fact that someone like that can infiltrate our department so brazenly means that the institution is fundamentally broken. And if the allegations that Commander Brandt was responsible for recruiting Joseph Solomon are true, then I fear that what happened with him wasn't an aberration."

"It was merely the tip of the iceberg," Paul asserted.

"If that is the case, then it's all the more reason for you to stay," Camille said. "The only way to fix what's wrong with the department is by having more people like you on the inside."

"I couldn't agree more," Paul said with a light smile.

Sullivan shook her head. "I appreciate that you both think so highly of me. But the issues this department has go way beyond my ability to fix. This investigation has only just begun. Who knows what else is going to surface that the public has yet to learn about. If there are more corrupt cops out there, particularly in the detective bureau, the department will open itself up to lawsuits, the possibility of cases being retried and even overturned, and a public who has lost all confidence in the system. When morale within the rank and file starts to deteriorate, and it will, more officers will opt for early retirement or will decide to quit altogether. Less police presence in the streets means more crime in the streets. Public confidence erodes even further. What you're left with is a department that is left in complete disarray. I'm sorry, but I'm not so sure I want to be a part of that."

Camille and Paul both nodded their understanding. Camille was about to speak when she was interrupted by her cell phone. When she saw that the incoming number had a 202 area code, she sighed and buried the phone in her pocket.

"Another one?" Paul asked.

"Yep."

"What do you mean by another one?" Sullivan asked.

"Ever since my name landed back in the news, my phone has been ringing nonstop with calls from people I used to work with at the Bureau. They were mostly calls of concern, which I appreciated. But then I started getting calls asking me to reconsider my resignation."

"And what was your response?"

"I didn't respond."

"Not to a single call?"

"Not even when the Director himself asked for a meeting."

Paul sat back in his chair and crossed his arms. "I told him that he couldn't have her back, no matter how much he begged."

"Did you at least consider it?" Sullivan asked.

"Not for a second."

Sullivan nodded. "With everything you went through there, I guess that's understandable. So then I guess I should ask you the same question that you asked me. What's the plan now?"

Camille waited a long time before answering. "First and foremost, there are two very important women whose gravesites I need to visit. After that, I'm not really sure. But I've gotten assurances from my dear father that he'll help me figure out what that path should be."

"I've already told you, I could always use a caddie," he said with a sly smile.

Sullivan laughed. "Whatever it is you decide to do, just make sure you don't go too far away. I realize we've only just met, but I kind of like having you around."

"You saved my life, Detective Sullivan. I'd say the feeling is more than mutual." Camille was silent for a moment as she let the gravity of the statement sink in. Detective Sullivan did save her life. There was a time when such an act would have meant nothing to her. But now that she realized hers was a life worth saving, her gratitude to Sullivan was boundless. As Stephen Clemmons had rightly put it, there were a lot of wounds to heal, and she was finally ready to begin.

"So you're promising not to go too far away?" Sullivan reiterated.

"I'm not going anywhere," Camille answered with a self-assuredness that had completely eluded her up to this point. "I've finally made it home."

More Titles by John Hardy Bell

GRISHAM & SULLIVAN SERIES
The Other Daniel: A Short Crime Thriller (Grisham & Sullivan 2)
The Darkest Point (Grisham & Sullivan 3)

SCOTT PRIEST MYSTERY SERIES
The Rogue Element

The Thin Wall (written as E.M. Parker)